Where the Heart Leads

Journeys of a Spirit Healer

Joe McMonagle

To all who walk the path of learning: may you find
wonder in the heights you reach, and
wisdom in the valleys you cross.

Contents

Chapter 1   1

Chapter 2   18

Chapter 3   25

Chapter 4   36

Chapter 5   45

Chapter 6   47

Chapter 7   61

Chapter 8   68

Chapter 9   76

Chapter 10   80

Chapter 11   84

Chapter 12   96

Chapter 13   101

Chapter 14   111

Chapter 15   120

Chapter 16   136

Chapter 17   156

Chapter 18   169

Chapter 19   179

Chapter 20   186

Chapter 21   196

Chapter 22   201

Chapter 23   205

Chapter 24   213

Chapter 25   224

Chapter 26   235

Chapter 27   238

Chapter 28   246

Chapter 29   250

Chapter 30   255

Chapter 31   270

Chapter 32   276

Chapter 33   284

Chapter 34   289

Chapter 35   297

Chapter 36   300

Chapter 37   303

Chapter 38   316

Chapter 39   324

Chapter 40   331

Chapter 41   337

Chapter 42   346

Chapter 43   360

Chapter 44   367

Chapter 45   375

Chapter 46   379

Chapter 47   384

Chapter 48   391

Chapter 49   399

Chapter 50   406

Chapter 51   419

Chapter 52   428

Chapter 53   440

Acknowledgements   447

About the Author   449

Chapter 1

Trapped! Shadows cloaked the surrounding forest, thick with danger. His heart pounded so hard it felt like it might burst. He stood motionless, ignoring the strands of auburn hair that fell over his eyes. Before him loomed a creature three times his weight, radiating menace. Its eyes, blazing with rage, locked onto him as though nothing else existed. The air reeked of musk, damp leaves, rot, and the sharp tang of animal droppings. He thought he'd been careful. He'd scanned the area when he first arrived, but hadn't detected any creatures, human or otherwise.

Thom Macirdan had set out that morning from the Acadium in Docha-leigh, beneath a cheerful blue sky. The air had been crisp and clear, sure to warm as the day went on, judging by Siptema's weather so far. It was Suin-dae, the third day of the weekend, when most people rested. But Thom couldn't stay inside another day. He had offered to gather a particular fungus for Principal Healer MacDonuld. The Rejuvenary's antibiotic supply had been running low, and the fungus was used to make it. Thom had met Mac, as she was called, when he arrived at the school. At first, she was skeptical about his healing skills, given his age. But once she learned he'd trained with Healer Rinbalden, she put him to work. He'd planned to ride Apollo, but the colt was helping Headgroom Duncan MacAuley train Aponi, a nervous filly orphaned at birth. Which meant walking. It was a long trek to the monarchs' reserve, but it did him good. He packed a bag with his supper (pasties and an apple), a knife, and two empty herb bags.

After harvesting a bag full of fungus, Thom had considered what to do next. As it had been too early to eat, he decided to search for herbs. Healers always needed goldenseal and bloodroot for infections. He'd also hoped to find yarrow, which helped stop bleeding. Before beginning his search, he'd assured himself that nothing stirred in the vicinity but a doe, a fawn, and a few birds. After collecting a good amount of each herb, he headed deeper into the forest, toward the sound of a creek, and stumbled upon a low cave.

He'd hoped to find saxifrage in the underbrush. Mac had explained its value for breathing and digestion. Thom had just begun placing sprigs into his third bag when a low, menacing snarl tore through the air. Only after did he realize the usual birdsong and rustling of leaves had fallen silent.

Such was the predicament he now faced. Barely ten feet away, a massive boar loomed, its rage coiled in every taut muscle. As it shifted, its sharp tusks flashed in the filtered light, a silent warning.

"Digi," Thom cursed in Glakkadian, a language he'd learned while living in the Glakkadeth Archipelago. He hadn't checked near the cave.

A second snarl ripped from its mouth. Then it charged.

Snatching up a branch, Thom swung it at the boar's snout. The crack of wood meeting flesh startled it long enough for him to call on Archangel Michael for strength and protection.

The boar's fury surged, palpable to Thom's empathic ability, which enabled him to sense the emotions of beasts and humans alike. Behind him came high-pitched squeals. Extending his senses into the cave, he realized it held boarlets. "Digi," he cursed again. *She's a mother and considered him a threat.*

The boar closed in. Gripping the branch like a sword, Thom thrust it toward her face, forcing her to step back. Could he reach her spirit to show her he meant no harm? He lowered his shields but couldn't make a connection.

Growling, she pressed forward again.

Knowing he worked better with a staff, Thom adjusted his grip on the branch to block her.

She clamped her powerful jaws down on the branch, snapping it in half.

Desperate, Thom hurled himself sideways, crying out as pain lanced into his left arm. Reaching the nearest tall tree, he scrambled up until he found a perch safely out of her reach. Panting, he peered through the leaves. The boar was gone, most likely in the cave.

Letting out a sigh of relief, Thom checked his arm and saw blood spreading across his tunic. "Turg," he muttered, this time in Dochalan, his native tongue. "I need to wash and wrap this."

He tuned his senses to the boar and her young. They were inside the cave, well away from its opening. Now was his chance to escape. Quietly, Thom climbed down and retrieved his bags and cloak. Pressing his right hand over the wound, he made his way to the creek.

Once there, he peeled off his tunic, shivering. He should've worn his singlet underneath. At least the bleeding had slowed. Reaching into a pocket, he pulled out a handkerchief and dipped it into the water. Flinching as the cold cloth touched his skin, he carefully cleaned the wound.

The handkerchief had been a gift from Rin, his healing teacher for the last five years. He'd given Thom several, insisting he stop wiping his runny nose on his sleeve. It came in handy now.

Working quickly, he crushed goldenseal root and yarrow leaves on a flat rock, mixing in a few drops of water to form a poultice. Before applying it, he cut off the left sleeve of the tunic and rinsed it as clean as he could, along with the handkerchief. He smeared the poultice on the wound, covered it with the folded handkerchief, and wrapped his arm with the damp sleeve.

Though it had one sleeve now, he pulled the tunic back on and fastened his cloak over it.

"That was close," he muttered, his heart pounding. "She could've killed me. How could I have been such a fool not to check the cave first?"

Still shaken, Thom decided to eat, despite his stomach being in knots. It would ground him. He dug into one of his bags and withdrew a meat pastie and apple, quickly devouring them.

Brushing the crumbs from his lap, Thom rose. Before moving, he lowered his third and fifth shields to search for nearby animals. This time, he sensed an energy pulling at him.

Don't! Don't, he warned himself. Yet he had to investigate. Someone—human or animal—could be hurt. He remembered this feeling from years ago when he sensed Rindo's suffering.

Letting the energy guide him, Thom reached a dense thicket of trees and bushes, packed tightly enough to form a wall. It almost felt intentional, as if the barrier had been built to keep things out. Or in.

By this time, the energy had grown stronger and strangely familiar.

"Are you sure you want to do this?" Thom whispered.

His healer instincts overrode caution, as he carefully parted a few branches. The dense foliage revealed limited glimpses of what lay beyond. A low sound—part hiss, part rumble—emerged from within. That's not a boar, he thought, relieved. But it didn't sound like any animal he knew.

Steeling himself, Thom lowered all his shields, even his natural one. Energy rushed in, raising shivers, and not from the cold.

"Whoa."

Whatever it was, its spirit was huge and powerful. He had to find out more. As he tuned in, his spirit-healing gift expanded, becoming more sensitive. Once again, his desire had triggered a change. The most appropriate word to describe this being was holy.

He sensed two smaller beings with similar energy nearby, though weaker. What are they? *Advisors, can you tell me?* he asked, mind-speaking. No reply came.

Thom used to call his advisors a divine team, but he liked the word 'advisors' more. Refocusing, a faint spark flickered at the edge of his awareness, fading fast. That's the one he was being drawn to.

"This might be dumb," he whispered, pushing aside more branches to make an opening.

I can hear you, a female voice said. *You might as well come through but keep your distance.*

"What?" Thom blurted, startled. Part of him screamed to run, but he couldn't. With a determined shove, he forced his way through. His cloak snagged on a branch and tore free, nearly choking him. When he raised his head, he froze.

A massive dragon stared, as long as the front of his house and much taller than him, though she lay on the ground. Jade-green scales shaded to gold along its body.

Thom gulped as he felt a probe. But unlike the one Samiltun had used on him shortly after they met, at his Da's pottery, it wasn't threatening. From the corner of his eye, he caught movement. Two smaller dragons turned toward him. Shattered eggshells lay nearby. Nadia Sanneh's books had said dragons lay eggs. She was the author of his favorite series, *Demba's Chronicles.*

He studied the baby dragons. One had yellow scales, shading to green; the other was blue, shading to gold. These were the lesser energies he'd sensed. But what of the spark? He spotted it nestled at the larger dragon's feet, nearly invisible as its gray color blended into the stone beneath it. He sensed energy flowing into it from the large dragon, keeping it alive.

Thommy?

He jumped.

Thommy!

He heard the voice in his mind, certain it came from the dragon.

"Um. How do you know my name?"

We met years ago. Don't you remember?

Thom stayed silent. Almost without thinking, he reached into his pocket and withdrew a small triangular object. Its color matched the dragon. Something impelled him to bring this precious treasure before leaving the Acadium. Remembering his dream from long ago, he realized it hadn't been a dream.

"Ari?"

Yes. That's what you called me. I'm Ariel.

"I met you when I was a little kid, didn't I?"

Yes.

"Your littlest... it's dying."

You sensed that, Ariel replied mournfully. *Her hatching was difficult. I've been feeding her energy, but it isn't enough. She needs more than I can give.*

"I feel that," Thom said softly.

I knew your spirit was strong when we first met. It's much stronger now. I wasn't sure what gifts would manifest.

"I'm pretty good at physical healing, but I'm better with spirit healing," Thom explained, itching to get closer to the ailing dragon. "Can I help your baby? Her aura's faded and colorless."

Hatchling, Ariel corrected gently. *We call them hatchlings at this age. But yes, please do whatever you can.* She rose and moved to the others, leaving Thom space. *By the way, you can use mind-speech. That's how I've been speaking to you.*

"Oh," Thom said, surprised. A part of him wanted to ask more, but the hatchling needed him now. He hurried to her side and placed his hand on her. She was cold and needed warmth. Without hesitation, he lay beside her, pressing his body close. Wrapping his arms tenderly around her fragile torso, he focused, channeling energy into her for several minutes.

Her aura now had hints of purple and green. The memory of nearly dying while healing Rindo flashed through his mind, reminding him he couldn't do this alone. Aloud, he called, "Archangel Raphael and healing angels, thank you for being here. Please join your energy with mine to help heal this little one."

A rush of energy flowed through him and into the hatchling, mingling with Ariel's steady pulses.

After a while, Thom felt the little one stir. His nose twitched from a faint spicy scent. It's *working*," he mind-spoke. *Her aura's stronger, and her breathing's more even. She's no longer on the edge of death, but I need to keep providing her energy until she's more stable. By the way, does she have a name?*

If she survives, she'll have to give it to you. That's our way.

Lying there, Thom struggled to grasp that he was curled around a dragon. *You're real,* he mind-spoke. *People said you were a myth.*

Indeed. We limit contact with humans. That wasn't always the case.

What is this place?

A dragon sanctuary, created generations ago as a resting place for my kind. We rarely use it now, being so near to human settlements here.

Then why?

My time was close. I knew I wouldn't make it home to lay my eggs.

When did they hatch?

Those two hatched a few days ago, she said, nodding toward the pair asleep. *My littlest struggled. Her shell was thicker, and she kept tiring out. I helped, but she wouldn't survive if I did too much. Breaking through the shell releases enzymes hatchlings need. She finally emerged last night.*

I see, Thom replied, continuing to channel energy into the hatchling. Drained from the long day, he relied heavily on the angels. But the combination was working. And she was fighting to live.

Thommy, she seems a little better, Ariel said. *I have a favor. I haven't been able to hunt. If I don't feed them and myself soon, none of us will survive.*

I go by Thom now. And you're right. She's strong enough for you to hunt. Food might help her if she'll eat it.

Good. With a glance at her other offspring, Ariel waddled to the edge of the clearing, where the ground dropped away. Spreading her wings, she launched into the air.

Thom faced the little one as a wave of light-headedness hit him. He needed food, too. Reluctantly, he pulled away and grabbed his bag. Inside was his last meat pastie, slightly crushed but edible.

As he ate, Thom's gaze drifted across the sanctuary. A smile tugged at his lips as he pictured his own—the one Sestra B had helped him visualize. He saw the river flowing by the mountain, his favorite tree, and the field stretching toward the distant forest. That place always brought him peace.

Sestra B—formally Sestra Berbera—was a member of the Liberventian religious community in Glakkadeth. She had taught him about his spirit-healing gift. She also shared her understanding of life, an individual's purpose, and the One—the name her faith gave to the supreme being. Thom now called the One 'God,' as she did, finding it less cumbersome than saying 'the One.' Thinking of her steadied him, much like his sanctuary did.

This sanctuary was nothing like his, other than the name. It was oblong, bordered on three sides by a thicket. Aside from the slope where Ariel had taken off, the ground was flat, a patchwork of gray stone, sparse grass, and dirt. The hatchling pair lay quiet, occasionally opening their eyes to stare at him.

"Meep," one of them squeaked.

"Your mother's hunting for food."

"Meep," the other replied.

Cute, Thom thought. Then again, maybe that wasn't the best word for something bound to outgrow him ten times over.

Swallowing the last of his pastie, he took a sip from his water-skin. The food and water helped. He felt more grounded. Maybe the hatchling needed water, he thought, making his way back to her. With her head on its side, he carefully poured small amounts into her mouth, hoping her natural reflexes would kick in. She swallowed a little, but most dribbled out the other side. Well, he tried.

Lying down beside her again, Thom wondered if he could wrap his spirit around her, like he was doing with his arms. Feeling agreement from his divine advisors, he imagined his spirit cocooning her.

When Ariel returned, she clutched two bucks in her foreclaws. *Any problems?*

No, your other hatchlings meeped, but seemed fine. This one is a little stronger, he said, sitting up with his hand on her flank.

That's good news. Strictly speaking, a few days after hatching, and once survival is certain, they're called dragonets.

OK, he said, unsure why she was telling him.

Thom, after we've eaten, my dragonets and I need to fly home.

Home? he echoed. Thom was still amazed to be speaking with a dragon. *I don't think this one is in any shape to move.*

She's not. I meant her siblings.

Can dragonets fly at a few days old?

Not really. They won't be able to do much more than take-off. I'll be carrying them on my back, which won't be easy.

Shouldn't you stay?

No. I have an important gathering to attend. I'll leave part of a buck, along with a heart and a liver. They're vital for us, especially one in her condition. If she doesn't survive, will you bury her? At home, we would have burned her remains, but it would need to be a large fire here, and that would attract attention.

Sure. But I'll make her well.

Thank you, Thom. You're a special human.

He reddened. Will you come back?

Doubtful. The sanctuary's far from my home. It's a lot to ask, but if by some miracle she lives, would you care for her?

Can I think about it?

Certainly, Ariel replied, before nudging her dragonets to feed. While she ate daintily, the other two tore into their portions, flinging blood and meat into the air.

Sitting beside the now-sleeping hatchling, Thom let himself think. He couldn't leave her to die. But what would he tell people at the Acadium if he brought her back? Especially Mac and Noiri? Until they saw her, they'd think he made her up. Worse, they might try to hurt her.

She already had his heart, and he knew he'd give his life for her, even without knowing her name. She was part of him, after only the little time they'd shared. But how could he get her to the Acadium? Sure, training had strengthened him, but not enough to carry her. And once there, where would she stay? Winter was coming. She'd need warmth, like any newborn, or newly hatched, in her case.

The biggest question, though: how would he care for her? He knew nothing about dragons, other than what he read in Sanneh's novels.

Thom?

And how was he supposed to teach her to fly? Maybe she'd figure it out, like instinct. But her mother wouldn't be around to help. This is completely crazy.

Thom!

And what about the academs? How would they react?

Thom Macirdan! You silly muffin-head.

Muffin-head? Did someone actually call him that? It sounded male.

At least you heard me, the voice continued.

Jesh? Thom mind-spoke back.

Jeshua was a member of his divine advisors; one he considered a brother. The good book called Jeshua 'Deu's only son.' But he'd learned from Sestra B that every incarnated being shared the same divine essence as him. Sestra said Jeshua embodied it like no one else had.

Yes. I've been trying to get your attention for a while.

Sorry. Do you need something?

No, you do. You're spiraling into worst-case thinking again. Follow your intuition. As always, we're with you.

That's not easy to believe, because you're.... wherever you are... and not here with me.

True. But you've got to, even if you can't see us. And trust the timing of events. Synchronicity often has divine roots. And now... it seems Ariel and the dragonets are finishing their meal. I think she's about to repeat her question.

Oh, Thom replied, noticing Ariel staring at him.

Are you willing to be her guardian?

Taking a deep breath, and despite butterflies in his stomach, Thom replied, Yes.

I wish I had time to teach you how to care for her. If you hear of anyone who works with birds, they might help. They're not mammals like us, but they're similar. Some things she'll know instinctively, like flying. However, given her condition, she may need more time before attempting to try. One day, she could feel drawn to come to our homeland.

OK, he replied, relieved that a few of his earlier worries were addressed.

Thank you. I hope we'll meet again, Thom. It's an honor to meet one such as you.

Someone else had said that to him once. He found it puzzling.

Thom watched as Ariel herded the two dragonets to the edge of the hilltop. She launched into the air and circled back to encourage them. The first, a male, Thom instinctively knew, leapt, flailed, and tumbled down the slope. He waddled back up, leapt again, and this time stayed aloft. The second dragonet, a female, hesitated. Ariel urged her on. She leapt and remained aloft.

Once both had settled on Ariel's back, Thom called out in mind-speech, *I'm happy I met you again and your dragonets. Have a safe flight home.*

Me too, and thanks again.

As they vanished from sight, Thom brought his attention back to the one before him, his charge. How would he get her back?

Jeshua, he mind spoke, *since my divine advisors are with me, as you say, please put your heads together and send ideas; that is, when you have heads,* he added, picturing their natural form as balls of light.

"Come on, little one," Thom said aloud. "Your mother's left you in my care. Let's get you well."

An hour passed. Her aura had strengthened, its colors deepening. She seemed more aware. Her once-gray scales now appeared magenta shading to green, though lacking luster. The tip of her tail was lighter, possibly gold, like her mother's. On her snout, an infinity symbol in the same hue was emerging.

"Let's see if I can get food into you," Thom said.

He pulled a knife from his bag, and crossed to the flat rock where Ariel had left the buck's remains. He cut out the heart and liver first, dicing them. He did the same to the rest of the meat. She probably wouldn't eat much, but it was best to be prepared.

Thom made several trips to bring the meat closer to his patient, setting aside a small portion for himself. He'd need a fire—not just for cooking, but warmth.

Sitting beside her, Thom held a chunk of the heart near her nostrils, hoping the scent might stir her appetite. At first, nothing happened. Then her nostrils twitched. She opened her jaws, and Thom carefully placed the meat on her tongue. As she swallowed, her eyes popped open: sapphire, like the gems he'd seen in Glakkadeth.

"There you are, little one," Thom said, pleased. "Since your head's sideways, I have to be careful. I don't want you to choke."

The dragonet blinked.

Yes, that's what she was now, knowing she'd live. She's amazing, he thought. He still marveled that she was his to care for.

Something pressed into his belly—her snout.

"I see you want more."

For a stretch, feeding became a game. Thom would place the meat on her tongue and quickly pull his hand back before she snapped her jaws shut. After a few bites, she adjusted her body so her head rested more upright.

When he offered the last piece, he said, "You ate everything. Good job! I hope you don't mind that I saved a little for myself?"

By this time, her eyes had begun to close, and her breathing had deepened.

"Rest now," Thom said. Sensing into her again, he noted the purple and green of her aura were clearer. Since a few gray spots remained, he intended to give her more energy, but he needed food first.

He gathered up fallen branches and used the firestarter in his bag to get a blaze going. After cooking the meat he'd set aside and eating, he felt better but tired. Curling up beside her, he resumed feeding her energy through body contact and soon drifted off to sleep.

Cold droplets struck the side of Thom's face, jolting him awake. Wiping the rain from his cheek, he sat up and gazed upward. It wasn't night yet, but dusk was near. To the east, dark clouds crept closer.

"Digi! I should've been back to the Acadium by now. Mac and Finnell will be missing me." Finnell, the academ healer he worked with in the Rejuvenary, would start fifth level this year. Assessing his situation, Thom knew he wasn't going anywhere. He needed shelter.

Scanning the area, he spotted the gap in the thicket where he'd fallen through. Nearby stood a tree with broad, overhanging branches, part of the thicket, but reaching far enough to offer cover. The dragonet needed a nest; she lay on hard ground that would soon become mud.

"If I move us there," he muttered, "we should stay mostly dry."

Thom collected a few leafy branches and dragged them under the tree limbs. Pulling some vines, he layered them on top. Testing the makeshift nest, he said, "Not great, but it'll do."

Moving to her side, he caught a faint whimper. "OK, little one. I'll get you out of the rain."

He figured his best option was to grab her by her shoulders. Lift with the legs, he reminded himself, echoing his father's advice from years of hauling sand for their clay mixtures. "I'm going to drag you to the nest. Drag a dragonet. That's funny," he chuckled.

Thom crouched, slid his arms under her back as far as he could, and lifted. "Ughhh...," he grunted, setting her down. She's heavier than he thought.

Meeting her gaze, he said, "Hey, sweetie, if you can help, I'll get you out of the rain."

She snorted in what felt like agreement. Her breath was now tinged with a metallic edge from the deer meat.

He tried again. As he lifted, the dragonet promptly rested her head on his shoulder and pushed up with her hind legs. Together, they waddled to the nest.

After making her as comfortable as possible, Thom realized she needed support for her head. Spotting moss on rocks nearby, he peeled off a few clumps and tucked them beneath her. He retraced his steps to where he had fallen through the thicket, retrieved his cloak, and returned to the nest. Settling beside her, he draped his cloak over them both.

The rain was falling harder now, and Thom was grateful for the shelter of the tree. Remembering the herb bag, he used it as a pillow. Sleep claimed him almost instantly.

Chapter 2

Jonathan and his cousin, Nedd, set out before sunrise. They'd been on the road for about a week from Gra-e-gra, where Jonathan lived with his family. Later today, they'd reach the home of Nedd's parents to deliver the goods in their cart. Afterward, Nedd would take him the rest of the way to the Acadium for his first year.

Sitting beside Nedd, Jonathan shook his head, strands of his light brown hair brushing against his cheek. He should have gotten to the school a week earlier, at the end of Aegisa. That would've given him time to learn its layout before the semester began. His acceptance letter had strongly encouraged it. But his healing teacher, Rafia, had needed help with a critically ill patient. He hoped the provost would understand. Rafia had always stressed that patients came first.

Jonathan surveyed the goods in the cart, proud of the beautiful tunics, trousers, and other cloth goods his family crafted. They made more than usual this time.

He pictured Aunt Betz and Uncle Dillen nodding in approval. They raised sheep and goats. Along with Jonathan's father, Conor—Dillen's brother—and Jonathan's other father, Tadg, they made an agreement. His family would craft the fleece and mohair into finished goods. They were all talented, except for him, at least with crafting. His talent lay in healing.

Mid-spring every year, Nedd carted most of the raw material to Jonathan's home. At the end of the summer, Nedd came back to collect half of the goods. Both families sold their shares locally.

"Jonny, are you daydreaming again?" Nedd asked, nudging him.

"Turg, Nedd! Don't call me that! How many times do I have to tell you? Call me Jonathan!"

"OK. OK," he said, holding up his hand in surrender. "You only told us three months ago, when we stayed with you on your birthday. I've been calling you Jonny since you were born. Hard habit to break."

"Try harder," Jonathan grumbled.

"I hear ya. But were you daydreaming?"

"No. I was counting how many garments we made this time."

"You must've put in long hours," Nedd said. "Mam and Paps can't wait to see what new designs your sisters came up with. But I figured you were thinking about the Acadium."

"I can't believe Lady Ghetham is covering my tuition."

"Well, you saved her youngest daughter last winter," Nedd said. "And also helped her servants and townsfolk who caught the sickness."

"But I couldn't save her husband," Jonathan said with a grimace. "I did everything I could. I thought I'd beaten it, but Lord Ghetham had a weak heart from a childhood illness. That's what got him."

"You did your best, and everyone says it. Did you even sleep?"

"Not much."

"How do you feel about going back to school after testing out last year?"

"I was shocked when my teachers said I'd learned all they could teach me. I'm not sure what more I can learn about healing. Rafia taught me about using my gift, but she couldn't do much with my other one. I don't even know what to call it. Anyway, it's not as strong as my healing gift. Probably not important."

Nedd shrugged. "Maybe someone at the Acadium will. Plenty of folks talk about your healing gift—especially the way you sense, as you call it, people's illnesses, even when you walk by. Honestly, it scares me. One moment you're chatting, and then you go all quiet. Jonny? There he goes again."

While Nedd had been speaking, Jonathan sensed two beings nearby, both exhausted. One, a female, had nearly died and was weak. The other, a male, wasn't in the best shape, and seemed to be channeling energy into the first.

"I'm needed... in those woods," he said, pointing.

"I'll pull off to the side."

"Thanks. Will you unhitch a horse?"

"Sure."

Once the cart had stopped, Jonathan jumped down, his slender frame landing easily. He searched through the goods for the saddle Nedd always brought. Strapping it onto a horse, he rode toward the forest.

Spotting a game trail, Jonathan followed it in. He focused on the two presences, letting their energy guide him, until he came upon a dense thicket. "What is it?" he muttered, as he tuned in more closely on the two. "The male's human, but I can't tell about the other."

Dismounting, he looped the reins over a low branch and looked for an opening. He soon found a break, marked by broken branches and crushed plants. Pushing through, he froze. A boy, likely his age, lay curled around a scaled creature with a long tail.

As Jonathan crept closer, his breath caught. Was that a dragon?

He shook himself and focused on the boy. A blood-soaked cloth was wrapped around his arm, which lay above his head. Using his gift, he determined it was a puncture wound and still bleeding. It needed cleaning, and the cloth had to be replaced.

"You idiot," he whispered. 'Why didn't I bring my supplies?'

At least the wound wasn't infected. He could help. Crouching, he placed his hand over the cloth and directed healing into it until the bleeding stopped. The boy didn't stir.

How's his energy? Jonathan wondered. Dangerously low and dropping as he fed energy to the… baby dragon.

He had to stop the drain. But first, he had to separate them. His gaze returned to the young one, whose eyes were open, watching him. Would she let him touch her?

Sending her reassuring thoughts, he slowly extended his hand and rested it on her side, channeling healing and strength into her.

"It's working," he whispered, relieved.

Now to the boy. Jonathan carefully eased him away, breaking the flow of energy. Resting his hand on him, Jonathan sent energy into his weakened body.

What else could he do before riding back to the cart for supplies? He looked around. The fire was nearly out. He rebuilt it quickly.

Anything else?

They both needed food. He also had to figure out how to tell his cousin about his patients, as they'd be transporting them.

Shifting his focus to the baby dragon, her eyes were still fixed on him.

I don't know if you can understand me, he mind-spoke, *but I hope you trust me now.*

The dragon blinked.

Did that mean she understood? He hoped so.

In case the boy woke before he returned, he needed to leave a sign to show he'd been here and meant no harm. He'd tied a blanket behind the saddle before leaving Nedd. He'd fetch it to cover them. It might smell, but that would tell the boy it was someone with a horse.

After draping it over the boy, Jonathan headed back. As he emerged from the woods, he saw Nedd had unhitched the other horse, happily munching leaves nearby.

"Ho, Nedd," Jonathan called as he rode up.

"Back at you, Jonny. I mean, Jonathan. Sorry. Did you find someone sick?"

"Two."

"Are they OK?"

"They're stable but need care. One's a boy with an injury. I need my bag."

"And the other?"

"Um...," Jonathan hesitated. "The other... there's no easy way to say this." He took a breath. "The other's a baby dragon."

"A what?"

"A baby dragon," he repeated.

"None of your stories now," Nedd said, skepticism thick in his voice.

"I'm serious. I saw hatched shells nearby, which means she's a newborn. That alone is amazing. But even more so—the boy was feeding her energy. He was in bad shape."

"I'm still having trouble believing this."

"I get it. Most think dragons are a myth." Hesitating again, Jonathan continued, "We need to bring the dragon with us."

"What?" Nedd sputtered. "What are we supposed to do with it?"

"She."

"What?"

"The baby dragon's a girl."

"Hmm," Nedd grunted.

"I think the boy's her caretaker. Maybe he has an idea where she belongs. Either way, I can't leave them. It would go against the healer's code."

"But you're not an official healer yet."

"No, but I've been acting as one for the past year. I have to follow the code."

Nedd sighed. "OK."

"Thanks. It'll take a while to figure out how to get the dragon back here."

"Don't dragons fly?"

"She may be too young for that."

"So the dragon rides in the cart."

"Along with the boy."

"I hope the horses can handle the extra weight."

"Haven't you hauled heavy loads before?"

"Yeah. But not a baby dragon."

"I'd better get back. Mind if I borrow your slingshot? They'll be hungry when they wake up."

"Go ahead," Nedd replied, pulling it from a bag under the cart bench.

"Do you have any rope? I can use it to rig a carrier."

"Front of the cart bed."

Jonathan mounted the horse and headed back to the thicket.

Chapter 3

Thom felt a nudge, followed by warm puffs of air against his face. Coming awake, he found the dragonet staring at him, her eyes keen and unblinking. Memory rushed back: Thom had agreed to be her guardian. Shifting, he realized he was no longer touching her. A blanket covered him, smelling of horse.

"Where did this come from?" His eyes landed on the fire; someone had stoked it.

His stomach rumbled. Maybe the dragonet was hungry as well.

"Meep."

"Did you hear my thoughts?"

She nodded.

How did he forget about mind-speech? Hi, little one. I don't have any food. I'm sorry. You finished the buck yesterday. I'll see if your siblings left any scraps.

Thom removed the cloak from the dragonet, and tied it around his neck. Picking up the blanket, he draped it over her. By the way, I can't keep calling you little one. Your mother said dragons choose whether to share their names. Would you tell me yours? Or whatever you want me to call you?

The dragonet was silent, before speaking. My name's Kamael*Ariraz. You can call me Kamael.

Thank you, Kamael. I'm Thom. Once I find food, I'll figure out how to get you to the Acadium where I live. I'll need to make a carrier to drag you along. It won't be comfortable, but I don't have many options.

Remembering his injury, Thom carefully moved his left arm. It was stiff, but pain-free. He knew it had bled more while making Kamael's nest, but the bleeding had stopped. He searched where the other dragonets had eaten and dug up a few morsels. After rinsing them with the little water left in his waterskin, he fed them to Kamael.

I know it's not much. Maybe I can catch a rabbit.

Kamael snorted.

I'll figure something out, he assured her, kissing her forehead.

"OK," Thom said, aloud. "What can I use to make a carrier?" Surveying the area, he added, "I can gather branches and use vines to tie everything together."

For the next while, Thom worked steadily. He wanted to get Kamael back to the Acadium as quickly as possible, hopefully before dinner. It was already mid-morning.

Once I finish this, we can get on our way, he mind-spoke. *I think we can make it back to the Acadium in four hours. I hope.*

But he knew he needed help. "Hey, divine advisors," he called out loudly, "if you can send someone to help me get Kamael back, I'd appreciate it. Thanks in advance."

Kamael gave him a curious look. Thom wondered if dragons had a spirituality or belief in divine beings.

Tying off the last vine, Thom stepped back to inspect his work. If he laid the blanket over the branches and secured it, it might be more comfortable.

He paused to check on Kamael. Her eyes were closed, but as he approached, they fluttered open. *I'm about done.*

She raised her head and sniffed.

Do you smell something?

Food?

That's the first time she mind-spoke to him, Thom realized. *Thanks, Kamael. Maybe you smell game. I'll see if I can catch it.*

All he had was a knife. Before climbing through the thicket opening, he grabbed a few rocks. He noticed the opening appeared larger. That would help when it came time to getting Kamael out.

Outside the sanctuary, Thom considered what to do. Dragons clearly had a keener nose, but he could use his gifts to sense if there was an animal nearby.

He hesitated. Was it fair to use them? His gift was for healing, not hunting. But Kamael needed food, and he had no other way to find it quickly. Swallowing his uncertainty, he quieted his mind and let his gifts search for life energy.

He sensed an animal immediately. Too large to be a rabbit. Perhaps a deer? Keeping low, he crept from tree to tree toward the presence. In a short time, he realized there were two energies—one was human; the other, a horse.

"Oh, divine advisors," he whispered, "please let that be the person who left the blanket."

Soon after, he spotted a figure on horseback through the trees. How should he announce himself? This might seem weird, but...

"Ho, the horse!"

"That's a new one," a male voice chuckled.

A boy rode toward him. Raising his hand, he asked, "Were you the one who left the blanket and built up the fire?"

"That was me. But... "Ho, the horse?"

Thom gave him a lopsided grin. "Best I could come up with to get your attention."

The boy smiled back.

His face almost glows, Thom thought. And those piercing green eyes. What about his aura? Lowering his fifth shield, he saw rich purple, green, and brown. He sensed the boy was strongly aligned with his purpose and highest self. Thom felt drawn to him and resonated with his energy. How was that possible when he didn't know his name? Then again, hadn't he felt that with Kamael? Weird.

"Um, hello."

"Sorry. Did you say something?"

"Yeah. Did you hear me from inside the thicket?"

"Actually, Kamael smelled you. Or, rather, she smelled your horse and hoped it was food."

"Kamael? That's the baby dragon's name?"

Oh dear, Thom thought, realizing his mistake. "I shouldn't have told you. Dragons don't share their names lightly. And the correct term is dragonet. What's your name?"

"Jonathan."

"Thom."

Jonathan stepped closer and extended his hand.

"Nice to meet you," Thom replied, shaking it. Whoa. He couldn't describe the feeling. Just that his touch was comforting and safe.

"Nice to meet you, too."

"Let me check with the dragonet."

"OK."

"Kamael wasn't real upset I shared her name. She remembered you helped us earlier. Please don't tell anyone."

"I won't. Did you just use mind-speech with her?"

"Yeah."

"I can mind-speak with most animals. I wonder if I can with Kamael, if she and you would let me."

"I didn't realize until her mother told me," Thom explained.

"I can't believe she's real. I always thought dragons were a myth."

"Me too."

"This might sound like a strange question, but do you have experience with dragons?"

"About a day. I stumbled upon her, her mother, and two siblings." Thom continued with a quick summary of how he ended up there.

"Interesting. How's your arm? I channeled healing energy to stop the bleeding, but I didn't want to do more without seeing it. I brought back bandages and other supplies."

"Thank you. You're a healer, too?"

"In training, I guess. On my way to the Acadium."

"Really," Thom said, surprised and pleased he'd have time to get to know Jonathan. "As for my arm, it's stiff and sore."

"Understandable. How'd it happen?"

"Got between a wild boar and her boarlets," Thom replied, frowning.

"Ouch," Jonathan winced. "Once we're inside the thicket, I'll take a look."

"Thanks. Could I ask you a favor?"

"Like what?"

"I need to get Kamael back to the Acadium since she can't fly. I was going to pull her on a carrier, but I'm worn out. The way I feel, it'll take hours."

"You're in luck. My cousin's driving me there. We need to drop off goods at my aunt and uncle's place first, but we can take you both."

"Whoa," Thom exclaimed. "Thank you, divine advisors!"

Jonathan jerked at Thom's outburst, and his horse tossed its head, snorting.

"Sorry. I'd asked my advisors for help. Now, here you are. Are you sure?"

"Yeah. But I'd like to talk to you about your... advisors."

A loud grunt echoed in their minds, followed by a clear, *Me.* Both were startled.

"You heard that?" Thom asked.

"Yep. I guess that answers my question."

Sorry, Kamael. I'll be right in, Thom mind-spoke. "You wouldn't happen to have any food?"

"Not with me. Half a loaf of bread in the cart; maybe an apple. But I do have my cousin's slingshot."

Did you hear that, Kamael? We'll get you food. But it won't be the horse.

"What did you tell her?"

"She had wondered if your horse was food."

"I'm glad you told me. I need to convince him she won't eat him. Kamael probably smells like a predator. I'll search for food as well."

"Thanks."

"I'll meet you inside."

Sometime after, Jonathan entered the sanctuary with two scrawny old rabbits and an injured and dying grouse.

"That was fast," Thom said.

"It felt like I was led to them."

Thom mind-spoke, *Thanks again, advisors.* Aloud, he added, "And thank you, rabbits and grouse, for offering yourselves as food for Kamael." He felt a surge of energy in acknowledgment of his gratitude.

Jonathan seemed puzzled but said nothing.

"Is your horse OK?" Thom asked.

"Tucker's fine. He trusts me. By the way, I brought him closer to the opening. When we get back to the cart, I'll have to do the same with Lady, the other horse. I'm sure she'll be fine."

"That's a relief."

"The tricky part will be the sheep and goats at my aunt and uncle's place," Jonathan added. "Hmm... I've got it. I'll send them off to sleep for a few hours."

"Impressive."

"I'm not exactly sure how I do it, and it doesn't always work," Jonathan replied, "but I've used it on patients."

"Neat. Thanks for the game. I'll feed Kamael."

"Can I check your wound after?"

"Sure."

Spotting the carrier, Jonathan said, "You built that. I can tie the end of my rope to it and the other to Tucker's saddle."

Thom cut the game into small chunks and fed them to Kamael, who devoured them.

"Ready for me to check you?" Jonathan asked.

"Yeah."

Jonathan unwrapped the cloth and removed the handkerchief. Bits of dried paste fell to the ground. Sniffing, he asked, "Goldenseal and yarrow?"

"Yes. Good nose. I was collecting them before I ran into the boar."

Studying the wound, Jonathan said, "It's healing well. Let me add a little more energy. It might ease your stiffness."

When Jonathan placed his hand over the wound, Thom felt warmth surge through it. "Thanks. You've got a healing touch."

After re-wrapping the arm with a clean bandage, Jonathan asked. "Ready to head out?"

"Yeah. Let me pack up. Then I have to get Kamael onto the carrier."

"Should we lift her together?"

"Um," Thom said, unsure.

Before he could say more, Kamael raised herself up, waddled to the carrier, and lay down on it.

"I keep forgetting she understands, even when we speak out loud," Thom remarked.

While Thom gathered his things, Jonathan checked the fire. It seemed out, but he spread mud over the coals to be sure.

"I'm ready," Thom said. "Can you help me carefully get the carrier through the opening? I want the trees and vines to grow back to keep this place hidden."

"Sure."

Grasping the carrier sides, they maneuvered it into the opening. A few branches bent; none snapped.

Once through, Thom covered the opening with fallen branches to conceal it until it closed naturally.

"Hi, Tucker," Jonathan said, patting the horse. Tucker snorted at Kamael's scent, before settling down. "I'll tie the rope to the saddle. Why don't you ride? He's strong enough to carry one of us."

"No, no," Thom said quickly. "He's your horse. You've done enough already—I can walk."

"Technically, he's my aunt and uncle's. And you've been pushing yourself hard by feeding energy to Kamael. It's about to catch up with you."

"How'd you know?"

"My healing gifts are pretty sensitive. They showed up early, and the local healers said they were unusually strong. When I found you, I could tell you were feeding her energy. It also looked like you were channeling someone else's—maybe the divine advisors you mentioned. After I gave you both energy, Kamael was tired but stable. You were nearly drained."

"Hmm," Thom said after a moment. "I thought that wouldn't happen again with my advisors' help."

Jonathan shrugged.

"My teacher, Rin, taught me how to avoid risking my life while healing. But I guess I was so worried about Kamael that I opened myself up more than I should have. And once I fell asleep, I couldn't stop the flow. Thanks for taking care of us."

"You're welcome. Now, mount Tucker. We should get back to my cousin."

As Jonathan led Tucker through the forest, he called back, "You said you're a student healer?"

"Yeah. I trained with Rin for about five years."

"Wow," Jonathan replied, eyebrows lifting. "Your gifts showed up when you were young, huh?

"About eight."

"Mine first appeared three years ago, when I was ten."

"You're thirteen?"

"This past Jauna. You?"

"In two months. You mentioned gifts. One's healing. What's the other?"

"I'm not sure," Jonathan replied. "It might be part of my physical healing. What about you?"

"I've got a strong physical-healing gift and some earth-sensing. But my most powerful is spirit healing."

"What's that?"

How could Thom explain it to another healer? "Since your gift's strong, can you sense illness?"

"Yeah."

"I can too, but not only the physical. I can see when a person's spirit is kind of sick, like their choices don't match their highest self." He didn't mention his truth-sensing or his recent ability to see images from Aponi's birth. He had told Noiri and Mac about them.

Jonathan was quiet.

"Did I upset you? I haven't figured everything out about this gift. Maybe I didn't explain it well."

"No. I'm fine. I needed to think. What you described sounds like my other gift—now and then I can sense when someone isn't living the life they're meant to."

"That does sound like mine."

"What's strange," Jonathan continued, "is that physical healing is my stronger gift. Based on what you said, it's like our gifts are reversed."

"Weird," Thom agreed, feeling tingling. *Gang?*, he mind-spoke his advisors. "But if you've got a spirit -healing gift, you might study with Mage Keenan, like me. Provost Gavin says she works with unusual gifts. When she asks about yours, tell her your other gift might be like mine."

"I will."

They rode on in silence, the horse's sway making it hard for Thom to stay awake. Jonathan's sweet. He liked him. A warmth stirred in his chest. Maybe they'd be in the same...., but he couldn't complete the thought before sleep took him.

"How did you first get into...?" Jonathan began, glancing back and finding Thom slumped in the saddle.

Chapter 4

"Thom, we're out of the forest," Jonathan announced.

"Huh?" Thom replied sleepily. "We're what?"

"We left the forest. You can see the cart... and my cousin."

"I slept the whole way," Thom said, rubbing his eyes. "Sorry. I should've stayed awake to keep you company."

"You needed the rest. I'm gonna run ahead and ease Lady in with Kamael. I'll shift things around in the cart to make room for you and her. Take Tucker's reins and wait here."

When Jonathan waved him on, Thom guided Tucker forward. Now that they were out of the trees, he quickened the pace. "Is everything OK with Lady?" he called as they neared.

"She's fine. Meet my cousin, Nedd. This is Thom—and his dragonet."

Nedd stared, his mouth open. "I guess part of me thought Jonny was pulling my leg. But I should've known—when it comes to healing, he wouldn't joke."

Thom dismounted.

"Let's get you both comfortable in the cart," Nedd offered.

"Once we're moving, I'll see about the bread, Thom," Jonathan added. "No apple, though—Nedd ate it."

"That's fine. Anything's appreciated. I can't tell you how grateful I am. The idea of hauling a dragonet back to the Acadium wasn't exactly appealing."

"I understand. Jonny did mention we'll be stopping at my folks' place before taking you on?"

"Yeah." Thom wondered how they'd react to Kamael.

Together, they lifted her into the cart. Thom climbed in after and made himself comfortable near the front.

Jonathan and Nedd untied the carrier from Tucker and left it by the roadside. After securing both horses, they climbed onto the bench and got moving.

Reaching under the bench, Jonathan pulled bread out of a bag and said, "Here. I've got water, if you need to wash it down."

Thom quickly gobbled it up before taking a drink. "That helped. Thanks."

"Sleep. We'll wake you when we're there."

Scooting down next to Kamael, he closed his eyes.

It seemed like mere moments when Thom felt someone shaking him.

"Thom," Nedd said.

"Are we here already?"

"Yes."

"I didn't realize I was that tired. Where's Jonathan?"

"At the house. He wanted to prepare my folks and take care of the animals."

In a short while, Thom spotted a figure ahead.

"That's Jonny. Looks like they're ready for us."

Nedd guided the cart to the farmhouse where Jonathan waited with an older couple and a young girl. Their loose tunics and dirt-smudge trousers hinted at a morning tending the sheep and goats. Thom guessed they were Aunt Betz and Uncle Dillen, and Nedd's sister.

"Welcome," Uncle Dillen called. "Jonathan told us everything. Quite a story. We'd like to hear more. This is my wife, Betz, and our daughter, Terza."

"Nice to meet you, Mr...," Thom began.

"Please call us Aunt Betz and Uncle Dillen," the woman cut in.

Trying to sound brave despite a tremble in her voice, Terza asked, "Can I get closer to your dragonet?"

Thom turned to Kamael, and after conferring, added, "She says it's OK."

"Did you speak to her mind to mind?" Uncle Dillen asked.

"Yeah."

"We know you can talk to animals, Jonathan," Aunt Betz said. "Can you talk to the dragonet, as well?"

"Yeah."

Now by the cart, Terza spoke, "She's really pretty."

Since Kamael was stronger, her color had deepened to a vivid magenta, shading to a forest green. The gold on her forehead and the tip of her tail remained faint, but Thom expected them to brighten soon.

"Does she have a name?" Terza asked.

"She does. But dragons decide who gets to hear it. It's their custom."

"How did you learn that?" Aunt Betz asked.

"From her mother. But I've no idea how to care for her. I doubt the Acadium has any books."

"I'll help you search," Jonathan offered.

"Thanks."

"Let's unload the goods," Uncle Dillen said. "I see your dragonet's resting on top of the pile."

Thom nodded.

"Nedd, grab a few old blankets to replace them," Uncle Dillen told his son.

"I'll get two farmhands to help," Terza added.

Thom alerted Kamael that they needed to move her.

The farmhands then unloaded the goods quickly, eyeing her warily, despite Thom's reassurances.

Admiring a jumper, Aunt Betz remarked, "These designs are beautiful. I've met people who'd pay well for this. Your family's truly gifted, Jonathan."

"Thanks, Aunt Betz."

"Jonathan," Thom whispered, "your cousin called you Jonny, but your aunt called you Jonathan."

"I prefer Jonathan," he replied quietly, clearly displeased.

"Thom," Aunt Betz said, "would you join us for supper? That is... if you can leave your... dragonet."

"Let me check." He was quiet for a beat. "She says she'd be fine, but she's hungry. Do you have anything I can give her?"

"We do. A wolf got into the pasture yesterday. Our watchdog chased it off, but not before it killed an ewe. Dillen skinned it this morning. Would your dragon like that?"

"Yes, but are you sure? I don't want to take food from your family."

"Yes. We butchered a sheep a few days ago and have plenty. I've got a big pot of mutton stew on the hearth."

"Thank you."

When Thom told Kamael, she tilted her head and parted her mouth slightly. Her ears, small and fin-like, quivered, and her eyes glowed with anticipation.

"I take it she's pleased," Aunt Betz said.

"She is."

"Follow me to our springhouse," Nedd offered.

Before Thom could do so, Jonathan asked, "Can I help feed her? I just want to show my aunt and uncle a few of the new designs first."

"Sure. I'll meet you back here."

Nedd then led him to a small building beside the house. Inside, a chill hit him, and Thom shivered. Meat and other food hung from hooks.

Seeing his reaction, Nedd said. "Paps and I diverted a stream and ran stave pipes underneath to keep it cool."

"That's clever."

Nedd grabbed a slab of meat, slung it over his shoulder, and carried it to a table outside. He was about to cut it up when Thom intervened.

"Would you mind if I say a quick prayer first? I want to thank the animal for helping another life."

Afterward, Thom explained the size of the chunks needed. Working together, they finished quickly. Terza arrived with two large bowls.

"Mam said you can use these to carry the meat to your dragonet."

"Thanks," Thom replied.

"Can I watch you feed her?"

"Sure."

As Nedd and Thom approached Kamael, Thom saw Jonathan waiting by the cart.

Kamael sniffed, her eyes lighting up.

"I'll see you inside," Nedd said.

"Thanks. Terza, stay a couple of steps back."

"OK."

"Jonathan, stand beside me, and hand me one piece at a time. Be careful. She's not always neat, and you may get spattered."

"Good to know."

As expected, Kamael devoured each bite.

"She was hungry," Terza noted, as her mother's voice rang out. "Coming."

"Yeah," Thom said. "Back when I found her, her siblings tore through their food quickly. Might be normal for dragonets."

"There were more?" she asked, her eyes wide.

"Terza!"

"Oops! I'm coming," she called, hurrying off.

"She's asleep."

"That seems pretty normal," Thom explained. "Is there somewhere where we can clean up?"

"By the barn," Jonathan answered, noticing the spatters on his tunic.

Thom finished a second helping of the stew, sopping up the gravy with a thick slice of warm, crusty bread Aunt Betz had just pulled from the oven.

"I see you were hungry," she said.

"It was wonderful. Thanks."

"You're welcome. If you don't mind me asking, Nedd said you wanted to pray before cutting the mutton."

"Yeah. To thank the sheep's spirit for feeding the dragonet. I learned that from the Glakkadians." He paused. Calling Kamael 'the dragonet' felt wrong. He needed a name others could use.

"Glakkadians?" Nedd asked.

"People in the Glakkadeth Archipelago. My teacher and I lived there for a few years. They believe everything shares the same essence, and every living thing has a spirit."

"Hmm," Jonathan said.

"Yes?" Thom prompted.

"That's nice. I'd like to hear more about what you learned from them."

"OK."

"Where's Glakkadeth?" Terza asked. "I never heard of it, or Glakadekians."

"Glakkadians," Thom corrected. "The Glakkadeth Archipelago is a group of islands southwest of our continent."

"What are they like? Do they eat weird food? Wear strange clothes? Do they speak like us?"

"Now, Terza," Aunt Betz said gently, "Thom and Jonathan need to get going if they want to reach the Acadium before dinner. If we can convince Thom to visit us again, maybe he'll tell you another time?"

"Happy to."

"I'll fetch two fresh horses," Nedd added.

"Let me put together a bag with apples and sweet biscuits for the road," Aunt Betz offered.

"I'd appreciate it," Thom said.

When Jonathan and Thom neared the cart, Kamael stirred, blinking sleepily. Her eyes met his, and he sensed a flicker of discomfort.

Are you OK? Thom mind-spoke.

I... leaked, she murmured.

Leaked?

Her eyes fell on the blankets, then away, as if embarrassed.

"Oh, dear," Thom said, noticing the wet spot. "Jonathan, do you have another blanket? She... uh... had to...uh... Sorry."

"What's wrong?" Nedd asked, arriving with the horses.

Thom pointed. "The dragonet peed."

"Ah. Jonathan, would you hitch the horses? I'll get more blankets."

When Nedd came back, they swapped out the soiled ones.

Are you comfortable? Thom asked.

Sleepy.

Rest then.

"All set?" Nedd asked.

"Yes," Thom replied, climbing into the cart.

Aunt Betz hurried toward them, with Uncle Dillen and Terza close behind. "You can't forget the food," she said, handing Jonathan a bag.

"Oh yeah. Thanks again. Nice meeting you." Thom noticed the two farmhands remained by the barn.

"You're welcome," Uncle Dillen replied. "Do your teachers know you're bringing a dragonet back?"

"No. And I wasn't supposed to be gone overnight either."

"I'd love to see their faces when you tell them," he said. "I'd suggest you tell them alone, Thom, while Nedd and Jonathan hang back with the dragonet. It was a shock when we heard. It's certain to be for them. And cover her when you arrive. No need to cause panic."

"Good idea."

Nedd urged the horses forward as the cart rumbled down the graveled road.

Thom checked behind and saw the family waving. He lifted his hand in acknowledgment before facing the road ahead. "Now I've got to figure out how to tell my teachers."

"Good luck with that," Nedd said, smirking.

Chapter 5

"Commander, did you find him?" Queen Niamh asked, swallowing a bite of beef pastie.

"No, your Majesty."

"I wish Rin were here," King Pethuric said, pacing their office in Cleirigh Hall. "Maybe he could've detected his energy like he did when he found Thom years ago."

"I know. But he's in Eiren, trying to make amends with Gabi for not showing up four years ago. That's why he offered to train her healers." She handed him a pastie. "Peth, eat. We've had nonstop meetings all morning, and you don't think clearly on an empty stomach, especially if we're going to figure out how to find Thom."

"True," he replied, taking a small bite. "We should at least send Rin a message."

"Mac and Noiri expected Thom back before dinner yesterday," Queen Niamh said. "Is that correct, commander?"

"Yes, your Majesty," she replied, standing at attention, dark brown hair brushing her broad shoulders. "Healer MacDonuld said he was collecting fungus in Glinurif Forest."

"It's possible something delayed him," Queen Niamh speculated.

"Maybe," King Pethuric said, "but we still haven't discovered which noble was behind Thom's kidnapping. What if they found out he returned? I don't like this. Not at all."

"Neither do I. Commander, you said your team searched the forest. Did they find any trace of him?"

"Subcommander Rycard's squad found cart and horse tracks near the forest, but no sign of him. Those could've been from any traveler. And Duncan said Thom walked."

"Cart tracks," King Pethuric repeated. "Anything else?"

"One guard reported seeing drag marks coming from the forest."

The queen frowned, meeting her husband's gaze. "Someone could've taken him. Send another team to examine those marks closely."

"I agree," the king replied.

"Immediately, your majesties."

"And Commander," the king added, "ask Provost Gavin to join. Maybe she knows a teacher or academ with tracking skills."

"Good thinking," the queen concurred.

"Will do," the commander replied, quickly exiting the office.

"Now, Peth, sit down and finish eating. Your pacing's driving me crazy," Niamh said.

Chapter 6

Nedd guided the cart to the left side of the Acadium, beyond the stone wall that enclosed the grounds. They stopped short of the side entrance—the same one Thom had entered with Paddi on his first day here two weeks before.

Thom mind-spoke to Kamael. *"I'm going inside to tell the provost about you. She'll probably be shocked.*

Why?

Most humans don't believe dragons are real.

Why?

No one's seen your kind for a long time.

Why?

"Jonathan, are you hearing this?"

"Yeah," he replied. "Sounds like Terza when she was 3."

"It's strange," Thom murmured. "She doesn't always sound that young. Maybe it's a dragon thing."

"Are you guys mind-speaking to her?" Nedd asked.

"Yeah," Thom replied. "I'm trying to explain what's coming, even though I'm not sure."

"That'll be a challenge."

Kamael, I can't explain. Can you trust me? Thom asked.

OK.

I'm covering you up in case anyone comes by. Stay quiet.

Kamael dipped her snout.

After making sure the blanket hid her, Thom climbed down. "I'll be back as soon as I can."

"Sure you don't want me with you?" Jonathan asked.

"Yeah. The provost might be angry, and I don't want her taking it out on you."

"OK."

Thom hurried toward the side door, his breath unsteady. *Ground to the earth,* he told himself. *Divine advisors, thanks for your help in advance.*

Stepping inside, he spotted Jena Ginnis, a third-year academ, seated at the same table where she'd been when he first arrived.

At the sound of the door closing, she shrieked, "Thom! Are you OK? Everyone's looking for you. You were supposed to be back before dinner yesterday. What happened?"

"Uh. I'm all right. Is Provost Gavin around?"

"She's with Healer Mac in her office."

"I'm guessing they're worried."

"That's an understatement," Jena said, "and I don't know why. It's not like you've been gone a whole day."

"Um. Thanks, Jena. I should go."

At the provost's door, Thom stopped, inhaled deeply, and grounded himself before knocking.

"Jena," came the provost voice, "I said no interruptions."

Thom eased the door open. "It's not Jena. It's me."

"Thom!" Provost Gavin and Healer MacDonuld exclaimed together.

The healer jumped up with such force that her chair toppled over.

"Where have you been? Were you kidnapped again? Are you hurt?" Provost Gavin fired off the questions in rapid succession.

"Can I come in?" he asked timidly.

"Get in here!"

Thom stepped inside, a little reluctantly, and shut the door.

Healer MacDonuld's eyes went immediately to his bandage. "You're injured."

"A little. It's healing well. Another academ helped. And no, I wasn't kidnapped."

"What academ?" they asked in unison.

"Jonathan. He's starting his first year here, too. I don't know his last name." He hesitated before adding, he's outside with the fungus and herbs I collected, Healer MacDonuld. I got a lot," he said, hoping to ease the tension.

"Why didn't he come in?" Provost Gavin asked, then waved it off. "Never mind. I need to inform the monarchs you're safe. They sent two search parties!" Her tone was sharp.

"Sorry for causing trouble. But... how did you learn I was kidnapped before?"

"When you hadn't returned," Healer MacDonuld said sternly, "I sought out Noiri. I wasn't very worried... until she told me thugs from here kidnapped you when you lived in Glakkadeth."

"Rin told me a few weeks ago," Noiri explained, her tone softening. "He, the King, Queen, and I discussed whether to provide you with special protection, but we wanted your time here to feel normal. When Mac told me you were missing, I went straight to Niamh and Peth."

"Oh no," Thom replied. "I'm really sorry. Like I said, I wasn't kidnapped. But something unusual did happen. Before you tell the monarchs I'm back, can I explain?"

Both were momentarily silent, before Noiri said, "Go ahead, but quickly."

Thom began recounting the events. When he mentioned the wild boar, Mac cut in.

"Your wound," she said, pointing at the bandage.

"Her tusk jabbed me as I escaped."

"I want to check it. And I'll need to meet the academ you mentioned."

Thom was now the one who fell silent, unsure how to bring up Kamael. Maybe being direct was best, so he told them.

"A dragonet," Provost Gavin repeated skeptically, her tone once again firm. "If Rin hadn't vouched for you, I'd say you were telling tales."

"I could hardly accept it myself."

"Are we supposed to believe you stumbled across a mythical creature?" Healer MacDonuld asked, her measured and unyielding. "You're trustworthy, Thom. But this is hard to swallow."

"Um...," Thom replied. "I can show you."

"What?" Provost Gavin asked.

"I brought her back with me. She's not old enough to survive on her own. I promised her mother I'd care for her."

"She's here? At the Acadium?" the provost asked, her eyes widening.

"Outside in a cart with Jonathan and his cousin."

"Very well, Academ Macirdan," she said, standing. "Take us to her."

Thom gulped, noting her displeasure. "Yes, Provost."

Hearing the sounds of people approaching, Jena lifted her head. "See, Noiri? Thom's OK," she said, failing to register the expression on the provost's face.

"Yes, I do, Academ Ginnis. "Go find Odhran and send him to my office. He's with the weapons trainers."

Odhran, whom everyone called Oddi, was the King and Queen's son. He was too young to be an academ, but occasionally studied there.

"Certainly, Provost."

As they stepped outside, Thom pointed to the cart.

He was relieved that Kamael remained quiet as they approached. Jonathan and Nedd had climbed down.

"Provost Gavin and Healer MacDonuld," Thom said, "this is the academ who helped me."

"I'm Jonathan Llewelyn."

"Ah," Provost Gavin said. "You sent word you'd arrive late due to an emergency."

"Yes. Nice to meet you, Provost," he said, offering his hand.

"Likewise," she replied, shaking it.

"Academ Llewelyn," Healer MacDonuld said, "you and I will need to talk, since you'll be under my tutelage. I'm Head-healer MacDonuld."

"Nice to meet you as well, Healer," he said, shaking her hand. "This is my cousin, Nedd."

The youth ducked his head. "Nice to meet you."

"Now, Thom," Provost Gavin said, disbelief evident in her voice. "Where's this mythical creature?"

Reaching into the cart, Thom lifted the blanket. "Provost Gavin, Healer MacDonuld... meet the dragonet."

She lifted her head and studied them with interest.

Kamael, these are Provost Gavin and Healer MacDonuld, he mind-spoke.

The dragonet blinked slowly and said, *Hi,* with an audible meep.

The provost and healer were stunned.

Are they OK? Kamael asked.

Probably. They're surprised you're real. "Noiri? Mac?"

"It's truly a dragonet," Noiri breathed, rubbing her eyes. "I can't believe it. But I am seeing him."

Mac remained silent.

"She's a female," Thom said. *Kamael, I haven't told them your name, but is there one I can call you instead of 'dragonet'?*

Kami.

That works, Jonathan mind-spoke to Thom.

Thom started. *We can mind-speak? How did you know?*

I didn't. I thought maybe I could, since we can both talk to her.

"What do you call her?" Mac asked, coming out of her stupor.

"Kami."

"Kami," Noiri repeated. "She has deep blue eyes, like she can see into your soul."

Thom hadn't considered that.

"And her coloring's beautiful," Mac added.

Thank you, Kamael replied, glancing down shyly.

"She said thank you," Jonathan offered.

"Wait," Noiri said. "You both can talk with her? Mind-speech?"

"Yes, ma'am," Jonathan replied. "I can speak with most animals."

"You and I must talk soon, young man," Mac said. Turning to Noiri, she asked, "When you meet with Jonathan to review his skills, would you include me?"

"Of course. Now that we're over our shock..."

"Speak for yourself," Mac cut in.

"What I was going to say, Mac," she continued, pointedly, "was that we can't stay here. Deliveries often come to the side door. But I have a place in mind—an old storage building behind the Acadium that's mostly unused."

"Thanks, Noiri," Thom exhaled in relief. He wasn't being sent away, and Kami was welcome. *And thanks, Divine Advisors, especially you, Sereh. I can't imagine what I'd do without your support.*

Sereh was Thom's guardian angel and had been with him his entire life, as well as in previous lives.

"Best cover Kami again until you get her inside," Noiri advised. "I'll meet you there. I need to get the key." Addressing Mac, she added, "I also want Oddi to fetch his parents."

"I assume you'll want them to dress down to avoid being recognized."

"Smart. I'll have Oddi pass that along as well. I'll see you shortly." With that, Noiri left.

"Thom, I want to check your arm," Mac added. "I'll get a few supplies from the Rejuvenary and then join you."

Thom, Jonathan, and Nedd stood before the barn-sized doors of a two-story stone building. Thom exhaled in relief. Kami would fit through those doors. She was small, but once she grew to her mother's size, a regular door wouldn't work.

Once Noiri let them in, they broke apart a few hay bales, fashioned a nest, and carefully placed Kamael in it.

Meanwhile, Nedd led the horses and cart out and secured them to a tree to the right of the building.

Is this OK? Thom asked.

Cold.

"Did she say something?" Noiri asked.

"She's cold."

"Use the blankets from the cart," Jonathan suggested. "I'm sure Nedd's family won't mind. I'll fetch them."

"Thanks. That should help."

"Do you know how warm she needs to be?" Noiri asked.

"No."

"I'll find Mac and see what we can do."

When Noiri and Mac reappeared, they were carrying an armload of blankets. Jonathan returned with Nedd, bringing a few more.

"We couldn't come up with anything better for now," Noiri said. "The king and queen are on their way. They want to see you for themselves, Thom, and meet Kami. We had to tell Oddi. He needed to understand why his parents had to dress down. He won't tell anyone."

"Uh... I guess that's up to you, Noiri."

He was adjusting the blankets to get Kami as warm as possible when the smaller door opened. In walked two adults and a boy, dressed in scruffy tunics and trousers with their heads and faces mostly covered. The man wore a floppy hat much like the one Rin had. The woman had a headscarf, and the boy wore a red cap. They appeared to be an ordinary family.

"Thom!" King Pethuric shouted, rushing over to him and pulling him into a powerful hug. "You're all right, aren't you?"

"Uh, yeah... but I'm having a little trouble breathing, Your Majesty."

"Sorry," the king said, releasing him.

Queen Niamh stepped forward, offering him a gentler embrace. "We're glad you're safe. You do have a tendency to disappear."

"Yeah," Thom replied with a sheepish grimace. "I don't mean to."

"Well, you'd be getting a stern talking to," Niamh continued, "if not for the... unexpected guest."

The boy, Oddi, stared wide-eyed at the dragon, his brown eyes bulging. He appeared about eight, with wavy, blond hair poking out wildly from under his cap. Thom recalled the mess his own hair used to be at that age, as it sometimes still was.

"This is Kami," Thom said. "Kami, this is Queen Niamh and King Pethuric, the leaders of our land. The boy's their son, Oddi."

Kamael lifted herself onto her unsteady forelegs, gave a small bob of her head, then collapsed.

"Did you teach her that?" Oddi asked.

"No. And I'm Thom."

"Nice to meet you," he replied.

"And who are these others?" Queen Niamh asked.

"This is Jonathan Llewellyn and his cousin Nedd, Your Majesties," Thom said. "Jonathan's starting his first year as a healer. Nedd drove us here."

Jonathan and Nedd bowed. "Your Majesties."

"No need for that in private," King Pethuric said. "Please, call us Peth and Niamh if you're comfortable."

"Thank you, your... um... Peth and Niamh," Nedd murmured.

"Thank you," Jonathan responded, amused by his cousin's awkwardness.

"You've probably told Noiri and Mac what happened," Niamh said. "But we'd like to hear it."

"Here, Niamh?" Mac asked.

"Yes. If we went to our office, word would spread that Thom's back. Given our guest, this place will do. Peth and I can sit on hay bales. I do have one request, Noiri."

"Yes, Niamh?"

"Since it's dinner time, could one of you bring us food to share? Oddi'd be glad to help."

"I would?" he asked. "But I want to stay."

"Yes, you would," Peth said firmly. Oddi frowned, but remained quiet.

"Certainly," Noiri said, grinning behind her hand.

"Thom, do you think Kami's hungry?" Mac asked.

Before he could answer, Kami nodded vigorously.

Peth blinked. "Kami understands our language."

"She does," Thom said.

"I'll go with Noiri and Oddi to get a slab of roast for her," Mac offered.

"Could you bring back a knife?" Thom asked. "And if there's a liver or a heart, Kami enjoys those."

Peth raised an eyebrow.

"Mamie, Da, can Thom wait to tell his story until I'm back?" Oddi pleaded.

Peth chuckled. "Yes, we can ask him, son."

"I'll wait."

When the three came back, Noiri juggled a basket of pasties, cheese, fruit, a pitcher of water, and cups. Mac carried a large bag and a bowl. Oddi lugged two buckets—grain for the horses.

"Did you wait?" Oddi blurted, handing the buckets to Nedd.

"Yes," Thom said, smiling. "But first, I want to feed Kami."

Mac set the bowl on a hay bale and pulled a knife from her pocket.

"Want help?" Jonathan asked.

"Yeah, thanks," Thom said. "Eat, all of you. Don't wait for us."

Accepting Mac's bag, Thom was pleased to find a liver, along with the roast. Kami's nostrils flared at the scent, and she let out a gurgle of excitement, drawing chuckles.

"If that doesn't prove she's harmless," Niamh said, "nothing will."

Kami made quick work of the food and soon after closed her eyes.

"She's a few days old. So she sleeps quite a bit," Thom explained.

At last, unable to resist Oddi's pleading eyes, Thom began his story between bites of pastie. When he finished, Noiri gave him a curious look.

"When you told us your story earlier," she commented, "you didn't mention meeting Ariel."

"Oh. I kept it short because I was worried about Kami waiting in the cart."

"It's incredible to think you first met Ariel as a toddler," Peth remarked. "I wonder if that's what Seer Lalia saw years ago?"

"It seems likely," Niamh said. "The stories my grandmother told spoke of dragons' wisdom. Thom, remember when Rin told you about her vision?"

"Yeah. About Ariel, I didn't remember until I saw her yesterday." Was it only a day ago? he wondered.

"Do you still have Ariel's scale?" Oddi asked.

"Yeah," Thom said, pulling it from his pocket.

"Can I touch it?"

"Sure," Thom said, handing it over. Facing the king and queen, he added, "Your Majesties... um... I mean, Peth and Niamh, you didn't seem shocked when you saw Kami. Did you already know dragons were real?"

Niamh replied, "Yes, but no one's seen any in centuries. We presumed them extinct. Over time, people believed they were myths. My ancestors chose to encourage that."

"Truly?" Noiri said, startled.

"At our country's founding, dragons were essentially our partners," Niamh explained.

"Partners?" Mac echoed.

"Yes. I believe the alliance ended not long after Cleirigh Hall was built, around 650. Most of what we knew was lost. Apparently, the building behind our residence was used for dragons and their riders to take off and land."

"Riders, Wow!" Thom exclaimed.

"How many were there?" Noiri asked.

"Not sure. Or why the partnership ended." Addressing Thom, she asked, "How many know about Kami?"

"Besides us, Nedd's parents, his sister, and two farmhands. My family doesn't, and neither does my sponsor, Paddi."

"Good. We want to avoid panic and keep her safe. For now, let's keep this quiet."

"OK. Can I ask a question about Paddi? It's not about COM."

COM—Covert Observers and Messengers for the Docha-leigh Commonwealth—was formed when Niamh became queen. Its members watched for anything that might affect their land.

"Hmm," Niamh said. "Rin told you about that?"

"Yeah. I sort of figured it out. Before he left, he told me Paddi was a member."

"OK," Niamh said cautiously. "What's your question?"

"When I met him, Padraic Byrne, at his sister's, he told me to call him Paddi. My Da said calling someone that isn't nice."

"I can answer that," Peth cut in. "His younger sister, Lida, who you've met, started it. She couldn't pronounce Padraic when she was little."

"It stuck," Niamh added.

"Back to Kami, hon," Peth said, "Keeping her secret won't be easy, especially with nosy academs."

"Hmm. Not to mention the amount of food she'll need. Let's discuss that at the residence. We'll need a meeting with a few key people, including the chief cook, a couple of hunters, and the commander. But yes, we need to be careful."

"Whatever you think best, Your Majesties," Thom said, using their titles given the gravity of the situation.

"Back to Kami's quarters," Peth said. "Thom, is Kami's nest sufficient?"

"I'm not sure. I'll ask her when she wakes. But Ariel suggested asking falcon trainers, even though dragons are mammals, not birds."

"Worth exploring," Peth replied. "Niamh, wouldn't there have been books or scrolls on dragon care?"

"Probably, but who can say if they survived?"

"I can check the Royal Library," Oddi offered.

"The Acadium's library is also extensive," Noiri added.

"Thom," Mac said, "skip working in the Rejuvenary these next two weeks before classes start. Split your time between searching and caring for Kami. I'll ask the falconers if they have any books about healing."

"Thanks, Mac. I also wanted to remind you I collected plenty of fungus, saxifrage, and other herbs."

"I'd forgotten. And I need to check your wound before I forget that again. Will Kami be good on her own?"

"She should sleep for an hour."

"Good."

"Jonathan," Noiri said, "go to my office now. I need to assign you a room. Tomorrow morning, you, Mac, and I will discuss your skills and coursework."

"Yes, ma'am."

"Nedd," Noiri said, "would you like to stay in a guest room tonight or head back to your farm?"

"Here, thanks. The horses and I could use the rest. They're to the right of this building. Is that OK?"

"For tonight, yes. Otherwise, you could house the horses in the Acadium stables. Sorry, I should've suggested that earlier."

"That's all right. Something else was on your mind."

Chapter 7

Thom spent the night with Kami. He didn't want her waking up in a strange place without him. Shortly before sunrise, she nudged him, demanding food. He hadn't slept well, and his neck ached from resting his head against her. Stepping outside, the sky was lightening in the east. Another clear and warm day was ahead.

Groggy, he went to his room, changed, and attended to his personal needs. Then he headed to the staff dining room, where the cooks continued serving meals until more academs returned. He hoped to find Noiri or Mac to ask about getting food for Kami.

Luck was with him. Both were there, along with Jonathan and Nedd, chatting at the same table.

"Good morning."

"Good morning, Thom," they replied.

"I see I'm not the only one up early."

"Nedd needs to get home to help with the animals," Jonathan replied.

"I understand. How are you all?"

"A certain guest has been on our mind," Noiri said.

Mac tilted her head. "Can I presume you spent the night with her?"

"And she's asking for breakfast?" Jonathan smiled.

"Yes, to both," Thom said.

Shifting uneasily, he eyed the kitchen doors. How was he supposed to get her food? Should he just walk in and ask? Had Noiri already spoken to the cook? And what would he even say?

"I don't know how much or how often she needs to eat," Thom admitted. "Yesterday, she ate three times. She nearly died after hatching, and I had to feed her energy to keep her alive."

"Interesting," Mac said. "Did that come from your spirit-healing gift?"

"Mostly," Thom said, leaving out his help from Archangel Raphael and the healing angels.

"I'd like to talk more about that," Mac continued. "I understand you'll be training with Mage Keenan and Brother Lamen. I want my work with you to complement theirs."

"OK," Thom replied. "Noiri, you said Brother Lamen gets back next week. I'm not sure about Mage Keenan."

"She'll be back today. I'd suggest you and Mac meet with her together. Mac, can you arrange that?"

"Certainly."

"Um... could I make a request?" Thom asked.

"Go ahead," Noiri replied.

"Can Jonathan join us? From what he told me, he might have a minor spirit-healing gift."

"Of course," Mac said.

"What's weird," Jonathan added, "is that Thom's biggest gift is spirit healing. His physical healing's strong too, but not at the same level. Mine are flipped."

"That's remarkable. And weird, as you say." Mac chuckled.

"Excuse me," Nedd cut in. "Didn't you say your guest was hungry, Thom?"

"Digi. She won't be happy I haven't brought her food yet."

"That's what we were discussing before you arrived," Noiri said. "After breakfast, I'm going to see Niamh and Peth to ask if the royal hunters might increase their quota and deliver the meat to the cooling larder. Mac and I have taken the head staff cook into our confidence. I'll introduce you."

"Cooling larder?" Jonathan asked.

"An academ invented it five years ago. Large ice blocks sit behind screens that vent into the larder. Ice porters replace them daily through hatches. One was added to the Royal Residence and an even larger one to Cleirigh Hall."

"Our family could use that," Jonathan said.

Thom shifted impatiently. "That's interesting, but can we go now?"

"Of course," Noiri replied.

"Thom, you haven't eaten," Jonathan noted. "I'll get you a couple of egg and cheese pasties and a drink. Juice or coffee?"

"I'd prefer a drink called Timbu, but none of you have heard of it. Juice, please."

"I've got to hear about that," Jonathan replied. "I'll bring your food after I see Nedd off."

"Oh, Nedd. Sorry. I don't know where my head's been."

"We do," the four of them said in unison, exchanging looks.

"Ugh," Thom groaned. "Of course. Thanks for your help. You were a lifesaver."

"You're welcome. Mam and I visit the city every few weeks, and the whole family comes every other month. I wouldn't be surprised if Terza wants to join us more often."

"Well, thanks again, and safe travels," Thom said, hugging Nedd, before following Noiri into the kitchen.

"Good luck in school," Nedd called after him.

Thom was feeding Kamael small chunks of lamb when the door opened and Jonathan walked in.

"How's Kamael?"

"I don't want to ask while Kami's eating," Thom said, as she swallowed another bite.

Better, she mind-spoke to both. *And I can eat and mind-speak at the same time.*

Thom blinked. Of course, she could. Kami's responses confused him, though. Sometimes she acted like a child; other times, as if she lived for centuries. *I should've known better,* he admitted to her. *You seem stronger this morning.*

I am.

"Do you think you can feed yourself now?" Thom asked aloud. "I'm happy to continue as long as you need, but once classes start, I'll have less time."

I don't know.

Kamael, Jonathan offered, *Is it OK if I feed you so Thom can eat?*

Yes, that's fine.

After Thom and Kami had finished their food, he and Jonathan were cleaning up when Mac entered.

"Good morning, beauty," she said to Kamael.

I like her, Kamael replied.

"She said she likes you," Thom relayed.

"That's sweet. Given what you said about Kami being weak when she hatched, I'd like to sense into her condition. I recognize you're her guardian, but as your advisor, I think it's warranted."

"OK."

He and Jonathan watched as Mac knelt beside Kami, placed one hand on her head, and rested the other lightly along her upper spine.

"Her brain's fully formed. Clearly, I've never examined a dragon, but structurally, it seems intact. And judging by the rapid signal activity I'm sensing, she'll likely be quick-witted."

Thank you, Kami replied.

"She said thank you," Jonathan relayed this time.

"You can sense brain signals?" Thom asked. "Rin taught me about them. I couldn't detect any. Jonathan, can you?"

"I don't know."

"Place your hand on her head, like mine," Mac instructed, indicating her fingers spread across the back of Kami's head.

Jonathan's eyes widened. "I can feel them."

"You do have a powerful gift, Jonathan," Mac said, sitting back to give him more space. "I'm only aware of a few who can do that. About Kami, unfortunately, I hear a crackle in her lungs. You said you tried to keep her dry during the rain?"

"I did my best," Thom said, brow furrowed.

"I'm sure you did. If she were human, I'd prepare her a medicinal tea. I still think it's worth trying. You'll have to work out how to help her drink it."

"I will."

"Her muscles are weak, too. She needs to be warmer."

"I was thinking the same," Thom said. "And I keep getting flashes of caves."

"Didn't you see images of Aponi's birth?" Mac asked.

"I did. Does that mean I can see past events for an individual as well as an entire species?"

"Maybe. Speak with Mage Keenan about that."

"Mac, Thom," Jonathan said, "can I check Kami's lungs too? I would've said something earlier, but I was kind of in shock about what Mac said about my abilities."

"Please," she said, moving further away.

"I feel the crackle. Can you, Thom?"

He stepped beside him, placing his hand next to Jonathan's, touching it briefly. Jonathan's skin was soft and smooth beneath his fingers.

Shaking himself, Thom refocused. "I do."

Jonathan moved his hand lower. "Her bowels are a bit irregular. OK if I try to help?"

"No," Thom replied, a twinge of jealousy rising. " I mean, yes," he corrected. Why hadn't he caught that? He'd been able to sense what was wrong with Mirabel years ago.

When Jonathan spoke again, he said, "Her lungs and bowels are better. I'm not sure if it's her age or because she's a dragon, but it required more effort than with humans or other animals. While sensing within her, I noticed something about her wings."

"What?" Thom asked, concern tightening his chest. Missing something else stung more than he wanted to admit.

"Her bones are fragile. The membranes might be too thin. But I haven't worked with birds."

"I'm not very familiar with them, either," Mac said. "But let me check."

"Kami had a tough hatching," Thom added. "But since her siblings flew off two days after emerging, I thought she'd be fine once she got stronger."

"The crackle's gone," Mac said. "Good job, Jonathan. And I share your concern about her wings. I'd suggest speaking with our falconer."

"Has he been told about Kami?" Thom asked.

"She. And no. I'll speak with Niamh about including her in our group."

"Thanks, Mac. Kami's mother did say a person familiar with birds might help."

"Once the falconer learns, I'd imagine she'll come as soon as she's available," Mac said.

"Back to getting Kami warmer. Maybe we could heat rocks and place them underneath wool cloths or canvas for padding. What do you think?"

"That might work," Mac said, rising. "I think I know how we can do that—with Mage Keenan's help."

"OK," Thom replied, curiously.

At the door, she added, "Jonathan, I'll see you in Noiri's office shortly."

"Yes, ma'am."

After she'd left, Thom said, "Kami's asleep. I'll go to the library to see if I can find any books."

"I'll meet you when I'm free."

Chapter 8

Thom had started on another row of books when Jonathan appeared.

"Any luck?"

"No. I couldn't ask the librarian either, because she wasn't told about our guest. When she offered to help, I told her I was learning the layout of the library."

Jonathan tilted his head. "Makes sense. Can I help?"

"Thanks."

Before long, Jonathan had found a book on raising geese, but nothing on dragons.

"I'm such an idiot," Thom said, smacking his forehead.

"Why?"

"Niamh said that dragons stopped being partners with people ages ago. Rin told me they built the Acadium around 900. That's over a hundred and sixty years ago. If there were books on dragons, they wouldn't be here."

"Good point. Should we stop searching?"

"For now. Maybe we'll find a book on falcons or eagles at another time. I hope Oddi's had better luck in his family library."

"Me too."

"I need to clean up. The upper shelves were dusty," Thom said, punctuating his comment with a loud sneeze.

"Deu bless you," Jonathan replied. "Or should I say, the One bless you?"

"I'll take both."

"I would've thought the librarian would be a stickler for cleanliness. Ours back home insisted on it."

"I'd imagine she's the same here. But this place is huge. Dusting's probably an academ's job, and no one's been assigned since Mei. Anyway, Kamael's breakfast also splattered me. Should've cleaned up first. Have you used the washroom shower yet?"

"Shower? Is that the closet where water sprays over your head?"

"Yeah."

"I saw one this morning and figured it was for washing clothes. Nearly got soaked when it started spraying. My fathers would love it. They complain baths take too long. I like baths."

"In that case, Jena Ginnis said there are soaking tubs in the lower level, next to the salle. One's for men, and another's for women. They're filled with bubbling hot water, perfect for sore muscles. Jena told me lots of academs head there after weapons training."

"Do they work?"

"I haven't tried them yet, but she swears they do. By the way, what room are you in?"

"440G, above the Rejuvenary."

"You're across the hall from me, 437G, on Quad Gallean."

"I'm guessing the G stands for Gallean."

"Exactly. Each room number ends with the first letter of its quad: Gallean, Lamond, Chanzie, and Diarg. Makes it easier to find people."

"And they're named after the mountains in Docha-leigh," Jonathan added.

"Oh yeah. Anyway, I'd like to hear how your meeting with Noiri and Mac went. Can you stop by my room after I shower?"

"Sure."

Thom lay on his bed reading the novel he'd borrowed from Paddi before coming to the Acadium. He surveyed his room. It was much larger than his alcove at home, and included a desk, wooden chair, wardrobe, and bookcase. He wished it had a comfortable chair, like in Sestra B's office.

On one shelf sat *Demba's Chronicles*. Rin had bought him the first book in the series years ago in Dridley to help him learn Glakkadian. It was also the city where he and Rin had taken a ship to Glakkadeth when he was nine.

Thinking of the series made him think of Mekial, his friend in Glakkadeth. He missed her a lot. Like him, she was a fan of the books. It featured dragons, and he had to assume his divine advisors had a hand in choosing it. He couldn't believe he was a guardian of a dragonet. It felt like a dream.

On top of the bookcase sat three objects. One was an angel carving with a repaired wing. He hadn't planned to buy it—he'd been looking for a gift for Khali, a girl from Dridley who helped him learn Glakkadian. But the shop owner accused him of being one of the thieves plaguing his store. Thom had been tempted to use his gift to convince him otherwise when the angel fell and broke. He and Rin believed his advisors had caused it to fall as a warning.

To the left of the angel sat his blue treasure jar, holding Ariel's scale. He was glad he now remembered when he got it. On the other side was the wooden carving of Apollo, a gift from Rindo, whom he'd healed when Rindo was three. The carving was lifelike. Impressive for a seven-year-old. He'd been happy to see Rindo and his family a few months earlier, since he'd been worried about the boy's health. Paddi, Rindo's uncle, hand-delivered Rindo's carvings to a local vendor to sell. Thom wondered if he could find the shop.

Settling back into reading, he lost himself in a world where divine beings incarnated as horses. He was reading about one attempting to rescue a child who had fallen through river ice, when a knock startled him.

"Come in."

"Sorry, I'm late," Jonathan said. "Mac wanted me to see a patient."

"That's OK," Thom said, closing his book. "An academ?"

"No, a carpenter working at the Royal Residence. Her apprentice was carrying a board and accidentally hit a box of nails. They flew everywhere, making her look like a pin cushion. A few went in deep."

"Ouch."

"Mac had seen how well I healed your puncture and hoped I could help."

"How'd it go?" Thom asked, sitting up.

"Good. Got all of them cleaned and closed. Mac said she was fit to return to work."

"That's remarkable."

"Hey, your room's the same size as mine. Wait..., you don't have a fireplace either?"

"Oh, right. I didn't notice since the weather's warm. No potbelly stoves either. I wonder how they heat our rooms."

Jonathan shrugged.

"Funny that Jena didn't mention it when she showed me around."

Jonathan tapped the padded window seat. "It looks like we all have one of these."

"I read there sometimes."

"Smart. Speaking of reading, are all your books for class?"

"No, most are part of two fantasy series. One's from my sponsor, Paddi. I'm in the middle of the second book now. The other's in Glakkadian, which includes dragons. Pretty amazing, huh?"

"Any care instructions?"

"Not that I remember. The author claimed she saw dragons flying. That inspired her story. I didn't believe it at the time."

"I wouldn't have either."

"Sit wherever. How'd your meeting go?"

Jonathan settled cross-legged beside him on the bed.

Thom blinked, glad he'd chosen a spot so close.

"Good. I've got a list of books to buy."

"I need a few more myself. What are you taking?"

They compared classes and found they shared math, history, and government. Jonathan had anatomy, while Thom was in second-level herbology.

"I heard we all have to take weapons and self-defense," Jonathan said.

"Yeah."

"Seems strange. Why would people like a historian or metal-worker need that? Don't they spend all their time indoors? I kind of get why healers like us might need it if we travel."

Thom shook his head. "I heard Declan, the armswarden, has to test us to determine our skill level."

"I'll be starting at the basic level, 'cause I've never trained before. Sounds like you have."

"Yeah. Rin taught me first. Then I trained on the ship and in Glakkadeth."

"I noticed you don't have a supervised rotation in the Rejuve-nary."

"No. Mac wanted me to wait until second semester." He was grateful. It gave him more time with Kamael. "Can you tell me more about what you pick up with your spirit-healing gift?"

"When I look at people, I sort of see a glow around them, even colors. But it doesn't last long."

"That's an aura. Yours is purple, green, and brown."

"What do they mean?"

"Purple's tied to the spiritual, green to healing and generosity, and brown to reliability, comfort, and connection to earth. Why don't you try viewing mine? Closing your eyes might help."

Minutes passed when Jonathan spoke again. I'm getting flash-es of purple and green. Maybe blue."

"Blue can mean honesty and truth."

"Where'd you learn it all?"

"Rin."

Jonathan was silent for a time.

Sensing his unease, Thom asked, "Are you OK?"

"Um... would you mind telling me how you ended up in Glakkadeth?"

Thom hesitated. What could he say? *Divine advisors*, he mind-spoke, *what do you think?*

Trust him, came the reply, along with the familiar tingling that marked their presence.

"Did you just check with your advisors?"

"I did. The thing is, only a few people were told. Rin, the King, and the Queen thought it best to keep it quiet."

"Never mind."

"No, it's fine. My advisors told me to trust you."

"They did?" Jonathan's eyes widened. "So... they know me?"

A voice Thom didn't recognize spoke in his mind. *Very well.*

Sereh, who's...? Thom mind-spoke.

You'll learn soon enough.

Not that again, he sighed. Divine beings didn't always give direct answers.

"I promise not to tell anyone," Jonathan said.

Thom shared his story, pausing occasionally to find the right words. He began with Lord Samiltun's scheme but chose not to mention his name, in case the monarchs preferred to keep it quiet. He spoke of the bandits, Rindo, and his kidnapping. He went on to describe how Sestra B had worked with him on his spirit-healing abilities and introduced him to the Glakkadian faith. He ended with how he, Mekial, and Budaj invented his favorite drink.

"Wow. I'm glad you told me about Timbu. You mentioned it before. I've never heard of chocolate."

"Me neither, at least not before Glakkadeth. And sorry for running off at the mouth. It's nice telling someone my age."

"I'm honored. You've gone through so much. I'm not surprised your teacher wanted you to learn self-defense and weapons. And the One Faith sounds... interesting."

"Yeah. Much of what they believe resonates with me. That's why I'm meeting with Brother Lamen at their local chapel."

"That figures."

A chime sounded from the hall clock.

"Oh," Thom said. "We've been talking a while. Let me check the time."

Jena had told him Noiri added the pendulum clocks, after the Acadium was enlarged, to help academs get to class on time. Before that, they used time candles.

When Thom got back to his room, he said, "it's an hour before noon supper. Want to help feed Kamael?" He hoped Jonathan would say yes.

"I'd like that. Bring a rain cloak," Jonathan added, peering out the window. "A storm's coming. I'll go get mine."

Chapter 9

Thom was feeding Kami the last of the meat when a knock sounded at the door.

"I'll get it," Jonathan offered.

"I'm Falconer Elspeth," a female voice said. "Are you Thom?"

"No, Jonathan. He's over there," he said, tilting his head toward Thom. "Has it started raining?"

"A bit," she replied, showing her spattered cloak. "The queen said we have an unusual guest."

"You could say that. Please, come in."

Thom saw a woman about his Mam's age in the doorway. Her short black hair clung to her narrow face and round chin.

"She's real," she whispered. "I knew Niamh wouldn't lie, but... this is incredible." She shook her head. "I'm sorry. She's really something."

Kami raised her head, baring her teeth, her eyes glowing with pleasure.

"She thanks you.... um, Falconer Elspeth. I'm Thom."

"Please call me Ellie. May I come closer? Mac said your dragonet's wings were weak."

"Yes. You can call her Kami. Do you think she's all right?"

Ellie slipped off her cloak, revealing muscular arms, and knelt beside Kami, examining her wings.

"I've never treated anything like her. Bird wings are mostly feathers over skin and bone. Hers are more like a bat's with those membranes. But I have little experience with them."

"Does that mean you can't help?" Thom asked, his disappointment evident.

"Oh, I think I can. I don't have Mac's healing gift, but I've worked with plenty of winged creatures."

"That's a relief."

"I'll need to lift her wings to examine them."

"Let me tell her," Thom said, focusing on Kami. After a moment, he added, "She understands."

"Did you... mind-speak?" Ellie asked, her voice edged with curiosity.

"Yes. We both can."

Ellie's eyes lit up. "Dare I hope? Can you communicate with other animals?"

"No," Thom replied. "I can sense whether they're sick, though."

"I can speak to most," Jonathan admitted.

"You could be a great help to us animal handlers... if Mac can spare you occasionally."

"I'll have to ask," Jonathan said.

"Fair enough. Now to business."

Ellie delicately ran her hands over the left wing, tracing the bones between each segment. Holding it steady, she slowly extended it.

Kami watched her closely.

Are you OK? Thom asked.

Yes. Her fingers are warm.

Thom and Jonathan remained silent as Ellie moved to Kami's right wing and repeated her examination.

After a thorough check, she said, "Her bones are fragile. Make sure you're giving her finely ground bone. For her muscles, she needs protein. Keep feeding her meat, especially organs. They're full of nutrients for growth and healing."

Kami's ears twitched, and she nodded quickly.

"OK," Thom said. "I'll tell the cook. What about her membranes?"

"I'd be guessing, but collagen might help. It builds cartilage in humans. Try fish, beans, peas, and lentils. Check with Mac to be sure."

"OK. Any idea how long until Kami's wings are strong enough to fly?"

"Months. But you'll see signs. Birds flap their wings to build strength, and even hop around."

Thom let out a breath he hadn't realized he'd been holding. "Thank you. I've been guessing at everything."

"If you need me again, I'm in the mews, at the left corner of the Keep."

As Ellie reached for her cloak, Jonathan nudged Thom. "Should we ask her about the heating?"

"Um," Thom said, "could you tell us how rooms are heated here? We haven't seen fireplaces or stoves."

Ellie chuckled. "You'd be amazed how many academs ask. When the monarchs added floors a few years ago, they replaced the stoves with radiators."

"Radiators?" Jonathan asked.

"Noiri's cousin, the queen of Eiren, had them in her palace. She and the king showed them to Niamh and Peth during a visit."

"But what are they?" Thom pressed.

"Metal panels with pipes inside that carry hot water from the boiler downstairs. One's tucked under the window bench in your room."

"The window seat. Of course," Thom muttered, shaking his head.

"I've got to run. My charges need tending."

"Thanks, Ellie," Thom called as she stepped out into the rain. Peering back at Kami, she was fast asleep.

"How do you think Kami will take to the new foods?" Jonathan asked quietly.

"Not sure. But we can explain it."

"Are you thinking a mash?"

Thom was happy Jonathan wanted to help with Kami's care. He already felt they were a team. "Yes. I'll mix in pieces of heart and liver along with the other stuff. Would you come with me to talk with Mac?"

"Sure."

"I hope you don't mind being late for supper. I also want to tell the cook what we need."

"No. Kami's more important."

They found Mac in her office. She confirmed Ellie's suggestions and promised to tell the cook.

Chapter 10

"That was good," Jonathan said, finishing his griddle cakes with a satisfied smack. "The honey made them even better. Fresh from the comb. Too bad there's not enough for the whole school. I'll miss it once we're in the dining hall."

"Fresh?" Thom asked.

"One of the maintenance women keeps a bee nook on the grounds that produces enough for the staff."

"I think you've got a little on your chin."

Jonathan reddened, wiping it on his tunic sleeve.

"I don't like honey," Thom said. "The syrup was good," he added, before burping. "Excuse me. I eat fast. It comes from growing up in a large family."

"I hear ya," Jonathan said. "I'm just as bad."

"Ready to go?"

"Uh huh. I'm glad it's not raining."

"Yeah," Thom said. "Did you see the lightning last night?"

"It woke me up."

"I sat on the window bench and watched for a while. It was extraordinary."

"Yeah, it lit up everything."

"I need to visit Apollo. Want to come?"

"I'd like that."

After dropping their dishes in the bins by the staff kitchen, Thom said, "Apollo's in the Keep stables."

"How do we get there?"

"There's a path by the side entrance leading to the back gate into the Keep."

When they arrived, Apollo was grazing with Aponi in the corral. He trotted over and gave a low nicker.

"Apollo," Thom said, "this is Jonathan."

"He's handsome. Is that a star on his forehead?"

"I thought the same thing." Without meaning to, Thom checked Apollo's spirit. It felt dimmer. "What's wrong?"

"Do you want me to try talking with him?"

"Please."

Jonathan's gaze softened before he answered. "He was worried when you didn't visit. Then he sensed people were anxious and rushing around. And he kept hearing your name."

"I'm getting that feeling now. Did Apollo tell you in words?"

"Mostly, and images—uniformed people exchanging words as they saddled their horses."

"That's like what I got from Aponi. The images. She had a difficult birth."

"Do you think it's part of my spirit-healing gift?"

"Could be. We can ask Mage Keenan." Focusing on Apollo, Thom said, "I'm sorry you were worried. There was an emergency." Resting his hand on her neck, he explained what happened. "We'll go for a ride this afternoon. I'll bring you an apple."

Apollo whuffed into his hair, then nuzzled him.

On the other side of the stables, Thom saw Duncan was free. "Let me introduce you to the head-groom. And I want to ask about Aponi."

"OK."

Walking over, Thom greeted him. "Hi, Duncan."

"Hi, lad. Apollo worked wonders on Aponi. She's calmer and even trusts us more."

"I'm glad. Sorry I didn't stop by yesterday. Something suddenly came up."

"Aye. I know how that goes."

"I want you to meet Jonathan. He's also gonna be a healer."

"Good to meet ye, lad."

"Nice to meet you, sir."

"None o' that. Call me Duncan, unless Noiri has me training ye. Once in a while, I teach academs how to care for horses. Might I ask, do ye have the same gifts as Thom?"

"Sort of. But they show up... differently."

"Well, if ye want to come with Thom to help, ye're welcome."

"Thanks."

Thom noticed Jonathan hadn't mentioned his ability to speak with animals. He wondered why.

"I'd best get back ta it. Stay outa' trouble," Duncan added, giving Thom a pointed look.

He guessed Duncan had heard about his disappearance. "Let me say hello to Aponi, then we can head back."

Aponi neighed as Thom approached. After introducing Jonathan, Thom sensed her spirit. It felt lighter. Jonathan checked her as well and found nothing wrong physically.

"Did you sense her spirit?" Thom asked. "I see it as a luminescence."

"I did, but it flickered. Since she's healthy, I'm guessing it's my spirit-healing gift."

"Maybe it'll get stronger when you work with it."

"Maybe."

"Let's get supper."

Chapter 11

The next morning, Thom carried a bowl of patties made with diced meat, fish, beans, peas, and crushed bone. The sky was clear, and the air fresh from the last storm. But he knew they expected another. He carefully stepped around puddles dotting the path as he made his way to Kami's building. About ten feet from the door, he spotted a woman with light brown hair tied in a long ponytail and a girl with shoulder-length brown hair. He didn't recognize either and slowed.

Had someone heard him mention Kami? Maybe she'd made a sound, and they'd come to investigate. Should he reverse course? That might look suspicious. He could pretend he was taking scraps to the compost heap. A kitchen assistant had said it was back here. To make it believable, he'd need to hide the bowl's contents. Deciding that was the best solution, he draped the end of his tunic over it.

Focusing more closely on the older woman, Thom noted her confident stance, but her plain tunic and trousers matched the girl's. The younger one, unlike the woman, kept eyeing the door. Best if he walked by and hoped they'd leave soon.

"Good morning," he said, starting past.

"You're Thom Macirdan, aren't you?" the woman asked.

Thom blinked, gripping his bowl tighter. "Um..., yeah," he said cautiously.

"I'm Mage Keenan," she added, extending her hand. "Mac sought me out yesterday. She told me about... our guest. We didn't want to go in without meeting you first."

"Oh," he said, releasing his breath. "Nice to meet you. Let me put this down."

"No need. You were worried. And... she didn't make a peep while we waited."

"What gave me away?"

"I have the gift of empathy... among others." Gesturing to the girl, she continued, "This is Tovah Maynik. She's going into her second year. We're hoping to find a solution to make our guest warmer."

"Nice to meet you, Thom," Tovah said.

"Same to you," he replied, noting her accent. It wasn't Glakkadian, especially since her fair skin didn't match most in Glakkadeth. Where was she from? He knew it would be rude to ask.

Mage Keenan opened the door and motioned Thom inside. The room felt dim after the bright morning light, but enough light filtered through the high windows to see clearly. Kami was on her forelegs, her snout twitching.

"Yes, I brought you breakfast, dear one. Same mix as yesterday but with more heart and liver."

It's not as good as plain meat, Kami complained.

I know. But we need to build up your wings. I did bring separate meat chunks.

Kami snorted.

Speaking aloud, Thom said, "This is Mage Keenan and Academ Tovah. They're here to make your nest warmer."

Kamael bared her teeth in a dragon-grin.

"I think she's happy to hear that," Mage Keenan concluded. "Don't mind us. We wanted to see the setup to help us brainstorm a few options."

"OK."

Thom had barely begun feeding Kami when she shoved her snout into the bowl, snatching a mouthful.

"Hungry, are you?"

When Mage Keenan spoke again, she said, "Thanks, Thom. We have an idea. I need to check with Queen Niamh and King Pethuric."

"Thank you, Mage Keenan and Tovah."

"Call me Kee. On another topic, Mac and I need to meet with you to discuss your gifts. I hear they're special."

"Um...," Thom mumbled, embarrassed. "Jonathan's joining us, isn't he?"

"Yes, Noiri mentioned that."

After they left, Thom noticed Kamael shifting in her nest. *Is something wrong?*

Itch.

Ah, Thom said, pressing his lips together. *Might be straw mites. Hopefully, Mac has lavender and rosemary in the Rejuvenary to sprinkle around.*

Soon, she replied, squirming.

I promise. Your colors are duller, too. I'll get a few things for cleaning your scales.

Kamael brushed her snout against his arm, a quiet gesture of gratitude.

Thom dropped the last piece of heart onto her tongue, and picked up the empty bowl. *I'll be back.*

As he reached for the door, it began to open. Thom froze, wishing it had a window. On the other hand, that would expose Kami to anyone walking by. Relief flooded him when Jonathan's face appeared.

"Good morning, Thom. Hi, Kami. Need help?"

"Yeah. Kami's itchy. Probably mites. I promised to take care of it. She could use a good cleaning… to shine her up a bit."

"I'll ask Mac if she has something that might help."

"Ground-up lavender and rosemary."

"Huh," Jonathan said, raising his eyebrows. "Did Rin teach you that?"

"No. Maden, the stable manager in Glakkadeth. I'll meet you back here."

They regrouped and got to work. First, they sprinkled the herbs. Next, they thoroughly scrubbed her scales with the brushes Thom had found. Mac had provided an oil with crushed chickweed, which they generously worked in with cloths. They treated her wings with extra care, dabbing lightly along their delicate membranes. By the end, Kamael's colors were almost glowing.

Better? Thom asked.

Yes, she replied, her mind-voice softer now.

Try keeping your wings outstretched? It'll help them dry, Thom suggested. *I think you're bigger. Your aura's definitely stronger.*

I noticed that, Jonathan added.

On Moon-dae, three days later, Thom met Jonathan in the staff dining room. They were finishing breakfast when Mage Keenan approached, her eyes bright with excitement.

"Thom, may I speak with you… alone? she asked, flicking her eyes toward Jonathan.

"Sure. If this is about our guest, Jonathan and his cousin helped me get her back."

"You're Jonathan. Nice to meet you. I'm Mage Keenan. Kee."

"Nice to meet you."

Realizing it was rude to stay seated, they both stood.

"What about our guest?" Thom asked, making sure no one was nearby.

"Her Majesty did a little… digging," Kee said, her grin widening. "Literally. There's an open area beside Raganni Hall, behind the Royal Residence. Under the dirt and weeds, she found sand. Lots of it."

"Sand," Thom repeated. "Would that be easier to…?"

"Heat," she finished. "Yes. Much."

"Do you want us to move some?" Thom asked, glancing at Jonathan, who nodded.

"Hold on. There's more. On another hunch, Niamh dug inside Raganni Hall. She even convinced Peth to help," Kee added, clearly amused. "He's not fond of getting dirty. They uncovered four large sand pits. There are probably more, given the building's size."

Thom was stunned.

"If we move our guest there, Tovah and I wouldn't have to reheat the nest as often. And she'd still be hidden."

"Neat ability," Jonathan remarked.

"That's perfect," Thom replied, nearly bouncing. "Jonathan and I are done. Can you show us now?"

"I thought you'd say that. Let's go."

"Um," Jonathan cut in, "we should put our dirty dishes in the wash bin first."

"Oh, yeah," Thom said, his face warming.

After clearing their dishes, they followed Kee out.

Once inside Raganni Hall, they took in the ceiling rising twenty feet. They were examining the pits when Niamh entered.

"I see Kee shared my little discovery."

"Yes," Thom replied. "It's perfect. What made you think of this place, if you don't mind me asking, Your Majesty?"

"We're in private. Again, call me Niamh. I remembered the soil in the open area beside the building was a mix of sand and dirt. Duncan and his horse handlers use it to train foals, but the sand always struck me as odd. When I dug deeper, it was all sand."

"But what about this building?" Thom blurted, wincing at his impatience.

Niamh gave him a pointed look but kept her tone even. "While Peth and I were digging in the open area, I remembered a story my Nana told me. She said riders once used the roof of Raganni Hall to mount their dragons. That got me wondering. I dragged Peth inside, and we dug more. Go over to the left wall."

Thom went to it and saw a plaque, its surface dull and darkened with age. In the center, a patch of copper peeked through, revealing the hall's name.

"Check the left edge of the writing," she urged, smirking. "See if you can clean there."

Thom narrowed his eyes, then wiped the grime with his sleeve, revealing a capital letter D.

"This isn't Raganni Hall," Niamh proclaimed. "It's Draganni Hall.

Thom stared at her, speechless.

"Are you saying the hall was built for dragons?" Jonathan asked.

"Not originally. I believe it was remodeled and renamed after the Royal Residence was built."

Shaking off his stupor, Thom said, "This is amazing. Thanks, Niamh." *And thanks, divine advisors,* he mind-spoke, certain they had a hand in this discovery.

"Since most academs arrive next Widna-dae," Niamh said, "I'd suggest we move Kami here in the next day or two. Kee, do you think you can get the sand heated by then?"

"Absolutely."

"What about the area outside?" Jonathan asked.

"Oh yeah," Thom agreed, "Ellie said that when Kami's wings are stronger, she'll need space to hop around to build strength before her first flight."

"I'll speak to our maintenance crew about putting up a fence; once she's healthier, she can use it to get fresh air."

"I hadn't considered that," Thom admitted.

"I'll let Duncan in on our secret. After all, he'll be losing use of the open area." Without another word, she walked deeper into the building along the same wall. Halfway back, she stopped and looked at its base. "Yes. Just as I thought," she said, her voice lifting with satisfaction.

"About what?" Kee asked, curious.

"Sorry. I remembered another story. One that my Pop-pop told me. About an injured dragon staying in a castle to recover. It had big doors that opened wide. I wondered if this building was that castle. Come and see."

They gathered around and followed her gaze. A narrow strip ran along the base of the wall.

Thom noted that its texture was peculiar.

"See the joint between these sections. I don't think this is a wall, but doors. And the strip's a metal track they slide on."

Crouching to examine it, Thom scraped away crumbling plaster. "Niamh's right."

Jonathan knelt beside him and picked at the plaster, revealing a round metal piece. "Is that a roller?"

"Yes," Niamh said, bending closer. "I'll have our crew work on this, too."

"Thanks, Niamh," Thom said quietly, trying to take it all in.

Before dawn, two days after the discovery, Thom, Kee, Tovah, and the monarch commander wrapped Kami loosely in a gray canvas and carried her to her new home. Niamh kept watch until they were inside to ensure no one was nearby.

Meanwhile, Jonathan kept the horses in the nearby stable calm, aware that Kami's scent would unsettle them.

When they reached the Hall, they eased her onto the hot sand. She stretched and rolled, indicating she appreciated the warmth.

Thom laughed. It was clear Kami was happy. "How did you make the sand warm?"

"I can raise the temperature of objects," Tovah explained. "Kee's helping me learn how to better control it."

"That's amazing," Thom said. "I'd like to hear more about your gift."

"Sure."

"You'll get the chance when the semester starts," Kee added. "All academs with mage gifts meet with me in a group. That helps me track progress and identify any similarities we can build on."

"That's brilliant," Jonathan said, who had just joined.

Kee's eyes twinkled. "Well, thank you."

Thom caught the faint pink in Jonathan's cheeks. *He blushes like me,* feeling warm inside.

"Magery is new for our land," Kee explained. "It started appearing in my generation. At first, no one knew what to make of it. When the monarchs found out, they invited those children to the Acadium. I started here when I was ten."

"So your gift showed up then?" Thom asked.

"The year before, actually. At the time, there were no mage-teachers. Peth heard the term used by a visiting diplomat from a northern land. Those of us with gifts studied with various people, including your teacher, Thom."

"So, Rin taught here?"

"When he had time."

Thom wondered how much, given his COM work.

"I like that other kids with mage gifts will learn from each other," Thom commented.

"Back to heating Kami's nest," Kee said, "Tovah and I will need to renew the sand's warmth every couple of weeks. We're hoping to find a longer-lasting solution that doesn't require as much channeling."

"What about Kami's food? We had an arrangement with the Acadium's chief cook."

"Oh, I forgot. Niamh spoke with Keelin, the Royal Residence cook, and set up the same arrangements. I already told the Acadium's cook."

"Thanks. Um... do I just walk up to the Royal Residence door?"

"Yes. The kitchen's off the back entrance, across from this building. You can't miss it."

"Thanks again."

"If you have any issues, come and see me. My office is 305L on Quad Lamond, facing Ninrise. That's the area in front of the Acadium."

Ninrise, the commonly used name for Noinín's Rise, was founded by Queen Noinín, a scholar herself.

"If you need me," Tovah added, "I'm in 436D on Quad Diarg, facing the quad."

"I appreciate it. Jonathan, want to come with me to get a snack for Kami and introduce ourselves?"

"I do."

That night, Jonathan lay in bed, replaying the day. He was glad he could help with Kami's move. Meeting Keelin had gone well. She'd been kind, but even that didn't mean as much as Thom asking him to join when he talked to her. Jonathan liked that, maybe more than he should, given how recently they'd met. Thom's open, honest face made a lasting impression, and not just because he was cute.

Jonathan wondered if Thom felt the same. He figured he might, but he'd been wrong before. It didn't turn out well.

Still, he wanted to spend more time with Thom, and their shared healing studies gave him the perfect excuse. Which re-minded him—he had books to buy, and Thom needed a few as well. Maybe he'd suggest a trip downtown together.

The next morning, Thom and Jonathan tried the library again. They came across a couple of books on eagle care, but nothing else.

"I was hoping Oddi turned up something in the residence library," Thom bemoaned.

They ran into him in the residence kitchen. His next plan was to check the archives of Cleirigh Hall.

"Let's search a little longer," Jonathan suggested. "What about asking your divine advisors?"

"Oh…duh. Why didn't I think of that?"

They were finishing noon supper, no closer to finding anything on dragons, and not convinced the books on eagle care would help. Thom was quiet for most of the meal.

To break the silence, Jonathan said, "Noiri told me the dining hall opens on Suin-dae. After that, we'll eat there instead of here."

"Oh," Thom mumbled. "Niamh said the other academs come back on Widna-dae. That means Eran and Ciarenn will be here. I can introduce you. They're my sponsor's kids."

"I'd like that. Um... you said you needed a few more books, and I haven't gotten mine. Since we had no luck in the library, what if we ride downtown after we're done? Duncan said I could borrow a horse."

"Good idea. I'm sure Apollo'd enjoy the ride," Thom said, perking up. "Let me brush my teeth and use the washroom. I'll meet you by the side entrance."

Chapter 12

The streets buzzed with life as Thom and Jonathan wandered around. Vendors called out their wares, and the scent of roasting nuts filled the air.

As they walked along the main road, Jonathan said, "It's strange the way it winds around instead of going straight to the Keep. Maybe it started as a cattle path."

"It might've, but there's a better reason. It was designed to prevent a direct route to the Keep in case of an attack. I wonder if anyone ever tried?"

Jonathan shrugged. "Maybe we'll find out in history class. But where'd you learn that?"

"Rin."

"Did you hear there's a parade along this road on the Summer and Winter Solstices?"

"Really?" Thom replied, clearly curious.

"It starts at City Bridge and goes all the way to the Keep. With bands and everything. And there's a big festival afterward in Ninrise: competitions, dancing, food."

"Speaking of food, want to get a snack before we buy our books?"

"Sure," Jonathan said, enthusiastically. "Let's go back to the main square."

As they neared, Thom stopped and nudged Jonathan's arm. "What's that?" he asked, gesturing toward the open door of a dressmaker's shop.

Inside, a young woman pumped a foot pedal beneath a metal contraption with a needle rising and falling quickly through fabric.

"It's a cloth stitcher," Jonathan said. "Noiri told me about it when we talked about my family's goods. She mentioned a new program—artifice crafting—where academs learn how to make tools for daily chores."

"It stitches fast."

"Yeah. But it wouldn't help with my family's designs. They hand-stitch patterns a machine probably couldn't handle."

"I get it. Let's find something to eat. Maybe a sweet biscuit."

"And a hot drink. It's gotten colder since the clouds rolled in."

Thom pointed to the right. "That vendor looks like she has both."

As they approached, a short, round-faced woman greeted them. "What can I offer you, young gentlemen, today?"

"We both want a hot drink... and a treat," Jonathan said.

"Well, I've got coffee and tea. But I recently added a new drink, Timbu."

Thom burst out laughing.

The vendor frowned. "Why are you laughing? It may have a strange name, but I assure you it's good."

"Sorry," he said, genuinely. "That was rude. It's just... I'm familiar with Timbu. Believe it or not, me and my friends invented it."

She raised an eyebrow. "I wasn't born yesterday. My cousin works in the Keep kitchen, and she said a dignitary from

Glakkadeth suggested it to the king. Word is, he's quite fond of it."

"He's not lying, ma'am," Jonathan said.

"It's true," Thom added. "It's made with chocolate and hot milk, isn't it?"

The vendor's expression softened. "Yes... but you're not claiming to be a dignitary or from Glakkadeth."

"No, ma'am. I lived there until Aprali, and brought a bag of pieces back."

"Maybe... but I still have my doubts."

Hoping to persuade her, Thom switched to Glakkadian and repeated his explanation.

"I didn't understand a word, but my cousin mimicked the dignitary's speech, ending her sentences like we do with questions. Yours sounded the same. Still, you're not telling me you've met the king and queen—you're a child."

"Well..." Thom paused. She had a point. How could he convince her? The image of the repaired angel statue on his bookcase flashed in his mind. *Don't worry*, he mind-spoke his advisors, *I'm not going to try using my gifts to force her*. Would she believe it if he mentioned he was an academ. But he hadn't had his first class yet, so he couldn't claim to have met the monarchs at a school event. Mentioning Paddi wasn't appropriate either, as that relationship might be a secret. And lying was out of the question. That would go against everything he believed.

But the vendor mentioned a dignitary from Glakkadeth. Perhaps that person had learned of Timbu through Musa Bittaye, who had captained the ship Thom sailed on to and from Glakkadeth. He and Mekial had introduced him to Timbu. Peth had said he planned to ask the captain to add a large supply to his cargo for Docha-leigh. The captain must have done so quickly for it to get into the hands of city vendors. Or maybe this vendor had gotten some through her cousin. How she'd gotten it didn't matter right now. His connection with Musa might work.

"Thom," Jonathan said, "she's waiting for a response."

"Sorry. You're right." Since nobody would believe he'd met the monarchs, he explained instead about his friendship with the captain and the cargo he carried.

"I see. Then a dignitary on board must've told the monarchs."

"Maybe," Thom replied. It wasn't impossible.

"So, would you like some?" she asked.

"Yes, please, for both of us."

As always, when people tried Timbu for the first time, Thom watched closely as Jonathan tasted the drink.

"This is great," he said, smacking his lips. "Like a warm hug."

Thom wouldn't mind hugging Jonathan. Where did that come from?

"You mentioned you wanted a treat," the vendor said. "I have cinnamon and sugar biscuits."

They walked away with one of each.

"Let's head toward the bookshop," Thom suggested.

They were a block away when Thom spotted two men standing outside a spirits shop.

He froze.

Is that... Samiltun? Thom's chest tightened.

Sensing into the man, Thom felt the same oily energy he encountered long ago. His body shook, and his cup of Timbu slipped from his hand, spilling down his tunic.

Jonathan had walked several paces ahead before he realized Thom wasn't beside him. He looked back. "You OK?"

Thom remained rooted to the spot, mute.

"Thom. What's wrong? You're as pale as a ghost."

"Sami..." Thom whispered. Lifting his trembling arm, he pointed toward the men.

Jonathan saw a tall, stout man in fine clothes standing next to another, dressed in a simple tunic and trousers, his arms piled high with packages.

"Who is...?" he began, but broke off at a sound behind him. Thom had dropped his uneaten biscuit on the ground and bolted back toward the square where they'd tied their horses.

"Wait!" Jonathan shouted, breaking into a run after him.

Chapter 13

A loud bang jolted Thom awake. He lay flat on his back, his arms and legs chained to a hard surface.

"You're finally awake, boy," a male sneered.

His stomach knotted with terror at the voice, and a chill swept over him. He knew that face.

"I see you remember me," Samiltun said, a cruel smile curling his lips. "Thought you'd get away? I don't know where you've been these past years, but I never forget an energy signature."

Even without the chains, Thom couldn't have moved. His body felt paralyzed.

"Many plans went into the dustbin when I determined your gift was minimal. You fooled me once. But not now. Your gift's strong. You'll serve me well."

"N... n... n... no," he stammered, bile rising and burning the back of his throat.

Samiltun stepped closer, his eyes gleaming. "What can you do? You're chained where no one can find you. I'm quite gifted, boy. No one's ever resisted me. You don't stand a chance."

Thom clenched his fists. "I w... will." His voice was weak, but his resolve hardened. Desperate, he strengthened his shields, making them slippery, like Rin had taught.

Samiltun let out a low, menacing chuckle. "I've grown stronger, too—strong enough to tear through shielding. Even yours."

The bone-chilling sound made Thom's insides heave. He knew. Samiltun had sensed his shields.

Without another word, the man turned to a nearby table.

Thom heard the unmistakable pop of a cork. Years of helping his healer mother made it quite familiar. His heart hammered. What's he going to do?

When Samiltun faced him again, he held a glass vial. "Now I have a means to make you cooperate." Seizing Thom's head, he forced the liquid down his throat.

Thom gagged, fighting it. Then his gut revolted, and he vomited—Timbu, biscuit, and even his earlier supper. Disgusting, yes, but he was grateful.

"Turg, boy!" Samiltun snapped. "You'll lie in your mess for the trouble you've caused."

He forced more liquid down Thom's throat.

"I'll be back in an hour when the valerian root has taken effect."

After he left, Thom took deep breaths to steady himself. His stomach roiled with the bitter remains of half-digested food and valerian root. It would help if he threw up again. But his body refused to cooperate. Anger raged within. He had to escape. But how?

Medelin hadn't taught him how to break chains. He had trained Thom in self-defense and weapons in Glakkadeth.

Thom tugged, but the chains held fast. He couldn't even wipe the foul smear from his face and tunic. Despair crept in. How had Samiltun recognized him? After all, he'd changed. The thought made his fear spike.

Samiltun'll force him to do awful things. He twisted and pulled until the cuffs bit into his skin, wrists and ankles throbbing. Exhausted, he sagged against the restraints, his breath shaky. His eyes drifted shut as the valerian root did its work.

Thom was awakened abruptly by a loud voice.

"Now I'll be able to break through your shields."

Terror surged. And just like the day in the pottery, Thom felt a probe pressing against him. This time, it slipped off his outermost shield. Maybe it wasn't hopeless.

Samiltun kept pressing, each probe sharper and more forceful than the one before.

Thom's shields held, repelling each attack. He was doing it—beating Samiltun. Then came a different kind of probe. Or was it a pulse? A faint voice followed.

"I'm here. Let me help."

"You're not trying to help," Thom insisted, his voice hoarse but steady. "You want to use me." A spark of defiance flared, and he successfully pushed back against the energy, relieved to find he had a little control.

"Perceptive for a child," Samiltun growled.

Thom felt the probe again, but it couldn't get past his shields.

"Perhaps another dose of valerian?"

As the door closed, Thom sagged, his limbs leaden and thoughts muddled. All was lost.

At the Acadium, Jonathan pounded on Thom's locked door. "Thom!"

No answer. Only a slow creak... creak.

"Thom, are you in there?" he called, straining to place the sound.

He pressed his ear to the wood, heart pounding. Nothing. Maybe the noise came from outside. What if he used mind-speech?

Thom, it's Jonathan. Can you hear me? Please... open the door.

"Turg!" he cursed.

If those idiots had watched the road, they wouldn't have crashed their carts, and he'd have been back sooner. Who were the men Thom saw? He looked terrified. Like he thought they'd hurt him. What if Thom never made it back?

He knocked again, more hesitantly. Maybe he wasn't inside. What should he do? His mind raced. He needed help.

Jonathan tore down the steps, leaping three at a time. Cold sweat clung to him, and his breath came fast and shallow. As he entered the Rejuvenary, he slowed out of respect for the patients. At Mac's office door, he paused for a moment before opening it and stepping inside.

"Jonathan, what...." she began.

"Something's wrong with Thom!"

"Is he sick?"

"No... don't think so... I thought he was in his room... not sure now... I'm scared."

"Slow down. Have some water. You're flushed," she said, handing him a glass. "Start again."

"We went downtown to buy books. Thom saw two men and froze. Then he took off. I thought he came here. But when I pounded on his door, he didn't answer. It's locked. What'll I do?"

"Let's go see the provost. She has keys to all the rooms."

In the gloom of his cell, the air stale, Thom sat slumped in a chair, chained. His head hung low as his fears spiraled. His shielding had failed, and Samiltun had broken through, leaving him powerless. Even his cries to his divine advisors had gone unanswered. He felt a failure, like when Lebrim died. The memory pressed down on him, cold and suffocating.

Didn't anyone miss him? Especially Jonathan. He thought they were becoming close. After leaving Glakkadeth and Mekial, he doubted he'd find another friend. But then came Jonathan: kind and generous. Why hadn't he found him?

Jonathan had been there when Thom saw Samiltun and his servant. He had to have noticed how scared he was, especially when he ran. Or maybe he was fooling himself about their closeness. Maybe Jonathan was just being nice, like he would be to anyone.

But... hadn't Jonathan sat on his bed when Thom told him about Glakkadeth? And he was helpful with Kami. He'd been sure they were friends. Maybe that wasn't true. Wouldn't they be searching for him by now?

It had to be at least two weeks since that day. Surely everyone knew he was missing—Noiri, Mac, Kee, Paddi. And what about Niamh and Peth? Noiri must have told them.

And Rin. Thom knew he was away, but wouldn't someone have told him he'd been... ? He didn't want to say it. But he was... kidnapped... again. The word struck him like a blow. Rin would be devastated.

Classes had probably started by now. He pictured academs running through the halls at the sound of the 'opportunity' bell. Jena had told him that's what the academs called it, a half-mocking salute to the teachers' constant reminder that learning was an opportunity. The name brought a flicker of warmth.

Would he ever see any of them again? His spirit plummeted. He was alone, abandoned. They must have all given up, even his divine advisors. He was helpless.

Footsteps echoed outside the door. Slow. Heavy.

Let it be the servant with water. Thom's mouth was dry, and his tongue, thick and swollen. The bitter taste of valerian root clung to the back of his throat. Hunger twisted through him. Samiltun had given him moldy bread yesterday. Or was it the day before?

He knew Samiltun wanted to use him. But for what?

On the table by the door lay a strip of leather. Thom knew it well. Samiltun liked to slap it against the bench where Thom had once been chained: thrap, thrap, thrap. He hadn't yet used it against Thom, but... the sound sent shivers through him.

The door screeched open, scraping against the stone floor, setting his teeth on edge.

A shadow filled the frame, lantern light flickering across hollow eyes and sharp cheekbones: skeletal and haunting.

"Time for another lesson, boy!" the voice rasped, edged with malice.

Outside Thom's room at the Acadium, Noiri unlocked the door. It wouldn't budge.

"Why won't it open?" Mac asked.

"I'm so stupid!" Jonathan blurted. "I can use my gift to tell if Thom's inside." Closing his eyes, he reached out. "He's there."

"Could he have blocked the door? Say with a chair?" Mac suggested.

"Possibly," Noiri said. She banged loudly. "Thom! Thom, open up."

Jonathan and Mac joined her, their pounding and shouts echoing down the empty hall. Normally, others would've come running. But no one else lived there yet.

After a time, they stopped, exhausted.

"Mac, can you tell if he's injured?" Noiri asked.

She drew in a quiet breath and focused. "His heart's racing, but I don't sense an injury. Jonathan, see if you can find out more with your spirit-healing gift."

He lowered his natural shield and tuned in. "Thom's shields are fully raised. I can't get through. It's strange, but even though I barely know him, it feels like I do. There must be a way. Let me think."

Mac and Noiri waited quietly.

Jonathan knew he'd failed to reach Thom using mind-speech. But maybe he could use the connection forming between them. It felt really real.

"I have an idea," he said, closing his eyes.

Time dragged.

Noiri shifted restlessly, whispering, "Do you think it's working?"

Mac's expression flickered. "Hard to say. That gift's new to me."

More time passed before Jonathan opened his eyes. "I think I reached him, but he pushed me out. His aura was a tangle of black and red strands, completely hiding his spirit."

"Since he's not physically hurt," Mac said, "it must be emotional. Jonathan, you said Thom saw two men. Did he say anything before he ran?"

"Sammy."

"Sammy," Noiri repeated. "Let's go to my office. Maybe Rin mentioned him in his notes to me."

"Can I stay here?" Jonathan asked, glancing at the door. "I don't want to leave him."

"I understand," Mac said. "But he's not in danger now, and we need you with us. If you recall anything else, it could help us find a way to reach him. We won't be long."

Mac and Noiri were seated while Jonathan paced.

"Sit," Noiri said.

"I can't. My legs keep twitching." Was he picking up Thom's distress, four floors away? His empathic gift was strong, but this felt deeper.

"Let me get you valerian tea," Mac said.

"I found the notes," Noiri added, pulling papers from a drawer.

When Mac returned, she handed Jonathan the cup.

"I don't think this will help," he muttered. His legs felt like they could run around the Acadium ten times.

"As your teacher, drink!"

He obeyed, doubtful.

"Anything in the notes?" Mac asked.

"No mention of Sammy," Noiri said, shaking her head.

"What about breaking down the door with an axe?" Jonathan asked, struggling to stay seated.

"If this is emotional, that might traumatize Thom more," Noiri replied.

"I agree," Mac said. "Jonathan, did the two men seem threatening?"

"No. But I'm not as good with that kind of sensing as Thom. I don't think they even noticed him."

"Perhaps Thom was afraid for another reason," Noiri commented.

"Could be," Mac said. "Should we tell Niamh and Peth?"

Noiri hesitated. "I'm not sure."

"Rin isn't around, is he?" Jonathan asked. "I bet he could reach Thom."

"No," Noiri said, tapping her lips. "Since Thom ran, he must've known it would be dangerous to be seen."

"Do the notes cover what happened to him before he got here?" Mac asked.

"No. They mention Thom's gifts came early, but not why. The names listed are Medelin, Sestra B, and Maden. People Thom trained with."

"Noiri, may I make a suggestion?" Jonathan asked, setting the empty cup aside, and realizing he felt calmer.

"Of course."

"My intuition says you should speak with Niamh and Peth. I keep going back to how they greeted Thom when they met Kami. It seemed like they knew more."

"I'll seek them out now."

"I'll go with you," Mac said.

"I'll check with Kami," Jonathan added. "Maybe she can reach him. After that, I'm going back to Thom."

As they left Noiri's office, they ran into Duncan.

"Something's wrong with Thom."

"We know," Jonathan replied. "How do you?"

"He rode in half an hour ago. Pale. Like he wasnae there. Soon as he dismounted, he ran off, no thought to unsaddle or see to Apollo. I tended him afore comin' here."

"We've no idea what happened, and we can't get in his door," Noiri explained. "Mac and I are going to see the monarchs."

"Mind if I join ye?" Duncan asked.

"Not at all," Noiri said. "You were the last to see him."

Chapter 14

"Again," Samiltun demanded, standing in Thom's cell, lit by two lanterns. "Make him completely loyal. So much that if I told him to kill himself, he wouldn't hesitate."

Thom felt sick each time he was ordered to twist another's mind. But he couldn't refuse; he'd learned that the hard way.

He hated himself for not meeting the young man's pleading eyes. The man couldn't have been much older than Bedum, Thom's eldest brother, dressed in tattered clothes that clung to his thin frame, his long hair tangled and greasy. Dragged from the streets a few days before, he'd remain filthy and hungry until Samiltun had full control over him.

Now that Thom cooperated, he was given small meals—thin soup and coarse stale bread—to keep up his strength. This was the second time today that he'd faced the man. Guilt ate at him.

"Do it!" Samiltun barked, snapping the leather strap. "You'd better succeed. I'm losing money."

Thom pushed into the man's psyche again, planting the belief that Samiltun was a god and must be obeyed. He remembered too well what happened when he hesitated. His back throbbed from his failure, the raw welts pulling with each movement.

"He'll follow your commands now, my lord," Thom said in a shaky voice.

"About time. My boys will have a few more for you tomorrow."

"Yes, my lord," he replied, bowing his head.

"Eat," Samiltun ordered, tossing him a crust of bread. "No more excuses."

"No, my lord," Thom mumbled.

After Samiltun left, Thom sagged, grateful he was no longer chained. How long had he been here? Three months? More? His bedding, a nest of discarded blankets, lay in one corner. A pail for his waste sat in another. Metal rings were fastened to the wall on his right. He'd hung there until morning.

Exhausted from the strain and fear, Thom crammed the bread into his mouth and swallowed it along with his torment. Then he dropped onto his blankets. Curled up in a ball, he rocked himself to sleep.

Stepping into the monarchs' office, the guard announced, "Your Majesties, Provost Gavin, Head-healer MacDonuld, and Head-groom MacAuley have requested an audience."

"Send them in," Queen Niamh said.

The guard ushered them in and exited.

"Good morning. This is a surprise," Niamh remarked, studying their faces. "Or maybe not so good? I'd offer you tea, but I'm sensing there's a problem. Duncan, since you're here, did someone get hurt riding?"

"No. The laddie... "

"Yes," Noiri interrupted quickly, flustered. "Not from riding, not physically. It's about Thom."

"Again?" Peth asked, setting down his quill. "I love the boy, but trouble seems to follow him."

"Peth!" Niamh chided, "Let's hear them out."

Mac explained the situation. Duncan described what he'd seen when Thom rode in.

"Thom said 'Sammy' before running off?" Niamh's fingers tightened around her cup.

"Yes," Noiri replied. "We don't know anyone by that name. Rin never mentioned him, not even in his notes. We were hoping you might."

Niamh exchanged a look with Peth. "We do. But first. Are you sure Thom's in his room?"

"Yes," Mac said. "Jonathan and I sensed him there."

"Good. Thom must've meant Samiltun." Her expression shifted as she told them why Rin had taken Thom to Glakkadeth.

"This... merchant," Mac said, nearly spitting the word, "tried to force Thom to use his gifts for him. Disgusting. Criminal!"

"Indeed," Peth replied. "We've been watching Samiltun for years. So far, he hasn't tried to influence another child. If he's broken the law, he's covered his tracks. No wonder Thom was terrified. He wasn't even nine when it happened."

"In that case," Mac said, concerned. "I think Thom's having a stress reaction. He may not be answering the door because he's caught in a nightmare."

"Poor thing," Peth murmured, shaking his head. "And you couldn't get in after unlocking the door?"

"No. We think he wedged a chair under the handle. We considered forcing the door, but we didn't want to traumatize Thom further. We're at a loss."

"What floor's he on?" Niamh asked.

"Fourth," Noiri replied. "Above the Rejuvenary."

"Could someone climb up the outside wall and get into his window?" Peth asked.

Niamh considered. "But if anyone sees them, won't it appear to be a break-in?"

"Maybe a maintenance worker could pretend to be patching grout near Thom's window," Peth suggested.

"That could work. Duncan, would you find the maintenance lead and explain? Don't give any details. Tell her we suspect a child is injured and unable to respond."

"Aye, I'm on it," Duncan replied, leaving the room.

"Has Kami been able to reach Thom?" Peth asked.

"Jonathan's checking now," Noiri answered.

"Good."

"We'll head back and try reaching Thom again," Mac said, and they departed.

"I feel for the boy," Niamh voiced quietly. "He's sweet and gifted. He's had a hard life for one so young."

"I know. I think he's given me a few gray hairs already. And he isn't even ours."

Mac and Noiri found Jonathan back at Thom's door.

"Any luck with our guest reaching Thom?" Noiri asked.

"No. But let me check again." He closed his eyes. "She's trying, but can't get through."

"You can mind-speak to her from here?" Mac asked. "That could be useful."

Noiri shared Peth's idea about a maintenance worker accessing Thom's room.

Jonathan rubbed his chin. "I don't remember if Thom had his windows open. I wish we could break through to him. I wonder if his divine advisors can reach him?"

"Divine advisors?" Mac asked.

Jonathan explained Thom's close connection to them and how he identified more with the One faith.

"Oh," Noiri said, her eyes lighting up. "Thom's supposed to train with Brother Lamen at the Chapel of the One on Refuge Square. Maybe he can get through."

"Didn't you say he wasn't due back until the end of the week?" Mac asked.

"Yes, but I'm hoping he got back early."

"What if he spoke to Thom in Glakkadian?" Jonathan added.

"That's brilliant. Both of you," Mac said.

"Would you ride there, Jonathan?" Noiri asked. "Take the main road to the second crossroad, then go right. It'll lead you into the square."

"I'll leave now," he said, sprinting toward the stairs.

"I need to tell the maintenance lead to hold off," Noiri added.

"I'll keep trying to reach Thom," Mac said. "By the way, that creaking we heard earlier... it's closer to the door."

Thom lay on scratchy blankets in his prison. The bitter taste of what Samiltun forced down his throat lingered, leaving his mouth dry hours later. He didn't know what it was, except that it left him foggy and unable to resist Samiltun's commands. Still, the tiniest sliver of control remained, enough for him to loosen its grip over time. Relief should have followed, but dread weighed heavily over him. Weeks earlier, he'd slipped and revealed that he was regaining control. Since then, Samiltun dosed him four times a day. The next dose was due soon.

Time blurred. Had he been imprisoned half a year? There was no way to tell, in his windowless room. His eyes had adjusted to the gloom, so he no longer ran into the waste bin. The first time, he knocked it over and had to clean up the mess with his hands, retching all the while. He wasn't about to use his tunic or blankets.

Everyone must think him dead. He couldn't bear to imagine what that had done to his family. Or to Rin and Jonathan.

There had to be a way out. For the thousandth time, Thom scanned the room for anything that could help him escape. In rare moments of clarity, he considered what might serve as a weapon. He'd once used a chair to defend himself in Glakkadeth. Perhaps Samiltun had guessed as much as he'd taken away the chair in his cell, leaving only a stool with legs too short to be of value. He'd even reviewed every technique Medelin had taught him for overpowering an opponent using his upper body.

Calls to his divine advisors, especially Jeshua, remained unanswered. Desperation gnawed at him. He strained until his head throbbed, reaching out with every fiber of his being for a flicker of guidance. Nothing came.

Footsteps thudded outside the door.

"Time for your next dose, boy," Samiltun said as he entered. "It's troublesome that I can't control you without the valerian, and even that wears off quickly. But I have new medicine." He held up a bottle, smug. "Mixed with valerian, it's supposed to keep you under for a full day. Paid good money to get mimosa bark shipped across the southern sea."

Thom groaned.

"Not that cost matters now. You've already earned me a small fortune, and I see it growing, which is why I need you to do as I say."

"It's wrong," Thom shouted, his voice rising. And once again, he'd given away that the drug's grip had faded.

"Wrong's relative. Now, drink. And don't try to throw it up. Remember the consequences."

He did.

The drink began to take hold as the familiar fog crept in. Thicker this time, like his thoughts were being smothered.

"No. Please, no," he cried, his voice weakening. *God, Jeshua, Metatron, Sereh... help!*

His condition gave his self-doubts room to pounce. *You're weak. You can't resist. Admit you're powerless. Obey.*

Samiltun's expression hardened, contempt flashing in his eyes before he strode out.

Let me help you. You're not alone.

What was that?

You're weak. You can't resist. Groaning, he rocked back and forth, attempting to use his last bit of control to silence the doubts.

Thom, let us help you.

Huh? His foggy mind struggled to make sense of the words.

You're weak!

Thom, listen to me. We're here to help.

Wait, that's Glakkadian, Thom realized, before the medicine claimed him.

It was early evening. Outside Thom's door, Jonathan heard a groan. "That's Thom. First sound we've heard."

For the past hour, Jonathan had been here with Brother Lamen, who'd been calling to Thom in Glakkadian at his suggestion.

"Keep speaking," Jonathan urged.

"Thom, it's Brother Lamen from the Chapel of the One. Sestra B wrote to me about you. You have a strong faith. The One is with you. Come back to us."

How could he be hearing Glakkadian? Samiltun didn't know he'd escaped to Glakkadeth. Thom shook his head, reality shifting like it had for a character in a fantasy novel he once read. He reached for the wool blankets that served as his bed. Except they were soft, rather than coarse.

New blankets? That made no sense. His stomach growled. And his back ached from the most recent beating.

Thom inhaled. Damp, stale air filled his lungs. He touched the blankets again. They were rough. Had he imagined their softness? Was he losing his mind? It had to be the medicine.

The One is with you.

The One is with me? How was he hearing this? Samiltun wouldn't say it. Neither would the servant.

Jeshua's trying to reach you. Your divine advisors love you. You're not alone.

The phrases echoed in his mind. They seemed clearer. Maybe this new medicine was wearing off. He ran his hands across the blankets again. They were soft. So was the floor beneath him. But how could the floor be soft? It was made of hardened dirt.

Dare he open his eyes? He didn't want to see the strap Samiltun had beaten him with hanging on a hook outside his cell. The punishment came after he tried to resist forcing another person, a woman this time, to obey Samiltun. But Samiltun had won. Shame for misusing his gift crashed into him, sudden and brutal as a battering ram.

Be open to the One! Be open, the voice pleaded in his mind.

The words were in Glakkadian again. Could he trust it? Should he open his eyes?

We're here.

The voice held a steady warmth that tugged at him. A breeze brushed across his face, carrying the fresh scent of leaves.

Impossible. His cell had no windows.

Wait! He wasn't curled in a ball. He was kneeling on soft cloth.

Steadying himself, Thom recalled one of Sestra B's favorite sayings: Courage is acting despite the fear. He could do this. Opening his eyes, he spied the pale wood of a headboard, a fluffy pillow, and a deep green checkered bedspread. He wasn't imprisoned in Samiltun's cell. He was in his room at the Acadium. But how?

It didn't matter. He was home. He was safe.

Chapter 15

"Skree-onk... ahemm... hrmmm... hrmm."

"That's new," Jonathan remarked. "The first sounded like a piece of furniture scraping, but the rest? Someone clearing their throat?"

"That'd be my guess."

"Thom! Let us in," Jonathan called. Lamen added his voice.

Thom recognized one speaker: Jonathan. But not the other, a man... who spoke Glakkadian.

Looking around, he realized his bed had moved. It was now a couple of feet from the door. His chair was wedged under its handle. How had that happened?

The pounding and shouting continued.

Thom stumbled to the door. After pulling the chair away, he reached for the handle when the door burst open and sent him sprawling.

"Oomph."

"You OK?" Jonathan asked, crouching beside him.

"Dunno," he mumbled. Behind Jonathan, he saw a dark-skinned man with curly black hair.

"I'm Brother Lamen, Thom... from the Chapel of the One," he said in Glakkadian.

"You're Brother La..." Thom began in Glakkadian, but as he pushed himself up, a wave of dizziness hit him, and he slumped down.

"Lamen," the man repeated, "Stay down, Thom." Switching to Dochalan, he added, "Jonathan, let's move the bed first. Then, we can get him into bed."

"OK."

Once Thom was settled, propped against the headboard, Jonathan asked, "How did your bed... ?"

"Dunno," Thom murmured, dazed. Was this real? Or was he only dreaming and about to awaken back in captivity?

Jonathan sat on the edge of the bed. Lamen claimed the chair.

"What happened?" Jonathan asked. "Why didn't you answer?"

Thom didn't reply. He surveyed the room as if seeing it again after years away: his wardrobe with his Acadium uniforms and the window seat above the radiator. His gaze lingered on the bookcase, holding *Demba's Chronicles*, the angel statue, the carved horse resembling Apollo, and his treasure jar.

"Is this real?" he whispered.

"Very," Lamen assured him.

"And you're not dreaming," Jonathan added.

"I don't... I can't," Thom stammered, struggling to believe he was free.

"What are you trying to say?" Jonathan asked, taking Thom's hand with care.

"He really didn't..." he began, breaking into racking sobs.

Jonathan wrapped his arms around him. "It's OK. You're safe. Just let it out." To Lamen, he added, "Would you tell Noiri and Mac? They may be in the staff dining room."

"Of course."

When Lamen returned with them, Jonathan was still holding Thom, who lay curled against him, with a tear-streaked face and semi-conscious.

"How is he?" Noiri asked.

"Exhausted. He hasn't told me what happened."

Mac stepped closer, studying Thom. "I'd rather not give him anything strong to help him sleep until we learn more. He's probably dehydrated. I'll bring water with crushed fennel seeds. It'll ease his nerves. And I'll bring one for you, Jonathan, as well."

"Thanks," he said, brushing a strand of damp hair from Thom's forehead.

"I'll let Niamh and Peth know," Noiri said. "Jonathan, you'll stay with him?"

"Definitely."

"Lamen," Noiri continued, "did you want to stay or go?"

"Go. I'll check in again in a day or two."

"Please do. I'll walk you out."

Once they were gone, Jonathan saw that Thom had fallen asleep. He eased him onto his back, pulled the chair close, and sat.

"I'm not leaving you, Thom."

Mac reappeared with two glasses. "If he wakes, get him to drink this. Are you staying through the night?"

"Yes."

"You'll need a better chair," she said, as Noiri stepped in.

"I ran into Oddi. He'll tell Niamh and Peth."

"Noiri, Jonathan's staying with him tonight. Can you help me move a stuffed chair from the quad's common room?"

"Sure," she replied, following Mac out.

A short time later, grunts and scraping echoed down the hall.

"This should do," Mac said as they positioned it by the bed. Noiri moved the desk chair back into place.

"Thanks," Jonathan replied.

"Make sure you drink your water," Mac admonished. "You're nearly worn out from all your worry and running about."

"Yes, Mac," he said, taking a sip to appease her.

After they left, he sank into the stuffed chair. He'd lit an oil lamp but kept the flame low so it wouldn't disturb Thom.

Staring down at his sleeping form, Jonathan wondered what kind of nightmare held such a grip that even their shouting and pounding hadn't woken him.

"What did you go through, dear one?" he whispered.

Samiltun loomed over him in the darkened room where Thom was chained once more. "If you think you can get away that easily," he jeered, "you're more pathetic than I expected."

It's not real, Thom told himself. It's not. He kept his eyes shut, not wanting to see the man. But he smelled the burning oil of the lantern Samiltun brought to his cell.

"I'm doubling the dosage. And hiring guards. You won't escape again."

"No, it can't be."

"It is. Expect another beating. Four days, no food," Samiltun laughed maniacally. "You'll rot in your own filth. That'll teach you."

"Please, no!" Terror filled him. His body began to rock back and forth, slowly at first, then building into a panicked rhythm, mindless and automatic. To any watching, he'd resemble a boy on an imaginary horse, desperate to ride free from this place of horror.

A groan woke Jonathan. He must have dozed off. It was still dark outside. Blinking, he realized the bed was no longer beside him, but pressed against the door. On it, Thom crouched on his knees, rocking.

How had he not heard the bed scraping across the floor?

"Thom, wake up! I'm here. Thom!" Jonathan cried, rushing to his side.

Thom met his gaze, his eyes wide with fear.

"I'm here!" Jonathan repeated. "Whatever you're dreaming isn't real. You're in your room, and I'm with you."

"Jonathan?" he whispered.

"Yes. You're safe."

"Safe?"

"Uh huh. Scooch over. I'm getting in. But first, take a drink," he added, handing him the glass Mac had left.

"Bleh," Thom muttered. "Licorice. I hate licorice."

"Drink a little more. It'll help."

Thom obeyed, then shifted to make space for him.

Jonathan pulled him close. "Now rest. If the nightmare returns, you'll feel me beside you."

The next morning, a woman's voice called, "Jonathan, is everything OK? We can't get in."

Jonathan lay curled behind Thom, his arms wrapped around his chest. Not wanting to awaken him, he whispered, "We're fine. Give me a second."

Carefully extracting himself so as not to wake Thom, he climbed out of bed, pushed one corner of it aside, and opened the door as much as he could.

"What was preventing us...?" Noiri asked, squeezing through the gap. "Oh," she said, taken aback at the sight.

"What?" Mac asked, following her in.

"Remember the creaking?" Jonathan asked. "It seems Thom's been rocking himself."

"Not unusual after trauma," Mac explained. "Has he said any-thing?"

"No."

"I have more fennel water and chamomile tea," Mac added. "It looks like Thom didn't finish his glass."

"He hates licorice."

"Chamomile should help. We'll bring plain water with the food."

"Great." Thom's breathing was slow and steady. Leaning down, Jonathan shook him. "Sorry to wake you, but Mac brought you tea."

"Huh," Thom mumbled, opening his eyes.

"He seems more rested," Mac said.

"After the nightmare came back and I climbed into bed with him, he slept soundly."

Noiri raised an eyebrow.

Not noticing, Jonathan added, "His aura colors have im-proved also."

"We've got to do something about this," Noiri noted, pointing.

Bending over him again, Jonathan said, "Thom, we need to move your bed."

"Move... my... bed?" Thom repeated, groggily.

"Yeah. You rocked it across the room. Let me help you to the chair."

After Thom was comfortable, Noiri, Mac, and Jonathan repo-sitioned the bed.

"I wonder if we should put a shoe under one leg," Noiri suggested. "It'll keep the bed from moving if Thom rocks again."

"Are you serious?" Jonathan asked.

"I am. I'll find an old shoe later. We'll be back soon."

Seeing Thom's eyes drooping, Jonathan said, "Let me get you back into bed. Noiri and Mac are bringing breakfast."

After some time, they came through the door carrying two trays. Noiri placed the one with folding legs in front of Thom; Mac set the other on the desk. Each held a bowl of porridge, bread with jam, and a glass of orange juice.

"How are you doing?" Noiri asked, noticing Thom awake.

"Tired, but OK, I guess. I feel kind of raw. My body's all wobbly."

"Food should help," Mac assured him. "Eat. Both of you. We'll be back in a while to check on you."

The next time they entered, they found Thom dozing, his breathing even. Jonathan sat nearby, gazing at him tenderly.

"He ate everything," Jonathan said. "And he's not as pale."

Thom stirred at the sound. "Oh. Hi, Noiri and Mac. I must've fallen asleep."

"That's good," Mac said. "Do you need anything else?"

"Washroom?"

"Oh, do you have to...?" Jonathan began.

Thom nodded.

"Think you're strong enough to walk?"

"Maybe. But would you help me get there?"

"Of course."

"I'd like to take a shower. I'm all sweaty."

"I can help. I'll grab clean clothes."

"Thanks."

Noiri leaned in. "Do you think you'll be up to telling us what happened afterward?"

"I guess."

"We'll take your dishes and be back at half past the hour," Noiri said.

Jonathan hesitated."Would you give us a bit longer?"

Supporting Thom, Jonathan guided him down the hall.

"You're shaky," Jonathan said as they stepped into the washroom. "Mind if I help you undress?"

"Probably best," he replied, blushing.

In the changing area outside the shower, Jonathan helped Thom out of his tunic, trousers, and undergarments. They were filthy and reeked. How had he not noticed? Of course, he'd been focused on Thom's mental state.

"Do you see any... scars... on my back?" Thom asked, his voice trembling.

"Scars? You have a brown mark halfway down on the left."

"That's my birthmark. Nothing else? No sign of being whipped or beaten?"

"Oh, Thom, I'm sorry," Jonathan said with compassion. "But no. Your back's smooth, even if it's dirty."

"It really wasn't... real?" Thom asked, exhaling a long breath.

"No. It definitely wasn't. I'll wait out here. If you get dizzy, call me."

Thom was sitting in the stuffed chair when he and Jonathan heard a sound at the door.

Rap rap rap.

"Come in," Thom replied.

"That was a stronger voice," Mac said, as she entered. "Glad to hear it."

"He was dizzy getting out of the shower," Jonathan added.

"Yeah...sorry about that," Thom said, lowering his head. "I had to lean on him to get dressed."

"No need to apologize."

"I brought a treat Peth believed might lift your spirits," Noiri said, entering behind Mac. "A pitcher of Timbu and muffins with chocolate bits."

Thom looked up, his face brightening. "Thank you."

After Noiri poured drinks and Thom and Jonathan had taken bites of the muffins, she asked, "Would you be up to sharing what happened?"

Thom told them everything.

Silence followed, as they absorbed it all.

Jonathan was the first to speak. "That's awful."

"Yeah," Thom agreed, struggling to believe it hadn't happened.

"You said Samiltun could control you with a concoction," Mac said. "I wonder if there's truth behind it."

"Search me," Thom replied.

"Do you remember what? I hope this doesn't sound callous. But it might help with some of my uncooperative patients."

"Valerian," Thom said, pausing, "and something called mimosa bark."

"I'll check into that. Impressive that your gift was strong enough to burn through it."

"Yeah. How's Apollo? I don't remember the ride back."

"Fine," Jonathan replied. "Duncan's giving him special care."

"What about Kami?"

"Worried. I can mind-speak her from here. You should try."

Thom fell quiet, then at last said, "It works. She was upset. I told her I was OK and that I'd visit soon. Will you thank Tovah for feeding her? Kami told me."

"I will," Jonathan said.

"How are you feeling now, Thom?" Mac asked.

"Stronger. But still tired."

"Sleep, then."

"Would you mind staying a little longer, Jonathan?" Thom asked. "I'm afraid the nightmare might come back."

"Not at all."

"And that's why I brought the shoe," Noiri explained. "Jonathan, help me lift one of the bed legs."

After placing the shoe, she asked, "Sorry to change the subject, but can I assume you never got your books?"

"No," Jonathan admitted. "I can get mine and Thom's tomorrow."

"If you need to go, I understand," Thom offered.

"I have another idea," Noiri said. "I know what Jonathan needs, and I can guess yours from your bookshelf, Thom. I'll have my assistant take care of it today."

"Are you sure?" Thom asked. "I don't want to inconvenience anyone."

"Stop your nonsense," Noiri quipped, her voice playful.

"We'll let you rest," Mac said. "I'll bring you a sleeping posset shortly, without fennel. Hopefully, it'll keep the nightmares away. Jonathan, do you need anything?"

"A shower and a change of clothes."

"I thought you preferred baths?" Thom said, smirking.

This time, Mac raised her eyebrows.

"It does take less time. I'll be quick."

"No rush," Noiri said. "I'll stay until you get back."

"I'll come back quickly," Mac added.

Thom, a male voice called. *Open your eyes.*

The voice was kind and warm. It definitely wasn't Samiltun, or even Jonathan. When Thom complied, he met a familiar pair of brown eyes.

Jeshua?

Yes.

Thom's breath caught when he realized where he was—his Sanctuary. He sat beneath his favorite oak tree.

How did I get here? I usually have to visualize it.

When he lived in Glakkadeth, Sestra B had guided her students in imagining a safe place where they felt most connected to the divine.

Sereh helped, Jeshua said.

Is she here? I don't see her.

Not yet. How are you?

Thom hesitated. *I think I'm better. Maybe.*

You do get caught in sticky situations more than most.

I know, even if it wasn't real, Thom said with a sigh. *It truly wasn't real?*

No it wasn't, Jeshua assured him. *After seeing Samiltun and his servant, your psyche reverted to the child you were when you met him.*

You mean... I was eight again?

That's what we believe. Although you hadn't seen him in years, your fear remained, yet mostly buried. Unfortunately, when Rel and I warned you before you left Glakkadeth, we planted a seed that deepened it. We're sorry.

Rel was Thom's higher self, Lightworker-Reliance.

It's OK, Thom replied. *I needed to be told. Was the servant under Samiltun's control?*

In a way. Through money. We were very concerned when we couldn't reach you. Sereh was frantic.

I was, came a voice behind him.

Thom watched as her glowing sphere transformed into a female form and sat beside Jeshua.

I thought I'd be able to reach you, Sereh said, her voice tight with concern. *But all I could do was speak to your friends' guardian angels. I asked them to seek out Brother Lamen.*

Oh. I heard Glakkadian when I was captured...um... was in my nightmare, he said, trembling. *I didn't think Samiltun spoke it. I guess it sort of woke me up.*

Sereh reached out and rested her hand on his. *I'm glad it helped.*

And you found your way back, Jeshua added.

How are you doing, now, with us here? Sereh asked.

Better. He met both their eyes. *I'm glad I didn't lose you. But..."*

Yes? Sereh prompted.

Thom hesitated. *Do you think it'll happen again?*

We don't, Jeshua answered. *But it would be good if you spoke with Brother Lamen about it.*

Why?

Besides being a spiritual director, he's trained to help people heal from trauma.

I've never met anyone who does that.

He'll be able to guide you through your feelings, Sereh added. *And not only about your nightmare.*

Thom shifted uncomfortably. *That doesn't sound like fun.*

One request, Jeshua said. *You may not like it.*

O... K..., he replied cautiously.

Try to have compassion for Samiltun.

Compassion? Jesh, how can I feel that after what he did?

I understand. But we—me and your other advisors—don't want your fear, hurt, and anger to harden into hate. Hate twists the heart. When it does, it becomes easier to justify harm... like Samiltun did.

Thom exhaled slowly. *I guess that makes sense.*

We believe Samiltun's hatred began when his mother was murdered. It drives him.

Thom frowned. But aren't there others who've been hurt who haven't done bad things?

Good question. Maybe their circumstances were unique. Please try, if not for his sake, yours.

I will, Thom answered, unsure he could.

Why don't you ask Uri to help? Jeshua suggested. *That's what you call Archangel Uriel.*

Yeah. Sestra B told me that Uri offers light to those trapped in darkness. That fits Samiltun. And me... for a while.

Jeshua nodded. We'll let you rest. Sereh, anything to add?

Yes. Let Jonathan help you. You try to do everything alone, and feel guilty when you can't.

OK.

He's very good for you. And sweet.

Thank you.

When Thom awoke, the room was quiet, bathed in soft afternoon light. Jonathan dozed in the chair. Beyond him, the hill leading up to the Keep plateau rose clearly through the window. No haze. No clouds.

A soft snort drew Thom's eyes back to his friend. His hand was tucked under his cheek, mouth slightly open. Sereh was right. *He's sweet.*

Thom recalled his visitation with Sereh and Jeshua. He did feel better, but decided that speaking with Brother Lamen seemed wise.

A familiar pressure told him he had to pee. He stood carefully. No dizziness. Not wanting to wake Jonathan, he decided to venture down the hall on his own.

Once he'd taken care of business, Thom slipped quietly back into the room. Jonathan stirred as he eased into bed.

"Thom," he said, rubbing his face and stretching, "Are you OK?"

"Yeah. Needed the washroom."

"You should've woken me."

"You seemed peaceful. And, before you say a word, I made it fine."

"Do you need anything?"

Remembering Sereh's admonishment, he said, "I'm a little hungry."

"It's close to dinner. Let's head to the staff dining room."

"Could I eat here instead? I'm not ready to be around a lot of people. "

"Mind if I join you?"

"No," Thom said, frowning slightly. "But you said staff dining room. Aren't we eating in the dining hall? Isn't it Mercha or Aprali?"

"Siptema," Jonathan said, blinking. "Why'd you think that?"

"In the… nightmare, I'd been with… him for over half a year."

"Oh, Thom," Jonathan said, his voice tinged with sadness. "I'm really sorry. It's Setr-dae, the day after we went downtown."

"I didn't miss any classes, my birthday, or Solstice Day?"

"No."

"I guess my mind's messed up."

"Whose wouldn't, after what you've been through?"

Thom sat silently, shaking his head.

Chapter 16

T hom tugged at the end of his ascot, muttering under his breath. It was Fwi-dae morning, the day of the school assembly, and he couldn't get the knot correct. The other academs had returned two days earlier, filling the halls with their chatter. Thankfully, he'd risen early enough to miss the crowd in the men's washroom.

The assembly would begin in less than an hour, followed by the welcome supper. Thom was still battling with his ascot when a knock came at the door.

"Come in."

Jonathan entered, dressed in his formal school uniform. "Are you ready?"

"I would be if I could get this blasted thing tied," Thom said, staring unhappily into the mirror.

"Let me see."

Thom showed his failed attempt.

"You're close, but the stitching should face front, and the ends shouldn't be even. I can fix it. Face the mirror."

Thom's heart pounded as Jonathan reached from behind to grasp the cloth. He made quick work of tying it, then spun Thom around to face him.

"Ooh," he swayed. "Dizzy."

"Sorry. You're quite dashing."

"Um, thanks," Thom replied, blushing. "You are, too."

He slipped on his gray waistcoat and dark blue tailcoat. Studying himself, he had to agree. He liked that the brocaded burgundy and gold ascot contrasted nicely against the darker fabric. If Rin were here, he'd laugh, as he had when he caught Thom admiring the outfit gifted by the Prezdan and his spouse in Glakkadeth.

"Let's head to Maginn Hall," Jonathan said. "I want to sit up front."

"Really? I usually sat in the back in my old school."

"Same here. But I got tired of the kids whispering and passing notes."

"That happened at mine. Once, I almost got in trouble when a student dropped a note near me. Before the teacher could see, I stepped on it."

"You never passed notes?"

"No. I didn't have friends. I was two years younger than most, and they didn't like me."

"I'm sorry," Jonathan said, sympathetically. "That's terrible. You're nice. And smart."

"Thanks," Thom mumbled, blushing again, but trying to hide it. "Let's go."

They descended to the first floor and entered an enclosed walkway leading to the glass-roofed atrium at the center, where Maginn Hall and Flynn Library stood. The walkway was one of four that divided the interior grounds into grassy quads. Each had windows at waist height, interrupted occasionally by doors into the quads.

The main walkway, wider and more of a corridor, began at the Acadium's front entrance. Jena had taken Thom down it during his tour. Photographs lined the walls: Provost Noiri Gavin, Queen Niamh and King Pethuric Cleirigh, and past provosts and monarchs of Docha-leigh. He'd been struck by how lifelike they were.

Thom was grateful for the crisp air. It kept him cool in his stiff uniform. Its many layers would be unbearable in the summer.

Reaching the atrium, he saw that a group of teachers had already gathered. Thom spotted Head-healer Macdonuld.

"You both clean up nice."

"Thanks, Mac," Thom replied. "The clothes are uncomfortable."

"I'm not surprised. You're a bit early, but feel free to go in."

As they neared the double doors, they passed a statue.

That's Joseph Henry Maginn," Thom explained. "Jena said he was a talented photographer who captured images of the leaders of other lands, including Eiren. The pictures we passed were his. His generosity helped complete the hall when the Acadium was first built.

"What about the statue by the library?" Jonathan asked, pointing across the atrium.

"That's Margaret Flynn. She was the first librarian. When the Acadium opened, she contacted her fellow scholars to gather book and scroll donations for the library."

"She must've known plenty. It's packed with books. I'm sorry we haven't found anything about..."

"Yeah. At least we have Falconer Espeth's help."

Inside the hall, a stage was to their left, with three tiers of seating opposite.

"How about if we sit on this end?" Thom suggested.

"Is that so we're closer to the door and the dining hall?" Jonathan said with a half grin.

"I heard the food'll be special. I want to be near the serving tables."

After sitting down, Thom noticed the school seal on the podium and the large banner behind it. The dark green seal had Royal Acadium embroidered in silver thread along the top edge. Its center was divided into four sections: an open book, a flying dove, a spiral, and an oil lamp. A plaque outside Noiri's office explained they represented learning, spirit, journey/growth, and wisdom. Along the bottom edge were the words, Founded, 903, Freas-a-chos, Docha-leigh, though most people simply called the city Freasa. His sister Meli, an artist, would have appreciated the imagery.

In front of them, just before the stage, lay the orchestra pit where academs tuned their instruments. Soon after, the music director entered, followed by Noiri and the teachers, who took seats on the stage.

The director led the musicians and the academs in the school song. New academs, like Thom and Jonathan, sang from the sheet music placed on their seats.

When the song ended, Provost Gavin stepped to the podium.

"On behalf of Queen Niamh, King Pethuric, and the faculty, we welcome returning and new academs. You all are quite beautiful and handsome in your formal uniforms. For new academs, it might seem odd to wear them today, but this gathering marks the start of our academic year. Our tradition calls us to honor it."

Tradition or not, it itched. Thom tugged at his collar.

"Each year is unique," the provost went on. "Full of opportunities to grow, learn, and be challenged. First-level academs, you're at the start of a journey to explore and grow your gifts. Continuing academs, you're encouraged to deepen your skills. Perhaps you'll discover new abilities."

"Huh," Thom grunted quietly. Some of us had that happen years ago.

"This year, you'll experience blessings, like making new friends. But you may face situations that once seemed impossible, even fantastical."

She gave Thom and Jonathan a wink.

Murmurs rippled around them. A few carried wonder; others, skepticism.

"We hope you'll be open to everything," she continued. "Trust that we, your teachers, will walk with you every step of the way. For those of you searching for your field of study, we'll help you explore your interests and consider your options. We want you to find a path that reflects your passion and brings you joy."

Thom thought of Nuala, whom he'd met at the monastery in Glakkadeth. Using his spirit-healing gift, he had sensed her unhappiness as a novice and her longing for the sea. When he and Rin had sailed back to Docha-leigh, she served as an apprentice sailor. She'd been radiant, and her aura reflected it.

He snapped back to attention. Noiri hadn't finished speaking.

"We don't want that happening again," she stated firmly. "Come to us, your teachers, if you're feeling desperate or thinking of harming yourself. Or at least tell a friend."

Oh no. What did he miss? He'd ask Jonathan.

"No one's gift or calling is better than another's," the provost added. "If we overhear jealousy or arrogance, we'll put a stop to it. Here, humility and gratitude are core values, and the monarchs lead by example."

Thom heard whispers that he couldn't make out.

"Ahem," she said, clearing her throat. "Our school motto is: *fostering your highest potential for the greatest good.* We want you to become your best self and use your abilities in service to others."

Jonathan leaned over. "I like that. Fits well with healers."

"I agree." It reminded Thom of what Rin and his divine advisors had told him.

"If you look around, you'll see how diverse our community is—academs of all shapes, sizes, skin tones, and physical abilities. Some speak Dochalan as a second language; others follow different faiths or philosophies. We go beyond respecting diversity; we celebrate it."

Thom heard Jonathan grunt. What was that about?

"And, before I forget, about your formal uniforms. You're only required to wear them for special events, and we'll tell you when. Now to practical details. New academs, we understand that it may take time to find your way. That might mean being late to class. What I always find strange is that you manage to get to the dining hall on time."

Laughter spread through the crowd.

"Anyway," she continued, "we make allowances for the first two weeks. After that, we expect punctuality from everyone; academs and teachers alike. It's a sign of respect."

"I like that," Thom whispered to Jonathan. "Back home, the elders never apologized for being late, but they punished us kids if we were, even when it wasn't our fault."

"By now, new academs have been assigned advisors... and all of you have your schedules. You've likely noticed blocks of time called 'service.' Academs offer service to the school, usually related to their field of study. For example, Culinary Science academs help in the kitchen and serve meals."

Thom spotted Eran two rows back. Her smile met his.

"Another example is healer academs," the provost added. "They assist Head-healer Macdonuld and others in the Rejuvenary. If you have questions about your assignment, speak to your advisor."

Thom's advisor, like Jonathan's, was Mac. They'd already discussed his assignment, preparing herbs and treatments. And he'd continue making jars for salves, since the school had two kilns for the pottery academs. He was glad he could continue using those skills.

"Finally," she said, "before I introduce the teachers, I want to touch on our school's more casual atmosphere, which stuns some parents. When we first met, I invited you to call me by my first name, Noiri. Your teachers will encourage you to do the same. We believe people of all ages can learn from each other. In our classes, we encourage discussion. Younger people can offer insights that older, and at times biased, minds might miss."

"That said, there may be occasions when you disagree with your teacher. If that happens, ask questions. If you still disagree, sit with it for a day or two. If there's no resolution, involve a third party, like another teacher, your advisor, or even me."

Smiling at the academs before her, Noiri concluded. "That's enough blathering. Let me introduce your teachers. Each will say a few words."

"I'm Professor Tavish Craigan," he began in a deep, resonant voice. "I teach metallurgy. You can call me Tavi. I'm obsessed with metals. Some say I've got metal on the brain."

Jonathan chuckled along with the other academs. As Tavi spoke, his thoughts drifted back to Noiri's comments about diversity. She hadn't mentioned people like him—those who didn't fit into the traditional ideas about boys and girls. It wasn't about attraction alone, but about what you valued and the roles others assigned based on gender. Thom had told him about Nuala's struggle with doing what people expected. It wasn't fair. He hoped Noiri's silence wasn't intentional. He was tired of dealing with prejudice. For now, he'd better tread carefully until he knew what she and the other teachers thought.

At the end of the assembly, Noiri invited them to make their way to the dining hall and their welcome feast.

As Thom stepped into the atrium, he heard his name called. It was Eran.

"Hi," he said, hugging her.

"Sorry I didn't come by earlier. A few of my friends monopolized me when I got here."

"That's OK."

"Did you still want me to introduce you to them? she asked, eyeing Jonathan.

"Oh… no thanks," Thom said, embarrassed. A few weeks earlier, when he was staying with Paddi's family, he'd been upset that Rin wouldn't be around and had figured he'd be all alone again. That's when Eran had offered to help him meet people.

"Ahem. I'm Jonathan."

"Nice to meet you," Eran said, giving Thom a teasing look.

"Sorry. Jonathan's first-level healing also."

"Yep. I'm looking forward to working with Mac."

"She's great," Eran admitted. "Treated some of my classmates' accidental burns."

"Where's Ciarenn?" Thom asked.

"He's around. He sits in the back of the hall with his friends, yet they're always first in the dining hall. I think they found a secret way in, but he won't tell me."

"Want to join us for the feast?" Jonathan asked.

"That's sweet. He's a keeper, Thom. But no. I'm helping in the kitchen."

"You'll miss all the food," Thom said.

"Nah. We get our own feast later, with special treats from the head cook."

"I'm glad," Thom said, fidgeting in his tailcoat.

"Stiff?" Eran said knowingly. "Once you take a seat, take off your jacket and hang it over your chair. It's allowed now that the assembly's over."

"That's a relief."

"And lose the ascot," she added. "Ciarenn always forgets, and it ends up covered in food. Anyway, I need to run. By the way, since we're friends, my classmates and I will rope you into tasting our food experiments."

"OK," Thom said, unsure what he was in for.

"Let's follow Eran's example," Jonathan said, grabbing Thom's hand and tugging him.

They exited the walkway near the dining hall and came to three sets of double doors, spaced between large interior windows. Sunlight streamed through the outer wall's windows, overlooking a quad.

They entered the first set of doors into a large rectangular room. To their left were swinging doors to the kitchen, where raised voices, clanging pots, and the clatter of plates could be heard.

The noise reminded him of the pottery at home. Thom's heart warmed; he already missed his family, even though it had been no more than a month since he'd seen them.

Jonathan nudged Thom. "It's got windows along the back wall. I like all the light."

"Me too."

Academs in white smocks arranged plates, bowls, and utensils on long tables along that wall. In front of them and to his right were round tables, unlike the rectangular ones in the monastery refectory. The sight brought Mekial and Sestra B to mind. He missed them, too.

"Let's pick a table," Jonathan suggested.

"OK."

As they neared an empty one, Thom heard his name.

Scanning the room, he spotted Ciarenn waving from a table with two other academs: one male, one female.

"Join us."

"Sure." Remembering his earlier slip with Eran, he quickly said, "Ciarenn, this is Jonathan. Ciarenn's Eran's brother."

"Nice to meet you," Jonathan said.

"This is Rilla and Ronan, my classmates," he replied. Rilla had long red hair tied in a ponytail. Ronan had short brown hair, a narrow face, and the beginnings of a mustache.

Thom noticed all three were dressed alike. "Ciarenn, aren't you wearing what you wore when we first met?"

"Yes. That morning, we had our cadet initiation at the Keep for those joining the Royal Guard. During our final year, we spend half our time with a mentor-guard while finishing our classes."

"Sounds intense," Thom said. "Thanks for letting us join you."

"It will be," Rilla admitted. "But to be honest, we had an ulterior motive in inviting you. At the welcome feast, tables with new academs get food first."

"Does that happen all year?" Jonathan asked.

"No," Ronan replied. "Just today. After that, tables are called in a specific order. We haven't figured out the system."

"We're sure that's intentional," Ciarenn added. "They want everyone to have a fair chance at the best selection."

"May I sit with you?" asked a female voice.

It was Tovah. "Please," Thom said. "Ciarenn, Rilla, Ronan, this is Tovah, second level."

A few more academs joined them, filling their ten-seat table as Noiri began speaking.

"Welcome again, academs. Our head cook and staff have prepared a wonderful meal. Throughout the year, our Culinary Science academs will serve dishes they create. Some may include ingredients from other lands—gifts from visiting dignitaries hoping they'll become trade goods. Today's meal doesn't feature those, but it will be marvelous, nonetheless."

"She's right," Rilla whispered, "Eran's a great cook."

"Don't tell her that," Ciarenn whispered back. "She'll get a big head."

"As is our custom," Noiri continued, "we begin by offering thanks to the cooks and to the animals and plants that contributed to this meal. For new academs, some of the animals were injured and wouldn't have survived. Others were taken by hunting parties tasked with maintaining species balance. After I offer the thanks, we'll take a moment of silence for those with a particular belief system."

Soon after, servers paraded out with steaming platters, bowls, and tureens—roasts, fish, chicken, potatoes, chopped green vegetables, and soup. Others carried beverages, baskets of bread, and butter.

Thom's stomach gurgled in anticipation.

Jonathan nudged him, "Hungry?"

"My stomach always does that. It's embarrassing."

An older male, likely a teacher, began calling tables forward. Much to Ciarenn's disappointment, theirs wasn't the first.

"Think Noiri caught on to our plan?" Rilla asked, laughing.

When their table was called, they filled their plates and returned to their seats.

Initially, everyone ate in silence, which Thom didn't mind. It gave him time to take it all in. This was the start of a new adventure. As always, he reached into his pocket and rubbed Ariel's scale. He'd done the same weeks earlier on the road with Rin, just before entering Freasa for the first time—a little excited and a little nervous. Back then, he'd had no idea he'd become guardian to Ariel's daughter.

"Finished already, Thom?" Jonathan asked.

"Huh? No. Thinking about all this."

Before he could respond, Ciarenn broke in. Shifting his gaze between Jonathan and Tovah, he asked, "I know where Thom's and the others are from, but what about you two?"

"Go ahead, Tovah," Jonathan said.

"Originally, the Vlodan Republic. When I was eight, we moved to Edin in eastern Docha-leigh, near the border. After I got accepted into the Acadium, we moved here."

That explained her accent. Thom almost asked why they'd left.

"What are you studying?" Rilla asked.

"Earth sciences."

"What about you, Jonathan?" Ronan asked.

"I'm from Arran, north and a little west."

"And the rest of you?" Thom prompted, glancing at the other four.

Everyone had enjoyed second helpings and the apple-rhubarb crumble for dessert. Thom had swallowed his last bite, and was wiping his mouth with his cloth napkin when Eran approached.

"Thom."

"What's up?"

"King Pethuric gave the head cook a small bag of chocolate bits to try. She loved them and added them to the pantry staples. We had enough for two trays of biscuits. I saved a plate for you and your table, but don't tell anyone else."

"Thanks, Eran." Thom couldn't mention he'd escaped to a foreign land, but he could say he lived somewhere else. To his tablemates, he said, "Some of you might not know I lived in the Glakkadeth Archipelago. That's where I first tasted a sweet called chocolate. These biscuits have pieces baked in."

In a flash, they were gone. Everyone agreed that chocolate was amazing, and said they couldn't wait to try Timbu.

They were about to get up when Noiri called for attention. "Before you go, I want to thank the cooks and servers, including the Culinary Science academs, for this delicious feast."

About twenty people emerged from the kitchen.

"Thank you for sharing your gifts. Once again, your skills have impressed us. I can't speak for the rest of you," she said, patting her stomach, "but I overindulged and may regret it."

Thom noticed many nodding.

"Without healthy food, we would not prosper. Now let's hope you academs are as eager to consume your studies. Consume your studies. Get it?" she chuckled.

Groans echoed around the hall, from academs and teachers alike.

"Well, I tried. Let's show our gratitude."

She began clapping, and the hall erupted in a standing ovation.

Once the staff was back in the kitchen, Noiri added, "Before you leave, please place your dirty plates, utensils, and glasses in the dishway bins. Enjoy the next few days. And be ready to start classes bright and early on Muns-dae."

After dropping off theirs, Thom and Jonathan were getting ready to leave when Eran ran through the doors.

"Thom, Jonathan."

"The biscuits were a hit," Thom said, "especially since they were warm. We all got glasses of milk to go with them."

"Thanks. Jonathan, you've got a smudge of chocolate on your ear," Eran commented. "At least, I think that's what it is."

"What?" Jonathan said, reddening.

Thom dabbed it off with a napkin.

"Thanks."

"Did you need me, Eran?" Thom asked.

"Yes. I want you to meet the cook and a few of my culinary friends."

After changing into comfortable clothes, Thom and Jonathan stopped by the residence kitchen to get supper for Kami. After she ate, she sprawled in the sand, eyes half-closed, and her maw curved in a goofy grin.

"Stay like that," Thom said, not wanting to disturb her contentment. "We're going to examine you."

Kami was finally growing, but her wings remained fragile... and dry. Thom retrieved the oil and cloths from a small cabinet Peth had found in the basement storeroom. The other day, he, Peth, and Jonathan had hauled it over to store supplies.

"I was shocked when Noiri hinted at Kami in her speech," Thom said as he dabbed oil beneath her right wing, near the joint.

"She probably wanted to prepare everyone. Not sure how many academs caught that. Kids can be pretty dense."

"I guess. I wish we could find books on dragon care."

"Let's ask Oddi if he's found anything."

"OK. I'm almost done with her right wing. How's the left coming?"

"Nearly finished."

Once they completed the task, Kami stretched her wings against the warm sand to dry.

"What are you up to this afternoon?" Jonathan asked.

"I need to check with Keelin about when the hunters will deliver more meat. After that, I want to ride Apollo... but not downtown," Thom added quickly.

"Because of your nightmare?"

"Yeah."

"I get it. If you need anything there, I can go for you."

"Thanks. I'm good for now. Want to come with me to find her?"

"Sure."

When they brought the bowls from Kami's meal back, Keelin was in the kitchen. Its size still amazed Thom. It held a broad hearth, two stoves, and a bread oven. Multiple sinks lined one wall, with a tall dish cupboard and cooling larder nearby.

"Hi, Keelin," Thom said.

Keelin, short and round-faced with a wheat-colored complexion, was kneading dough. Her straight black hair hung in a braid down her back.

"Does Kami need more?"

"No. She's fine... and sleeping. I wondered if you knew when the hunters would bring more game."

"Tomorrow. Why?"

"Livers and hearts are especially good for young dragonets."

"I'll keep that in mind. Hard to believe we have a dragon here."

"I can introduce you," Thom offered.

"Um... My Gran-Da used to tell stories about 'em—fierce creatures he said."

"Kami's not fierce," Oddi interrupted, suddenly popping up beside them.

"Where'd you come from?" Jonathan asked.

"My room. Hoping for a snack. It's been ages since supper."

"It hasn't been long, young man," Keelin replied. "But maybe one biscuit."

"Two?" Oddi asked, giving her his best sad face. "One for each hand."

"Oh, Deu, how can I resist?" she said, handing them over.

Grinning, Thom asked, "Oddi, can we talk with you?"

"OK," he replied, breaking off a piece of biscuit and popping it into his mouth.

Oddi led them to a two-level library. Two walls were lined with bookcases, and a third held a fireplace flanked by two stuffed chairs, where the King and Queen sat reading.

"Oh... Your Majesties," Jonathan blurted, starting to bow. "Sorry to disturb you."

"Jonathan," Peth said, "Please call us by our first names in private."

"Oh... um... OK," he replied, his face reddening.

"Oddi, are you eating a biscuit?" Niamh asked.

"Yes. Keelin said it was OK."

"That's fine. Could you give me one? I'm hungry. Always am, now that I'm carrying two little ones."

Thom hadn't realized Niamh was pregnant. She'd worn loose clothing when she visited Draganni Hall. Opening his senses, he confirmed it.

"How 'bout if I get you one instead?" Oddi offered.

"That'll do."

"How's Kami?" Peth asked.

"She's finally growing," Thom said. "But her wings remain fragile. We added the food Ellie recommended. Hopefully, it'll help. And thanks again for finding the cabinet, Peth. It's perfect."

"You're welcome."

"By the way, a crew will replenish the sand outside Draganni Hall tomorrow," Niamh explained. "They'll put up the fence the next day. Kami will hear a little noise. Sorry for the delay."

"Thanks," Thom said. "I'll ask her to stay quiet while they work."

"Did you need something?"

"From Oddi. We want to check if he found anything in the archives."

"Ah. If he had, he'd have told you already," Peth said. "But he's here now."

"What took you so long?" Niamh asked.

"Keelin wanted me to bring you tea," Oddi replied, juggling a hot cup and a plate of biscuits.

"She's always thinking of me," Niamh said fondly.

Setting them down, Oddi added, "Can I have one of yours?"

"Sure, but only one. Jonathan and Thom have a question for you."

"Any luck finding a book?" Jonathan asked.

"Nope. The archivist took me to the oldest stuff, but there's not much before Cleirigh Hall was built."

"I should have realized," Niamh said. "Even Nana didn't know what happened to the earlier records. You were respectful to Sir Tadhg, weren't you, Oddi?"

"Yes, Mamie. He wouldn't let me touch anything. The books were all brown. And there were even scrolls. But we have more boxes to search."

"Thanks, Oddi," Thom said, trying to hide his disappointment.

"Anything else?" Peth asked.

"Would it be OK if Jonathan borrowed a horse? I want to take Apollo out."

"Absolutely," Niamh replied. "Duncan trusts you."

"Thank you," they said, before leaving.

Thom and Jonathan started out riding east of the plateaus and soon came upon the river that flowed under the City Bridge. It must've turned north near Freasa's edge.

Farther on, it curved east again. At the bend, they spotted a stone building, where workers were setting a large wheel in the water.

For the next hours, they traveled at a relaxed pace, passing farms where some harvested grain, and others tended cattle. Though Harvest Day was over a month away, Jonathan explained that oats and barley ripened earlier. They saw men and women repairing a barn, and beyond, a boy, perhaps a few years younger than Thom and Jonathan, with his dog watching a flock of grazing sheep.

It had been a good afternoon. As the sun dipped lower, shadows stretched long across the ground.

"It's getting close to dinner," Thom said. "We should head back."

"I'm starving. Hard to believe after all I ate at supper."

"When Bedum was my age, Mam used to... bemoan... her word... how much he could eat."

"Bedum's your oldest brother?"

"Yeah."

"My Pa used to complain, also," Jonathan added. "Pa's the main cook in our family. My Da tends to burn things."

Chapter 17

"Jonathan," Thom called, pounding on his door. "Ready for breakfast?"

It was the first day of classes. The morning was cooler than the weekend had been, but the sky was clear. The past three days had been restful. Thom and Jonathan explored the Acadium, read, rode, and, of course, cared for Kami. None of the other academs knew she existed. Moving her to Draganni Hall had helped.

Thom took his self-defense and weapons test today. If Kami had stayed where she was originally, someone might've stumbled on her. Or the shouting and weapons clashing might've startled her into making a noise. He wasn't even sure what she'd sound like. Would she roar if scared or angry? Cry when upset? Did dragons even have tear ducts? And what would a laugh sound like?

How he wished he could find a book that told him. He supposed he could ask Kami, but reading about dragons would help. He knew they were intelligent, based on his time with Ariel. Did dragons have a language? A writing system?

"Jona..." Thom began, knocking again just as the door opened. His hand smacked Jonathan's nose.

"Ow... someone's impatient," he said, rubbing the spot. "I said I was putting on my shoes. Didn't you hear me?"

"No… sorry. "I was thinking."

"About?"

"Our upcoming testing. And Kami," he whispered. "I'm glad she's at the Keep."

"Worried that people might find her?"

"That… and other things." He went on to share what was on his mind.

"Having books on dragons would help," Jonathan agreed.

"Uh huh. Are you ready to eat?"

"Yeah," Jonathan said, annoyed, "I yelled that through the door, too."

"Sorry."

"Apology accepted."

"Let's head to the dining hall," Thom said, glancing at the clock on the wall near the quad common room. "It's early. Hopefully, we'll beat the crowd."

They hadn't yet figured out the quickest route to the dining hall, which was on the opposite side of the Acadium from their rooms. Yesterday, Thom had learned there were 600 academs at the school. It could hold 1000. He couldn't imagine that many.

Late morning, Thom exited the side entrance and followed the path around to the back of the building. The training yard, a hard-packed stretch of ground, was at the back right corner. He'd changed into a simple, close-fitting shirt. The loose-flowing tunic of the school uniform would have gotten in the way during testing.

His early morning had passed quickly. Math had gone well; his Glakkadian lessons in that subject had prepared him. History followed. The teacher began with an overview of Sandrim, the continent on which Docha-leigh was located. She promised they'd soon study the kingdom's founding and the migration of the first peoples. Thom wondered if those early settlers had ever seen dragons.

Jonathan had joined him for math and history, but their schedules split after that. He wasn't sure what Jonathan had next. Maybe an herb class. After supper, Thom was due at the Rejuvenary to grind herbs and prepare treatments.

At the yard, He noticed academs exiting through a back door on the lower level. Thom hadn't known about that. He'd use that next time.

A group of boys and girls had already gathered. Some were chatting; others waited alone, shifting from foot to foot. They varied in size and build. A few were tall and broad-shouldered. Two boys seemed older and stronger. One had close-cropped light brown hair. The other was dark brown, brushing his shoulders. Thom doubted they were his age. Maybe their gifts had taken longer to appear. Rin had said most showed up around twelve.

He no longer found it strange that girls were present. Training alongside Mekial and other girls in Glakkadeth had cured him of the silly belief that limited fighting to boys.

"Attention, first levels. Line up in four rows of five along the back wall," called a man with sandy hair. He was lean but muscular, and as Thom passed him, he noticed how massive the man's wrist seemed compared to his. From the assembly, he knew the man was the armswarden and the head of training. Four others stood nearby, likely assistants. Two were Ciarenn's age.

Falling into his usual pattern, Thom joined the back row. At the front, he spotted the two larger boys he'd seen earlier.

"My name's Declan Heugh," the man continued. "My assistants and I will test your stamina, self-defense skills, and familiarity with weapons, like knives, swords, and staffs. Some of you will have no experience. That's expected. I factor that in when assigning training groups." Pausing, he reviewed those before him. I see we've got some strong academs this morning. Strength is an important component of self-defense."

Thom observed the same two boys flexing their muscles.

"But strength isn't everything," Declan added. "It doesn't guarantee stamina. I've seen academs flip opponents twice their size. That's why we consider body type. I'm naturally lean. It takes effort for me to build and keep muscle. Others bulk up more easily. Then there are those with athletic builds, with broad shoulders and narrow hips. They build muscle quickly, but are prone to gaining weight. Those academs will do more running and fat-burning exercises. And all of you should expect to sweat."

Thom's expression grew thoughtful.

"To reiterate why everyone trains, including scholars, chefs, and healers," Declan continued, "everyone travels. And travel often brings danger."

"But what about people who stay in one place?" asked a short boy from the row ahead, his voice cracking.

Thom heard a few snickers. He felt sorry for him. Thankfully, his voice had already changed. He hated it when people laughed at things you couldn't control. He remembered Kevar and the kids from home laughing at his small size when he was younger.

"That's a fair question," Declan replied, frowning at the noise. "I suspect you haven't been to many cities, lad."

"No, sir."

"The truth is," he continued, "even if you don't travel, bandits and thieves are everywhere, including here in the capital. It's important to be able to protect yourself and help anyone who needs it, especially the elderly and young children."

"I'll do my best."

"I trust you will. You wouldn't be here if you weren't willing to try. If you've trained before, you're aware you'll get scrapes and bruises. Sometimes a small cut or gash might happen when you're working with knives and swords. Even wooden practice swords can leave a mark."

Thom exhaled at the mention of practice swords. He didn't like using edged weapons. Thrusts, counter-thrusts, and feints made him uneasy. He preferred techniques like deflecting a blade or spinning to avoid an attack. Knives were easier to tolerate since he used them at meals.

Declan went on. "We have salves and bandages for minor injuries. For anything more serious, go to the Rejuvenary. But that shouldn't be necessary if you follow instructions. For bruising, hot baths help," he said, pointing to the door from which others exited the building. "Inside are two rooms with large soaking tubs. The water's treated with mineral salts to ease soreness. That's enough instruction for now."

Declan studied the group to confirm they were paying attention. "We'll divide the twenty of you among me and my assistants. Each will go through a series of weapon assessments. Before you begin, understand this: there's no grading. No one fails. By the time you graduate in six years, every one of you will be well-trained."

Thom was assigned to one of the assistants, a young man about Thom's height with curly blonde hair. His group started with a stamina test—running laps around the Acadium.

On his third lap, he slipped on the pebble path and fell. As he pushed himself up, he heard a grunt behind him. The two large boys were approaching. As they passed, he couldn't tell if they were laughing at him.

He got up, brushing pebbles from his scraped hands and knees, and resumed running. By his fifth time around, Thom could feel it. His stamina wasn't what it had been. Rin had kept him training on their return voyage to Docha-leigh, but in the four-plus months since he disembarked, he'd lost his edge. A few academs continued running, but the two weren't among them, he noted with a smirk.

Back in the training yard, the others in Thom's group were lifting sandbags. The assistant approached.

"I'm Barran, sixth level."

"Nice to meet you. I'm Thom."

"I'm impressed you managed five laps. I saw you fall. Are you OK?"

"Yeah. Just scrapes."

"When you're done, be sure to clean them. Dek told you we have salves for them. We don't want them getting infected."

"I've got those in my room. I'm an academ healer."

"Ah. You look like you've trained before."

"Yeah. But not much since Mei."

"Off for the summer?"

"Something like that."

"What kind of training?"

"Running and lifting sandbags. Movement routines, but I can't describe them. And I trained with staff, knives, and swords."

"A solid mix. Would you show me the movement work?"

"Sure. Like I said, I'm out of practice."

Thom began his routine, but midway through, he lost his balance on a spin. "Sorry."

"Don't apologize," Barran said. "Up until that point, your movements were like a dance. Dek teaches something similar here, but not to that extent."

"That's funny. When I first started, I also told my teacher it felt like a dance. He said it's important to move smoothly and make quick changes without losing balance."

"True. I'll mention it to Dek. Let's move on to weapons."

"OK. I'm all right with the staff, less with knives and swords. I've never done archery."

"I'm fairly skilled with all of them. That's part of Royal Guard training."

"Are you in Ciarenn's class?"

"Yes. Let's begin with the staff. Head to that open corner. I'll grab us a pair."

After returning, he handed one to Thom. "Start by showing me how you move with it."

Thom ran through a routine Medelin had taught him. As he progressed, his body remembered more than he expected, and increased his speed.

"Very good," Barran said. "Now, let's spar."

As Medelin and Rin had taught, Thom focused on the trainer's eyes, watching for signs of a strike. After a long, well-paced exchange, Barran broke through mid-twist and tapped Thom's right leg.

"Digi," Thom muttered, rubbing the spot.

"Sorry. You were doing so well that I slipped into my usual sparring habits."

"That's OK. I expect bruises."

"Fair enough. One question. Did you just say 'digi?' Is that a curse?"

"Um, yeah. I picked it up somewhere."

"Well, you underestimated your staff abilities. Better than some of my classmates, even if you're a little weak on your right side. Overall, you did well."

"Thanks."

"Let me check your sword and knife work," Barran continued. "I'll grab the equipment and have another assistant cover my group for a bit."

Thom was running through another routine when Barran came up to him.

"Nicely done. I liked how you kept switching directions. You didn't get dizzy?"

"A little."

"OK, I brought two practice swords and a few knives."

After the drills, Barran put the weapons away and rejoined him. "You're decent with knives, but they're not your strength. The scrapes on your hands probably didn't help. You're better with swords, likely a carryover from your staff ability. You're going to be a hard academ to place."

Thom waited quietly, sensing Barran was weighing his next words.

"For sword and knife work, you're at a third-level skill. But with the staff, you're at sixth."

"I am?" Thom replied, unsure what else to say.

"Would you mind waiting here?"

Thom grabbed a cloth and wiped the sweat from his face. He watched Barran walk toward the armswarden, who had just finished sparring with the small boy. Thom saw Declan shake his hand. He must be skilled.

After a short wait, Barran beckoned Thom across the yard. As he approached, he heard the armswarden speak.

"Niall and Oran, run a few more laps. And do so every morning before breakfast, five days a week."

Thom saw he was speaking to the two large boys. Niall and Oran. So those were their names. Arrogant, definitely, but were they mean? It didn't feel right to check their auras.

"You're Thom," Declan said, offering his hand.

"Yes, sir."

"Declan or Dek," the trainer corrected. "First names, like Noiri said. Barran tells me you're skilled with the staff. How long have you trained?"

"Since I was about nine."

"I'll get back to my group," Barran said. "Good sparring, Thom. Hope we do more."

"Me too," he replied, his pride swelling.

"Four years," Dek said. "That's a long time... and unusual. Can you tell me the circumstances that led to that?"

"Um...," Thom hesitated. Once again, he wasn't sure how much he could reveal about his time in Glakkadeth.

"I can see you're uncomfortable answering. I won't press. You're probably tired, but I'd like to spar with you. Care to give it a try?"

"Um, yeah. I could use a drink first."

"Certainly. There's cool water with ginseng. And grape juice. Have a seat on the bench."

Thom rested while Declan tested one of the girls. Her well-defined muscles reminded him of Mekial.

When Declan finished, he motioned for Thom.

Handing Thom a staff, he picked up another. It was well-worn but sturdy.

Thom wondered if it was made from hickory, like his own. He left his staff in his room, not wanting to stand out among the other academs. When he first received it, an image of a majestic tree flashed in his mind. He smiled at the memory. He'd bring it next time.

"Ready?" Declan asked.

"Yes, trainer," Thom replied, uncomfortable using the first name of a teacher he'd just met.

"Enough," Declan declared. "Well done. You held your own for quite a while."

"Thanks." Thom noticed others watching him, including Niall and Oran. Both were frowning. He hoped that wouldn't lead to trouble.

"You started slow," Declan continued, "but after several minutes, you found a good rhythm. Like Barran said, your right side is weaker, but you caught every jab. I agree that you're at a sixth-level skill with the staff. For knives and swords, I trust his judgment. As for archery, you'll train with the first levels."

"Thank you, Dek," Thom said, realizing he was silly not to use his first name, especially since he did with the king and queen.

"Go and clean up. I'd also recommend time in the soaking tub."

As Thom walked to the door, he heard Declan mutter. "Curious, that one."

When Thom reached the tub, three others were already there, but there was plenty of room. Before climbing in, he checked that his scrapes weren't bleeding. He yelped when his wounds hit the surface, stung by the minerals. As usual, his face reddened. Would he ever stop doing that?

The sting quickly gave way to tingling, like what he felt when talking with his divine advisors.

Settling into the water up to his neck, he sighed. The heat bathed his tight muscles and bruised body. Clearly, he hadn't trained in a while.

He was nearly dozing, eyes half closed, when a voice stirred in his mind.

Wake up!

"Huh, what!" he blurted. Thank goodness he was alone.

It's Jeshua.

Hey, Thom replied, in mind-speech. *Did you see me? I think I did OK.*

You did. Dek and Barran were impressed. As was Rel.

I'm not in the greatest shape.

No, but you haven't lost everything. Besides your training with Medelin, remember the running around we did on the monastery grounds?

Yeah. But I was the only one running. You were only in my head, you know. It was fun.

Speaking of which, don't forget to make time for play. You often get hyper-focused when something's new, usually because you're afraid of failing.

I'll try.

Don't stay in much longer. You'll wrinkle up like a prune.

I won't, he said, hearing him chortle.

Climbing out, Thom pulled on his sweat-soaked clothes. Next time, he'd remember to bring a change.

After undressing in his room, he tossed his clothes into the laundry bag in his wardrobe. With his scratches tended, he threw on fresh clothes. Supper was nearly over; he'd better hurry before the food was gone. He was due in the Rejuvenary soon. Mac would likely ask him to prepare more ointment and salve—a necessity created by the day's training assessments.

The sun slanted through the window, signaling late afternoon, the same day as his testing. Thom sat at his desk reviewing his math and history homework when there was a rap on his door.

"Come in."

"Hi, Thom," Jonathan said, stepping inside. "Want to go to dinner?"

"Sure. I was going over my assignments."

"I did that earlier. We've got loads to read for history. At least we have a few days."

"Yeah. I'm curious to learn about other lands. We didn't cover that in school when I was younger."

"Mine didn't either. Don't forget. We're supposed to write an essay about the people in one of them. Will you write about Glakkadeth?"

"Not sure. How was your training test with Dek?"

"OK. They told me I'm in good shape because I ran six laps around the school without losing my breath. But like I told you, I've never trained in self-defense or weapons."

"I'll be starting from scratch in archery."

"Shall we head down?"

Chapter 18

Thom rode downtown mid-morning on Turi-dae, headed to the Chapel of the One to meet with Brother Lamen. He'd seen him briefly the day after waking from his nightmare. It was Lamen who had suggested they have their first real meeting today.

Two days earlier, on Tas-dae, he and Jonathan had met with Mac and Kee to discuss their spirit-healing gift. Thom had described his, including saving Rindo, truth-telling, and his recent life-imaging ability.

Mac was especially intrigued by his Rindo story and the involvement of his divine advisors. Thom even explained how he channeled energy into Kami in the dragon sanctuary. Not surprisingly, neither knew of it, despite the fact that Mac had been to the forest.

When Thom mentioned the tingling sensation he felt when connected to his advisors, Jonathan said he'd experienced something similar while tending patients with his mentor at home. Additionally, Jonathan shared his own imaging abilities when communicating with animals.

After listening closely, Kee and Mac had agreed that Jonathan had the same spirit-healing gift, only not as strong as Thom's. Mac added that the next time Jonathan worked in the Rejuvenary, she wanted to sense into him to observe his gift. She'd do the same with Thom once he began working with patients. Then Kee told them when the first mage class would meet.

Nearing the chapel, Thom spotted a fenced yard between it and a large stone building to the left. Hitching posts, a water trough, and hay bins marked it as a holding area for horses and carts. The yard lay empty.

Aware that his visit might last over an hour, Thom removed Apollo's saddle and gave him a rubdown using one of the brushes hanging on the fence. He tied him off with a lead rope, leaving enough slack for him to reach the water and hay.

"I'm meeting with a monk here," he told him. "You remember the monks at the monastery in Glakkadeth? Like Maden? She helped with your birthing."

Apollo whinnied.

"I'll be back later."

Before stepping into the chapel, Thom noticed the carved symbol above the entrance—the same one he'd seen at the monastery: a spiral, like the school seal, but with wavy lines. He knew the lines represented the spirit flowing through.

Inside, he felt transported back to that place. Although smaller, the chapel also featured a central altar made of dark wood, draped with a white cloth. Several candles burned steadily on it, casting a warm glow. The benches, arranged in a circle, reminded him of the hard ones from his chapel at home. Except these had padding. As in Glakkadeth, finely stitched banners of angels hung on the walls.

At the back, he spotted a door. Nearby was a small table, behind which sat a man with dark skin and wiry black hair. He appeared to be in his late twenties.

As Thom approached, the man looked up from what he was writing and asked, in accented Dochalan, "May I help you, young sir?"

From his features and speech, Thom could tell he was from Glakkadeth and replied in that tongue. "Good morning to you, sir. I have a meeting with Brother Lamen."

The man's jaw dropped.

Thom enjoyed his reaction.

When he finally recovered, he said, "How do you know my language? You speak it well, and your accent's perfect."

"I lived in Birkemi for four years."

"Birkemi," he repeated, his eyebrows lifting. "Did you live near my monastery, Holders of Lumen-anima?"

"No. My teacher and I lived on the southeast side. But I've been there. Another one of my teachers was a member."

"What was your teacher's name?"

"Sestra B."

His grin widened. "She taught me two classes when I was a novice. I haven't seen her in years. Oh, where are my manners?" He set his quill down and stood. "I'm Brother Zakari, but call me Zak."

"Good to meet you. I'm Thom."

"And me, you," Zak said, slightly bowing his head. "I'm amazed at how well you speak Glakkadian."

"Thank you," he said, resisting the urge to admit he picked it up quickly.

"I miss home. And a few foods your land doesn't have."

"Like?"

"Chocolate for one," he said, wistfully. "The monastery cook made the best biscuits using bits of it. A monk who recently came back from home said there's a new baker who adds them to buns and makes a drink with them. That didn't exist when I lived there."

"Timbu," Thom said, laughing.

"Yeah. That's what she called it. You know it?"

"You could say that." He explained his involvement, including how it got its name. He shared that the monarchs now imported the chocolate bits, and told him about the vendor who sold Timbu. As he spoke, a shiver ran through him, recalling his encounter with Samiltun soon after he met her, and the nightmare that followed.

"I'll seek her out today," he said, his eyes bright with anticipation.

Thom glanced at the book Zak had been writing in. "Might I ask... is that a journal?"

"It is. The monk who told me about Timbu mentioned a visitor to the monastery who kept one. Now that I'm living in Docha-leigh, I thought I'd do the same. I'll have to add something about you."

Thom didn't reply. He suspected he was the one the monk meant, and wondered how he'd come up in conversation.

"You said you're meeting with Lamen. I'll let him know you're here."

"Thanks."

As Thom waited, he noticed the absence of incense. He didn't mind; one whiff usually sent him into a sneezing fit.

Standing there, he felt at home. His time in Glakkadeth had changed him physically, mentally, and spiritually. His beliefs in Deu, whom he now called the One or God, had shifted. So had his belief in himself. He was more confident, despite the doubts and fears that occasionally crept in.

The people in Glakkadeth had been wonderful, from those at the monastery to Mik, Prezdan Modu, and his husband, Gallen. Before he and Rin left, they'd been awarded medals for service to the land. The whole thing embarrassed him. He kept the medal tucked away in a drawer and had even considered leaving it at Paddi's.

As his Acadium sponsor, Paddi gave him a place to stay during school breaks when there wasn't time for him to get home. The journey from Freasa to Potai-cruth required a week, and some breaks weren't long enough. Now, as Kami's guardian, he wasn't sure he'd go home often.

Thom grew up in Potai-cruth with his parents and seven siblings. His father, Uric Macirdan, was a potter, and his mother, Winni, a healer.

The door opened, pulling Thom from his thoughts. Zak stepped out, followed by Brother Lamen.

"Good to see you again, Thom," Lamen said, his eyes crinkling with warmth. "You appear well."

"Thanks. I feel better than I did last time."

"I'm glad. Please follow me," he said, leading him through the doorway.

"Good meeting you, Thom," Zak called. "Hope to see you again."

"You will."

They made themselves comfortable in two stuffed armchairs in Lamen's office, which formed a sitting area with a small table between them. Nearby was a desk, chair, and bookcase. The setup reminded Thom of Sestra B's office.

"Zak's quite impressed with your Glakkadian," Lamen said. "I gave him leave to get a cup of Timbu. I'll have to try it myself."

"It's good. But I'm biased."

"Now. How are you... really? Still having nightmares?"

"Wow. You don't waste time. No general questions about what I learned from Sestra B?"

"We'll get to that. I'm not sure you're aware that I specialize in helping people who've experienced trauma. And even though what happened to you was imagined, the impact was very real."

"I'd say."

Thom hesitated. Should he mention Jeshua and his divine advisors? Since Lamen would help him develop his spirit-healing abilities, he ought to know. And given how direct Lamen was...

"Jeshua told me about your work," Thom confessed.

"Is that a teacher at the Acadium?"

"No. He's... um... the son of the One in your holy book. He's one of my divine advisors."

"That Jeshua?" Lamen said, his eyes widening.

Should Thom tell him about his relationship with him? His intuition shouted yes.

"Jeshua's like a brother. He told me that he and I—well, my higher self, Rel—shared lifetimes together."

"Now, it's my turn to say wow. Like all monks in my community, I have spirit guides and a guardian angel, but I've never heard of anyone with Jeshua on their team. I assume you learned about higher selves from Sestra B?"

"Yeah. I might as well mention my other advisors."

"Please do."

"Well... the One, Archangels Metatron, Raphael, and Orion, my guardian angel Sereh, and a few spirit guides. But I chat most often with the One, whom I call God, Jeshua, and Sereh."

"That's quite a group. Did you get the idea to call the One 'God' from Sestra B?"

"Uh huh. They're the ones who stepped forward. I think it's because of my calling as a spirit healer."

"Let's save that for another time. For now, back to my original question. Nightmares?"

"One. Last Muns-dae night. It didn't last long, but when I woke up, the bed had moved a little. Not as much as it could've since Noiri put a shoe under a leg. I must've rocked myself again."

"I see. If you weren't aware, your body's trying to escape." Lamen paused, a flicker of realization crossing his face. "I'm speaking Glakkadian. I must've slipped into it after hearing you speaking with Zak. Is this OK, or would you prefer Dochalan?"

"Glakkadian. It reminds me of my friends there."

"Good. About the nightmares, they'll lessen in time. Talking with me will help."

"OK."

"I also want you to understand that your body might shake suddenly. That's a response to a trigger. It's your body's way of shaking it off."

"That already happened."

"Go on."

"The other day, I overheard another academ healer asking Mac why she wasn't mixing valerian root with the chamomile herbs. It's usually added to help patients sleep. She said it didn't work well for the patient she was treating. It was me. As soon as I heard that, I started shaking. Thankfully, no one noticed."

"You were worried they would?"

"Yeah. I don't want anyone else knowing about my nightmare. I feel like a baby."

"First, even adults have nightmares. Second, don't dismiss the idea of sharing it. As a healer, doing so could help others with theirs. But as a teenager, you've got a lot going on, and emotions are all over the place."

"I get that. But I'm not a teenager yet. I turn thirteen in Nuvima."

"Can you say more about your reaction to valerian root?"

"It was in the liquid Samiltun forced..." Thom corrected himself, "that I thought Samiltun forced on me after he... fake-captured me."

"Don't change your wording," Lamen said gently. "For you, it was very real. That's part of healing."

For a while, they discussed the nightmare, his feelings, the sights, smells, and sounds, including what Samiltun had said. Then Lamen guided him through a meditation, calling on Thom's advisors to further his healing.

Thom went on to speak about his gifts, focusing on his spirit-healing abilities, and how his beliefs had changed. One key example was reincarnation. The Iosan faith didn't teach it, while the One faith did.

"You've endured so much in these past years," Lamen said. "The connection between your spirit-healing gift and your beliefs is striking. As new abilities emerge, or existing ones expand, we'll explore how they shape your choices."

"I hadn't thought about that."

"Well, you've been here two hours. I don't want to keep you longer or you'll miss supper. Let's start with twice-weekly meetings for the first few weeks and then adjust as needed. Would Muns-dae and Turi-dae at this time work?"

"Not Muns-dae morning. I have back-to-back classes up until supper on that day."

"I have an idea. But first... after living in Glakkadeth, did you like our food and its spiciness?"

"Oh, yes. It took time to adjust. Some days I drank a lot of milk and Rin's herbal remedies. But by the time I left, I loved it."

"What if you came for supper on Muns-dae, and we met afterward?"

"That'd be great. Sometimes, Dochalan food tastes bland. But... I do enjoy the Acadium food," he added hurriedly.

"Perfect. Before our next meeting, pay attention to any feelings, reactions, or nightmares tied to your abduction." Lamen paused, smacking his forehead. "I can't believe I missed this. You were abducted twice—first by Vern and Finn, as Sestra B mentioned in a letter, and then Samiltun, even if that one wasn't real. Some of your reactions now might trace back to the first. I need to reflect on that."

"I'll write about it in my journal," Thom added.

"You might talk with Jonathan," Lamen suggested. "You two seem to be growing close."

"I will. Thanks, Lamen. I'll see you next time."

After escorting Thom back to Apollo, Lamen returned to his office, thinking about Thom and Jonathan's friendship. He suspected it might become something more. But maybe they're not old enough for hormones to stir. If he was correct, they'd face this land's discomfort with same-gender relationships. His parents were of opposite genders, but half his classmates at the monastery had same-gender parents.

"Lamen," a male voice called.

"Yes," he replied as Zak stepped into his office.

"You're afternoon appointment canceled. Some crisis at home."

"OK. Ready for supper?"

"Yes. And thanks for letting me get some Timbu. It was quite good."

"Timbu," Lamen muttered. "Thom's an unusual lad." He recalled how Sestra B had written as much in the same letter, including that he was full of surprises. So far, she'd been right.

"Did you say something?"

"Come on. Callum promised to save us seats."

Chapter 19

"Not acceptable," Samiltun said, irritation sharp in his voice as he glared at the teen before him.

It was the last week of Siptema. Earlier that morning, he'd ridden through the city streets toward the Traders Quarter, where his modest business sat. Mud puddles dotted the ground from rain two days earlier, and his horse had splashed through one, speckling his trousers. The monarchs had recently launched a road improvement initiative, tedious work from what he'd seen: pouring crushed stone and spreading tar. Progress was slow, especially near his home. Apparently, the crews were now working in a poorer quarter, part of the monarchs' misguided belief in treating everyone equally.

What a load of gutterdung! he thought, glaring harder at the boy. *They should focus on neighborhoods like this one. We're creating jobs!*

Samiltun wore the simple brown cotton trousers and tunic favored by other traders, rather than his usual linen. The sole hint of his status was the gold ring on his finger, etched with his family crest and inherited from his deceased father, a lord.

Years ago, that lord had had an affair with Samiltun's mother, a cook at an upscale inn. When Samiltun was thirteen, the lord's wife discovered it. Soon after, his mother had died, and many of its patrons had gotten severely ill. A bumbling constable blamed poor sanitation and shut the inn down. Samiltun ended up living on the streets. That's when his gifts began to emerge.

Back then, he'd gone by Rue, short for Ruefell. He survived by stealing and sleeping wherever he could. At sixteen, the lord learned of his situation and, out of a lingering affection for Rue's mother, adopted him. His wife was furious. The couple had no children, and she'd hoped the title would pass to a relative.

Only after moving into the lord's manor did Rue learn the truth: the wife had his mother killed. He overheard a stablehand talking with a housemaid about it. The wife had instructed one of her attendants to hire a poisoner. Undetected, he laced an almond cake his mother had been preparing with powder from black cherry leaves. Bent on revenge, Rue developed his gifts until he could compel a thief to kill the wife and her attendants. The lord died in a hunting accident years later, leaving Samiltun the title.

Since then, Samiltun had worked hard to command the respect that came with his position. His servants and employees all knew this, though his pawnshop and home were a far cry from the life most lords enjoyed. The shaking boy standing on the other side of the desk, and wearing second-hand trousers and a patched tunic, had to be reminded of his place.

That one was currently his deputy, or DP, of eight children Samiltun had assembled two years earlier. They were his Finders, as he liked to call them, because they found goods for him. It didn't matter where: on the streets, in a stranger's pocket, or inside a wealthy home.

Once a week, he came to collect the shop's earnings and the goods the Finders had gathered. His DP was responsible for delivering the latter, which he was doing now.

"Didn't you check these?" Samiltun barked. "See the monograms on the handkerchiefs? Or the label on the tablecloth? That was custom-made at the finest textile shop here!"

Of utmost importance was that the items couldn't be linked to him. Any connection would ruin everything.

"And this ring!" Samiltun sputtered, spittle striking the boy. "It has the maker's mark."

"I'm a-sorri, saur," the boy mumbled, head lowered, not even wiping the wet from his cheek.

"And what do I smell? Didn't you wash this week?"

"Ya, saur," he replied, sniffing his armpits. "But I been runnin' all ova. I did chek um. Mebbe the marked stuff got mixed wit' the utter stuff."

"You wear decent clothes and get paid for being my DP," Samiltun snapped. "I could replace you. Do you want that?"

"Nah, saur. I'll do better. I does make sure da others git the right stuff. I was a-hurryin'. I herd yeh was cumin' two days early. I tol' em to hit the streets where the wealthy folks buy stuff."

"You're not blaming me, are you?"

"Nah, saur. "Ony 'splainin'."

"Take these away," Samiltun growled, gesturing to the traceable items. "Drop them somewhere. I'll be back next week and will expect twice as much."

"Ya, saur," the boy said, bowing and backing out the rear door into the alley.

Samiltun sat in his office at the back of the pawnshop. He never worked the shop himself, having no interest in dealing with the dirty, pathetic miscreants who required his services. He'd hired two women for that, and would soon be reviewing the shop earnings with one of them, Veena. Using his gifts, he ensured they remained loyal and didn't steal from him. The same went for the Finders.

Maybe it was time to replace this DP. He couldn't remember his name, not that it mattered. Some of the children would age out soon. His DP was the oldest, close to fourteen. Samiltun preferred the Finders between six and twelve. The smaller and more innocent-looking, the better. Adults tended to pity them and paid less attention to their belongings when they were near, assuming they were harmless.

A week ago, one of the littlest had snatched a gold necklace from an elderly woman who bent to help the girl after a staged fall. That necklace was already being melted down, soon to be recast as jewelry for sale. The older children were better suited for quick grabs from shops and homes.

Samiltun was pleased with how cleverly he maintained his crew. Their clothes were in fair shape, and he fed them enough to keep them skinny, but not starving, avoiding notice of constables and the busybodies who ran the orphanages and soup kitchens. The monarchs' other belief that everyone had a right to food and shelter annoyed him. It was a good thing a few kids slipped through the cracks, like those abandoned by thieving parents and taught to distrust authority. All it required was manipulating one unsuspecting child to begin recruiting more.

His gift was so strong that he simply had to refresh control over his people twice a year at the Summer and Winter Solstice gatherings. The events cost more than Samiltun liked, but they were an easy way to ensure everyone's silence.

Thoughts of his gifts led him to think of the Macirdan boy he'd failed to control some years back. He couldn't believe he'd misread the boy's abilities. Since then, he hadn't found another with a strong enough gift to exploit. Three years ago, he moved to the capital, convinced he'd find more gifted children in a larger population. After selling his manor west of Potai-cruth, along with its tapestries, furniture, and most of its horses, he could only afford a modest house; prices were far higher here. A small sum remained, which he invested foolishly and lost.

Focusing on the remaining goods the DP had left, he began assigning value. They'd fetch a tidy sum. Not that he'd tell the boy. His growing wealth had allowed him to hire two servants, and he was nearly ready to purchase a manor. He was about to outgrow his current quarters and had his eye on a fine property at the city's edge. But more coin was needed. And wealth alone wasn't enough.

Samiltun craved power.

With it, he could control Docha-leigh and rid it of the undesirables. He pictured himself sitting on the throne, replacing the bleeding-heart monarchs, with nobles groveling at his feet and foreign dignitaries offering tribute. Shifting on the padded chair in his office, an absurd luxury in this place, he sighed, savoring the vision.

A soft tap sounded at the door.

"It's Veena, sir."

"Enter."

"Is now a good time to go over the books?"

"Yes."

Samiltun was instructing her to raise the interest on the carpenter's tools when a bald, medium-height man, in a worn tunic and trousers, barged into his office.

"Dergin," Samiltun barked. "Where are your manners? I told you to knock. If you want the pay Marten gets, act more civilly."

"But I gots sumpin' 'portant to tell ya."

"What did you say?" Samiltun asked, his expression hard. "I expect proper speech."

"I... um... have sum...pin...," he said, frowning before continuing. "Marten... has...a message for... you."

"Better. Work on it. Veena, we're done. I'll be heading home soon. Leave the earnings in the usual place."

"Yes, sir," she said, exiting through the inner door to the shop.

"What's the message?"

Marten...thunks...thinks, he's founded....found...two kids what gots... thet haves gifts."

Samiltun shook his head. "You're saying Marten's found two children with gifts."

"Ya, sur. They's twins."

"Did he say what the gifts were?"

"Sumpin about findin' coins an' metal."

Hmm, possibly earth sense, Samiltun mused. Maybe they can find gems. "Where's he now?"

"Watchin' the home, seein' ifn' they use theys gifts agin."

"And he's sure this time. I don't want another waste of time."

"Ya, sur. He din't want to risk gettin' chained agin, like afore."

"What's the family's situation?"

"Poor, sur. They's hev many kids. Mebbe eight. And the mutter's expectin'."

"Where do they live?"

"Prun-shees."

"Ah," Samiltun said.

That quarter lay in the city's northwest section, where poorer families lived, often several to a home, sometimes above shops. The buildings there were a mix of old and new. The newer ones followed the monarch's recently instituted Good Housing law. It was a short ride from here.

Chapter 20

With a free hour after supper, Thom sat in his quad's common room, gazing out the window. Red, orange, and yellow leaves swirled in gusts of wind. Now that it was mid-Uctiba, the weather had become colder. He always appreciated autumn, though he didn't like how quickly it gave way to winter. Even so, his birthday was a month away. He'd be thirteen. Jonathan had also asked what he wanted. He was currently helping in the Rejuvenary. Thom was jealous.

He liked coming here. It gave him a break from being alone and a chance to interact with others, although no one else was present at the moment. Each floor had a room like this at its four corners. This L-shaped room, located where two hallways met, had windows on two sides, large study tables, and a few stuffed chairs, identical to the one in his room.

A week ago, he learned Noiri had decided every academ's room should have one. He was glad. He didn't want special treatment. The chair was quite cozy; he'd fallen asleep in it more than once.

A strong wind blew through a window, snuffing out the oil lamp and scattering his notes. He jumped up, shut it, and scooped up the pages. Taking a taper, Thom stepped into the hall to light it from a wall sconce before returning to relight the lamp. Outside, dark clouds were gathering.

"It's gonna rain," he muttered. He didn't need Rin's some-times-unreliable weather-sense to determine that.

Thom wished Rin was around. They hadn't seen each other since they said goodbye at Paddi's home in Aegisa. He wondered if Rin knew about his nightmare... and about Kami.

"Kami!" Thom shouted. The coming storm would be the worst she'd faced. *Kami, he mind-spoke, are you OK?*

Loud noises.

That's the wind. It might get stronger, and it's probably going to rain hard. It'll surely get louder. Are you warm enough?

Yes. Can you stay with me?

No. I have class with Kee soon. You've met her. She and Tovah heat your sands. Thom pictured them in his mind, hoping Kami could tap into it.

I remember.

I'll be back before dinner with another meal.

OK.

Thom picked up a quill and his journal and opened it to a blank page. He hadn't written since a few days after he first met with Lamen. Writing helped him sort his thoughts, as did talking with his divine advisors before bed.

On clear nights, he loved sitting in his window seat, gazing at the two moons—one pink and one blue. An astronomy academ had told him the smaller, closer pink moon orbited their planet in a circular path. The blue one, farther out, followed an elliptical path. She even said they sometimes aligned. That'd be amazing to see.

Bringing his attention back to the page, Thom wrote a single letter: G. He always started that way. He'd begun keeping a journal when he was eight, after his best friend Davi moved away.

Back then, he didn't give it any thought. Later, he learned G stood for God. Sestra B believed it was because he had a strong bond with God, solidified at his pre-incarnation meeting.

He wished he could remember what had happened during that meeting. But forgetting was intentional, past lives included, to ensure each life began fresh. Lamen had said some things weren't completely forgotten, like trauma. And that the next life offered a chance to heal it.

His attention shifted back to his journal, and Thom resumed writing: *Classes are in full swing. I'm getting used to the schedule, and can now get to my classes on time. G, you'd think that since the Acadium is square, I wouldn't get lost. I did. Twice. But I've figured out the best routes. Some stairwells can get packed. I'm a fast walker, but some academs move so slow they're practically going backward, like my Da says.*

Last week in history, our teacher, Risteard Colgan, who we call Rish, told us that a widow with two daughters and a son founded Docha-leigh. She came from a land south of Eiren, which is now mostly unpopulated. Its leaders had become corrupt, and when disease struck, their neglect caused it to spread. The widow lost her youngest boy because of it. And guess what? Her name was Niamh. That's our queen's name. Isn't that something? Desperate, she convinced a ship captain to take her on as cook in exchange for passage across the sea.

Rel watched from the divine realm as Thom wrote in his journal. When Rel (they) incarnated as Thom, part of their spirit did too, keeping them forever connected. Like all beings here, Rel was genderless. They met Thom about a year before, as humans measure time. Jeshua had brought them to Thom's Sanctuary after a monk Thom couldn't save had died.

Thom's jottings about the land south of Eiren reminded Rel of their previous incarnation, Celes. She was an apprentice healer who died unexpectedly from the plague Thom mentioned. Rel had been quite upset. Celes hadn't fulfilled her calling, and it had taken extra effort for Jeshua to calm them. After Rel had processed her death, Archangel Metatron, who oversaw light-workers, agreed to let Rel incarnate again sooner than usual to continue their training. Thom now carried the same calling, with a few variations.

Rel focused on Thom again, who hadn't moved from the stuffed chair.

G, Thom continued, Rish explained that Niamh and her family had settled in a small village. Unbeknownst to them, bandits raided it a few times a year, but the villagers soon saw her as a savior. Her husband, a soldier, had died challenging the corrupt leaders before the plague struck. Ahead of his time, he'd taught his wife and daughters self-defense, something the leaders had forbidden. Their son was yet a toddler.

During one raid, Niamh and her daughters defeated the ban-dits, even tracking down their lair and destroying it, reclaiming the stolen goods. The villagers named her headwoman, and as a result, more people came to live there. Over time, the village became Freas-a-chos, and the land, Docha-leigh. That's when they named Niamh queen. Freas-a-chos means serve and protect, and Docha-leigh means hope and healing. I like that. It fits with my calling. I want people to feel safe and hopeful as they discover their passion.

Oh, and there weren't nobles in those days. That started when the queen honored those who'd provided a great service to the people. Passing on titles to children came much later.

I'd better stop. My next class is with Mage Keenan. We call her Kee. Thanks for watching out for me, G, and to all of you, divine advisors, for doing the same.

Thom, Jonathan, and Tovah entered the classroom together. The chairs were arranged in a circle, with the desks pushed to the side. Kee was chatting with a girl with copper-toned skin and high cheekbones.

"Oh, there's Cat," Tovah said, pointing to the girl. "She's in my level. Wait until you hear about her gift! I'm gonna say hi."

Thom and Jonathan sat as two more academs walked in—one was a dark-skinned boy with straight black hair; the other, a girl with short, thick hair, redder than Thom's auburn, and with lighter skin.

Thom asked, "Do you know them?"

"No."

Once everyone was seated, Kee greeted them. "Good afternoon. You all look bright and cheery for the start of a new school year. This is our first group session for academs with uncommon abilities. Welcome! We'll meet each month to discuss your unique talent and any changes that have occurred. To start, please share your name and level, when your gift appeared, and a brief description. Helean, would you start?"

"OK. I'm fourth level. My gift showed up when I was fifteen, the summer before last. I was outside after a fight with my Ma about my hair. I wanted to cut it, but she insisted long red hair was more attractive. She said, for the umpteenth time, that while I lived in her house, I'd do as she said."

Thom nodded, along with the others. Parents everywhere used the same threats.

"Anyway, a storm came up. I was running back to the house when I got struck by lightning."

Thom and Jonathan, along with one other, gasped. Clearly, the rest had already heard this story.

"I didn't die, obviously," Helean said, her voice full of mischief. "It went through me into the ground. You should've seen my hair, standing on end! Sparks were shooting from my fingers when I ran inside. Ma went all hysterical. After hugging me, she cut my hair," she added with a chuckle.

"OK, Helean," Kee said, nudging her back on track. "Your gift?"

"Sorry. Something was different. I could see energy charges, not just in storms, but also people and animals."

"Kee," Thom said, raising his hand. "Can I ask Helean a question?"

"Yes."

"I'm Thom, first level. Do you see a person's life spirit, their soul, like me?"

"I'm not sure. I see sparks moving back and forth really fast. Why?"

"My gift lets me see a person's life spirit. I'll explain more when I share my story."

"Helean, why don't you mention what happened earlier this year," Kee prompted.

"In Jenua, I was coming from my room when I saw a man carrying an unconscious girl into the Rejuvenary. I'm not a healer, but something drew me to follow. The healers were pounding on her chest, yelling that her heart wasn't beating. I must've been possessed or something, 'cause I pushed them out of the way and placed my hand over her heart. Suddenly, sparks shot from my hand, and it started beating."

"Wow," Jonathan and Thom exclaimed together.

Would that ability have helped Lebrim? Thom wondered. No. It was his time.

"Thanks, Helean," Kee said. "Mardu, you're next."

"That's me," said the boy with the straight black hair. "I'm third level. My gift showed up over the summer. I've always had good eyesight, even in the dark. Last Jauli, Mam lost her wedding ring. She'd taken it off while cleaning and somehow knocked it off the table. When I checked under the stove to see if it was there, I squinted hard, and my eyes did something weird—I could see through the wooden floor, all the way to the ground."

Thom shook his head, amazed again.

"My parents thought I was making it up, so they had my sister take something into the bedroom. I couldn't see her, but when I told them it was a spoon, they were shocked."

A gust of wind rattled the windows, followed by a thunderclap. Several academs yelped.

"Check them," Kee called over the noise. "Make sure they're all closed."

Thom felt the thunder roll through him. Helean must've felt it as well, spotting her by the window, motionless.

"This one's stuck," Cat said.

Another gust hit, pushing the stuck window open further. Papers flew, and the lamps blew out, leaving everyone in near-darkness.

Thom saw the shapes of Jonathan and Kee struggling to force the window shut as rain poured down, lit briefly by a flash of lightning.

"Everyone, stay where you are," Kee shouted. "Tovah, can you feel your way to the table by the door. There's a ceramic container with tapers. Light one from a sconce in the hallway."

"OK," she said, sounding unsure.

"We'll resume once the lamps are lit," Kee assured them.

When Tovah came back, she reported, "All the sconces are out."

Another flash lit the room. A deafening thunderclap followed, drawing a scream from one of the academs.

Kee was silent for a moment. "Hand the taper to Helean. I want her to try something."

"I'm by the door, Helean," Tovah called.

Thom heard shuffling.

"I've got it."

"Let's see if you can light it," Kee said.

"Are you sure?"

"Yes. To be safe, go to the container, dump out the other tapers, and put yours in."

"Done."

"Now, picture a spark moving from your finger to the taper. Hold the intention that one spark is...well...sparked. Pardon the pun."

Thom groaned, but considered Kee's words. Sestra B had said the same thing about working with his gifts. He must've blinked, because the taper was lit.

"Neat," the academs chorused.

"Great job, Helean," Kee praised her. "Let's light the lamps."

Once the room was lit again, Kee said, "Let's resume. You're up, Catori."

Thom noted she was the girl Tovah had called Cat.

After she described her uncanny memory for everything she read and heard, Thom, Jonathan, and Tovah told them about their gifts.

Thom dropped his satchel off in his room and grabbed his rain cape. Time to feed Kami.

Descending the stairs, he reflected on what Catori had shared after the introductions. She belonged to an indigenous tribe that lived in southern Docha-leigh. Her name meant spirit. Like him, she had divine advisors, but she called them elders. She spoke with them often, and with ancestors who passed, which was something, especially because her gift allowed her to remember people's stories word for word.

Thom was touched by how they responded to his gifts. They leaned in, especially Helean, as he described the colors, swirls, and patterns in auras. And when he explained his ability to truth-tell and sense when someone was living their purpose, they were on the edge of their seats. Jonathan's advanced healing abilities also impressed them to no end. Their curiosity grew when he explained that he and Thom had what he called flip-flop gifts.

Chapter 21

Stepping into the Royal Residence kitchen, Thom said, "Hi, Keelin."

"Hi, Thom. I thought you'd be coming by. Good thing you wore your rain cloak."

"Yeah. It's coming down steadily. Sorry for dripping on your floor."

"It's fine, Oddi did earlier. It comes when kids are around."

"I didn't mean to," he said, entering.

"Hi," Thom greeted him.

"I know, Oddi," Keelin said. "There are rags by the door—for perpetrators to clean up after themselves," she added with mock sternness.

"Oh," Thom replied, "I'll wipe up my mess."

"That wasn't aimed at you, but I'd appreciate it. I've got two hearts and livers for Kami, and I ground the meat for you. All that's left is for you to add the extras."

"Thanks. You didn't have to."

"I had time."

"Thanks again. After wiping up his drips, Thom went to the cooling larder and grabbed the two bowls of meat from the usual spot.

"Can I help?" Oddi asked.

"Sure," Thom said, showing him how much crushed bone, peas and lentils to add to the meat.

"This is fun," Oddi remarked.

Minutes later, when they finished, Thom said, "Well done."

"Can I help feed Kami?"

"She mostly feeds herself now. But sure. I think she'll remember you."

"I promise not to get in the way."

"Oddi," Keelin called. "Don't forget your rain cloak."

"I won't."

Opening the door to Draganni Hall, Thom called, "Kami, I'm here with your meal. A little wet. Oddi's with me and wanted to help. Do you remember him?"

She nodded.

"How are you?" Thom asked, setting down a bowl and motioning for Oddi to place his next to it.

OK. So glad the booms and blink-blink lights are gone!

Switching to mind-speech, Thom replied, *I understand. They're loud, but usually not dangerous. Was the sand blowing around?*

Sometimes, Kami answered, pointing her snout toward the sliding doors.

"Oddi, check the doors and see if there's any wind coming through."

When he reached them, a gust blew, and a soft whistle came through the cracks.

"Kami's right," Oddi said. "Look, the sand's swirling."

"Could you look for rags and stuff them along the bottom?"

Oddi found a few and wedged them into place.

"That's good," Thom said. "You've already been a big help."

Thanks.

"Did Kami just thank me?" he asked.

"She did. You heard her?"

"Yeah. That's neat."

Kami, can you talk to anyone? Thom asked.

Yes.

That's handy. It's nice and toasty in here, and I'm soaked. The rain got under my cloak. Mind if I lay it over your sand to dry?

No.

"Oddi, is your cloak wet?"

"Not really."

"You can share my nest, Kami offered.

Thanks, Thom said. He laid out his cloak and motioned for Oddi to hang his on a wall hook.

Food now, Kami insisted.

"I think she's hungry," Oddi said, pointing to the drool at the edge of her mouth.

Do I smell good meats?

You do. Keelin set them aside for you. She even ground your meat.

Kami rolled her tongue in anticipation.

"Oddi, bring me the bowl with the mash. Leave the one with the hearts and livers where it is. They're her treat.

"Ewww."

"I get it," Thom replied. "But dragons love them, and they help young ones grow. We'll give them to her after she finishes the mash. She likes me to toss them in the air and she tries to catch them."

"I can do that," Oddi said, his eyes sparkling.

Kami ate everything, even licking the bowls clean.

Looks like you enjoyed that, Thom said with a smirk.

Yes, Kami replied, tilting her head and opening her mouth in what he recognized as a smile.

Are you OK with the storm?

Yes. The booms are thunder, aren't they? And the blink-blinks are lightning."

Yeah. But how do you know that now?

I'm not sure. I suddenly remember things. Was I in a storm after I hatched?

You were. But it wasn't raining as hard, and there wasn't any thunder and lightning.

You met my Mama, didn't you?

I did. And your brother and sister.

What happened to them?

They had to leave. Your Mama asked me to care for you.

Will they come back?

I'm not sure.

I feel... connected to them. Maybe to other dragons. But it's not strong.

Thom wondered if what she felt was anything like what he did with his advisors. Then he frowned, thoughtful.

"It's sad Kami doesn't have her Mama," Oddi said.

"Yeah." He felt a nudge. Kami's snout pressed against him.

You stopped talking to me.

Sorry. I'm kind of confused. Sometimes you sound like a child. Other times, older.

I dunno. Maybe 'cause I'm a dragon.

See. That sounded more like a child.

Kami shook her head.

Are you OK if we go now? Thom asked.

Uh huh. I'm gonna sleep.

Thom kissed her forehead and pulled on his mostly dry tunic, as did Oddi. Picking up the bowls, he handed one to Oddi and said, "Thanks for your help."

"Welcome. Can I help feed her again? That tossing game was fun."

"Sure."

As Thom stepped to the door, he glanced back. Kami's eyes were closed, a soft, raspy snort escaping her. He hoped she wasn't getting sick. She'd been through enough.

Grasping the handle, he opened the door. The rain had picked up again.

"Turg. We'd better run!"

Chapter 22

Even though the Royal Residence wasn't far from Draganni Hall, Thom was soaked again by the time they entered the kitchen. So was Oddi.

"We're back, Keelin," Thom said miserably. No one was there. "Where do you think she is?"

"Probably putting dinner on the table."

"Oh. I'd better run. I didn't realize how long we stayed with Kami."

"Eat here. We always have plenty. Mamie and Da won't mind."

"Oddi, is that you?" a woman called from deeper inside. "Dinner's on the table. Keelin's about to serve the soup."

"Mamie. Thom's here. He was gonna run back to the school, but I told him to stay."

Niamh and Keelin stepped into the kitchen.

"Thom, you're all wet," Niamh said. "Please eat with us. Keelin, grab a few towels. I'll add a place at the table and serve."

"Certainly," Keelin replied, hurrying off.

"Oddi, run up and change into dry clothes," his mother added.

When Thom entered the dining room, he saw the table set for five, dwarfed by the room's size. His hair was damp, and to his dismay, his cowlick refused to lie flat.

"That darn hair again, huh, Thom," Peth teased, raising his eyebrows.

Thom blushed, remembering when he'd first met Peth and Niamh in Aegisa at Paddi's home. Peth had admitted he also struggled with his hair as a child. "Are you sure it's OK I eat with you? I don't want to intrude."

"You're not," Peth assured him, gesturing to the empty seat across from Oddi. "There's hot vegetable soup and warm bread."

"Thanks."

They ate in silence for a while, with nothing but the clink of spoons against bowls.

"How's Kami?" Niamh asked at last.

"She didn't like the thunder and lightning. Wind got through the cracks in the sliding doors and blew the sand around. Oddi handled it."

"I did. I even helped feed her."

"Thanks again. Kami's fine now. She's had a full meal and is sleeping."

"Cracks," Niamh frowned. "We'll need to fix that. I'll speak with the Commander and see if she can find a worker we can trust. We'll get them sealed before winter."

"Thank you, Niamh," Thom said sincerely.

"You've finished your soup," Peth remarked. "Have more. And another slice of bread."

The warmth of the soup seeped into Thom. He hadn't realized how much the dash outside had chilled him.

"How are Kami's wings and her weight?" Niamh asked. "Ellie said you were feeding her a mixture to thicken them."

"Yeah. I haven't noticed much of a change. She is putting on weight. But she's not as heavy as her siblings were in the dragon sanctuary."

"Dragon sanctuary?" Niamh echoed. "I think my Nana used that phrase in one of her stories."

"Oh, right. I don't think I mentioned that's where I found them." Considering his last chat with Kami, he asked Oddi. "You still haven't found any books or papers on dragons, have you?"

"No. Nothing's in the archives."

"Or in the Acadium library," Thom added.

"What's going on?"

"Kami and I were mind-speaking. Sometimes she sounds like a kid... other times, a teen."

"How old is she now?" Peth asked.

"About six weeks."

Niamh's gaze went distant.

Peth tilted his head. "What's wrong, luv?"

"Thinking about Nana again. When tucking me in at night, she'd tell me stories her gran told her. I vaguely remember one where a young male dragon, older than Kami, got injured in a snowstorm. Somehow, he knew how to repair his wing and make it home, even though no one had taught him."

"How did he know, Mamie?" Oddi asked.

"I asked Nana that, too. She said dragons share knowledge... or memories. Maybe that's what's happening with Kami."

"Maybe. I wish I knew more."

"I'll try to remember anything else she told me."

"Can you tell me those stories?" Oddi asked.

"I'd also like to hear them," Peth added.

"Of course."

"Thom, I can take notes," Oddi offered.

"I'd appreciate it. And thanks for dinner."

"Wait!" Oddi blurted. "You can't leave before dessert. Keelin made chocolate popovers."

"Well then, I'm definitely staying."

Chapter 23

Almost two weeks had passed, and the sun hadn't yet risen, when Thom was startled awake. Today, Uctiba 32, marked the first day of a four-day weekend celebrating a successful harvest. The school always held the celebration on the last Fwi-dae of the month.

During his meeting with Lamen yesterday, Thom had noticed a new chapel banner. It showed an angel with curly black hair and wearing a burnt-orange tunic with a geometric pattern. A lion was depicted beside her. Lamen said she was Archangel Ariel, whose name meant lioness of God. Odd that Kami's mother bore the same name. The archangel, Lamen had explained, had a strong connection to their planet, Talamh, fitting for a harvest banner.

Today's supper would be the Acadium's harvest feast. Tomorrow, Thom and Jonathan would join the Byrnes for a second celebration.

With no classes, Thom had planned to sleep in. What had woken him? He stayed quiet, listening. "Something's gonna happen. And big."

A week ago, he'd told Lamen about his occasional flashes of prescience. They'd started after his first encounter with Samiltun. But when did he learn he had that ability?

He went quiet again. An image rose: he was sitting with... oh yeah, Sereh, Jeshua, God, and Metatron. They told him. Back then, he called Jeshua 'Iosa,' and God 'Deu.'

"Oh, wow. I finally remember one of my earliest divine visitations."

A dark-feathered bird struck his window, making him jump and bringing him back to the unease that had woken him. Bad omen? Coincidence?

Thom would be thirteen in less than two weeks. But why a premonition about that? Noiri always held a special supper each month for birthdays. Nuvima's celebration would fall two days after his.

He sat up, heart pounding. What if Samiltun did try to kidnap him? His breath quickened, and he felt on the verge of panic.

"Remember the meditation Lamen and Rin taught you," Thom said aloud.

He planted his feet firmly on the floor, imagining a rope anchoring his core to the center of the earth. Its strength steadied him, slowing his breath and heartbeat.

Thom often fixated on worst-case scenarios, like Mekial had said on the beach in Glakkadeth. Maybe everything would be OK.

"Gang," Thom said to his advisors, looking upward, "could you give me a hint what this is about?" He wasn't sure why he continued doing that. Lamen had explained that the divine realm existed all around them, just in another space. But old habits hung on, probably from the Iosan elders who insisted heaven was up and hell down.

"Well, I'm not getting back to sleep now. Might as well clean up. No one'll be in the washroom."

"Thanks for inviting me to the Byrne's," Jonathan said, as he and Thom left the school grounds heading to Paddi's home. "I would've gone to my aunt and uncle's, but they left last week to visit my family."

"You're welcome. Eran suggested it. With most academs gone, it didn't seem fair for you to be here alone."

"Thanks again."

After a stretch of quiet riding, Thom said, "That's their place ahead on the left. The one with reddish-brown stone, three stories, and a portico."

"It's beautiful. Paddi must do well as a textile merchant."

"Probably."

"I wonder if he's familiar with my family's goods."

As they rode through a pair of stone pillars, a man around Thom's father's age, with graying hair, and a teen with wavy blond hair came out to meet them.

"Is that Paddi?" Jonathan asked, pointing toward the man.

"No, Griffin, the head servant. The other's Benn, who cares for the horses."

"Good to see you again, Thom," Griffin said.

"And you. This is Jonathan. He's a first-level healer like me."

"Nice to meet you."

"Are Eran and Ciarenn already here?" Thom asked.

"Yes. They arrived last night. Please come in. Benn will curry your horses."

"Thanks, Benn."

Stepping into a two-story entrance hall, Thom noticed a paint-ing by the wooden staircase—a middle-aged woman with chest-nut hair. He hadn't seen it on his last visit and guessed it was Paddi's late wife. Ciarenn had her aquiline nose.

Paddi entered from a nearby room. "Greetings, Thom and Jonathan."

"Hi, Paddi," Thom replied, giving him a hug.

"And welcome, Jonathan. I'm glad you could join us."

"Thank you, sir," Jonathan replied, bowing.

"None of that. Call me Paddi. Join us in the sitting room."

Inside, Thom spotted Eran and Ciarenn. "Hi, guys. You came yesterday?"

"Yeah," Eran said. "You could've too."

"Thanks, but I didn't want to be away from... um..." Thom replied, realizing he almost mentioned Kami.

"What?" Eran asked. "Homework? I'd heard you did yours on the day it was assigned?"

"I do."

"Thom's helping me with my history assignment," Jonathan added, quickly.

"Thom," Paddi said, "you haven't met my oldest, Iosef. He was away the last time you visited."

"Nice to meet you," he said.

Iosef, like Eran, resembled Paddi, with dark brown hair and a straight nose with a slight hump.

"Good to meet you, Iosef," Jonathan said.

Thom caught a small grin on Jonathan's face.

"Thom, Jonathan," Paddi said, "help yourselves to a drink, ges-turing to a table by the wall. "We have berry juice, hot apple cider, and Timbu."

Both of them chose cider. As Thom poured it into cups, he whispered, "Thanks for covering."

"Any time. Do you think you should tell Paddi?"

"Maybe. As he sat down, he gave it some thought. Although Paddi was a member of COM, Niamh and Peth wanted to keep Kami's existence to as few people as possible. And what about his kids?

"Iosef," Jonathan asked, "where'd you get your jumper?"

"Last autumn, I was scouting towns for clothing sellers. I found this in a trading store. The designs are intricate, don't you think?"

"I do. My sister made it."

"What?"

"Does it have a Llewelyn Crafts label?"

"Yeah."

"Llewelyn's my surname," Jonathan explained. "My family makes jumpers and other clothes from the fleece and mohair we get from my aunt and uncle."

"Exquisite work," Paddi added.

"Thanks."

"I asked the shopkeeper where it came from," Iosef said, "but he couldn't tell me. The owner was off that day."

"My aunt and uncle's ranch is an hour's ride north and a little west of here," Jonathan said.

"Would they mind if I stopped by next week?"

"I'm sure it'd be fine. I can give you a note and mention I met you today, with Thom. They met him when... oh."

"What?" Eran prompted.

"Paddi," Thom cut in, "when we left the Barrelson's a few months ago, Rin said you were part of the same... advisors' group."

"You know about that?" Paddi asked, frowning.

"Um," Thom said, shifting uncomfortably. "I figured it out from a few things Rin said."

"Are you talking about COM?" Ciarenn asked.

"You've heard of it?" Thom said, surprised.

"COM?" Jonathan repeated.

"Thom," Paddi said, "I told my children because of a few unexpected trips and late-night meetings. Can I assume Jonathan's trustworthy? Sorry to ask."

"That's OK," Jonathan said, his gaze shifting to Thom.

"He is. Jonathan saved my life a few weeks ago."

"I beg your pardon."

"I didn't," Jonathan said.

"It felt like it."

"Please explain," Paddi said.

Thom told them about his nightmare, his belief he'd been kidnapped, and how Jonathan snapped him out of it.

Eran, Ciarenn, and Iosef sat open-mouthed. Paddi's expression didn't change.

"Rin told you about Samiltun, huh?" Thom asked.

"Before he left. I wish you'd told me sooner, but I was away when it happened."

"I can't believe you went through that," Eran said. "But... I don't think that's why you and Jonathan stumbled earlier."

"You noticed?" Jonathan asked.

"What'd I miss?" Ciarenn said.

"They both started to say something, then stopped," Iosef explained.

"You caught that?" Thom said.

"What about the advisors' group?" Jonathan interrupted.

"Oh, Rin and I are part of a covert advisors' group for the monarchs," Paddi said, giving him a brief explanation.

"Back to the question," Eran pressed. "What didn't you say?"

Taking a deep breath, Thom told them about Kami.

If their jaws had dropped before, now they hit the floor. Paddi's included.

"Come on," Ciarenn protested. "You're saying there's a baby dragon at the Keep."

Before Thom could answer, Eran jumped in. "Thom, I know you like fantasy. But everyone says dragons aren't real."

"I'd have said the same," Paddi added, "if I didn't know you were honest. Has Rin heard?"

"No, unless Niamh and Peth wrote him."

"If the baby dragon's real, prove it," Ciarenn demanded.

"Ciarenn," Paddi said, sharply. "But I'd like to see it as well."

"Her," Thom corrected. "And baby dragons are called drag-onets. Come with us tomorrow morning when we feed her. It'll have to be early, before the other academs get back. We don't want anyone else to know."

"Why not now?" Ciarenn asked.

"Because we're about to eat our Harvest supper, you dolt," Iosef said. "Meggie and Pel spent days preparing it."

"Speaking of food," Eran said, "didn't you say you have to feed Kami three times a day? You're staying overnight, so who's...?"

"Oddi's handling it," Thom replied.

Pel entered, clearing his throat. "Supper's ready."

That night, Thom and Jonathan sat on Thom's bed.

"How do you think Niamh and Peth will feel about us telling them about Kami?" Jonathan asked.

"Hopefully, fine. Since Paddi's in COM and his kids have been told, they understand the importance of secrecy. Anyway, everyone will hear about it once Kami starts flying."

"True. Her wings are definitely stronger. Ellie said it might take a couple of months."

"Yeah." Thom walked to the window. It was clear, but cold outside. "I hope she doesn't want to try during the winter."

"I agree," Jonathan said, before joining him and looking out. "That's a steep hill."

"It leads to the Acadium. You can see part of the wall."

"Oh yeah."

"I'm worried about Kami. I wish we had instructions."

"We'll figure it out."

While Thom appreciated Jonathan's support, he felt unsure. "Ready for bed?"

"Yeah. Um… my room's next door, but… would you mind if I stayed? I have trouble falling asleep in new places."

"That's fine. "You take the right side of the bed. I'll take the left."

The next morning, Jonathan and Thom were not the first ones up; they found Eran in the dining room. Paddi had asked Meggie and Pel to serve breakfast early.

"Did you both… sleep well," she said with a sly grin.

"Yeah," Thom said, grabbing a muffin with chocolate bits.

"Yes," Jonathan replied, meeting her gaze.

Chapter 24

Jonathan had gotten up early, just as the sky was lightening. Outside his window, someone was walking toward the library. He pressed his hand against the glass. It felt cold, and his warm fingers left a faint imprint. Frost blanketed the grass; it was supposed to warm up, at least for mid-Nuvima.

Afternoon classes were canceled for teacher meetings. Good thing, 'cause it freed up the time for Thom's party. Gazing upward, Jonathan mind-spoke to Thom's divine advisors, *If you had a hand in that, thanks.* He envied Thom's connection to them. Did he even have a guardian angel? Now and then, he imagined he'd visited with a divine being in his sleep, but all he remembered was a single word: sense.

Enough musing, Jonathan told himself, glancing at his list. There was quite a bit left to do. First, he checked the kitchen staff to ensure they had everything Eran needed for the cake and sweet pastries. Back in his room, he grabbed more decorations and headed to their common room. Jonathan knew Thom spent time there after supper, but not usually before, which meant he wouldn't see anything.

By the time he finished decorating, the room matched what he'd envisioned. Emmett, an artist who lived in their quad, had cut out letters reading 'Happy Birthday Thom,' and made them appear three-dimensional. Late last night, they'd strung them across the room.

Opening the quad door, Jonathan heard movement, but saw no one, especially Thom. He was probably feeding Kami. He didn't want to risk getting caught out of his room. Thom usually came by when he was ready for breakfast.

Rap rap... rap rap rap.

"Come in, Thom," Jonathan called.

"Ready for breakfast?"

"Always. How's Kami?"

"Mostly fine. She doesn't like the cold much. So she was grateful Kee and Tovah had reheated her sand yesterday. I need to thank them. I was even sweating by the time I left."

"Winter's almost here. Happy birthday, teenager!" Then he broke into the birthday song."

"Thanks so much. You have a beautiful voice."

"Thank you. Do you feel like a teenager?"

"I've kind of felt like one since I was six. That's one of the reasons the other kids made fun of me."

Jonathan's voice tightened. "That shouldn't happen here. Noiri wouldn't stand for it. Let me grab my books."

"You're taking them to breakfast? We usually get them after."

"I have to see Mac before class."

"About a patient?"

"Not sure. Someone, maybe Mac, slipped a note under my door last night asking me to stop by. Let's go."

As usual, the dining hall was quiet when they arrived; few academs had come down yet. They quickly loaded their plates with eggs, sausage, and buttered toast, and dug in. By the time they finished, the room was bustling.

Standing in the doorway, Thom said, "A lot of people wished me happy birthday. Strange that no one from our quad did. Maybe they don't know."

Jonathan shrugged, annoyance crossing his face. They should have.

"I'm being silly. It's not like I'm a kid and need everyone to say something."

"They'll find out on Setr-dae, at the Acadium birthday feast."

"Thanks again for singing to me. That was really sweet."

"You're welcome."

"You off to see Mac?"

"Yeah. I'll see you in government class."

Morning classes dragged by for Jonathan, as he kept mentally running through his task list, worried he'd forgotten something.

He was finishing his last bite of supper when Thom whispered, "Jonathan, want to come with me to feed... ?"

"I can't. Mac asked me to stop by again."

"That's the second time today. What did she need you for earlier?"

"Oh... um," Jonathan hesitated. He didn't want to lie, but he couldn't tell Thom the real reason. "She had a question about a treatment I did." It was true, even if most of the conversation had been about the party.

"A patient?"

Jonathan froze, eyeing Tovah in desperation.

"Mind if I go with you, Thom?" she asked. "Um. I want to make sure the sand's temperature is still warm enough."

"OK. I'll see you later, Jonathan?"

"Definitely." He gave Tovah a nod of thanks.

Sometime after supper, Tovah and Thom were walking down the hall when he said, "You want to see our quad room. Aren't they all pretty much the same?"

"Our's, on Quad Diarg, faces the back," Tovah said lightly. "I wanted to see your view... if that's OK."

"I guess," Thom replied, puzzled. Their hall was unusually quiet, especially since academs had the afternoon off. Opening the door, he was met with a loud cry.

"Surprise! Happy Birthday, Thom!"

He froze. Jonathan stood grinning, with Eran, Ciarenn, and Paddi behind. "I can't believe you're here."

"We wouldn't miss it, son," Paddi called.

"And everyone from mage class... and our quad," Thom added, spotting Oddi.

"Mamie and Da couldn't come," he explained. "But I was gonna."

"Thanks, Oddi. The decorations are beautiful. The streamers! And the sign with my name. Did you do this, Jonathan?"

"Some. Emmett did the lettering. He's really talented."

"It's amazing. Thank you, Emmett," Thom called to the older boy with dark hair and a narrow nose.

"You're welcome."

"I can't believe this," Thom remarked.

"That's not all," Jonathan said, his eyes twinkling. "We have a few... guests."

"You don't mean... our... guest?" Thom whispered.

"Of course not. Look to the right."

"Redik and Meli!" Thom shouted. "How?"

"Redik had business here for Da," Meli said, stepping forward, her light brown hair in a ponytail. "I convinced Mam and Da to let me come. And I brought a few of my paintings to show a gallery owner."

Redik, with shoulder-length brown hair, was one of Thom's older brothers. When Thom returned home from Glakkadeth that summer, he learned Redik no longer helped Da make pottery, but traveled to promote his wares and take orders. Meli used to help too, until she'd discovered a passion for painting.

"I'm glad you're here," Thom said, tears spilling over.

"None of that," Redik teased. "You cry at the drop of a hat."

"Oh, shut it, Redik," Meli said, rolling her eyes. "He's a healer. Healers have hearts."

"Sorry," he said, softening.

"Where's Brigid?" Thom asked. Brigid was Redik's girlfriend.

"She's working with Da on a big commission."

"And Mam had a problem patient her apprentice couldn't manage," Meli added. "That's why they couldn't come. But they sent gifts."

"Thanks," Thom said, blinking back more tears. "Apprentice?"

"She brought her on right after you left," Redik explained.

"You have a few more guests," Jonathan said, now pointing left.

"I don't think my heart can take this."

The crowd parted, revealing two people he hadn't been sure he'd see again.

"Rin! Mekial! I can't…" he cried, breaking into sobs.

"Happy Birthday, Thom!" Rin said.

"Surprise!" Mekial added, rushing up to him.

Thom kissed her umber-toned cheeks, then buried his face in her black, shoulder-length braids. "How are you here?"

"How do you think?" she replied with a smirk. "Captain Musa gave me a lift. And Rin met me in Dridley and brought me the rest of the way."

"But that's a long trip for my birthday."

"I'm not just here for that. I've come to enroll."

"I thought you were going to the Guard Academy in Glakkadeth."

"That was the plan," she replied in Glakkadian. "But a couple of months after you left, Modu and Gallen visited the monastery. You wouldn't believe the stir they caused. After everything you did for our people, they felt I deserved a chance to do the same. And asked if I'd study here."

"And you said yes," Thom replied in the same language. "But what about your training?"

"Rin said I could train here."

"You did?"

"Yes. Modu, Gallen, and I had spoken before we left, but I wanted time to consider. And I needed to speak with Niamh and Peth." Switching to Dochalan, he added, "Now, isn't it time for the birthday song?"

"Of course," Thom said, realizing everyone was watching.

After a lively, slightly off-key rendition, Thom was led to a giant chocolate sheet cake, and blew out the candles.

"What do you think?" Eran asked after he had his first taste.

"Sho goo!" he said thickly, before swallowing. "I love the raspberry filling. Did you make it?"

"I did," she replied proudly. "And I baked a few vanilla cupcakes and apple pastries for anyone who doesn't like chocolate, if you can believe that."

"Thank you, everyone. This is all just... wow."

"Jonathan's a great organizer," Tovah said, coming up beside him. "He's been running around like a maniac all week, making sure everything was ready."

"You can say that again," Meli added as she and Redik joined them. "He wrote Mam and Da a month ago about the party. Didn't think any of us could come. But it was nice of him to alert us."

"He did?" Thom said, eyebrows lifting. He spotted Jonathan across the room. "Excuse me."

"You were surprised, huh?" Jonathan asked.

Thom grasped his hands. "Very. I can't tell you how much this means," he said, his eyes misting again.

"I understand. That's why I put so much time planning it."

Thom was drawn into his sparkling eyes, grateful to have found such a sensitive and caring friend. In just a few months, he felt a bond he couldn't imagine losing.

"Thom?"

"Um...thank you," he stammered. "Did you send a letter to Rin?"

"No. Mac told me this morning that Rin and Mekial were staying at Paddi's. She knew about the party and thought I might want to add something... or someone unexpected. Mac let me skip my Rejuvenary shift to go tell them. Griffin brought them up in a carriage."

"I can't believe this," Thom said, shaking his head. "I keep saying that. Sorry."

"It's OK."

Mekial joined them and said in accented Dochalan, "You've made lots of friends. Remember when we visited the beach, and you didn't believe you'd make any?"

"Yeah."

"And what did I tell you?" she teased.

"Something about how good things might happen too, not just bad."

"Exactly. Not only have you made new friends, but you've got me back. Oh, and Khali says hello; her uncle's ship docked in Dridley."

"Thanks. How's she doing?"

"Good. Her brother now helps her sell Sweet Spice Twisters. Back to you. Any disasters or adventures? You've been here, what, two months? But we are talking about you."

"Would you excuse me?" Jonathan said. "I need to check on the drinks."

He did need to, but more than that, he wanted to give Thom time alone with Mekial. He knew how much she'd meant to him. If Jonathan was honest, he felt jealous, not of their closeness, but of the time they'd shared. Now that she was here, he couldn't help but worry Thom might have less time for him.

"Jonathan," Eran called, "Come grab a piece of cake."

"Thanks."

"Thom seemed surprised."

"Yeah."

"Nice job keeping it secret. I heard no one from your quad wished him happy birthday at breakfast. Idiots."

"Thanks for holding this," Meli said, as she approached.

"You're welcome."

"None of us have been able to celebrate with him since he was eight," she added.

"I know," Jonathan admitted.

"That's why it was hard for Mam and Da not to come. Da felt guilty, but the client was paying extra to have his pottery pieces completed quickly."

"Got it."

"And the problem patient wouldn't obey Mam's apprentice," Meli continued. "Mam felt she had to stay in case he did something stupid."

"I'm sure Thom understands. I'm glad you and Redik made it."

"Meli, I heard you're an artist," Eran said. "Can you show me your paintings?"

"Sure. I have them back at your house."

Thom enjoyed chatting with Mekial. It felt like old times, and gave him a chance to keep up his Glakkadian. He asked about her brother Budaj and her two mothers. The name Timbu had come from the three of them—T, M, B, each of their initials.

Mekial updated him on life at the monastery, including Sestra B, Maden, and the others. They'd just finished talking about a new sword technique Medelin had taught her when Tovah approached.

"Mekial," Thom said, "this is Tovah. She's second level."

"Good to meet you."

"And you," Tovah replied. "Thom's mentioned you in mage class."

"Mage class?"

"It's because of my spirit-healing gift."

"Ah. I hope this doesn't sound rude, but do you have an accent? Mine's pretty strong."

"Good ear," Tovah said. "My native tongue is Vlodinian."

"The Vlodan Republic," Mekial said.

"You know it?"

"From world history class."

"I'm impressed," Thom said. "I hadn't heard of it until I met Tovah."

"I understand you're enrolling here. What'll you study?"

"Weapons and self-defense. And government and diplomacy stuff. I'm meeting with Provost Gavin tomorrow."

"She'll ask you to call her Noiri," Thom explained, "like we do with all our teachers."

For the next hour, Thom enjoyed mingling among the other guests when Emmett approached him.

"I wanted to give you your gift. It's a small watercolor and ink study of you in front of the Acadium."

Thom unwrapped the painting, and his eyes widened. "This is... wow. I mean, you're an incredible artist, and I love it. The way you painted me looking up, like something's in the sky, and the glowing spots around me. It gives me tingles."

"That's the weird thing. I didn't paint them. They appeared while it was drying."

"Oh. Thank you."

Thom didn't say what he was thinking; that the painting showed him looking up at Kami, out of frame, sometime in the future when she could fly. The glowing spots might be his divine advisors watching over him.

"You're welcome," Emmett said, embracing him. "There's... something about you."

Soon after, Thom dragged Meli over to meet Emmett and show her the painting. They both fell into talking about what inspired their art, oblivious to those around them.

He finally made his way to Mac and Noiri, who had stopped by. They wished him well and snatched a piece of cake before heading back to their meetings.

As the guests began to leave, Rin pulled him aside.

"Thom, I heard a few things from the monarchs. Can we talk somewhere in private?"

"My room's a few doors down."

Chapter 25

Thom sat on his bed, while Rin claimed the stuffed chair.

Rin glanced around Thom's room. His eyes landed on *Demba's Chronicles* and the repaired angel. He remembered the story behind the statue.

"It means so much that you and Mekial are here," Thom said. "I know COM keeps you busy."

"It does," he replied, brushing aside his dark brown hair, now streaked with more gray.

"You didn't forget your floppy hat, did you?" he asked, a playful glint in his voice.

"I did not, you silly boy. I can buy one for you if you'd like. I'm in the capital all next week. But first, how about a proper hug?"

"Please."

Rin blinked. Thom now stood eye-to-eye with him. When they first met, Thom had been quite small for his age, and Rin wasn't exactly towering. He barely reached five and a half feet on a good day.

"I do have COM duties, but I cleared my schedule once Niamh approved Mekial's training here. Modu and Gallen are her sponsors. In their last letter, they asked me to say hello and thank you again for the Timbu. It's become a major export, especially to lands with winters."

"I'm glad. It's popular here. Vendors started selling it back in Sipt..." he said, his voice fading.

"Was that when you thought Samiltun kidnapped you?" Rin asked, noting the way Thom's eyes dropped.

"You knew?"

"Niamh wrote me. Are you sure it was Samiltun?"

"Yeah. I could feel his slimy energy."

"I'm sorry. Your shields are stronger than when I last saw you."

"Thanks. Kee has me working on them. But when I was in the nightmare, they didn't hold up."

"How are you now? You had a hard time after Vern and Finn kidnapped you."

"I've talked about it with Brother Lamen at the Aaliswan chapel. He helps people through hard things, even if mine wasn't real."

"I'm sure he said that didn't matter."

"Yeah. Jonathan's helped, too. He stayed with me the first couple of nights after I came out of it. He's a healer like me. Well, honestly, he's better than me. And he has a little of the spirit-healing gift. Isn't that weird?"

"What do you like about him?"

As Thom listed Jonathan's qualities, a scene flashed through Rin's mind—Lightwork-Reliance's pre-incarnation meeting, which his own higher self had attended. Half listening, he recalled that Jonathan's higher self, Lightworker-Sens, had been there. God had spoken of an opportunity for them, likely discussed in the private meeting Rin's higher self hadn't been invited to. Now, something stirred in him—an inner knowing that fleeing with Thom to Glakkadeth, where same-gender love was more accepted, had set the stage for that sacred opportunity to unfold.

Holding that awareness close, Rin said softly, "He sounds like a special lad."

"He is."

Rin wondered if Thom was aware of his attraction to Jonathan.

"I have something else to tell you."

"About the Keep's most unusual guest?"

"How?"

"Niamh mentioned her in the same letter that explained your nightmare."

"Want to meet her?"

"I'd love to."

"It's almost dinner, and Kami's expecting food. Do you know where Mekial, and my brother and sister are? I'd like to introduce them as well."

"Mekial's probably in her room. 423L on Quad Lamond."

"Great. I'll see if Jonathan's around. Then we can get her."

"Your siblings are in the guest wing on the first floor," Rin added.

Thom knocked on Mekial's door, with Jonathan and Rin behind.

"Yes?" she replied, opening it. "Oh, Thom, Jonathan, and Rin. Now that I've finished unpacking, I realize I need warmer clothes."

"We can go downtown tomorrow," Thom said.

"Thanks. What's up?"

"I want you to meet someone."

"Another academ?"

Thom shook his head. "You'll see."

"This isn't one of those pranks like we used to play on Budaj, is it?"

"No. You have a cloak?"

"Yeah," she said, grabbing it from a hook behind the door.

After collecting his brother and sister, Thom led the group out the side door and up the hill. Stopping at the rear door of the Royal Residence, he said, "Wait here. Jonathan and I will be back."

When they came out, Meli said, "That was fast."

"The cook, Keelin, had the food ready... and wished me happy birthday."

Before they reached the door to Draganni Hall, Thom mind-spoke, *Hi, Kami, I've got your dinner. I'm bringing others I want you to meet.*

OK.

As they entered, Thom said, "Rin, Mekial, Redik, Meli, meet Kami. Kami, this is Healer Rinbalden, my teacher, and Mekial, my friend from Glakkadeth. The others are my brother, Redik, and my sister, Meli."

Kami tilted her head and opened her mouth slightly.

"That's how she smiles," Jonathan explained.

"A dragonet," Mekial said. "She's... amazing."

"Uh huh," Thom replied.

"Kami says she's happy to meet you," Jonathan added.

"You know mind-speech?" Rin asked.

"Yes. With Kami and most animals."

"I can only speak to Kami," Thom said. "And to my divine advisors."

"Ah."

"That means Nadia Sanneh didn't make it up," Mekial concluded. "I was right, Thom. You didn't believe it."

"I don't think she ever cared for a dragonet. Or she would've written about it. Dragons once had a relationship with humans in Docha-leigh, hundreds of years ago. But we haven't found any records."

Jonathan looked toward Redik and Meli, who were still, with their mouths open. "Are you two OK?"

"Redik? Meli?" Thom said, hoping to break them out of their stupor.

"Umma—umma—umma," Redik stammered.

"She's real," Meli breathed. "You said there were dragons in Sanneh's series... but I didn't think..."

Kami snorted, drawing attention back to her.

"Thom," Jonathan interrupted. "Kami's getting impatient."

"Sorry, Kami. Jonathan, will you help?"

"Sure."

After eating, Kami curled up and closed her eyes.

Redik had mostly recovered by then, his head shaking in disbelief.

"You gonna be OK, Redik?" Thom asked.

"Yeah," he mumbled.

Rin, quiet up to that point, spoke. "I see purple and green in her aura, and some blue. It's strong, even for her small size."

Thom frowned. "Oh, I haven't checked that in a while."

"Any shapes or patterns?" Rin asked

"Yeah," Thom said, his voice full of excitement. "The purple's moving in swirls, expanding and contracting. The blue forms overlapping patterns. Jonathan, are you getting any of it with your spirit-healing gift? Try holding an intention to see it."

"I see the colors, but the patterns are blurry."

"Seeing the designs confirms your spirit-healing gift," Rin said. "Kee told me another academ showed up with a mage-like gift this year, besides you two. That means that kind of gift is increasing. Last year, Tovah was the only academ who discovered a gift. I wonder if that means something."

Thom shrugged. "I need to take the bowls back to the kitchen before going to dinner, if that's OK."

"Of course," Rin said.

Thom had just entered the door when he overheard Keelin speaking to Peth.

"I can certainly heat up some Timbu. That'll be nice on a cold evening like this."

"Thanks, Keelin."

"Hi, Peth. Keelin," Thom said, stepping into the kitchen. "I'm returning the bowls."

"Please set them in the sink. I'll take care of them."

"Happy birthday, Thom," Peth said. "How was your party?"

"Great. I'm glad Oddi could come."

"As are we. Folks might've had a hard time enjoying themselves if we attended anyway."

"I understand," Thom said, as Niamh walked in.

"Were you feeding Kami?" she asked.

"Yes, with Jonathan. We introduced her to Rin, Mekial, Redik, and Meli."

"How did they respond?" Peth asked.

"My siblings were shocked. Mekial was caught off guard. And thank you for suggesting she study here."

"You're welcome. With her skills, she'll be a great fit. What about Rin?"

"He acted like it was nothing."

"Where is he?" Peth asked.

"Oh, turg," Thom cursed. "He and the rest are waiting outside."

"In the cold?" Niamh asked. "Thom, you should've invited them in. I'll get them."

Once all were inside, everyone was talking at the same time, except for Redik and Meli, who were struck dumb.

"I heard the noise," Oddi called, joining them. "What's going on?"

"Hey," Peth yelled over the cacophony. "We're a bit much for Keelin while she's preparing dinner. Let's give her some space. Keelin, can you stretch the meal enough to feed everyone?"

"Certainly. I'll add more vegetables to the soup and heat up a few more loaves of bread."

"Let's move into the sitting room," Niamh suggested, leading them down the hall.

Dinner lasted for hours, filled with many stories, including those about Rin, Niamh, Peth, and Gabi's antics as academs. Keelin had made a large pot of Timbu and, to Thom's embarrassment and gratitude, another birthday cake. Carrot this time, since he'd already had chocolate. By the end, Oddi had fallen asleep at the table.

Everyone except Rin made their way back to the Acadium; he stayed behind to speak a bit longer with the monarchs. After leaving Redik and Meli at their guest rooms, Thom, Jonathan, and Mekial paused on the landing between their quads.

"Thanks for introducing me to Kami," Mekial said. "I'm shocked I met the queen and king on my second day in Freasa."

"Well, it just seems fair," Thom said, "I met Modu and Gallen."

"I guess. It's late. I'd better get to bed. Good night."

"Good night, Mekial," Thom and Jonathan said together.

After she closed her door, Jonathan asked, "Thom, could you come to my room? I have a present for you." He hoped Thom would like it. He spent hours trying to figure out what he would like best. And he wanted it to be personal.

"You didn't have to, especially after the party."

"I wanted to," Jonathan said, opening his door and gesturing him in.

"Nice. You have a view of the quad. I wonder if Kami could land there when she can fly."

"Maybe. Have a seat."

Thom claimed the desk chair. "Funny that Rin said she seemed small. How would he know?"

Jonathan shrugged, pulling the stuffed chair closer. "How big were her siblings?"

"Not quite twice her size. And they were stronger, since they could fly. I worry about her. Maybe something's wrong. I wish we could find out."

"I know. Can I give you your gift now?"

"Oh, sure."

Jonathan went to his wardrobe and pulled something out wrapped in purple cloth. "Happy birthday, Thom!"

"I love the wrapping. Purple's my favorite color."

"Meli told me."

Thom untied the twine. From the shape, he guessed it was a novel. But when he unwrapped it, it was leather-bound, not typical for a book.

"Turn it over."

Thom's eyes filled with tears. It was a journal. Embossed in gold at the bottom: Thom Macirdan. Beneath that: Spirit Healer.

"So you like it?"

"It's beautiful," Thom said, pulling him into a hug.

Jonathan held him close, breathing in his scent—a hint of spice from Kami and Apollo, mixed with sweat, and a pure and clean smell, not quite of this world. An image flashed before him: mountains, a river with a bubbling hot spring, and a meadow edged with distant trees. The word 'Sanctuary' came to mind.

What was that? It didn't resemble the dragon sanctuary where Jonathan had found Thom and Kami.

Thom stepped back, wiping his eyes. "Thank you. I'll treasure it."

"You're welcome."

"Please sit. I have news."

They both sat on his bed.

"At the party, Paddi told me he visited my family. He was impressed with our goods and made an investment."

"What kind?"

"He gave my aunt and uncle money to buy additional sheep and goats, hire more help, and expand the barn."

"That's great."

"That's not all. He even traveled to my home. He gave my fathers' money. Some of its to hire craftspeople, and the rest to build a two-room shop for making and selling goods."

"How does your family feel about it?"

"Excited. Paddi said two of my sisters are already developing new designs specific to his clients."

Thom hesitated. "Um... did Paddi say anything about your... parents?"

"You mean about having two fathers?"

"Yeah."

"Not a word. Maybe Paddi's met same-gender couples in his travels."

"Maybe." Changing the subject, he asked, "How many siblings do you have? I know you have two sisters. Sorry I didn't ask sooner."

"That's OK. I have five: an older sister and brother, Jianess and Iosef, and three younger sisters, Cailen, Leende, and Caitlann. "What about you? Redik and Meli are older?"

"Yeah. And another older sister and brother, Deena and Bedum. My younger ones are Reta, Kavan, and Alli."

"We both come from big families," Jonathan said, yawning.

"You're tired, and you did so much. We both should get some sleep. Thank you again for the party and the gift. Can I give you another hug?"

"Please."

"Sleep well," Thom said as he opened the door to leave.

"You, too."

Chapter 26

"Rel? Have a moment?" Lightwork-Sens called into the space designated for Lightworker-Reliance in the divine realm.

"Of course. I just checked on Thom. Big day yesterday, especially with Healer Rinbalden and Mekial showing up."

"I saw that."

"Thom was touched by what your incarnate did for him."

"It meant a great deal to Jonathan, too. He'd been crazy all week getting ready for the party, and hardly got any rest. I'm glad he's sleeping in."

"Is there something you need?"

"Yes. To talk about what's going on between them."

"Go ahead."

"I keep thinking about your pre-incarnation meeting. Specifically, our private talk afterward with God and Metatron."

"I remember. When God explained our unique opportunity, I was intrigued. I'd never been in a same-gender relationship in my incarnations. You said one of yours had?"

"Two incarnations ago."

"How was it?"

"Difficult. Brinde discovered her attraction well before adolescence, and her culture didn't accept same-gender relationships.

When she was fourteen, her father died, and soon after, her mother fell ill and couldn't work. As the oldest, she had to raise her younger siblings. Brinde had a touch of a healing gift, which became her livelihood. Strong-willed, she fended off potential beaus and avoided marriage, but she lived a lonely life."

"That must have been incredibly difficult."

"It was. But I was proud of her resolve. When God proposed a same-gender relationship... well, I'm just hoping it will unfold more positively."

"Makes sense."

"Jonathan knew who he was attracted to from eleven onward. Having two male parents made it easier."

"But they're young, Sens. Thom's only thirteen."

"So's Jonathan. But in some lands, people once married at twelve."

"True."

"Be assured that Jonathan's not thinking of proposing. He's fairly certain of Thom's leanings, and hopes Thom has feelings for him."

"But Thom hasn't sorted things out yet."

"Exactly. That's why all of Jonathan's party planning had an edge, including his birthday gift."

"Why are you telling me this?"

"Because it might come out sideways. Jonathan would never consciously push, but I wanted you to be aware. He doesn't have Thom's relationship with angels and guides. He hasn't even identified his guardian angels yet. So, he doesn't have a team to ask."

"Thom could help with that. But regarding attraction, he's been thinking about it since Glakkadeth, and has noticed he's more drawn to men, including your incarnate. However, the Iosan elders' teaching on the topic holds him back. At least, Jonathan and he have a strong friendship to build on."

"They do. Anyway, I wanted you to understand the state of things. Jonathan has a kind heart, but he's not perfect."

"I understand. Since they're both healers, they're especially sensitive. And it's something the way their gifts complement each other."

"Jonathan calls them 'flip-flop' gifts," Sens added, their glowing sphere pulsing—the divine version of a grin.

"Cute name."

"Yeah. I'm glad they discovered that. It's brought them closer."

"I agree."

"That's all I wanted to say. Mind if I stop by once in a while?"

"Not at all. I should've reached out to you."

"It doesn't matter. Thanks for your time. I'll see you around."

Chapter 27

A soft glow punctuated the darkness, illuminating a lone figure hunched over a wooden chest, rummaging through its contents. Many items were moth-eaten. "Another stupid dress," he grumbled, tossing it aside. Around him lay a scatter of antiquated dresses, trousers, waistcoats, and other oddments pulled from more than half a dozen chests, their lids fallen where he'd tossed them aside.

"Hrgh—hrgh—hrgh," Oddi coughed. He should've brought water. The air in the storeroom beneath the Royal Residence was thick with dust and age. No one had likely been down here since before he was born, eight and a half years ago.

The Solstice celebration was two weeks away. A few days earlier, he and his parents had set up the tree, draping it with silver garland, shiny baubles, and an angel on top.

Back to the task at hand, Oddi reached into the chest before him, determined to find the belt once worn by his mother's Pop-pop. She'd said its silver buckle was oval, adorned with Solstice symbols. As a girl, she used to trace the abstract depiction of pine trees, a stag, and what she believed was a red bird, oddly large for the scene.

He'd been searching for days with no luck. His mother said her grandfather wore the belt with his royal regalia during parades.

She said he'd been an adventurer who loved taking risks. Oddi wanted to be like him, especially now that he was taking her place in the parade. He couldn't wait. He'd wear a special blue waistcoat and trousers and hoped to find the belt to honor him. His mother had been pleased when he told her that.

Oddi's mother was very pregnant, due at the end of Jenua. Except for meals, Healer MacDonuld had ordered her confined to bed for the remaining weeks. They hadn't told him why, but he knew his parents were worried. His mother had suffered two miscarriages and lost a daughter a few days after birth. She blamed herself.

"Turg," he muttered aloud. Another dead end.

Last week, lying on his bed after dinner, an image of the buckle had flashed in his mind, along with the word 'storeroom.' He'd overheard his parents mention foresight and wondered if he might be developing it. He hoped so. Not wanting to be wrong, he hadn't told anyone.

Sometimes, when he was around Jonathan, Thom, and Tovah, he felt kind of boring in comparison. His parents often reminded him he was smart and loved deeply, but it wasn't the same.

Several days after the vision, following a visit with Kami, it returned. That's what drew him here. He was frustrated he hadn't found it yet.

Oddi stretched, coughing again. History class would start soon. His parents considered it important for him to learn about their land, as visiting dignitaries frequently asked him about Docha-leigh. He'd better grab his sheepskin gloves, woolen cloak, and fur cap. The last time he'd run to the Acadium without them, his mother wasn't pleased. He didn't understand why. He always felt warm.

He shoved the chest aside and picked up his lantern to leave when a loud crash sounded behind him. Spinning around, he swung the lantern toward the noise. A large wooden panel had toppled, likely dislodged when the chest hit its base. Raising the light, he saw a bricked-up section behind it.

"That's weird," Oddi muttered. "Why would they patch a wall with brick? The section was large, ten feet high and half as wide. Curious, he stepped closer, pushing aside a few more chests. The mortar looked old, some of it crumbling.

When he pressed one of the bricks, it moved, then dropped into the darkness with a dull thud. He held the lantern near the gap, but couldn't see inside. "I'll come back tomorrow after breakfast with a chisel and tack hammer." He'd borrow them from his Da's tool chest. His father liked fixing things around the residence when he could.

The next morning, Setr-dae, having the whole day free, Oddi set about uncovering what lay beyond. After two hours, he had widened the opening enough to crawl through. This time, he stacked the removed bricks neatly on his side of the wall.

Putting his tools aside, he picked up one of the two lanterns he'd brought and carefully climbed through. As he stepped down, his foot slipped on something uneven. Steadying himself, he raised the lantern, revealing the brick he'd dislodged the day before.

About five feet ahead was a wooden door. Raising the light, he saw a raised figure carved on it. Leaning closer, he whispered, "Kami?" Each overlapping scale was precisely shaped. He shivered. "I hope this isn't a tomb. I don't want to find bones."

To the right of the carving was a metal lever. He pressed it, but nothing happened. Bracing himself, he pushed harder. The lever moved, but the door wouldn't budge. 'Use your whole body.' That's what Dek told him last summer when he struggled to push a stone-loaded cart. Gritting his teeth, he pushed once more and heard a faint hiss.

"Finally," he exhaled. Oddi pushed again with a loud grunt. The door shifted with a grinding scrape, then stopped, leaving a twelve-inch gap. He made a face; the stale heaviness coated his mouth. Back through the hole in the wall, he grabbed his waterskin for a quick sip and retrieved the lantern he'd left behind. Returning, he picked up the first lantern and squeezed through the opening.

A chill greeted him, like the cave he and his father explored last year. The scent was stale and papery, more like dried leaves than mold. "There must be books in here." The space felt sacred, urging a whisper. His heart quickened in anticipation.

Raising the lanterns, he peered into the dim space ahead. Light flickered across shelves lining the nearby walls, but beyond that, the room vanished into shadow. It felt vast.

At the first shelf on the left, he found rows of dragon sculptures: some in flight; others crouched. Below them sat trophies. Squinting, he read the stylized titles on a few: Fleetwing, Champion of Maneuverability, Distinguished Scholar, Esteemed Healer.

On the next shelf were racks of medallions. He picked one up. A dragon was imprinted on one side. The other held a king's face.

Further in, shelves were stacked with banners in purple, yellow, green, blue, and red.

"I can't believe it," Oddi said, his mouth agape. "All this stuff."

He crossed to the other side of the room, where shelves held scrolls and books. Reaching out, he hesitated, recalling the archivist's warning about how fragile older books could be.

Carefully picking up a book titled *Dragon Heroes*, Oddi opened it to the first page. An illustration showed a red and green dragon. Below it: 'Known as Solli.'

"That's a weird way to write someone's name."

The opposite page read, 'Her name was self-chosen because she bore the colors of the Solstice. Solli had earned a medal of honor for saving the monarchs' heir when a sudden fire swept through the Keep in 396. The entry added that the new Keep was later rebuilt in stone.

Paging through another, this one about battles, he found an account of the clash in 653 he'd recently studied. His history book hadn't mentioned dragons or dragon commanders. The omission had to be deliberate—someone wanted dragons erased from the chronicles.

He picked up a third, *The Wisdom of Uriendi*. The dedication page read: 'In honor of my friend, Uriendi. Many called him Peacock for the way he strutted his beauty. Despite that, Uri was humble. The wisdom in these pages should be taught to the entire populace of Docha-leigh, from monarchs to the youngest orphan. His sayings, stories, analogies, and poems reveal his holiness. I miss your brilliance, your humor, and your love. But most of all, I miss our time together. Soar with the angels, dear one. Your friend and riding companion, Eefa.

"Wow," Oddi exclaimed, forgetting his earlier resolve to whisper. "Dragons sound like the human heroes I've read about. Maybe there are books about training them. Thom's gonna go crazy when I tell him."

His stomach rumbled. He was starving. Mamie always said he exaggerated about needing food, but he couldn't help it. Besides, it was time to share what he'd discovered—and get something to eat. Supper was probably close.

In his rush, once through the hole in the brick wall, he kicked an unopened box. The belt with the buckle tumbled out. Snatching it, he sprinted up the stairs, two at a time. Bursting into the back hallway, he dashed past Keelin's office, the laundry, and a broom closet, then ran into the kitchen and nearly collided with Keelin.

"Oddi. There you are! Your father's looking for you. I'm about to dish out supper. Your mother's eating in her room from now on. Your father decided you both would join her."

He bounced on his toes.

"Your clothes and face are filthy," she continued. "What have you gotten into?"

"Dragons are real," Oddi said, his eyes gleaming.

"Of course they are."

"No, I mean there used to be more dragons here," he said urgently. "I found a room with books, medallions, and all kinds of dragon stuff."

"Slow down, and tell..."

"Wait," he cut in. "Is Mamie OK?"

"Talk to your parents. But first, wash up and change. Be quick about it."

Running into his parents' room, Oddi found his mother with a tray on her lap, and his father seated in a chair beside her, his own untouched on a small table.

"How do you feel, Mamie?"

"Managing. Mac was here and told me to rest more and drink plenty of nettle leaf tea. It wouldn't be so bad if I didn't have to waddle to the washroom so often. But I'm fine."

"Oh," Oddi replied, uncertain. His parents rarely kept things from him. But he wondered if she was saying that to make him feel better.

"Sit," his father said, gesturing toward the desk. "Keelin's bringing your tray. Where were you?"

"I found a dragon room," Oddi blurted.

"A dragon room?" his mother sputtered, tea splashing onto her quilt.

"Oddi," his father said quietly, "not so loud."

"Sorry. But yeah."

"Here's your tray, Oddi," Keelin said, entering and placing it on the desk.

"Oddi was telling us what he found," Peth explained.

"Mind if I stay?"

"No," Niamh said.

Keelin noticed the wet quilt. "Let me change that first."

When Niamh was comfortable, Oddi shared what he'd discovered.

"So, it wasn't all destroyed," Niamh remarked.

"From your description, it sounds quite big," his father commented, "maybe even to the back wall of the residence. But I'm certain there's no door on that outside wall."

"It was probably covered over," Niamh added.

Fixing his gaze on Oddi, his father said, "After we eat, take me there."

"Yes, Da. Should I find Thom?"

"Not yet. I'd like to see it first. By the way, did you find the belt?"

"Oh, yeah. It's in my room. Like you said, Mamie, the buckle had trees and a stag. But I think the bird's a dragon."

After inspecting the room and being equally awestruck, his father gave Oddi permission to tell Thom. Oddi was just getting ready to run over to the Acadium when Thom and Jonathan walked in.

"Hi, Oddi," they said together.

"Foun'drag'roo," he shouted, everything running together in his rush to tell them.

"Sorry. What?" Thom asked.

"I...found...a...dragon...room," Oddi repeated slowly, his eyes wide with excitement.

Chapter 28

"**I** can't believe this," Jonathan said for the tenth time, taking another book from the shelf.

"What now?" Thom asked, annoyed.

"A medicinal—with treatment suggestions and plant drawings. I've seen some of these near the dragon sanctuary. I've got to show Mac."

"Sorry I lost my temper. I'm frustrated we haven't found anything on dragon care."

"That's OK. I'll keep looking. Where's Oddi?"

"In the storeroom, cleaning up. When Peth saw the mess, he made Oddi straighten it. He did assign a few discreet servants to clean this room tomorrow after all the years of disuse."

Jonathan was examining a dragon sculpture when he heard a yell. "Are you OK?"

"Yes! Yes! Yes!" Thom shouted gleefully. I finally found the books."

"Where are you?"

"At the back."

Jonathan spotted him crouched in front of an open, dark-colored, waist-high cabinet, holding an open book. Thom wore an unrestrained grin, his brown eyes sparkling.

"Come closer," he whispered, almost reverently. "This is about dragon development. It mentions the first stages of life Ariel described to me: hatchling and dragonet. But it goes on to list those after: juvenile, flareling, and adult. It even has drawings."

"What's a flareling?"

"Beats me."

Leaning over Thom's shoulder, Jonathan said, "Whoever drew these was talented. What are the other books?"

"Two on care. Several on training, covering things like pairing a human with a dragon and coordinating them for battle."

"So people rode and fought on dragons?"

"Sounds like it."

"I'll explore around here."

"OK," Thom said, flipping through the pages.

Further into the room, Jonathan found a tarpaulin covering a large pile in one corner. Under it were partly decayed saddles, straps, blankets, and pads.

"I found old riding gear and stuff," Jonathan called.

Thom joined him. "I wonder if any can be repaired."

"Huh," Jonathan grunted, staring toward the back.

"What?"

"I think I see something interesting over there," he said, disappearing into the gloom with his lantern.

"Did you find something?"

Jonathan was running his hands along an uneven part of the wall. "It's a sliding door. Or it was."

Thom stepped beside him. "Like the one in Draganni Hall. But I've run past that wall plenty of times and never saw it."

"Maybe it was plastered over. Let's search for it when we leave."

"Good idea."

They stayed a while longer before heading back to the Acadium, each carrying a few of their findings, like treasures, because, in truth, that's what they were.

Before noon the next day, Thom, Jonathan, Mac, and Ellie were gathered in Mac's office, poring over three books and a scroll. Off to the side sat empty trays from an early supper.

"This scroll's nearly falling apart," Mac said, carefully holding its corners. "It mentions a contract between Docha-leigh's first queen and the dragon tribe overseeing Sandrim peoples. Niamh was right."

"I can't believe dragons lived all over this continent," Thom remarked, glancing up. "There has to be some reason why they disappeared, and the room was sealed."

Mac shrugged.

"Ellie and Mac," Jonathan said, "there's mention of a medicine like the one we made for Kami's wings."

"I'm glad we were on the right track," Ellie replied. "Anything else standing out?"

"Yeah. One entry describes how to use bacteria to treat colds and pneumonia."

"Interesting," Mac said. "A healer in Eiren wrote me last summer about bacteria that can fight other bacteria. Does it say where to find it?"

"In soil near swamps or mangrove forests. I've never heard of mangroves."

"They grow along the coast," Mac explained. "We've got swamps west of here. What's the bacteria called?"

"Streptomyces."

"Can I see? It might help humans."

Jonathan shook his head. "It's limited to birds."

"Oh well. Worth a shot."

"I'll check into it," Ellie added. "Falcons can get sick when the temperature drops fast."

"Thom, you're quiet," Mac noted. "What's keeping you engrossed?"

"I'm reading about dragonet growth. It lists signs when they're ready to fly: fluttering wings and hopping. Ellie, when we first met, you mentioned that for birds. I didn't see them with Ariel's other offspring, but that was different. I haven't noticed Kami fluttering. Have you, Jonathan?"

"No."

"It says play builds wing strength. And tossing a ball or something helps them learn to grasp prey."

"Speaking of flying," Mac said. "I'll talk with Niamh and Peth about having the leatherworkers examine the saddles. Hopefully, they're repairable. But Thom, don't you have to feed Kami before your next class?"

"Yeah," Thom replied, closing the book. "Jonathan, want to help?"

"I would, but Ellie asked me to help her in the mews."

"One of my falcons isn't eating. I'm hoping Jonathan can figure out why."

"OK," Thom said. "Mac, can we keep these here? I don't want other academs to find them in my room?"

"Of course. Now off with you."

Chapter 29

I t was Solstice morning, clear, but very cold. The week before, evergreen garlands had been hung along the walls, and poinsettias placed throughout the building. Yesterday, booths and competition areas were set up around Ninrise.

Thom was lacing his shoes when he heard someone at his door. Rap rap rap.

"It's me. Can I come in?" came Jonathan's voice.

"Sure."

"Good. You're up."

"I didn't sleep well."

"Worried about exams?"

"Nah. They were hard, especially history. So many dates and events to remember. But I think I passed. Weird how easily I remember tons of herbs and their uses."

"About Kami then?"

"No. Anyway, I'm looking forward to checking out the booths. Eran told me she and a few classmates will have a big urn filled with Timbu and baked treats at their booth."

"I'm excited about the parade, especially the musicians."

"Oddi's real excited about riding with his Da on the royal carriage."

"Too bad Niamh can't be in it."

"Yeah, Mac said she shouldn't," Thom explained. "Oddi mentioned Niamh'd had losses before. That must've been awful. Makes me think of Lida Barrelson. One of her twins died during childbirth."

"That's rough."

"According to Oddi, his mother always wears a long gown in the parade, kind of iridescent, and a crown that sparkles like icicles."

"You like that word."

"I guess. I learned it in Glakkadeth."

"Did you want to feed Kami first?"

"No. I'm starving."

"We'd better get a move on."

With stomachs full of porridge, cinnamon pastries, and Timbu, Thom and Jonathan stepped into Draganni Hall.

Good morning, Kami.

I smell something good.

The hunters brought in extra deer, Thom explained. *So there are plenty of hearts and livers.*

"I do like that they mostly use older animals," Jonathan said.

"Speaking of which, I want to thank their spirits first."

Afterwards, they watched as Kami dug into the bowl with the meat mixture. As usual, she saved the organs for last.

Mind if we check your wings while you eat? Jonathan asked.

No, Kami replied, swallowing a mouthful.

"They seem thicker," Thom said. Sensing into the webbing, he added, "Blood flow's strong and even."

"I agree. How do you feel, Kami?"

Scratchy, she replied, using a claw to rub her tail.

"Let me check there," Thom said. "A few scales are graying. That's normal when new ones are forming underneath. I'll apply some oil to soothe the area until they fall off."

Kami sighed as Thom treated her. While he worked, she finished the first bowl, then moved on to the second, heaped with organ meat.

Once the bowls were empty, Jonathan collected them. "I'll take these to the kitchen and come back. Then we can head to the parade."

"Sounds good."

Thom was rubbing another patch of gray-tinged scales when a wave of heat surged through him, starting in his hands. It wasn't from Kami or the sand. A sudden knowing settled in: he'd be needed here.

"Ready?" Jonathan asked, when he returned.

"I can't go."

"What?"

"I need to stay."

"You'll miss the parade," Jonathan complained. "I even picked the perfect spot."

"I'm sorry."

"Could you check with your advisors?"

"I should've thought of that." *Hey Rel, Sereh, Jesh,* he mind-spoke, *did I just get a premonition, or am I misreading it?*

"Anything?" Jonathan asked, his voice tight.

"Not yet. I don't always get answers immediately. Go. Maybe Tovah or Mekial would go with you?"

"I guess," he replied, sounding disappointed.

"Afterwards, you can tell me everything. We'll check out the booths together." Unless, he wondered, it wasn't a premonition.

"All right. Where should I find you?"

"Eran's booth," they said in unison, laughing.

After Jonathan left, Thom inspected other areas of Kami's body for additional signs of shedding.

Kami, would you roll over? I want to check your underside?

OK, she said, complying.

Yep. Some of your scales there are dull.

He worked his way along her belly and legs, then paused. *I'm out of oil. I'll get more from the Rejuvenary. How are you feeling?*

Tingly and sleepy.

Divine presence? Or maybe she's feeling the glow people experience after a massage. His Mam offered those to anxious patients after a healing.

Thom was replacing the stopper in the oil jug in Mac's office, when she entered.

"Oh, Thom. Weren't you going to the parade?"

"I had planned to, but Kami's about to shed, and she's scratching like crazy." He didn't want to mention his premonition. "Aren't you going?"

"No, I've seen plenty. And I'm watching our few patients, so the staff can go."

"That's nice of you. I'm heading back to finish applying the oil. I'll explore the booths later with Jonathan."

"Did you hear they made an ice rink in one of the quads?"

"No. Must not be mine, or Jonathan would've mentioned it."

Chapter 30

It was late morning, and Thom had finished oiling Kami's body. His advisors hadn't yet responded. Maybe it wasn't a premonition. Now he'd missed the parade, and Jonathan would be angry with him.

Kami snored, and Thom was wiping his hands when Mac rushed in.

"Good, you're still here," she said, her voice tight with urgency.

"What's wrong?"

"Niamh. She's gone into labor early, and there are complications. We need you."

As they ran toward the residence, Thom asked, between breaths, "Are... the king... and... Oddi back?"

"No. But Rin's with her. And he's asking for you."

"Rin's back?"

"Late last night."

As they scrambled to the second floor, a moan of anguish met them.

"I can't lose them, Rin," Niamh cried, her voice weak and strained.

"We'll do everything we can to make sure the three of you live," he assured her. "The bleeding's under control. Drink your raspberry leaf tea. It'll help with the delivery."

Thom and Mac stepped into the bedroom. Niamh's reddish-brown hair was in disarray. Strands plastered her sweat-damp face.

"Good," Rin said, watching her sip from a mug.

"All this tea's going to make me pee the sheets."

"We'll deal with it," Mac said.

Hearing her voice, he turned and saw Thom. "I'm glad you're here. Let's talk by the window so we won't disturb Nim."

"What's going on?" he asked, curious about Rin's name for Niamh.

"She felt a sharp pain and started bleeding from her vagina," Rin explained. "I got it to stop, but she's in a tremendous amount of pain."

"What can I do? I've never delivered a baby."

"That's OK. Mac and I do. I'm hoping you can connect with the twins' spirits, like you did with Rindo and his sister. Their cords have detached from the uterine wall, and the babies aren't moving. They won't survive if they're not born soon. But their heads aren't positioned correctly. Mac and I tried to adjust them, but it hasn't worked."

"I'll do what I can."

"Thanks."

Back at the foot of the bed, Rin said, "Nim, Thom's going to reach out to the twins and help them find their way into the world."

"Please," she whispered, her voice trembling with desperation.

Thom carefully sat on the right edge of the bed, placed his hands on her belly, and immediately sensed the twins. Both were horizontal: the boy was at the top of the womb, the girl at the bottom. He shared this with Rin and Mac.

"That's what we detected," Rin said.

Footsteps pounded up the stairs. Peth and Oddi burst in, Jonathan close behind.

"Are they...?" Peth gasped, his eyes welling.

"We're doing everything we can," Mac said.

"I asked Thom to help," Rin added. "Jonathan, I'm glad you're here. Would you assist?"

"Of course."

"Mac, you and I focus on Nim, to help her stay calm and breathe through the contractions," Rin added.

"What can I do, Thom?" Peth asked, his voice low and strained.

"Hold your wife's hand. Oddi, place yours on her shoulder. Send your love to her and the twins... and pray for divine support."

"We can do that."

"Where do you want me?" Jonathan asked.

"At my back. Place your hands on my shoulders. I think it'll help our spirit-healing gifts link."

OK, *gang*, Thom mind-spoke to his advisors. *We need your help. Rafe, you and the healing angels especially.*

Rafe was the nickname he'd given to Archangel Raphael.

Lowering his shields, Thom detected two intertwined streams of light green energy flowing from Mac and Rin. Good, he thought. That'll strengthen her.

Jonathan mind-spoke to Thom. *They're getting a little air through their severed cords—but it won't last long.*

Thanks. OK, little ones, I need you to move. Call on your higher selves and guardian angels for help. He hoped this would work.

Which way? they asked in unison.

Good question. Girl twin, since your head is closest to the canal, move counter-clockwise.

OK. You can call me Tressa. That's what they'll name me. My twin's Terrin.

That'll make guiding you easier. She spoke with surprising maturity, Thom thought. It was probably her higher self coming through.

Just then, Niamh groaned.

"She's having another contraction," Mac announced. "Long ooohs and low grunts, like we practiced, Niamh."

"Can I push now?" she gasped desperately.

Mac looked at Thom, who shook his head.

"Breathe through it, Nim," Rin encouraged.

"Her passage is ready, at least," Mac said. "A good sign, Peth."

Jonathan, add your healing energy to mine? Thom instructed. *Let's give them a gentle nudge.*

Thom felt Jonathan's gift reinforcing his—and the steady presence of Rafe and the healing angels. The twins moved some, but then stopped.

That's good, Tressa and Terrin. Keep going.

Tressa's feet are kicking my head, Terrin grumbled.

Well, your feet are hitting my face, she shot back. *There's not much room in here.*

Thom nearly chuckled. Now, they sounded a bit younger. *OK, let's do this together.*

Another contraction might help, Jonathan suggested. *Since our gifts are joined, I think I can signal Niamh's spirit.*

Brilliant.

A low groan escaped as another contraction passed through Niamh's body.

"You're doing great," Rin encouraged.

"Can I push now?"

"Not quite yet," Mac replied.

Thom sensed the twins had moved but stopped again.

They're running out of air, Jonathan warned.

I can tell. Gang, what do I do? Blessed Mother, can you help? Thom hadn't called on her before, but in a moment like this, it made sense—an ascended being in the divine realm who understood childbirth.

I'll try. These two have important missions. Open your spirit further, and you'll see. Remember what Rin told you months ago: intuition and intention. You're facing something new. You need another ability. Put forth an intention.

Thom found his spirit extending far beyond his body, as if part of him was traveling to the divine realm. He'd never gone there intentionally before. Ahead lay a chamber with luminescent, rippling walls, filled with seated figures. He felt drawn in, pulled toward a seat beside Rel, and a few other familiar faces.

There you are, Thom, God said. *We know you're in a tricky situation. But before you start worrying, Rafe, and the healing angels continue supporting the twins. And remember, time doesn't exist here. You'll be fully back in your body faster than the blink of an eye.*

Thanks for the reminder.

Looking around, he saw beings of many shapes and sizes, all in human form—chosen for its broader communication options—and with both genders represented. Some wore trousers and shirts, others long gowns. They were quite colorful.

Let me continue, God said. *You're attending an emergency follow-up to the pre-incarnation meetings of Princeps-Vir and Vatis-Augur.* He gestured to the female and male figures, both in matching beige shirts and trousers.

Unsure what else to say, Thom ventured, *Nice to meet you.*

We already have, Vir replied. *I'm the higher self of Tressa. Augie is Terrin's.*

Oh. Your incarnates—or soon-to-be—are trying hard to move so they... or you can be born. Why am I here?

Two reasons, declared a man with a golden complexion and shoulder-length black hair, seated to the left of Augie. *I'm Archangel Raziel.*

Thom admired his purple tunic and golden stole.

One of my duties, Raziel continued, *is mentoring those with a strong spiritual disposition who aren't called to be lightworkers. Augie's my student.*

Let me add, said the woman with rich, dark skin, dressed in a forest green gown, and sitting to Vir's right. *I'm Archangel Ariel. I'm known for fierce determination and mentoring future leaders. Princeps-Vir is my student.*

Ariel's the name of my friend, Kamael's mother.

I'm well acquainted with her. She's a wise soul, and another of my students, albeit incarnated in a unique form.

Wow. A higher self born as a dragon. That's wild.

Back to the reasons, God interrupted. *Vir and Augie's incarnates will manifest special gifts as they approach adolescence. We won't mention the circumstances, but if people don't change, your land could face great danger.*

Thom frowned. *I assume I'll be involved?*

Likely.

Why do I always attract danger? What's going on, Rel?

It does seem that way, they replied. *But I assure you that's not the case.*

He shook his head, resigned. *Not to be difficult,* he said, smirking, *but... will I remember all this?*

Laughing, God replied, *Good one. I enjoy your humor. Yes, you will. You may even guide the twins as they grow. After all, you'll be considered their uncle.*

I like that, Thom replied. *I already have two nieces. What's the other reason?*

In the second row, Archangel Metatron stood. *As you might guess, this crisis is awakening another spirit-healing gift in you.*

Metatron? I didn't realize you were here.

I thought it important, given your new ability to witness others' pre-incarnation meetings.

Oh no. Thom didn't want to reject it, but could it activate at any time? Speaking, he asked, *Will it happen when I pass someone in the hall? There are hundreds of academs. I don't want to walk into a wall if it kicks in. And you remember, I get overwhelmed pretty easily with new abilities.*

We do, Rel replied, patting his leg sympathetically.

You'll be able to control it, Metatron assured him.

Anything else? Thom asked.

That's it, God said. *Thanks for coming.*

Thom felt himself pulled back into his body.

"Why isn't she having more contractions?" Peth asked, his voice tight with worry.

"I don't know," Mac replied.

"Trust Thom," Rin assured him.

Tressa and Terrin were in the same position as before the visitation. *Jonathan, would you reach out to Niamh's spirit again?* Thom asked. *Her body needs another contraction. One more could be enough to get them better placed.*

On it.

As the next contraction passed through Niamh, Thom sensed the twins shift. Tressa's head was now aligned with the birth canal.

Great job. Jonathan, tell Rin that Niamh can start pushing.

"Push, Nim."

Before long, Tressa emerged with a wail. Thom then directed his attention to the other twin.

OK, Terrin, time to adjust. You've got more room now that your sister's out.

Finally. But I don't get to enjoy it, he quipped. *I'm out of air.*

Rafe, Jonathan, can you lend me your energy? Thom mind-spoke. *I'm tired.*

We don't want you to pass out, Jonathan replied, fatigue also evident in his voice.

Almost immediately, Terrin shifted into position. Relieved, Thom asked Jonathan to pass it on.

Terrin's delivery took longer, but soon a shock of red hair appeared, followed by the rest of him.

Thom raised his shields and withdrew from Niamh's spirit in time to hear Mac say, "They're both small, but healthy."

Thom opened his eyes. "She's right. Tressa and Terrin will be fine."

"How do you know their names?" Peth asked. "Nim and I didn't tell anyone. Not even Oddi."

"Their spirits told me."

"I knew your gift was unique," Peth murmured. "But experiencing it firsthand, it's hard to wrap my head around."

"I can sympathize," Thom said. "How's Niamh?"

"She's OK," Rin replied. "Exhausted, but OK."

"Why can't I hear Terrin?" Niamh asked anxiously.

"He's just quiet," Mac said. "His hazel eyes are wide open. Feels like an old soul."

Thom silently agreed.

"And what color are Tressa's eyes?"

"Blue," Oddi said, finally speaking. "And her hair's brown—hardly any at all."

Mac swaddled both newborns and laid them gently in Niamh's arms.

"They're... perfect," she whispered.

Peth eyes shone, tears streaming down his face.

"How are you, Thom?" Jonathan asked.

"Tired."

"Same here."

"Go rest in our guest room," Peth offered. "It has a large bed. I hope you don't mind sharing."

After a good nap, Jonathan opened his eyes. Thom was still asleep. The room was cozy, with a well-appointed desk and chair, and a maroon settee with a side table near the fireplace.

Thinking back, Jonathan could hardly believe what had happened. Linked to Thom, he'd partly witnessed Thom's spirit journey to the divine realm. He caught no more than fragments, yet sensed something profound had occurred.

Before Thom's spirit reentered his body, Jonathan had glimpsed another divine gathering. A male figure did most of the speaking, and the word 'sense' hovered around him. There was something familiar about the figure. Jonathan felt certain it was important.

"Hi, Jonathan," Thom whispered.

Rolling onto his side, he replied, "Hi, Thom. Did I wake you?"

"I'm not sure. You seemed deep in thought."

"I was."

"About the twins' birth?"

"Yeah. Can we talk?"

"Sure. I need to use the washroom first. They have an indoor one, like the Acadium."

"I'll go after."

When Thom didn't return immediately, Jonathan wondered if he'd forgotten. He was about to search for him when the door opened.

"Sorry I took so long," Thom said, his hair damp. "Hope you weren't dying to go. They had a shower, and I felt the need to clean up. Not that I was dirty. It felt right, sort of, like I was releasing the experience."

"I'll do the same."

When he came back, Jonathan found the bed remade and Thom at the desk staring out the window.

"Are you checking with Kami?" Jonathan asked.

"Oh dear, what time is it?"

"Late afternoon, maybe?"

"Turg. Let's check with her together?"

"OK."

Kami, it's Thom and Jonathan, Thom mind-spoke. *Sorry, we didn't feed you.*

That's OK. Oddi did.

We'll thank him, Thom replied.

He said you saved his baby brother and sister's life, Thom.

Not only me.

I could tell something was happening. Your energy got really big, and part of you went somewhere holy.

You could tell that?

I knew your spirit traveled as well, Jonathan added.

I didn't realize.

I'm going back to sleep, Kami said.

Rest well. Facing Jonathan, Thom asked, "Are you ready to talk?"

"Yeah."

"So, you were at the pre-incarnation meeting?" Thom asked.

"That's what it was? I wasn't sure. It flickered in and out. I think I saw it because we were linked."

"Sounds right. God just told me I could tell you about it," he said, then described what happened.

"Wow," Jonathan said in awe. "Some visitation. That's what you call it, right?"

"Yeah."

"I read the Solstice marks the shift from darkness into light," Jonathan added, "and it creates an opening between humans and the divine realm. Maybe that's somehow connected."

"Where'd you read that?"

"A spiritual book I found in the library. My family's not very religious, so I started reading on my own."

"I'm glad. And no wonder you're curious about spiritual stuff," Thom said, then growing quiet for a moment. "Seriously, what do I do with this new ability?"

"You told me you believed your calling started before you were born. Could it have been decided at your pre-incarnation meeting?"

"Duh. I should've realized that."

"I might've seen part of mine. Jonathan went on to share what he'd experienced.

"Thanks for telling me. About the word 'sense,' I think it's a name: Sens, Lightworker-Sens, your higher self."

"Whoa. That's why he felt familiar."

"I had the same reaction when I met mine."

"What are you going to tell the others?"

"I can't say anything about the twins' gifts, but I can tell Rin, Mac, and our mage class about my new ability."

A knock sounded at the door.

Jonathan answered. "Hi, Oddi. Come in."

"Hi, guys. I heard voices. Da told me not to disturb you until you were up."

"Thanks," Thom said.

"I fed Kami while you slept, and read to her about a dragon hero named Solli. I borrowed the book from Mac."

"I appreciate it."

"Da wanted me to invite you to dinner with Mac and Rin. Me and Da are eating with Mamie and the twins in their room. They're really tiny... and pink."

"And you're a big brother now," Jonathan added.

"Oh, yeah."

"Big job," Thom said. "You'll be watching out for them before long."

"Really? I could do that."

"But you said dinner, Thom remarked. "I didn't realize it was that late."

"How's your mother?" Jonathan asked.

"She's mostly sleeping, but I think OK. That's what Mac said. You should prolly check yourself."

"Let's."

Stepping into the bedroom, they found Niamh awake. Mac and Rin were helping her sit up, and Keelin held a tray with soup and bread.

Thom hadn't noticed the furnishings earlier. Along with the bed where Niamh rested, and the large wicker bassinet holding the twins, the room featured a sitting area with two cushioned chairs by a fireplace, a bookshelf on one wall, and several family portraits. One showed Niamh and Peth with a baby, likely Oddi. They'd need a new one now. Rich red, black, and gold rugs warmed the wooden floor, adding a quiet elegance to the space.

"Thom, Jonathan," Niamh said, her voice a little stronger, "please, come in. I can't thank you enough for saving Tressa and

Terrin. I was vaguely aware of something happening, but the pain got in the way."

"We were glad to help," Thom replied.

"You're still weak," Jonathan added. "Your aura colors are dim, but they'll be vibrant after a few days' rest."

"Very good," Mac said approvingly, meeting Rin's gaze.

"Here's the tea, luv," Peth said, entering. "Black tea this time."

"That's a relief. I know the raspberry helped, but it reminds me of the pain."

"I'll bring your trays in a moment, Peth and Oddi," Keelin said. "Dinner's ready downstairs for the rest of you."

"We're going to eat here with Nim," Peth added.

"We understand," Rin replied.

"It's nice that you're using my school nickname again," she remarked.

"I heard Rin calling you that," Thom said. "What with your name pronounced Neev, I couldn't figure out where Nim came from."

"Oh. Rin, Peth, and Gabi started it in school, because I was nimble at dodging their pranks. It helped when Oddi was a toddler. He was quick. As soon as I turned my back, he'd take off. But he never got far."

"I did?" Oddi asked. "I don't remember."

"We do," Peth said, chuckling. "I wasn't as nimble as your mother."

Keelin spoke up. "I'll bring your food up shortly, Peth and Oddi."

"Thanks," Peth replied.

"Let's give them some privacy," Rin said, guiding the rest out.

Following after him, Jonathan leaned toward Thom. "Now you can tell them about your new ability."

"Yeah. Tomorrow, let's explore the festival."

"I'm looking forward to it. Think you'll try to go home during school break?"

"No. Even with a fast horse, I wouldn't have much time there. I want to stay close in case Niamh or the twins need me. And then there's Kami."

"Good point."

"I might spend a couple of days at the Byrnes'. Eran said you're welcome to come."

"I'll take you up on that," Jonathan said as his stomach growled.

"Nice to discover that others have a talkative belly," Thom said, nudging him lightly.

Chapter 31

Dermot Lodan wandered through the festival booths. He hadn't been able to come yesterday because his father insisted he tend the horses, including one that had come up lame the day before. He resented it. That was a stablehand's job. And because of it, he'd missed the parade.

Not that he cared for the pageantry. It reminded him of his grandfather, Deda, a shrewd businessman with strong opinions and a no-nonsense way about him. Deda always rode in the parade with the trade contingent. As a child, he'd wave madly when he passed, as Deda nodded back. Dermot was trying to be like him. He started calling him Deda instead of Grandda, as his parents preferred, after reading papers on his grandfather's desk and discovering that's what he called his own grandfather. It felt right, and more personal.

Deda had established the family business when he was Dermot's age, amassing wealth quickly, even if it meant dealing with shady types. He used to say: 'You do what you have to do.'

Ten years before, one deal ended his reign, so to speak, since he considered himself the king of business. A nosy healer named Rinbalden, favored by the monarchs, exposed his clever arrangements. Dermot's resentment burned so hot that, four years ago, he spent his life savings hiring lowlifes. Their job: ruin the healer's reputation. When the first attempt failed, he had them forge evidence and stage a kidnapping. He never heard from them again; he only knew his money was gone and the healer's reputation remained intact.

These days, his focus wasn't the healer. He wanted to be in charge. Tired of taking orders, especially from his self-important older brother, Dermot felt ready. He knew horses and was well-trained. His father had praised him for finding a dealer who sold top-quality whole oats at a lower price. He was sure his brother was jealous.

Passing a group of kids in a snowball fight, Dermot laughed when one snowball sent the snowman's head tumbling. He would've done that once. He'd always had a strong throwing arm.

"Where to next?" he muttered. "Maybe something to eat. And a warm drink."

The festival was busy this year, Lord Samiltun noticed as he strolled among the booths in his cashmere cape, lined with gold silk and dressed to impress. His Finders crew would have plenty of chances to lift coins and jewelry, especially with revelers distracted by the activities. That reminded him of the twin girls he'd hired as servants two months ago. His man, Marten, had been right about their gifts. And their parents had welcomed the extra income. The girls now boarded at his home, giving their parents more space and fewer mouths to feed. Their parents fawned all over him when they first met.

Samiltun passed a jeweler's booth, eyeing the display.

"Sir," the vendor called, "I have quality diamond rings."

Shaking his head, he walked on. He appreciated them, but even with the profits from his Finders and the pawnshop, they were more extravagant than he could justify. Clothing was his one exception. He had to appear wealthy to attract the wealthy. He needed more money, mostly for bribes. Then, power would come through blackmail, which he thoroughly enjoyed. He recalled the arrogant banker one of his Finders had spotted in an out-of-the-way inn, with a much younger woman who was clearly not his wife. Samiltun had rewarded the Finder, and, in turn, the banker had 'rewarded' Samiltun for his silence. The fool didn't realize that his silence came with a time limit.

Lately, Samiltun had considered becoming a goods broker. He appreciated quality merchandise and liked the idea of setting prices.

His thought drifted back to the twins. Samiltun was certain they had the earth-sense gift. At eight, it hadn't fully activated. Maybe he could nudge it along. What a godsend it would be if they could detect gold, gems, and even diamonds.

He almost laughed at his use of the word. He'd stopped believing in any god after his mother was murdered.

It was early afternoon, and Rin walked through the booths. Before supper at the Acadium with Mac and Noiri, Rin had checked on Nim and her newborns. Yesterday had been a close call. If they'd died, it would've devastated the family and cast a shadow over all of Docha-leigh. They were beloved. Fortunately, all were doing well.

He had two goals: sweets and unfinished business. He couldn't deny himself the new chocolate treat Eran and her classmates had created: a dense, chewy cake. He'd heard that one had walnuts; the other, peppermint.

The unfinished business was more serious: uncover who had hired Vern and Finn to kidnap Thom in Glakkadeth. Before being sent to prison, Finn had said their employer, a young man no older than twenty, had gone by the name, Mitch Justan. But his description was frustratingly vague: shoulder-length brown hair, brown eyes, and a lean build. Not exactly rare traits.

Since Rin was certain the real target was him, he'd decided to scan people for auras showing signs of dissatisfaction and malice. But no luck. Plenty of the former, none of the latter. And was this man even the one in charge? Or did he report to an older relative?

Earlier, Rin had caught sight of Lord Samiltun and followed him, watching for signs that he was seeking young people. His fury over what Samiltun had tried to do to Thom years ago hadn't faded. Then again, that interference had triggered Thom's gift early. Rin knew Thom and Jonathan were here this morning. He hoped they hadn't crossed paths.

Dermot lounged by a food booth, sipping a cup of Timbu and munching on a second chocolate walnut square. He'd never tasted chocolate before and wanted to convince his Ma to buy some. He savored the last bite as a merchant in a cashmere cape approached. His eyes were drawn to the man's gold ring with a crest, proof he was a lord.

In contrast, Dermot wore a brass signet ring his mother had given him at thirteen. It had come in handy when a man attacked him outside a tavern in Prun-shees Square. He drank there because it was a place his brother wouldn't go near. The ale was cheap, but it dulled his anger toward him and his father, who disapproved of Deda's choices. With great satisfaction, he remembered the mark his ring left on the thief's face.

"Lord," a young woman at a booth called out, "would you like something to drink or eat?"

"What do you have to drink?"

"Cider, coffee, tea—and a new drink that's all the rage, Timbu. It's made with hot milk and something called chocolate, imported from the Glakkadeth Archipelago."

"Chocolate," the lord repeated, "Might I presume the cider is hot as well?"

"It is, sir."

"Eran," a boy in a school uniform called from the back, "Need more squares?"

"Yes, thanks, Colin."

She remained quiet before saying, "Sir, I could offer you a taste of Timbu to see if you like it."

"Go ahead," Dermot suggested. "It's good. And the squares are great. I've had two." He hesitated about whether to introduce himself. His father was always seeking new customers. But how could he bring up the business?

The lord looked his way.

"I'm going to take a few to my father. He runs a horse ranch," Dermot added, realizing as he spoke that his attempt wasn't the greatest.

"Interesting. What's your name?"

"Dermot Lodan."

"Lord Samiltun."

"Nice to meet you, sir," he said, bowing. "I help my Pa find other horses to breed with, to strengthen our stock." In truth, he'd only gone with his brother a few times. They'd have to let him take the lead soon.

"That's important work," Samiltun said.

"Yes, sir. You should try the Timbu."

Facing Eran, Samiltun said, "Young lady, I'll try a sample."

"Certainly," she answered, pouring him a small measure.

Samiltun tasted it. "It's good. But I'll stick to black coffee. Do you have sweet biscuits with some of that chocolate?"

"Yes. How many?"

"One."

After receiving his drink and biscuit, Samiltun addressed Dermot, "Good to meet you, Mister Lodan. Perhaps I'll visit your family's business."

"Please do, sir. I'm sure I can get my Pa to give you a good deal."

As the lord walked away, Dermot stood a little taller. Being called Mister Lodan pleased him. In that brief exchange, this lord had recognized his worth more than his father or brother ever did.

Chapter 32

The past three months had flown by. Tressa and Terrin were thriving. They'd put on weight and were hearty, a testament to Niamh's strength and her breast milk.

Late afternoon, Thom was on his way to feed Kami. He'd trained earlier with practice swords, and his sparring partner, Mekial—now an assistant trainer—had broken through his defenses more than once. His torso and arms were a patchwork of bruises. She'd apologized, but he knew that having her hold back wouldn't have done him any favors. Even a soak in the hot pool, followed by a massage from Jonathan, hadn't fully eased his aches. It was sweet of Jonathan to offer. After he ate dinner, Thom planned to finish his reading quickly and go to bed early. That's why he was feeding Kami now.

When he arrived at the dining hall, the others were already seated, waiting for their table to be called. He slid into an open chair, just as someone's stomach rumbled.

"I heard that," Tovah said, nudging Mekial beside her.

"We all did," Jonathan added.

"I'm starving. Weapons training was brutal," she explained. "After working with Thom, Dek had me spar with Ciarenn, Rilla, and Ronan. They graduate in Mei."

"That'd be a challenge," Thom said.

"Dek introduced the sparring switch-up Medelin used in Glakkadeth."

"The one where one person plays the victim and the others, attackers?"

"Exactly. I was the last victim and already tired. Rilla landed a shoulder strike when I overextended, and she clipped my leg when I didn't recover fast enough. The others came close."

"How did Dek rate you?" Jonathan asked.

"Pretty good." She was about to continue when a voice rang out.

"Can I have your attention, please?"

It was Eran.

"My classmates prepared today's meal with a spice called sun-shi. It's citrusy and hot. An ambassador from Naisuun introduced it to the monarchs, who suggested we try it here. We used the spice in a tangy glaze on crispy chicken bites, served with jasmine rice, and roasted broccoli with sweet root shavings. The rice helps with the heat. For those sensitive to spice, we offer an orange-glazed chicken option. Everything's clearly labeled. We hope you enjoy it."

"Do you think this'll be better than the last thing she and her friends had us try?" Jonathan whispered to Thom.

He was talking about luma, a smooth, starchy paste that tasted a little sweet and earthy, and came from an island directly south of Docha-leigh. Neither of them cared for it.

Thom gave a small shrug.

Once they sat down, each with a portion of the sunshi and orange-glazed chicken, Jonathan asked, "Who's trying the hot one first?"

"You, Mekial," Thom prodded.

She speared a piece of chicken and bit into it.

Everyone watched.

"It's nice. Lemony. Not spicy. I don't... wait... my tongue's tingling. That's kind of neat."

"Tingling?" Tovah said, "Probably not like Thom's."

"Nope," Mekial replied after swallowing. "Oh. Now ith numb. 'S not Glagga... foo'. She swallowed a quick spoonful of rice. "The heat's going away, and I can feel my tongue again. Cleared my sinuses. I like it."

Jonathan frowned.

"Let's try it together," Thom said to him. "Once we're full healers, we'll be traveling around and eating all sorts of things. Might as well get used to it."

Afterward, they all agreed they liked it, mostly. Even Jonathan and Tovah said it was good, though neither ate as much as he and Mekial. Having ice cream for dessert definitely helped.

A few days later, walking toward the Keep and Kami, Thom smiled. He was now treating patients. His shifts varied. Sometimes they'd be in the morning, others overnight. He was particularly sensitive to patients having nightmares, offering comfort and a valerian root tincture to help them sleep.

With his new ability to tap into a person's pre-incarnation meeting, Thom felt more connected to those in the divine realm. At one point, he wondered if a deceased relative was reaching out; it was a bit unnerving. He shared it with Lamen and Kee, who encouraged him to stay open to how the ability might expand, reminding him that his advisors supported him. Next time he saw his father, he'd ask if he knew anyone named Kurdane.

Stepping into the royal kitchen, Thom heard the clatter of pots and dishes. "Good afternoon, Keelin."

"Good afternoon, Thom. There's more organ meat for Kami. How is she?"

"Well. Now that it's almost Aprali and the weather's warmer, she spends most of her time outside. She's been cooped up since Siptema, as my Da calls it."

"I wouldn't like that either."

"Is Niamh here?"

"In the sitting room with the twins. I'm sure she wouldn't mind if you went in."

"Thanks."

Thom walked down the connecting hallway to the sitting room, where Niamh sat facing the bay window. The room boasted a brick fireplace, two bookcases, navy chairs, and matching sofas with tables between. A floor globe sat in one corner. Oddi, who was now studying geography, had pointed out the Glakkadeth Archipelago to him.

Thom cleared his throat. As Niamh swiveled her chair toward him, he blushed and started to back away. "I'm sorry. I didn't realize you were breastfeeding."

"Please stay," she replied, draping a white shawl over her shoulder and one of the babies. "Tressa got hungry again. She eats twice as much as her brother. Where does it all go? I guess I know, since we're constantly changing her nappies. What can I do for you?"

"Would you mind if I check the twins' auras?"

"Please do. I have to admit I've been curious."

Terrin lay in a crib beside Niamh's chair. Thom checked him first. Swirls of purple, turquoise, and white shimmered around him, reflecting his divine connection and radiating peace and reverence. He turned his attention to Tressa, now being burped, and saw brown, blue, and yellow, suggesting sturdiness, loyalty, and leadership. Both auras also included bright green waves, signifying good health. He shared with Niamh some of what he sensed, careful not to mention their callings.

"So Terrin might have a spiritual leaning," she mused. "I like that. Peth and I have become a bit more religious since you and your divine advisors saved them."

Thom dipped his head.

"I like the qualities you mentioned for Tressa," Niamh continued. "Thanks for confirming they're healthy. I haven't told anyone, but I have nightmares about them dying. I don't think it's about their birth. It feels more like a warning about their future. And that terrifies me. I don't know if you're aware, but I have a touch of prescience."

"I didn't," Thom replied, unsure whether to mention he did too.

"Did you need something?"

"To tell you that Kami's been spending time in the fenced area. Thanks again for setting that up. She likes being out there and keeps staring up at the sky."

"Do you think she might try to fly soon?"

"Maybe," Thom replied, explaining a few signs.

"Do your books say how much time typically passes between a dragonet's hops and her first flight?"

"Two weeks to a month."

"We'll have to decide how to tell people about her. I'll talk with Peth and Noiri."

"Thanks."

"Are you headed to see her now?"

"Yes."

"I'll tell you what we decide. Keep us updated on her activity."

Not long after, late in the afternoon, Thom stepped through the sliding doors of Draganni Hall into the fenced area, carrying Kami's food, and froze. She was bounding about wildly, flapping her wings.

You're hopping," he mind-spoke, stating the obvious.

I want to fly.

Today?

No. Need to practice.

Images filled Thom's mind: dragonets chasing each other, an adult dragon tossing a stick to a diving youngster, and one gnawing on a large bone with emerging fangs.

"Where did those come from?"

Just popped into my head.

"I'm a knucklehead," Thom said, smacking his forehead. "The training book said dragons share a collective consciousness and can access others' memories, living and dead. Maybe that's what's happening."

Maybe.

Thom set down the food. *I'll figure out how to help. Eat. I'll go and grab some dinner. Hopefully, I'll get inspired by the time I return.*

As he headed to the Acadium, ideas swirled. He could chase her around the yard. Maybe Oddi and Jonathan would help. He eyed a stick along the path as something to toss. Too risky. One poor throw could injure someone. There had to be a better option.

When he reached the school, he realized something: if Kami wanted to fly, she probably didn't need the special food mix anymore.

Thom was eating with Mekial and Tovah when Jonathan arrived.

"Hi, all."

"How's the patient?" Mekial asked.

"Kendra's good. While training, she landed face-first in poison oak. By the time she reached the Rejuvenary, it'd spread over her arms and legs and affected her breathing. I reduced the swelling, especially on her face. Mac and I applied an oatmeal-baking soda paste."

"Hearing that makes me itch," Tovah said.

"Jonathan, I was telling Mekial and Tovah that our guest is... itching to get airborne," Thom added.

Mekial groaned. "Bad pun."

"Do you mean?"

"Yeah. She needs to flex her... um... arms... and leg muscles." Thom leaned in, whispering about the images Kami had shown him and his chat with Niamh.

"Think Oddi'd have an old ball?" Mekial asked.

"Maybe. Want to come back with me after we eat?"

They did.

When they arrived, they found Kami walking the perimeter of the fenced yard.

"I'll drop off the bowls and see if I can find Oddi," Thom said.

"We'll see if Kami'll chase us or us her," Jonathan suggested.

When Thom rejoined them, with Oddi in tow, he was carrying a deflated cloth ball. Apparently, it'd been the victim of a garden rake.

"Is she flying yet?" Oddi asked excitedly.

"Thankfully not," Jonathan replied. "Hopping and running around. Thom, did Kami's siblings hop before their first flight?"

"No. One struggled to lift off at first but eventually made it. Ariel had to get home."

"We've been playing tag," Mekial explained. "She makes the cutest chirr-snort when she's having fun."

"What's the ball for?" Tovah asked, stepping back into the yard from the hall.

"It'll help her learn how to grasp with her claws, like she'd do when hunting. I read it trains her to stretch her neck and snap at prey."

Oddi shivered. "That makes me squirmy."

For the next while, Oddi chased Kami around what he began calling the play yard. The others alternated tossing the ball for Kami to catch. With her small fangs, the ball was a little worse for wear by the end.

Chapter 33

A week passed. Thom and Mekial finished the afternoon training early. Dek had introduced them to new weapons: a cudgel and truncheon. Although no longer used in combat, they helped improve coordination and worked distinct muscle groups. While their sword training provided a solid foundation in footwork, both struggled with the speed and control required by these blunt weapons.

Thom needed to see Niamh and Peth, and hoped they were in their residence. Mekial came along. They found Keelin in the kitchen.

"Are Peth or Niamh around? Oddi said they ended their workday early on Fwi-dae to enjoy the weekend."

"Let me check."

When Peth came in, with Keelin trailing behind, he asked, "Can I presume this is about Kami?"

"Yep."

"Follow me. Niamh's in the sitting room with the kids."

As they entered, she greeted them, "Welcome, Thom, Mekial. Where are Jonathan and Tovah? I heard you usually stick together. You know, we still haven't met Tovah."

"Sorry. She's visiting her family," Mekial replied.

"Jonathan's with his aunt, uncle, and cousins," Thom added. "They came into the city this morning.

"Can I presume Kami's ready to fly?" Niamh prompted.

"Yes. Her hops are much longer. One carries her across the play yard, as Oddi calls it."

"Leave it to him," Peth chuckled.

"We believe she'll try in the next few days."

"That pushes things a bit," Peth admitted. "Niamh and I have been talking about how to inform others. We only want to tell a few key people."

"I have an idea that might give us more time," Niamh interrupted. "When Kami's ready, Thom, could you instruct her to fly behind the plateaus instead of downtown? That way, she'd be flying over farmlands with fewer people. And if she flies high enough, people might think she's a bird."

"I can do that."

"But we're facing a conundrum," Peth added.

"What do you mean?" Mekial asked.

"Most people in Docha-leigh don't believe dragons are real. We're worried about extreme reactions. The first could be that many will want to see her."

"I don't think she'd want to face a crowd," Thom said.

Mekial tapped her chin. "We could tell her beforehand."

"Couldn't there be a sign-up, like when academs have to meet with teachers?" Oddi asked.

Niamh replied, "That's a possibility."

"What's the other reaction, Peth?" Thom asked.

"That people might fear her, and even try to harm her."

Thom stiffened. "I hadn't thought of that."

"Couldn't we protect her with guards?" Oddi asked.

"Another possibility. You really are thinking this through," Niamh said.

Oddi preened at her praise.

"But we'd need level-headed guards who'd be comfortable with her," Niamh clarified.

"Whatever you think is best," Thom said.

"Let us know when she's ready to fly."

The following morning, Jonathan, Thom, and Mekial had breakfast with the Llewelyn family at a city inn. As they were finishing, Terza asked, "When can we see Kami?"

"Terza," her mother cautioned, "we may not be able to. She's living in the Royal Keep, and we don't want to disturb her. She might not remember you anyway."

"That's OK," Thom said. "We can visit her. We'll go through the Acadium grounds. He'd already told them about Kami's intent to fly.

"Please, Mam and Paps," Terza pleaded.

"OK," her mother answered. "But you and I need to sell some goods, and your father and Nedd have errands."

At Draganni Hall, Thom led them into the play yard. Kami was staring at the sky, her wings twitching.

Kami, Thom mind-spoke, *do you remember Uncle Dillen, Aunt Betz, Nedd, and Terza?*

Yes.

"She remembers you," Thom said. "You can get closer if you want."

"She's bigger," Terza said. "Can I touch her?"

At Kami's assent, Thom replied, "Sure."

Placing her hand below Kami's ears, she scratched.

Thank you, Terza, Kami mind-spoke.

"I heard her in my head," she said excitedly.

"Oh, right," Thom remarked. "She can do that with anyone she wants."

Nedd's mouth dropped open.

Uncle Dillen gave a low whistle. "Well, I'll be..."

"She's truly amazing," Aunt Betz said, her eyes shining.

Thank you. I want to fly.

"Do you feel strong enough?" Thom asked.

"For a short flight."

Thom explained Peth and Niamh's concerns.

I understand. Tilting her head, her eyes became distant.

"What is it?" Mekial asked.

I can become invisible.

"Did that just come to you?" Thom asked.

She nodded.

"Jonathan, could you run to the residence and see if Peth, Niamh, and Oddi are around? I think they'll want to see this."

In no time, Oddi burst into the yard. "She's gonna fly!"

"Quiet, Oddi," Peth warned, as he and Niamh entered behind. "Thom, it's a bit sooner than we hoped."

I can become invisible, Kami repeated.

Peth shook his head. "That's unexpected. Not only mind-speech, but invisibility."

"That simplifies things," Niamh said. "In that case, we can hold off telling anyone else."

"I agree," Peth concurred. Noticing the others, he added, "And who do we have here?"

"Oh, sorry," Jonathan said, introducing his family.

"May she give flying a try?" Thom asked.

"Yes," Niamh said.

Before Thom could tell her to go, Kami flapped her wings and lifted off. Within seconds, she mostly faded, leaving a faint silhouette.

We can see your outline, Kami, Thom mind-spoke.

I'll try to fix that.

They watched as she disappeared into the distance, now completely invisible.

"How long will she fly?" Terza asked.

"Not long," Thom said, recalling what he read in the training book.

They sat and got acquainted while they waited. When they heard flapping, their eyes lifted to catch flashes of gold in the sky. Thom recognized them as parts of Kami's tail. The rest of her, he knew, was magenta shading to green.

"She's having trouble staying invisible," Uncle Dillen commented.

As she descended, they turned away to shield their faces from the flying sand.

"Your tail was a little visible," Thom said,

Tired and hungry.

"I'll check if Keelin has organ meat."

Kami flopped down, her wings splayed.

Chapter 34

It was mid-Aprali. Thom jolted awake and grunted. The sky beyond his window was beginning to lighten, promising to be a pleasant spring day. Had a sound from a neighbor woken him?

He luxuriated in the softness of his bed. Quieting his mind, he opened his senses in case a divine message was trying to come through.

Something significant's going to happen today.

This wasn't from his divine advisors. They felt different. Maybe his prescience gift? He sensed stirrings of it a few times over the past month, but he hadn't been sure.

Repeating the words, Thom was certain it was true. But what would happen? His breath quickened from anxiety. Once again, he heard Mekial's voice in his mind: 'It doesn't have to be bad.'

He closed his eyes, but sleep wouldn't return. Rising, he grabbed his clothes and headed to the washroom. When he got back, the hour was early, so he picked up his journal and an inkstave from the side table and dropped into his comfy chair.

The new writing instrument had replaced the quill. Invented by a clumsy metallurgy academ and two classmates, it held a refillable ink reservoir. Thom appreciated the convenience, even though it also smeared if he wasn't careful.

He began writing:

Hey G. I had a meeting with Brother Lamen yesterday. While he was finishing a letter, I noticed a book about the Akashic Records. I remember seeing one in Sestra B's office. Lamen said the records hold memories and information for all existence: past, present, and future. I wonder if it's like the consciousness Kami's been tapping into.

Most of our conversation, though, was about reincarnation, even dragon reincarnation. One book said dragons could live hundreds of years. I can't imagine that. But if they reincarnate, do they have pre-incarnation meetings?

Lamen also said that if someone dies before fulfilling their purpose, they sometimes incarnate soon after.

Why does that sound familiar? Thom scratched his head, but continued writing.

I told him I couldn't remember more of my pre-incarnation meeting. And I'm not getting any others yet. I'm not really sure why I have this ability. Can you tell me?

Thom, a voice said in his mind.

"God? Is that you?" He knew God had no gender, yet he continued associating a male voice with God, a lingering effect of the Iosan elders' teachings.

Indeed.

"Will you answer my last question?"

I will, but you won't be satisfied.

"I get it."

To answer your first, first, God chuckled. *All animals, fish, birds... and even dragons, have their version of pre-incarnation meetings. In them, they discuss what they might contribute to the universe or dimension they'll enter, including whether they'll interact with the population or even serve as a source of food.*

"That's why it's good to give thanks to them before meals."

If only it were more common. I especially wish those who kill animals recklessly would consider the impact on their species.

"I get it. So you're not against hunters."

Not if they respect animals and nature, and help ensure a healthy balance of their species.

"I see." Hearing footsteps in the hall, Thom said, "I'd better head to breakfast and bring Kami hers. I hope she had a good night."

About your new ability, God added, you'll understand its value in time.

"And there it is—my unsatisfying answer," Thom remarked, smiling. "Thanks for the chat."

Any time.

Now that Kami was flying, Thom and Jonathan met Mekial and Tovah in the dining hall as servers brought out the food. The foursome ate quickly, then rushed to the Royal Residence to fetch Kami's meal. She'd grown three times her original size, which the book said was normal once dragonets began flying. Her appetite increased right along with her flight time.

Kami could stay airborne for over an hour and remain fully invisible the entire time. The first time she managed that all the way through a landing, Thom was alone. Exhausted from the flight, she'd forgotten to warn him, and her wingbeats blew him into the fence, leaving him bruised. She'd apologized profusely and promised not to forget again.

"Good morning," Oddi said as they entered the kitchen. He always joined them to help.

"Good morning," they all replied, and got to work.

They unloaded the food from the cooling larder and chopped it up. It went faster because the pieces didn't have to be as small.

In the play yard, Kami was already flexing her wings, stirring up a cloud of sand that forced them to turn away.

"Hey. Stop the flapping," Thom yelled. He winced. What if someone nearby had heard?

"We have your breakfast," Oddi announced, once she stopped. They dumped Kami's meal into the food trough.

A week earlier, an academ metalworker had made it for a class assignment, thinking it might be useful for watering the Keep's horses. Duncan had thanked her. Since he'd been let in on Kami's existence, he knew it would be perfect for holding her food.

Facing Thom, Kami said, *Fly with me.*

"Excuse me?" he asked, unsure he'd heard her correctly.

I want you to ride with me. Now over seven months old, Kami sounded like an older teen, which was typical for a juvenile, according to dragon lore.

All five stood like statues, their mouths open, wide enough to fit a large apple.

Oddi was the first to speak. "Neat! Can I ride you sometime?"

Maybe. But you'll need to be older and taller. Addressing Thom, she asked, *Didn't you say you had an old dragon saddle?*

"Uh huh," he replied, recovering from the shock. "One of Duncan's stablehands repaired the straps and stitched in new leather."

Kami stared at him, intently.

"Didn't you want breakfast?" he asked nervously. He wasn't sure he was ready to fly.

No. I don't want to fly on a full stomach.

"But I have class in an hour," he protested.

"Thom," Jonathan said, "your class is with Mac. She'll understand."

"She would," Mekial and Tovah chimed in.

We won't fly long.

"Do it," Oddi said. "I'll help you carry the saddle from Draganni Hall."

With the saddle firmly secured and Thom strapped in, Kami asked, *Ready?*

"I guess," Thom said, less than enthusiastic.

Facing the back of the Keep, Kami flapped her wings. Sand swirled. The others cupped their hands over their eyes but kept watching.

Each wingbeat threw Thom back. The leather straps bit into him, but kept him from being flung off. If he ever did this again, he'd need to add padding.

Suddenly, Kami was airborne.

As she climbed, her wingbeats quickened. Thom felt as if he was riding a bucking bronco, like the kind he'd seen once at a horse dealer with Da and Bedum. His stomach churned. He didn't want to throw up on Kami, but he wasn't sure he could stop it.

Are you OK?

Um, Thom gulped as some of this morning's griddlecakes surged into his mouth. He forced it down, wincing at the acid burn. Any thought of his class vanished.

Am I too heavy? he mind-spoke, knowing Kami couldn't hear his voice over the wind.

No. I can carry more. When I'm higher, I'll find a thermal and won't need to flap as hard.

Thermal?

Rising air. Didn't Tovah say one of her teachers covered that in her weather class?

Oh yeah. Thom gulped again as a piece of sausage came back up. "Yuck." He shouldn't have eaten.

Found one.

The ride smoothed out. As his stomach settled, Thom began enjoying the flight. He could've used warmer clothes. Should he look down? Would it terrify him? He finally did. Farmland stretched below, neat and well-kept. Some fields held cows and sheep, smaller than Rindo's carved toys. The few people outside were ant-sized.

Kami flew a bit longer when Thom asked, *How far are we going? Mac won't mind if I'm late, but I don't want to miss the whole class?*

Not far. I have a stop to make.

Is that smart? You're invisible, but I'm not. What if someone sees me?

You're invisible, too, because you're riding me.

Thom saw it was true. Daring to release one hand from the saddlehorn, he touched where his leg should have been. It was there, just hidden. Kind of bizarre and cool at the same time.

OK. But can we go somewhere no one will see us?

Yes.

Ahead, Thom spotted a forest and realized Kami was taking them back to the dragon sanctuary.

Have you been here alone before?

No, I wanted to come with you.

Landing, Thom unstrapped himself and climbed down. The hedge he and Jonathan had passed through had grown thick. No one would ever discover this place existed.

I can smell my Mam, brother, and sister.

After all this time? Thom couldn't smell anything. Dragons must have a sharper nose. Were the shells still here? Checking the ground, he didn't see them.

Are you OK?

I miss my family.

Did you want to fly home? he asked. He hoped she wasn't leaving, but it had to be her choice.

No. It's not time. But I know where they are.

Thom was relieved.

I smell food, Kami said, pointing her snout toward the cliff where Ariel and the two dragonets had taken off.

Thom walked over and peered down. A short distance below lay a small fawn, its head at an unnatural angle.

I see it.

Dragging it back up, Thom whispered, "Thank you for providing sustenance for Kami. I'm sorry your life was short." To Kami, he said, "I thought you didn't want to eat before flying."

This isn't much.

After Kami finished, Thom climbed back into the saddle, and they launched into the air.

In no time at all, they landed in the play yard. It was empty. Everyone was likely in class. The food trough was covered, and the bowls were gone. One of his friends had done that. He was grateful. *I hope your food's not rancid.*

It isn't.

"What are you gonna do?"

Eat. Then sleep.

Later, on the way to supper, Jonathan, Mekial, and Tovah pulled Thom into a quiet corner. He recounted everything, punctuated by their cries of 'wow,' 'amazing,' and an occasional gulp. They were late for the meal, but no one cared.

Chapter 35

T he pendulum clock chimed three. Outside, darkness and steady rain made everything feel foreboding. The downpour, like his mood, had begun two days ago, and he feared neither would ease until finals ended on Mei 12.

That afternoon, Dek had required them to train outside instead of in the salle. When Niall and Oran complained, he'd told them they might have to fight in worse conditions.

Rubbing his bleary eyes, Thom sipped his tea, now cold. After everyone had gone to bed, he'd snuck into the staff dining room and brewed a pot to help him stay awake. He was exhausted, but he couldn't remember all the noble ranks or how to address each properly. Their teacher had told them about the time a guard had called a particularly disagreeable duke, 'My lord.' Rin had spent weeks calming him. A private dinner with the monarchs and the duke's family had finally smoothed things over.

Thom groaned and drew the oil lamp closer. His eyes burned. The page before him was covered with solid lines linking titles to territories, and dotted lines showing the hierarchy among nobles.

"Duke outranks an earl. Unless it's an archduke, which isn't the same as a prince but is above a marquess. I should remember this. He banged his head on the desk.

He was confident about his Advanced Herbs and Treatments exam. History felt fairly solid as well. But Nobility and Protocol terrified him.

For first-semester exams, Thom had aimed for Distinction across the board. After all, he'd been two levels ahead of other students his age at home. He'd earned Distinction in Herbology, Mathematics, and Weapons training, but only Merit in the rest. Better than Pass, at least.

He was determined to reach his goal this semester. Rin and the monarchs had given him a scholarship, and he couldn't risk losing it. Even with his father's business doing very well, he doubted they could afford next year's tuition.

"Enough waffling," Thom grumbled, rubbing his eyes again. "A marquess outranks an earl, who outranks a baron. But where does a viscount fit?" He flipped through his notes searching for an answer.

Thom, a male voice said.

"Is somebody else up?" He heard nothing.

"Where's that page?" He rummaged for his rankings sheet. "A viscount is higher than... "

Thom, it's Jesh.

"What?"

It's Jesh.

"Don't bother me!"

Thom.

"Leave me alone! I need to study!"

The oil lamp flickered out, leaving the room in darkness.

"Turg!"

Stop, Jesh said gently. *You're not thinking clearly. You need sleep.*

I don't want to fail, Thom pleaded, switching to mind-speech. *My Nobility exam is the day after tomorrow. I've gotta get this.*

I understand. But you'll do fine.

You don't know, Thom shot back. "I can remember this. I will," he said into the darkness. "The viscount is lower than the baron... no, that's not right. I need my list. Where's that taper?"

He felt around for it, planning to use his memory of the room and hall to light it.

A wind rattled the windows hard, stopping him.

Now that I have your attention, Thom, Jeshua said firmly, *get in bed and go to sleep.*

But...

You've been at this too long. And you need to play. Remember the fun we had in Glakkadeth? And our chase around the divine realm with Metatron and the others?

Yeah, Thom said wearily.

And last weekend, you ignored Jonathan, Mekial, and Tovah when they begged you to ride Apollo. Even Kami couldn't get you to fly again.

It's just...

You've been pushing yourself. Sereh, Rel, and I have seen it. Rest will clear your head.

I am tired.

Get some sleep. And take time to play tomorrow.

I'll try. Thanks, Jesh.

Good night, Thom.

Chapter 36

S amiltun sat at his cherry wood desk in his manor office. He'd purchased the estate two months earlier. The furnishings were solid and respectable, despite not being the finest. He planned to upgrade them once his wealth grew.

Spread out before him was a glittering array of jewels: garnets, rubies, sapphires, and one diamond.

Lena and Leesha, twins, had discovered them using their unusual gifts. Samiltun had hired a childminder, Eilidh Stewart, to watch them—valuable property in his eyes.

Soon after confirming the girls' talents, he hired Siomon Connemara, a mineralogist and expert in land formations, with a knack for finding gold and silver veins, and gem-rich sites.

Samiltun picked up a sapphire and held it to the light. Its facets caught the glow of the nearby lamp. He sighed, satisfied. The twins were earning their keep. To avoid the suspicion that might arise if he flooded local jewelers with his finds, he sold the gems to brokers who traveled to the neighboring Vlodan Republic. Apparently, buyers there were willing to pay handsomely for them, especially for larger stones.

Tap tap.

"One moment," he called, sweeping the gems into a velvet bag. "Enter."

The twins stepped in. They'd celebrated their ninth birthday the day before. Samiltun had thrown a modest party, enough to earn their family's gratitude. It was a small investment to keep their parents agreeable and the twins loyal.

Even so... they'd smiled brightly when they unwrapped the green ribbons. A flicker of emotion stirred in him. He ignored it.

"Lena, Leesha, what brings you here?"

"Sir, we're sorry to disturb you," Lena said, "But Leesha and I wanted to thank you for the party."

They were four and a half feet tall, and identical, but Samiltun knew it was Lena who'd spoken. She was more vocal. Both wore their red hair in ponytails, tied with the ribbons he'd given them.

"No trouble," he replied.

"My sister also wanted me to thank you for the book."

Leesha covered her mouth shyly.

"We both like reading about the older girl's adventures."

"No problem." One of his servants had suggested it—purchased from a peddler's cart. It was a way to keep the girls occupied in the evenings, when Samiltun had other matters to attend to.

"Thank you, sir," Lena said.

"When does Connemara take you on your next adventure?" Samiltun already knew, but he wanted to see if Connemara had told them. The man was so obsessed with treasure hunting that he often forgot to share details.

"Next Widna-dae," Lena said. "Miss Stewart is having us study volcanoes and kimlite pipes."

"Kimberlite pipes," Leesha whispered.

"Oh, yeah," Lena admitted. "What she said."

"Off with you," Samiltun urged, waving them away. "I'm sure you have work to do."

"Yes, sir," Lena replied. The girls curtsied and left the office.

Volcanoes and kimberlite pipes. What was that about? Samiltun knew Connemara often suggested study topics. This one piqued his interest. Was it related to his order to search for diamonds?

He'd begun wondering if the twins' gifts might be able to compress carbon into priceless stones, an idea that could increase his wealth exponentially. Perhaps he could use his gifts to push theirs. Surely, there were deposits nearby.

Pouring the gems from the bag once more, Samiltun brought the lone diamond to his eye, appreciating how it sparkled.

Chapter 37

Thom, Jonathan, Mekial, and Tovah were nearing Thom's home. His parents had invited them to spend a month together after school ended. They'd set out on Mei 14, two days after finals. Everyone had done well, including Thom. He hadn't earned Distinction in every subject, but he had in Nobility and Protocol. He could hardly believe it. Jesh had been right.

"Tovah," Jonathan called back, "congratulations on getting the Distinction award in Geology. I heard you got a perfect score."

"I did. Please don't make a big deal. My parents already did before we left, even to our neighbors. It was embarrassing."

Thom glanced behind at Mekial, riding alongside Tovah. "Congratulations on earning Distinction in Government and Weapons Training."

"Thanks. Same to you, Thom and Jonathan, especially for receiving the Queen Noinín Academic Prize. I heard it isn't awarded every year."

"It might have had to do with you saving Niamh's twins," Tovah added.

"Maybe," Jonathan said. Wanting to change the subject, he added, "The sixth-level graduation was impressive."

Picking up on the cue, Thom jumped in. "As was the ceremony for those entering the Royal Guards. Paddi's smile was so big when Ciarenn got his badge that I thought his face might crack."

"Rilla and Ronan's family seemed equally proud," Mekial added. "All three are very skilled with defense and weaponry."

They rode in silence for a while before Tovah remarked, "We've been lucky with the weather. Mild for late spring."

"I'm glad we weren't pestered with gnats," Thom added.

Jonathan smirked. "Funny. You're not mentioning the fly that got into our tent last night and wouldn't leave you alone."

"Ugh. It made me half mad."

"Half?" Tovah asked.

"Careful," Thom replied. "I know where you sleep."

"No problems in our tent," Mekial said, a twinkle in her eye. "We both slept soundly."

Jonathan, Mekial, and Tovah had borrowed horses from the Acadium stable. Thom, of course, rode Apollo.

Late that morning, Thom brought the group to a stop. "I wanted to warn you. My family likes to hug. My mother might ask you to help with the gardens. And I'm certain my father will suggest you try your hand at pottery."

"That's fine," Tovah replied, and the others agreed.

Riding down the path leading to his home, Thom noticed the flowers were in full bloom and the air thick with their sweet scent.

"Beautiful gardens," Mekial said. "All those colors, like a rainbow."

"That's my younger sister, Reta," Thom explained. "She has a strong earth-sensing gift and loves working in the soil."

"I'll have to talk with her about it," Tovah said.

"It shows," Jonathan added. "My fathers would be jealous. None of us kids were any good at gardening. Most of us had a brown thumb, if not black. Once, I even killed a cactus. I'm happy that doesn't apply to treating patients."

"You can say that again," Thom said.

"That again," Jonathan echoed.

"You're weird."

"I hope that's not a problem," Jonathan said with a wry grin.

"Nope," Thom answered fondly.

"OK, boys," Mekial cut in. "If you're done joking, we should probably let your family know we're here."

"Hey, Macirdans," Thom shouted.

Kavan burst out of the front door, followed by his youngest sister, Alli. Thom had first met her after returning from Glakkadeth, but she'd reacted to him like a stranger. Did she remember him now? She'd just turned four. Her birthday gift was in his saddlebag.

"Hi, Thom," Kavan yelled, his brown hair as messy as ever, a lock falling over one of his eyes.

"Hi. Has Mam seen your hair? She'd tell you to brush it."

"Already did," he smirked. "Didn't help."

"Hi, Alli," Thom said, noticing her peeking out from behind Kavan's back. "Do you remember me?"

"Uh," she mumbled, shuffling her feet.

"Come on, Alli," Kavan urged. "It's Thom. Your older brother!"

"That's OK, Kavan. Alli, I'm sorry I missed your birthday. I brought you a present."

"Present?" she asked, her eyes lighting up as she stepped forward.

"I'll give it to you inside."

By then, his parents had come out, along with Meli and Reta.

"Jonathan, Mekial, Tovah, good to see you again," Meli called, hurrying over to each as they dismounted. "And you, Thom," she said, wrapping her arms around him.

"Thanks, Mel," Thom replied, extracting himself from her embrace.

"Good to see you all," his mother, Winni, said. "We feel like we know you from everything Redik and Meli shared. We'll save the rest of the hugs when we're in the house."

"Welcome," Thom's father, Uric, added. "Kavan, Meli, help Jonathan, Mekial, and Tovah with their horses. Since Redik and Brigid mostly stay in the city, their stalls are free. Thom, I assume you want to groom Apollo."

"Yes, Da."

"How's Kami?" Meli asked. "And who's feeding her?"

"She's fine. Oddi's handling that, and keeping her scales shiny. Kami's showing a little vanity about her looks, even though no one can see her when flying."

"And you ride her? That's sound scary and incredible."

"It is."

"I want to hear everything," Kavan insisted.

"Sure. We'd better get the horses stabled first."

Seated around the long wooden table, Thom asked, "So Redik and Brigid are in the city? We didn't pass them on the road."

"They're not there now. Redik found a new trading post a few days' ride south," his father explained. "The owner wants to carry my pottery."

"That's great."

"Mekial, are you visiting your family this summer?" Meli asked.

"Not enough time. But I met Thom's teacher, Brother Lamen. He's from home and invited the four of us for a few suppers. Real Glakkadian food."

"I missed its unique spiciness," Thom said.

Jonathan volunteered, "Tovah and I are starting to like it."

"I'm glad," Thom remarked. "If we ever visit, you won't have a problem."

"You say that now," Mekial teased.

"But if I hadn't had problems at first," Thom countered, "we wouldn't have invented Timbu."

"You invented that," Kavan exclaimed.

"Didn't I tell you last year?"

"No," Meli answered.

"Sorry. Mekial, you tell them."

She had just finished sharing the story when they heard the sound of hooves outside and a woman shouting.

"Mam, Mam!" Deena rushed in. "You have to help. Liv's been hurt. Bad."

Her husband, Rian, followed, carrying a young girl, pale and limp. Their oldest, Dana, trailed behind.

"Come," Winni said, leading them down the hall to her healing room. "Thom and Jonathan, join us."

After Rian laid Liv on the treatment table, Winni examined her.

Thom noticed dirt clinging to his niece's tangled blond hair and streaking her cheeks. "What happened?"

"I... I... ran over her with our cart," Rian stuttered, guilt etched across his face. "I was heading out to deliver a dresser and two chairs. I didn't... see her."

"I'm sure," Thom said.

"Her trachea's crushed," Winni informed them, her voice tight.

"She has a few broken ribs," Jonathan added. "And a punctured lung."

"Her spirit's wavering," Thom warned. "It's like she has one foot here and the other in the divine realm."

"Do something, Mam!" Deena cried, ignoring him.

"Thom, you wrote about saving the queen's twins," his mother said. "Can you two help? I can heal bones, but not a trachea or a punctured lung."

"We'll see what we can do," Jonathan promised.

"Please try," Deena begged. "I can't lose her." She looked up and cried, "Why are you punishing us, Deu?"

"We'll do our best," Thom said. At the door, Thom spotted Mekial standing behind the others. "Would you let Mekial in?"

As she stepped around them, she asked, "How can I help? I'm not a healer."

"We can use your strength. Put a hand on each of our shoulders, and imagine your energy flowing into us."

"Thom," Jonathan said, "you take the trachea. I'll handle the lung."

"Jonathan, what should I do?" Winni asked.

"Check for internal bleeding. And stop it if you find any."

Thom placed his hands near Liv's upper neck. Using his mind voice, he called on Archangel Raphael and the healing angels to bolster his gifts with theirs. As warmth spread through his hands, he sent green energy into the damaged area. The crushed section spanned an inch. He needed to expand it. Could he slip a shield inside? But the shields he was familiar with were external, for protection or gift control.

Go ahead. Imagine it, a voice said.

Rafe?

Gently, he encouraged. *Make it smooth and flexible.*

"She's breathing a little easier," Winni noted.

Thom heard a sob behind him, but stayed focused on expanding the tiny shield. He could feel Liv's trachea resisting. It wasn't holding shape. He needed help.

Ask Mekial, Rafe prompted.

"Mekial," Thom said, with deliberate calm. "I'm sending you an image of what I'm doing. I've never done this before. If you get it, can you imagine your strength holding it in place?"

"But what about Jonathan?" she asked.

"I'll lend him my energy," Tovah offered, squeezing into the room.

"Thanks," Thom said.

"I'm getting it," Mekial replied. "Yes... I see."

"Perfect. That frees me to support her spirit. Oh dear. Her grip on the earth is slipping."

"No, no, no," Deena cried, dropping to her knees. "She can't die. Please, Deu. I know I'm sinful, but Liv's innocent. She doesn't deserve this."

Rian was weeping, his head bowed.

Winni met her husband's eyes. "Uric," she said delicately. "Take Deena and Rian into the other room."

Helping Deena up, he guided them out.

Liv, it's your Uncle Thommy, Thom mind-spoke. *I'm here. We're doing everything possible to help you heal.*

An image flashed in Thom's mind: a gathering centered around a woman with cascading blond hair. Was this Liv's pre-incarnation meeting?

Hi, Thom, an unfamiliar female voice replied. *Yes, it is. I'm Liv's higher self. It was always a possibility that she'd die young.*

Thom found himself thinking about Lebrim again.

I'll do what I can, he assured her, sending loving and healing energy into Liv. *Mekial, how's the shield holding?*

Startled to hear Thom's voice in her mind, she answered aloud, "It resisted some after you pulled out, but I imagined adding another shield over yours. It seems to be holding."

"Good," he said, then checked her spirit. "Liv's more connected to her body now. Let me anchor both shields before we pull out."

"Tovah and I can help," Jonathan stated.

"Thanks. Mam, any internal bleeding?"

"In her brain and abdomen. I stopped it and repaired a few muscle tears."

"Excellent."

"Her skin's becoming more pink," his mother observed, sighing with relief.

"The puncture's also sealed," Jonathan added, shaking his head. "I think Archangel Raphael helped. Tovah cauterized it."

"And the shields are secure," Thom confirmed. "Now for the ribs. "Mam, Jonathan, let's do that together. Jonathan, take the lead."

When they finished, Winni said, "Reta, get a cloth to wrap Liv's chest. We need to keep her ribs stabilized. Jonathan, put a pot of water on and add rosemary and thyme. The herbs are in the cupboard."

"Of course. The steam should ease her lungs."

"Thom, would you get Deena and ...?"

Before she could finish, she rushed in, "Is she OK? Will she live?"

"She's healing... and resting," Winni whispered. "The trauma drained her. Recovery will take time. You and Rian can stay, but everyone else... out."

Seated around the table again, sipping the tea that Meli had made, Jonathan, Thom, and Winni explained what they'd done.

"When Thom asked me to lend my strength to his shield," Mekial said, "I was shocked. But somehow I ended up creating my own."

"I was surprised, too," Tovah admitted. "I didn't think my ability to channel heat could be useful for healing."

"Thank you all," Rian said, guiding an unsteady Deena down the hall.

Thom noticed that Rian seemed a bit better. He hoped guilt wouldn't eat at him. Unfortunately, Brother Lamen lived too far away to help.

"Deena, take my seat," Kavan offered.

"Thanks."

"Is Livie OK, Mama?" Dana asked, speaking for the first time.

"Yes," Rian replied.

"Before we left, she opened her eyes and smiled," Deena said, tearing up.

"Then why are you crying? she asked. "And why couldn't Elder Ouna save her?"

"What about the elder?" Meli asked, narrowing her eyes.

Thom was glad Meli raised the question, recalling Deena's claim last Jauna that the elder was divinely touched. He'd likely have lost his temper asking about this so-called saint.

"Deena insisted we take Liv to her first," Rian explained.

"But she wouldn't help," Deena whispered. "She said I had to accept that Liv was going to die... and that it was either my sin or Liv's that caused it."

"Excuse me?" Uric sputtered. "She blamed you..."

"Yes. It couldn't have been Liv's fault—she's a child—but it could've been me. I fail Deu often. I must've broken a commandment for Deu to punish me."

"Deena," Rian cut in, "I was the one driving the cart."

"But I told her to go outside. If I only waited..."

"Deena, do you truly think Deu would do that?" Jonathan asked.

Again, Thom was glad someone else had said something.

"She's an elder."

"Sweetie," his mother said, "I realize you respect her, and you can believe what you wish, but please consider the possibility that she's wrong."

"I don't know."

"Deena," Rian cut in, "I haven't spoken against that elder until now. She wiped her hands of our daughter, like she was nothing. She didn't even offer to pray. Yet, Thom, Mam, Jonathan, and his friends healed Liv."

"But..."

"I'm not done," he said, his ire rising. "Last year, you told me you feared Thom would go to hell because of his beliefs. Do you really think Deu would have let him help if he wasn't right with Deu?"

Thom wasn't trained like Lamen, but he figured Rian channeling his guilt into anger would be a good thing.

Deena stayed quiet for a few moments. Finally, she looked up. "I'll... think about it." Her voice was softer now. After another moment, she added, "Thanks, Thom... and all of you for saving Liv."

"You're welcome," Thom replied.

Her fingers fidgeted with the edge of her tunic as she glanced at the others. "I haven't met your friends."

After introducing them, Thom determined that a change of subject was in order. Crouching before Alli, he said, "Happy Birthday!" then pulled a long package from his bag.

"A dolly," she squealed, as she tore the wrapping away.

Weeks later, the foursome prepared to leave the Macirdans.

"Thanks for the birthday party," Mekial said. "I love the scarf you knitted, Mrs. Macirdan."

"Mekial, call me Mam," she insisted. "You all can. And you're welcome."

"Thanks for teaching us how to make pottery," Tovah said to Thom's father. "I liked working with the clay."

"Thom thought you would, given your gift," Uric replied.

"Thanks for your hospitality," Jonathan added. "I hope we weren't too much trouble."

"Not at all," Mam said. "Be sure to bring the tin of sweet biscuits I made for your family. Don't let your siblings eat them all before your fathers get some. And you either, Tovah."

"I won't, Mam," Jonathan replied.

"Same here," Tovah chimed in.

"Thom, are you flying to Jonathan's?" Redik asked.

He and Brigid had arrived two days earlier. The sleeping quarters were tight, but they made do.

"We're stopping at Jonathan's aunt and uncle's first, but yes."

"It's amazing Kami's flying, and that you're riding her," his father said. "I hope to meet her someday."

"I hope so, too, Da."

"What about you, Mekial?" Meli asked.

"I'm staying with Tovah's family for the rest of the summer."

"We'd better get going," Thom said.

After hugs were exchanged, the foursome set off.

"That was a great visit with your family, Jonathan," Thom said, scrubbing a particularly dirty section of Kami's wing. He and Jonathan had gotten back to the Acadium not long before.

Like horses required after a long ride, Kami needed a thorough cleaning. Jonathan had gotten her food from Keelin, which Kami had quickly devoured. She was now half asleep.

"I'm glad," Jonathan replied. "Your family's big like mine. But I did worry. We call ourselves the 'Loud Family' because everyone talks over each other."

"Well, you know mine does. Growing up, I'd escape to the loft to get a break from the noise. Why do you think I took Alli on so many rides with Apollo?"

"I should've figured that out. Speaking of Apollo, are you going to visit him after we're done here?"

"Yeah. He knew I'd be gone a while. And Oddi promised to treat Apollo to apples if he could ride him. Apollo was fine with that."

"Thanks again to you and Rindo for the carving," Jonathan said. "I love how Archangel Raphael's hands are on the healer's shoulders while the healer's are on the patient."

"I'm glad you liked it. When I wrote to Rindo last Nuvima, I asked if he'd make it a little abstract. His parents gave him suggestions."

"It's beautiful. Do you think Tovah and Mekial are back yet?"

"No. Tovah's family enjoys spending a lot of time at wildlife parks. Apparently, the Vlodan Republic doesn't have them. Mekial was excited. I don't think they'll be back until the beginning of Siptema."

"So we've got over a month on our own. That's great. We did promise Mac we'd gather herbs. But maybe we can explore downtown more."

"Sure," Thom said. "And for the herbs, what if we fly to the dragon sanctuary?"

"I'd like that. I have to admit, I almost threw up when Kami flew us to my aunt and uncle's."

"Been there."

Chapter 38

J onathan paced his room, his chest tight and his thoughts spinning. About a month remained before third-level finals, and he should've been finishing his paper on the nervous system. Instead, he was unraveling—and not because of a patient or the pressure of studies.

No, the past two years had been quiet, at least compared to his first. That year had felt like one crisis after another. If every year had been like that, he would've exploded.

That's how he felt now.

Because of Thom.

Jonathan dropped onto his bed, gripping the edge of his mattress. Why can't Thom admit he was attracted to boys? To him? Sure, the Iosan elders strictly preached about relationships between opposite genders. But Thom wasn't Iosan anymore. Not really.

"What's his problem?" Jonathan shouted.

"You!" a male voice bellowed. "I'm trying to study."

"Sorry," he called back, his mind already returning to Thom. He'll be sixteen in six months. How could he not know by now?"

After dinner, he and Thom had tried studying in their common room, but a bunch of academs were talking. Jonathan had suggested going to one of their rooms. They ended up in Thom's.

Sitting side by side on the bed, they reviewed their notes. Thom's hand kept brushing his. Once could've been an accident. By the fifth time, Jonathan knew it wasn't, and he'd snapped. His words to Thom came rushing back.

"Would you stop it? Do you get what you're doing to me? Grow up! How can you be so stupid? You're so smart about most things, but..."

Thom had stared at him, his eyes full of confusion and hurt. Then Thom had apologized without even understanding why. Jonathan had stormed out after shouting the worst thing:

"I don't want to be your friend anymore!"

Jonathan buried his face in his hands. What had he done? He couldn't face Thom tomorrow. He'd skip classes. Thankfully, he wasn't assigned to the Rejuvenary. That, he wouldn't miss. Maybe he'd go to that park Eran had mentioned—the one she and Thom visited when he first came to Freasa. He needed to clear his head.

"But how could Thom not know?" he yelled again. It wasn't his place to push. "Turg! Why not?"

He knew why. Pa had told him how he'd lost his first love that way, before he'd met Da.

Jonathan got up. He wanted to kiss Thom. It had taken every ounce of self-control not to grab him and press his lips to his. His head was ready to burst. And his heart.

"Arrggh," he shouted, resuming his pacing.

He whispered, "Lightworker-Sens, what am I supposed to do?"

Jonathan didn't expect an answer, but he hoped. He needed to make sense of this. Raking his hands through his hair, he gripped it briefly at the roots.

"It would almost be easier if I never saw him again," he whispered, his words heavy with despair.

But even as he said it, he knew it was a lie.

He needed something to help him sleep. Valerian root tea would do.

Bright skies greeted Samiltun the following morning as he stepped out of his manor. The snow had finally melted. Winter had been long and harsh, slowing the twins' efforts to locate gems. They'd found nothing near the city's eastern edge, yet he remained certain a hidden hoard awaited him. Was it their failure... or his? Of course, it wasn't his. He simply needed to push them harder. Offering them a little gratitude might boost their motivation.

Yesterday, he'd spent the morning with his Finders crew. With his income up, he no longer needed them, but he believed anyone careless enough to get robbed didn't deserve their goods. Success had made him more generous with the crew: more food, better clothes, which helped them blend in among the wealthy. His new DP excelled at feigning innocence laced with sorrow, and trained the others accordingly. They were doing well. He even felt a bit of fondness for them.

Nonsense!

Caring made him soft. Enough lollygagging. He had a meeting with Connemara today to hear about new gem sites.

Tovah had been struggling with her gift lately. After her comparative faiths class, she dropped her books off in her room and felt intense heat spread through her body. She hadn't been walking fast, and her room was cool, despite it being late Aprali. Usually, she only felt energy flow out of her stomach when using her gift. Her flushed state brought back the morning a month ago, when she'd woken to find her clothes and bedding damp.

She quickly removed her tunic, wiped down at the basin, and changed into a dry one. She was grateful to have a washbasin in her room. Last summer, while the academs were away, metalworkers extended the washroom pipes, adding one to every room.

Reflecting on her faith class, Tovah felt a surge of delight. She appreciated learning how others viewed the world and life. Thom and Mekial told her about the Aaliswan belief, including that each person carried the One's breath, which she understood as the soul. She admired the Lumenventian's community's mission to help people remember their innate goodness and discover their purpose. Reincarnation confused her, but Mekial reassured her that some Aaliswans didn't believe in it. Next week, they were covering her family's faith, Ludaisan. She was glad her friends would learn about it.

Mekial came to mind again. She was really nice, and Tovah was fond of her and grateful her family had gotten to know her. On their camping trip, she'd been helpful, chopping firewood and washing pots after meals. She often talked about growing up in Glakkadeth and had even started teaching Tovah Glakkadian. Thom had lent her his Glakkadian grammar books. When using the workbook, she had to resist the temptation to peek at his answers.

Her thoughts drifted back to her gift. She needed to speak with Kee soon.

The same day, Thom sat in Lamen's office. He opened his eyes, the meditation fresh in his mind. Lamen had just guided him to sense that all things were made of the same divine stuff.

"How was that?"

"Well," Thom began, "I felt connected to the birds and deer. Their energy felt like mine. It's the first time I've seen animals in my Sanctuary."

"Good. What about the trees, plants, and flowers?"

"That was harder. I understand they're alive, but it's strange to think we're connected."

"And the earth, mountains, and water?"

"I couldn't feel anything. You'd think I would with water, at least, since it moves. I tried hard."

"Did you push yourself when it wasn't working?"

"Probably."

"And, what did I say?"

"Pushing comes from my mind and takes me out of the present."

"And?"

"It ungrounds me, if that's a word."

"Maybe," Lamen said with a half-smile. "You do tend to do that when a task doesn't come easily. That's the opposite of what this practice calls for. Relax. Let the connection emerge."

"OK."

"Anything else you want to tell me?"

Thom shook his head. He didn't want to bring up his rift with Jonathan. They hadn't spoken since that night two weeks ago, and he couldn't figure out why. It hurt.

On the ride back to the Acadium, he distracted himself by thinking about what was coming up. Exams were near, and he dreaded them. No matter how often he tried to convince himself otherwise, he worried he'd forget everything once the test began. His teachers had praised his work, and Mac was pleased with his help in the Rejuvenary. His physical-healing gift had grown. Not as much as Jonathan's. No. He wouldn't be jealous. Each person had their own gifts.

He planned to spend most of the summer with his family. Kavan had written about a hidden spot down the hill from home where Kami could stay safely, a place he'd stumbled upon during a winter whiteout. Thom was eager to help his Mam with patients and work clay beside his Da.

He let his mind rest, trusting Apollo to find the way. For the rest of the ride, Thom tuned into the energy around him through his earth sense. Without effort, tingling spread through his body, and he finally felt an expansive oneness with everything. He longed to share this with Jonathan.

At the recommendation of his friend, the Baron, Samiltun agreed to meet with a horse dealer at the Peat Inn, one of Freasa's most expensive establishments. The man was searching for an anniversary gift. Baron had suggested Samiltun might have something.

He did need a few horses, including one for himself. He wasn't sure of the breed of his current mount, taken five years ago from the old manor. Now, Samiltun wanted a horse strong and proud, and one that matched his status as a shrewd merchant.

Dismounting in front of the inn, he handed the reins to a groom and stepped toward the door held open by a porter. The flower boxes at the front of the building caught his eye, splashes of color whose scent lingered in the Mei air. Shaking himself, he mumbled, "Focus."

"Welcome, Lord Samiltun," the innkeeper greeted him. "Merchant Lodan and his son are already seated in a private room. Please follow me."

"Lord Samiltun," said a tall, muscular man with dark brown hair and a trim beard, rising to greet him. "I'm Andrey Lodan," he added, extending a hand. "This is my younger son, Dermot."

"Good to meet you, sir," Dermot said, standing.

"Same to you, Lodan, young man."

"We met briefly over a year ago at the Disime Solstice fair," Dermot offered. "You were at a food booth deciding what to drink, and I suggested Timbu."

Samiltun frowned. What? Did this boy think he remembered everyone he met?

"Why don't we sit?" Andrey said quickly. "What would you like to drink? I'll be covering the cost of our meal today."

When the meeting concluded, Samiltun left the inn satisfied. In exchange for five horses, including a purebred Muiragan mount for himself, Lodan would receive a raw diamond from the most recent vein the twins had discovered. Lodan planned to have it cut by a trusted jeweler for use in several pieces. His son spoke little during the meal, but what he said revealed he was knowledgeable. Samiltun sensed envy, perhaps resentment, toward the older brother, who held a more prominent role in the business.

Enough of that. He shifted his attention to the next expedition. In two days, Connemara would take the twins to a newly discovered cave: one he claimed was ideal for pushing their gifts to the limit, and making diamonds.

Chapter 39

"Aaaaaaaaaagh," Oddi screamed, jerking upright in bed. It was still dark outside.

Footsteps pounded down the hall, and his door flew open.

"Oddi, are you OK?" his Da asked, breathless at his bedside.

"I...I don't know," he replied, wiping sweat from his face.

"Your pajamas are soaked."

He tugged at his shirt, which clung to him. His pants were no better. "Yuck."

His Da sat beside him. "Did you have a nightmare?"

"It didn't seem like one. It was scary, but it felt real."

"Was it about your birthday next month?"

"No."

"What do you remember?"

"That's the weird part. I always forget my nightmares. This time, I can picture every bit of it."

"Tell me."

Oddi's mother rushed in, catching his last words. "Sorry I didn't come immediately. The twins were crying. Keelin's with them. What happened?" she asked, sitting on his other side.

"The city was on fire. Buildings were shaking. A few collapsed. People were running and screaming. Some had blood on their faces and clothes."

"Did you see yourself?" Mamie prompted.

"No."

"Peth, it could be a foretelling," Niamh suggested. "Kee mentioned Oddi might have the gift."

"A foretelling," Oddi echoed, his blue eyes wide.

"We'll speak with Seer Trethlyn."

"OK. But I saw one more thing."

"What?" his Da asked.

"Thom. Flying on Kami."

"We definitely need to talk with Trethlyn... and Thom," his mother added.

"Think you can get back to sleep?" Peth asked.

"Maybe."

"Let's get you out of those wet clothes first," Niamh said, reaching for his waistband.

"I've got it."

"I used to change you all the time."

"Yeah, but I can do it now."

After breakfast, Thom tossed another pair of trousers onto his unmade bed to pack. He was flying home this afternoon. Strange how casual it seemed to think that. He wouldn't be flying with Jonathan. The last time felt like ages ago—before that awful night when things changed between them. He'd loved the feel of Jonathan's arms around him, even with both of them strapped in. Mekial had told him that Jonathan had left earlier that morning.

His eyes traveled around the room. What else should he take? His staff, definitely. He needed to continue his exercises. Maybe Meli would spar with him if he could find a long stick for her. His gaze landed on the bookcase where his treasure jar sat. It was staying. He hadn't added anything since his guardian angel sent an owlet to drop a feather so many years before.

A month before his fight with Jonathan, Thom had helped him connect with his own guardian angel. The next day, a blue feather blew into Jonathan's face during training. That night, he dreamed of an angel wearing that color.

After strapping the bag closed, Thom proceeded to make his bed. Jonathan used to say that a tidy bed made the whole room seem neater, even if everything else was messy. He sighed. He had to stop thinking about him.

He was pulling up the bedspread when a wave of vertigo hit, and he sat down abruptly. Thom sensed he should lower his latest shield, his sixth, meant to protect him from overwhelm, now that he felt connected to all things. Archangel Michael had suggested it last year. A disturbance pulsed through him, its source unclear. He lowered the rest of his shields, hoping for clarity. Nothing came.

Gang, he mind-spoke, *if there's anything you can tell me, I'm open. And thanks in advance.*

He was about to drop books off when a knock came at the door.

"Come in."

Noiri entered, sweat staining her tunic, unusual for the provost. Her hair was tied back. Wisps clung to her flushed face.

"Niamh and Peth asked for us."

"Is everything OK?"

"Not sure. A guard found me, and said we're to come to their small audience chamber."

"OK. I need to stop by the library first."

"I'll head to Cleirigh Hall once I've cleaned up. I came straight from a run."

When he arrived at the chamber, Thom identified himself and then passed through the guards stationed outside. Stepping inside, he said, "Good morning, Niamh and Peth. Oh... and Oddi."

"Good morning," Peth replied. "Help yourself to Timbu. We always keep it on hand, even in the Spring."

"Thanks."

Thom poured himself a mugful. The Acadium and Keep recently added mugs to their dishware, preferring them since they held more than a cup, and didn't require a saucer. He grabbed a cinnamon twist as well. Just as he bit into it, Noiri entered, accompanied by an older woman with gray hair pinned in a bun.

"Oh, good, you're here," Niamh said, rising. "Thanks for coming. Please, have a seat. Thom and Trethy, first, some introductions. I think you'll find them quite interesting."

A puzzled expression crossed Thom's face.

"Do you remember the supper at Paddi's before your first year?"

"Yes."

"And the visions we told you about?"

"I'm still shocked anyone would have one about me."

"Is this the boy we saw all those years ago?" the older woman inquired.

"It is. Thom, this is Seer Trethlyn, one of the people who had them."

"Wow. Um...thank you. If not for you, Rin might never have found me."

"No thanks necessary, young man. Seer Arion, Lalia, and I often wondered what became of you. Are you as gifted as we believed?"

"Um," Thom mumbled, embarrassed.

"He is, Trethy," Peth answered. "Even if he is too modest to admit it. He's saved lives, including our twins."

"We didn't think it was our place to ask."

Thom stayed quiet.

"Speaking of gifts," Niamh added, "that's why we brought you here. We believe Oddi's had his first foretelling. And it's disturbing."

Thom found it curious how closely she echoed the word he'd thought earlier.

"Tell them what you saw, Oddi," Niamh encouraged. "Trethy, feel free to ask questions."

After a thorough exchange, during which the seer drew out all she could, Trethy shook her head.

"Does that mean you don't think Oddi had a foretelling?" Peth asked.

"Actually, I'm certain he did. But I didn't like what he saw. And I can't quite believe that Thom will fly on a mythical creature."

"Oh," Thom said, glancing at Niamh and Peth, who nodded. "The dragon's real. Her name's Kami."

"Hmm."

"You don't seem surprised, Seer Trethlyn," Thom commented.

"I've heard quite a few unusual visions to be taken aback by much these days. And please call me Trethy."

"We apologize for not telling you sooner," Peth added. "We haven't told many to avoid panic."

"I understand."

"Back to Oddi's vision," Niamh continued. "It seems like the fire causes buildings to collapse. But we have no idea how it starts, when, or where."

"Sorry," Oddi muttered.

"It's not your fault," Trethy assured him. "When Lalia first had visions, she couldn't give much detail either. It's promising that your gift enables you to hear. We'll help you strengthen it."

"Thanks... I think," he said, his voice unsteady.

"About the fire," Peth interrupted, "Should we send inspectors to check on building safety?"

"Where would we send them?" Noiri asked. "Freasa has quite a few buildings."

"True."

"What if we put the fire brigades on high alert?" Niamh suggested.

"Do they even know about foretelling?" Trethy asked.

"They don't," Peth replied. "We've kept that quiet for security reasons. But we could ask them to run fire drills."

"Brilliant," Niamh said. "I'll send a message to the fire chief."

"Sorry to cut in," Thom said, "but in Oddi's vision, he saw me riding Kami. Does that mean she'll be visible? Or only to him because he met her?"

"Can you check?" Noiri asked.

"Worth a try," Thom said, closing his eyes.

Everyone fell silent. This time, Trethy looked puzzled.

Coming out of his chat with Kami, Thom said, "She thinks Oddi saw us because they've spent time together."

"Good," Peth said. "Any other questions, Thom?"

"My turn to interrupt," Trethy said. "What did you do?"

"I can use mind-speech to talk with Kami," Thom explained.

"That's some gift," Trethy said.

"Are we done?" Niamh asked. "I want to find a messenger."

"One more thing, if you don't mind," Thom said. When she shook her head, he added, "I had an unusual... incident earlier." He then gave a brief account of it.

"Thom," Trethy asked, "I knew you had earth sense from our visions, but it seems like you have a touch of prescience?"

"I do."

""All right," Niamh said, standing. "Thanks for coming. Please watch for smoke or any other signs of danger, especially if you go downtown. Thom, let us know if you have any further incidents. We'll tell you if Oddi remembers anything more or has another vision."

Heading out, Thom knew his summer plans were now delayed. He sighed. There was no telling when the event in Oddi's vision might occur. But if it happened soon, and the fire and damage were limited to one part of the city, there might be time for him to fly home for a while.

Chapter 40

After a leisurely supper at a city tavern, Samiltun rode toward the cave where Connemara and the twins were extracting diamonds. The heat was wicked. Before leaving his manor, he'd ordered his servants to fill three waterskins. He didn't want the girls collapsing, though the cave would likely be cooler.

Wiping sweat from his brow, he shook his head. He'd considered delaying the work until the weather broke, but there was no relief in sight. A potential client was offering a substantial sum for a five-carat diamond, and he was determined that the twins would find one today.

Samiltun kept his pace slow so the gelding wouldn't overheat; he'd have preferred to ride Phoenix, his purebred buckskin with a black mane and tail, but wanted to keep him out of the sun. He'd named him after a horse he loved as a boy, one that belonged to the innkeeper where his mother worked, and that the stable manager had let him ride occasionally.

As he passed below the Keep plateau, he smiled faintly. Life had been hard back then, but he'd been happy, remembering how his mother often said, 'Love you, Rue.' That was until... No. He wouldn't think about it.

"Get out of my way," Samiltun snapped at a group of older women chatting in the road.

"I thought we'd gotten through," lamented Spirit-guide Resolute, Ruefell's higher self.

"For a little while we did," Turil replied, his guardian angel.

"True," another being said—the higher self of Ruefell's mother. "He even remembered my incarnate used to call him Rue. Those were good years. Rue's father made sure she had a secure position. It's deeply upsetting that Rue paid to have the wife and others killed."

"Not to mention his own father."

"He was bitter."

The three gathered in Resolute's dwelling, watching as Ruefell rode across the city.

"He's shown kindness toward Lena and Leesha," Turil added. "His heart seemed to open a little."

"I agree," Resolute replied. "But then memories of his mother surfaced again, and his heart hardened."

"Perhaps it's a beginning," Turil offered. "Let's keep sending him love, and reminders of who he once was."

Samiltun traveled a little-used road that skirted the left side of the plateau. He studied the mountain beyond, where a sheer rock face marked an ancient break. Eventually, he reached a clump of trees beside a tethered horse and cart. After securing his own, he stepped behind the trees and approached the rock face, where a cave lay hidden. From the front, the entrance was invisible, concealed by a slab. It revealed itself by circling to the right.

Inside, lanterns lit the cave, stretching back a hundred yards to where the twins were working.

Hearing him approach, Connemara called out, "Lord Samiltun, Lena and Leesha are making progress. They've already found a few diamonds. There's quite a bit of carbon, and I'm certain we'll find rich veins."

"Good."

"Lena, Leesha, come greet Lord Samiltun."

The twins crawled out of an opening barely four feet high and three wide.

"Good afternoon, sir" Lena greeted him.

Leesha gave a quick curtsy, which was comical given her smudged tunic and trousers. Curiously, the dirt on her clothes was identical to her twin's, even down to the marks on their cheeks.

"I heard you found more diamonds."

"Yes, sir," Lena replied. "We wanted to tell you what we figured out about our gift."

"What's that?"

"When we hold hands, we kind of feel the carbon in the walls. Mr. Connemara said diamonds come from pressed carbon. Leesha wondered if we could help press it more, remember?" she said to her sister.

"You think you can make more diamonds?" Samiltun asked, recalling his earlier hopes.

"We did. Small ones at least," Lena admitted, pulling slivers from her pocket. "We made a few, but it wore us out. We ate the leftover bread and were about to try again when you came."

Could he use his gift to boost their energy? "Girls, how are you feeling now?"

"Starving," Lena said. "But there wasn't any more food."

"I've got a few apples and a bag of biscuits with the chocolate bits you like. Would that do?" He caught himself wondering why he had the sudden urge to indulge them. Then again, if it meant more diamonds, it was an investment.

Leesha nodded so fast it was a miracle her head stayed on.

"Come and sit."

The twins quickly devoured the food, washing it down with water.

"Ready to try again?" Connemara asked.

"Yes, sirs," Lena replied.

"I'll stay out here and send you energy," Samiltun said.

Once in place, Lena called, "We're ready."

Samiltun pictured a cord linking him to the twins and began channeling energy, careful not to overextend himself. The sharp chip of metal on stone reached his ears.

After some minutes, Connemara called, "How's it going?"

"Something's happening," Lena replied. "We feel pressure around the vein. And it's warmer in here."

Samiltun maintained the flow. He was certain this would work.

"Sir, it's Leesha. We have more slivers and they're bigger."

Leesha's voice caught him off guard. Until now, Lena had done most of the talking.

"Good job, Leesha… and you, Lena," he called.

But slivers weren't enough. Samiltun wanted stones over a thousand carats. With unlimited wealth came the power and control he craved. No one would mistreat him again. He knew where that came from.

His first year after adoption had been good, but everything changed after a visit from the sister of his father's late wife. His father didn't disown him, but he treated Samiltun like a servant, assigning him chores like cleaning the stalls and working in the kitchen. His father never called him Rue again.

"Sir? Sir?" Connemara repeated. "Do you want Lena and Leesha to keep going?"

"Hmm. What was that?"

"Should the twins continue?"

"Yes."

After some time, Lena called out, "It's working. There's a spot where the carbon's all packed together. It feels like it's ready to turn into diamonds, but we're getting tired again."

"I was going to say that," Leesha complained.

"I have an idea. I'm coming in."

"OK," Leesha said. "But be careful. The opening has sharp rocks."

"I will," Samiltun assured her. She's worried about me. It unsettled him.

Crouching low, he crawled in, scraping his knees. His trousers would be ruined, but if it worked, it wouldn't matter.

Samiltun placed one hand on each girl's shoulders and resumed channeling energy. The effect was instantaneous. He truly was quite brilliant.

"There's more pressure now," Lena said. "I can feel larger pieces forming."

"Push more," he urged. "I want stones bigger than your fist."

"We'll try," Leesha answered.

It was risky, but Samiltun channeled even more energy. He had to. Sweat dripped from his brow as he noticed how damp their clothes had become.

"It's working, sir," Lena informed him. "I'm not sure how much longer we can do it."

"Stay with it," he coaxed. "You can do this. I'll be able to help your family more. Give it your all!"

A low rumble echoed, and the chamber shook.

The girls screamed.

Acting on instinct, Samiltun threw himself over them as the shaking intensified.

Rocks crashed from the walls and roof. One of the girls cried out as a stone struck her arm. More fell, with several hitting Samiltun's back.

Everything went black.

Chapter 41

Thom was about to climb onto Kami for an afternoon flight, when he froze. A deep unease gripped him, as if the land itself was sending him a warning.

The ground lurched. He threw his arms around his whimpering dragon. In the distance, horses whinnied in terror. The shaking worsened, feeling endless. Oddi's vision was coming true.

Loud cracks split the air, followed by crashes and the sharp tinkle of glass. From the Royal Residence? Thom hoped the family was safe.

When the shaking stopped, silence fell, brief and eerie. Then came the screams. He had to help.

"Kami, are you OK?"

Mostly.

Thom felt her lungs heaving beneath him. "Are you sure?"

Yeah.

"What was that?"

An earthshake. That's what I remember they're called. They haven't happened in a long time.

"I gotta see if anyone's hurt."

Go.

When he left the play yard, a thick cloud of dust rose ahead. A tower atop Cleirigh Hall was gone. He smelled smoke. In this heat, fire would spread fast. Where to first?

Check on the family, came a voice.

At the back entrance of the residence, Thom saw the twisted frame. He hurled himself against the door, but it wouldn't budge. A thin wail rose from within.

He ran around to the side where the sitting room windows were. Shattered glass littered the ground; shards clung to the window edges. Now he could hear babies crying. He had to get in.

Stripping off his tunic, Thom used it to clear the remaining glass from one window, then draped it over the sill. He carefully crawled through, not wanting to cut himself.

As he dropped to the floor, another earthshake began. The walls heaved and shuddered, the motion rolling beneath him like the ocean swells he and Mekial had ridden years ago. He grabbed a chair for balance as books tumbled from a shelf. The room was in chaos: smashed vases, mug shards, and pieces of the mantle clock scattered across the carpet. A side table had fallen on the playpen. Thank God it was empty.

"Can anyone hear me?" Thom shouted.

"Who's there?" came a male voice.

It sounded like Peth. "Thom."

"I'm in the kitchen. I need your help with Keelin."

Thom dashed down the hall, carefully stepping over photographs of the twins, Oddi, and the whole family. In the kitchen, pots, pans, and broken dishes covered the floor and counters. Keelin lay moaning beneath the tall cupboard. Peth crouched beside her.

"Help me move this."

Thom could only see her head and left foot, the leather shoe dusted with grit but sitting at a natural angle. He moved to the side across from Peth.

"Help me," Keelin whispered, her eyes wide with fear, and her skin the color of chalk.

"We have to be careful," Peth said. "If it tilts, it'll crush her foot. We need to lift it off."

"OK," Thom replied, hoping he was strong enough.

"On three. One, two, three."

Thom strained. The cupboard barely lifted.

"Aaagh," Keelin cried before passing out.

"Turg!" Peth cursed. "We need help, but I don't think anyone's coming soon. Let me think."

While he did, Thom scanned her. A bump rose on the back of her head, but his focus snapped to her hidden right leg. He could sense it was crushed and bleeding.

Archangel Raphael and healing angels, we need your help. Thank you for joining your gifts with mine. Energy surged through him as he directed it into Keelin's body.

She has damage to a few of her organs, Thom, came Rafe's voice in his mind.

Thanks. I need to check her spirit.

Thom dropped his fifth shield. Her spirit had a gray tinge, but she wasn't dying. At least not yet. Returning his attention to her leg, he sensed a dish shard jabbing her upper thigh, near her groin. From his anatomy class, he knew a main artery ran there.

"I have an idea," Peth said. "I'll move to your side. If we tilt it together, I might be able to pull her free."

"OK."

"Together, on three."

They lifted the cupboard higher, but when Peth dropped one hand to pull her free, Thom couldn't hold its weight on his own.

Hey, Thom called to his divine advisors, *which one of you can lend me strength?*

"Another idea. Use the wooden stool to prop it up," Peth said, pointing to one overturned nearby.

"Hello-oo," Thom called aloud toward his advisors again. "A little help, please."

Peth stared at him, brows drawn, clearly baffled by his outburst. Then he stretched toward the stool and grabbed it.

Once they had one corner braced, Peth said, "Now lift the bottom. Go."

"O...K..." Thom huffed. He really needed more strength training with Dek.

"Good," Peth said, pulling the cook clear.

Thom dropped the cupboard with a groan and examined Keelin. Blood gushed from her leg. Crouching, he pressed his hands over the wound and spotted the shard, now dislodged and lying on her trousers. "I need cloth for a tourniquet. And something to tighten it."

"Right," Peth said, snatching an apron from a hook and a long wooden spoon from the counter, before handing them over.

Thom had secured the tourniquet when Niamh rushed in with one twin. Oddi was close behind, carrying the other. Both, now two and a half, were crying. Tressa was pointing to her arm and repeating, "Owie."

"I heard a crash," Niamh said, breathless.

"We're OK. Thom dropped the cupboard."

"I'm glad you're here."

Thom noticed a bruise forming on Terrin's arm; right where Tressa pointed at hers. Kee had explained that twins were aware of what the other felt. He didn't detect injuries on Oddi. But a cut drew his eye. "Niamh, your forehead."

"It's nothing." She stepped toward Keelin. "That's a lot of blood! Oddi, take the twins to the library. They shouldn't see this. And be careful, books likely have fallen."

After he left, Niamh asked, "How is she?"

"Not good," Thom said. "Her liver and bladder are damaged, and her leg's crushed. At least the bleeding's stopped. I wish Jonathan or Mac were here."

"You're all we've got," Peth said.

"Since she's still unconscious, can we move her to the sofa in the sitting room?"

"Certainly," Niamh said. "I'll clear a path."

Peth and Thom were about to lift her when two guards, a man and a woman, ran in.

"Your Majesties, are you OK?" they asked.

"Yes. But Keelin's not," Peth replied.

The female guard gasped. "That's bad."

What about Oddi and the twins?" the other asked.

"In the library, Cetrin," Niamh said, addressing the male guard. "A table fell on their pen and hit Terrin's arm, but Tressa and Oddi are fine."

"Tamsin," Peth asked, "can you and Cetrin carry Keelin to the sitting room?"

After they laid her on the sofa, Cetrin asked, "Anything else we can do?"

"Check on the twins," Niamh said.

"Certainly," he said, then left.

"I need to check Keelin over more carefully and clean her up, but I could use a wet cloth."

"I'll get one," Oddi said, just then stepping into the room. "Guard Cetrin's with Tressa and Terrin. He's playing with them to keep them distracted. As usual, Tressa's in charge. And Terrin keeps talking to someone we can't see."

Sounds like their gifts are showing early, Thom observed. "Do you have any healing supplies? When she wakes, I'd like to give her valerian root to keep her sedated."

"We don't," Niamh said. "How stupid of us. Some monarchs we are."

"Nim... hon," Peth said, "we'll sort that out another time."

"I can run to the Acadium and ask Healer Mac," Oddi interrupted, rushing back in with the wet cloth. "I want to help."

"Slow down, Oddi," Peth warned. "We don't want you tripping over debris."

"Tamsin, did you come from Cleirigh Hall?" Niamh asked.

"Yes."

"How bad is it?"

"Terrible. A whole wing's gone where the tower fell. Cetrin and I didn't stay because we were sent to check on you."

"Oh Deu!" Niamh whispered in horror. "That means many injuries... deaths. Which wing?"

"The diplomatic wing, Your Majesty," Tamsin said.

"I don't think many were staying there. Do you, Peth?"

"Most should've left by now. We'll find out. What about the lower levels? Workers might've been in the storage rooms."

"I don't know, Your Majesty," Tamsin replied.

"I'm going to the Hall," Niamh said. "They need to see we're willing to help."

"Um, Niamh," Thom interrupted, "let someone check your injury. At least cover it with a bandage."

"OK," she conceded.

"I'll come as soon as I can," Peth said. After she left, he asked Thom, "Any change?"

"Her spirit's stronger, but I could use another healer."

"I'm here," Jonathan said, running in with a bag. "I've got valerian root and other medicines."

"I thought you went home."

"I was at my aunt and uncle's when the earth shook. I rode back to the Acadium as fast as I could to help."

"What's happened there?" Peth asked.

"The building's intact. There were minor injuries from what I saw, since most academs had left. But the Rejuvenary's a mess. Broken glass and jars everywhere. Mac said the last patient was discharged yesterday."

"Is she on her way to the Hall?" Peth asked.

"No, she's gone downtown with an academ healer."

Peth exhaled sharply. "What's the situation there?"

"My cousin and I came from the north, so I didn't see everything. But I passed homes with cracked walls and broken windows. As I rode up to the school, I saw smoke and fire in the southwest. Couldn't tell where exactly."

"I've got to find out," Peth said.

"Can I go with you, Da," Oddi asked.

"No. Stay with your sister and brother, since your mother and I won't be here."

"OK," he said, then blurted, "Another one's coming."

Before Peth could respond, the ground shook.

"Hold on!" Tamsin yelled.

When it stopped, Oddi asked, "Why does it keep doing that?"

"We'll talk to Geologist Aoife Ashlin," Peth said, "Now I'm torn. I want to know if more shakes are coming, but I'm not sure if you should find your mother or come with me."

"Oddi should go with you," Thom said. He wasn't sure why. He just felt it.

"OK. Oddi, let's go. But do exactly as I say. If you sense another shake, tell me so we can warn others."

"OK, Da," he said, following him down the hall toward the front door.

"Jonathan, did you see Kee at the Acadium?" Thom asked.

"I did. Tovah was with her. They were deep in conversation, but I didn't stop."

"Tamsin, can you find them? I don't have any authority, but Archangel Ariel suggested they could help elsewhere in the Keep."

"Archangel…" Tasmin muttered, shaking her head. "On it."

"Jonathan, can you help with Keelin?"

"What do you need?"

Thom couldn't tell if Jonathan was still upset with him. For now, he had to focus on Keelin. "Her liver and bladder were injured. See what you can do. I'll focus on her leg."

Jonathan went to work.

When Thom looked up again, Jonathan was lifting his hands from her abdomen.

"Both are repaired. As is a tear in her lower intestine."

"Good," Thom said, hesitating. How… are you?"

"Need food. My energy's low. You?"

"Same. I hope Peth and Niamh don't mind us raiding their pantry."

"I'm sure they wouldn't."

"Could you get us something? Also, Keelin's coming around. Would you put on a pot of water for valerian tea for her?"

When Jonathan returned with tea, bread, and cheese, Keelin was conscious, insisting she had to make dinner.

"Keelin," Thom said quietly, "you're hurt. Take deep breaths and drink this." He looked at Jonathan. "She's in shock and has lost so much blood. Her heart's racing."

"We need her kidney to produce more blood. You eat. I've got this."

When Thom finished, Keelin's skin color had improved. But her right leg worried him. Pointing, he said, "Her calf muscles down to her ankle are crushed. "What do you think?"

Jonathan crouched beside her foot, removed her sock and stocking, and brushed his fingers across the sole. The skin was already cool, faintly bluish. "No nerve response. It can't be saved," he said, shaking his head sadly.

Thom's chest tightened. It was hard to accept—Keelin was a good friend. But this injury was beyond repair.

Guard Cetrin entered. "Is there anything I can do? The twins are napping."

"Yes," Thom said. "Go to the Rejuvenary and see if someone can help us carry Keelin there? We'll watch the twins."

"Will do."

Chapter 42

After settling Keelin, Jonathan and Thom began treating the injured as they arrived. Two maintenance workers had been struck by falling debris on the lower level. A third, their coworker, had been crushed and didn't survive. Keep guards had brought them in. Thom recognized one of them.

"Ronan. You've got a cut on your cheek."

"Yeah. Niamh told me to get it checked when we brought the others."

"How are Ciarenn and Rilla?"

"They're at the Keep, searching for the injured," he said, his voice catching. "We found... others... their bodies were... " He doubled over and vomited. "Sorry."

"I'll take care of that... and your gash," Thom said, placing a hand on his arm.

He had tied off the last stitch when he heard a cart outside. Mac and Mekial entered, carrying a teenage boy on a makeshift litter fashioned from a torn blanket. His breathing was shallow and labored.

"Jonathan, his lungs—he was in a burning building," Mac called. "Can you help?"

"Certainly," he said, hurrying over.

"Two academ healers, and one full healer, Kirren, are on the way," she added.

"That's a relief," Thom said. "Mekial, you're not with Tovah?"

"No. Her gift's grown. She can sense what's happening underground, even when a building's collapsed. She thought I'd be more useful downtown. That's where I ran into Mac. Thom, bringing the injured here on foot or horse was too slow. Could Kami help with the seriously injured?"

"Smart. I'll tell Kirren I'm needed elsewhere."

"The worst is in Prun-shees quarter. I'll meet you there."

"No, you're coming with me."

"But... I've never..."

"Sorry. I should've taken you up before."

"It's fine. You like going with...," she said, glancing at Jonathan bent over the girl.

Thom hadn't realized anyone had noticed. "You can guide us to the injured," he said, avoiding mention of flying.

"How are you doing back there?" Thom yelled.

"Great," Mekial called, excited. "Am I holding on too tight?"

"You're good."

She whooped, then fell quiet. "I shouldn't be happy, not with people hurt or worse."

"I see smoke and fire ahead."

"To the right is a large courtyard with a healer's station."

"I can't land Kami there."

"Let's get closer."

"There's a warehouse with a gated yard," Thom announced. *Kami,* he mind-spoke, *can you land there?*

It'll be tight, but yes.

It was difficult, but at least the wind wasn't blowing smoke their way.

"I hope the owners don't mind," Thom said after both had climbed down. "Who's treating the injured?"

"Healer Sean Finnell."

Thom had worked with Finnell before he graduated and set up shop downtown.

"Let's find him." *Kami, we'll be back... with at least one passenger.*

OK.

They slipped through the gate and ran to the courtyard. Thom spotted Sean near a row of covered bodies.

"Sean," he called.

"Thom? Can you help? I've got one academ healer, but I need your gifts."

"Of course. I have quick transport if someone needs to get to the Rejuvenary fast."

"I don't follow."

"I'll show you when it's needed."

"Time to search for more injured," Mekial said.

She ran two blocks toward a building with cracked walls and a canted doorway. Flames licked at one side.

"Help," a woman cried from a third-floor window. "My children and I are trapped!"

A dirt and sweat-covered man pounded on the door. "I'm coming, Shayla. I'll get you out. I promise."

"The smoke's getting thicker," she yelled, coughing.

"I'll help," Mekial said.

Together, they pushed the door wide enough to squeeze through. A fallen beam kept it from opening fully.

Mekial eyed the twisted stairway, half-buried in debris but usable.

"We're in, Shayla," the man called.

"Sir," Mekial said, "I'll clear a path. Can you find something to douse the flames upstairs?"

"I hope so." He dashed to the kitchen basin.

When he returned with a sloshing bucket, Mekial had pushed aside enough debris to begin to climb. "Let's go."

Staying close to the intact posts, they carefully ascended to the third floor, where broken wood planks and roof shingles blocked a door.

"We're by the door, Shayla!"

"DaDa," two young voices cried. "It hurts to breathe."

"Dev," Shayla cried, "the fire's from the shop next door. Our wall's on fire. Hurry!"

They removed the blockage, but the doorframe was warped.

"Turg," Dev muttered.

"Together, on three," Mekial shouted.

They burst in. Shayla and the children ran to Dev, hugging him.

Mekial grabbed the bucket and flung the water at the flames, but it barely helped. "We've got to get out!"

"She's right," Dev replied. "Miss, lead us down."

They moved quickly. Once on the first floor, a fresh jolt rocked the building.

"Not another one," Shayla wailed.

Overhead, beams cracked. Mekial knew everything was about to come down. "Digi! We'll be crushed," she screamed in Glakkadian.

With no time to think, she raised her arms, picturing a larger shield than the one she'd created to heal Liv. "Help angels," she cried. A blue-robed angel appeared in her mind. Power surged up her legs, into her body, and out her outstretched hands as the ceiling collapsed.

When the rumbling stopped, they were untouched, but surrounded by wreckage: crumbled walls and flooring, and splintered furniture.

They were alive. How did she do that? *Archangel Michael, did you help?*

I did, Mekial. I'm certain Thom mentioned me.

Yeah.

Like you once told him, you're purpose is to protect. Your gift finally emerged. I'm your teacher now.

That's great, but how do we get out? The fire's getting closer.

You'll figure it out. Everything you need is in front of you.

"How did you do that?" Dev asked.

"I don't know. We need to move, and fast," Mekial said, switching back to Dochalan.

Her eyes swept the room. The path to the door was now impassable. Twenty feet to the left, faint light filtered through a window, partially hidden by a sofa. Two boards leaned over it, forming an inverted V.

"We can crawl through to the window."

"But isn't part of the roof blocking it?" Dev asked.

"It's our only option."

At the window, Dev and Mekial smashed the glass, which somehow remained intact.

"Dev, the fire's spreading," Shayla yelled, panicked.

"Quick. Push the debris," Mekial grunted, throwing her weight against it, as flames crept closer. *Archangel Michael, a little more help?*

It's coming.

A section gave way, revealing a soot-smudged face. "Give me your hand," the man called.

"Ciarenn?" Mekial asked.

"Yes," he said, helping them through.

"How?" she said, dumbfounded.

"King Pethuric sent us into the city. I was heading to the healer's station when I heard screams."

"Thanks. You saved us."

"And you, miss," Dev said. "I'm sorry. What's your name?"

"Mekial."

"I can't thank you enough, Mekial... and Ciarenn," Shayla added.

"You're welcome."

"You're not from Docha-leigh, are you?" Dev asked.

"No, the Glakkadeth Archipelago."

"How'd you get here?"

"I'm studying at the Acadium. Let's get you to the healer station. They'll check you over and give you food and water."

"Thank you."

"Our home's gone," Shayla moaned, staring at the building now fully engulfed.

"But we're alive," Dev said.

"Let's go," Ciarenn added. "Your kids are ready to drop."

Three academs ran past. One of them was Catori, Tovah's classmate. Mekial had met the other two at Thom's party, two years before, but their names escaped her.

"Cat!" she called.

All three stopped. "Mekial?"

"Ciarenn, I'll catch up."

"OK."

"You're back," Mekial said. "Didn't you go home?"

"Yeah. But we live outside the city. My family's fine. I went to the Acadium to help and met Helean and Mardu there," she said, looking at the two beside her. "Kee asked us to search for people trapped in their homes."

"She's the mage teacher?"

"Yeah. Mardu can see through walls. And Helean's hands glow." Helean demonstrated.

"That should be a big help. Be careful."

"We will," she said, running off.

Samiltun groaned as he came to. His head throbbed, his back screamed, and blood trickled down his neck. A weight pressed into him, but his legs were remarkably free.

"Lena! Leesha!"

"Mmph bmff," came a muffled reply.

"I don't understand." As he sat up, rocks slid from his back. All was dark. He coughed in the dust-filled air. "Girls?"

"We couldn't breathe," Lena gasped, straightening from where she'd been hunched over her sister. "I'm OK. Leesha?"

Samiltun heard crying.

"My arm hurts bad," Leesha whimpered.

He felt for her arm and traced it to where it met an obstacle. It was pinned. "Lena, help me."

As they shifted a rock to free it, Leesha sobbed. A groan echoed beyond the chamber, muffled by the stone blocking the opening.

"Connemara!" Samiltun shouted.

"Yeah," came a low reply. "My ankle's broken."

"We'll deal with that soon. Did any lanterns survive?"

"Not nearby," Connemara grunted. "I see one farther down."

"Can you reach it?"

Samiltun heard dragging sounds.

"Got it. The chamber opening's blocked."

"Try clearing it."

While rocks shifted, Samiltun checked Leesha's arm again. A bone jutted from her forearm, now faintly visible in the shaft of light.

Lena swallowed hard. Leesha cried louder. He had to cover the wound.

"I can see you," Connemara said.

"Grab the cloth from the food. I want to wrap Leesha's arm."

"Here it is," he said, pushing it through the gap.

"We'll get you help once we're out. Connemara, I'll help make a bigger opening."

After clearing a section, they made the opening big enough to crawl through. Samiltun passed Leesha out first. Lena followed.

"She's covered in blood," Lena cried. "And she fainted."

"The cloth should slow the bleeding." Samiltun peered toward the tunnel bend. "It's lighter down there. Lena, see if there's another lantern. And if the entrance is blocked."

"I don't want to leave Leesha."

He was about to go when something caught his eye in the chamber, a glint. Diamonds? He had to find out. "Please, Lena."

"OK."

Samiltun needed a distraction. "Connemara, gather your things and the girls as best you can. I need to grab the girls' tools. Pass me my bag. I think I have a firestarter. I'll tear a strip from my tunic."

Connemara gave a grunt. "I'm gonna use part of mine for a sling for Leesha."

Samiltun didn't answer. He tore the cloth, rolled it tight, and lit it. The light revealed diamonds scattered across the ground—some the size of a pebble, others nearly three inches wide.

Hearing Connemara tend to Leesha, he quickly scooped the stones into his bag. It bulged, but with Connemara's ankle and Leesha's state, he doubted anyone would notice.

"I'm coming out. If you can find a broken beam or something, we'll have a torch."

Samiltun crawled from the chamber, wincing at the movement.

With the added light, Connemara found two pieces of wood. He handed Samiltun the shorter one and kept the longer as a crutch.

Torch raised, Samiltun saw Lena approach with a second lantern, dented but amazingly still lit.

"Is the way open?"

"Mostly."

Outside, they found the horses dead and the cart crushed under rocks.

"We'll have to walk," Samiltun said. "Lena, lead the way. Connemara, follow. I'll carry Leesha."

Mekial was handing tea to a patient when she spotted four figures approaching, two men and two girls, one being carried, when another tremor struck. The ground rolled beneath her. With nothing to grab, she dropped to her knees and heard a scream. The girl on her feet had fallen, along with the man leaning on a makeshift crutch.

She pushed to her feet and ran toward them. "Sean, more are coming," she called, pointing. All were coated in black dust. Her eyes fixed on the man carrying the unconscious girl; he grimaced with each step. His clothes marked him as a merchant. It was refreshing to see. When she'd passed through Dridley two years before, she'd seen such people ignore the needy.

Sean reached the group just as she did. "Let me carry her," he said to the merchant. "There's a cot in the corner."

Mekial turned to the other girl. "Are you OK?"

"I hurt my foot when I fell."

"Sean can check it after he sees to..."

"Leesha. We're identical."

Mekial wasn't surprised she couldn't tell, with the dirt on their faces. "Let me help you up." She glanced at the man with the crutch. "Is it broken?"

"I think so."

"Ciarenn," Healer Finnell called, "can you help this man to a cot?"

"Will do."

Facing the first girl, Mekial asked, "What's your name?"

"Lena. Can I stay with my sister?"

"Of course. I'm Mekial."

Samiltun sat on an overturned crate, his bag strapped to his back despite the pain. Sipping chamomile tea, he watched Sean tend Leesha. She hadn't stirred, and he was worried. He also kept an eye on the constables wandering about. Another had arrived, helping a woman with a bloodied cloth around her head.

"Lord Samiltun," Connemara said from a nearby cot, "do you think we caused the shake?"

"What?"

"Do you think you and the twins did... this?" he asked, eyeing the smoking ruins.

"Shh. I don't know." Samiltun did know but wasn't about to admit it. "How is she?" he called to Sean, the question slipping out before he could decide if it came from concern, guilt, or fear of losing a useful employee.

"Stable, but she needs advanced care. Mekial, another patient for the Rejuvenary."

"Understood. I'm afraid you won't be able to go with her, sir."

"That's fine," Samiltun said, clamping down on his emotions as a constable passed by.

"I'm going with her," Lena insisted.

"I'll be back," Sean said to Connemara. "You'll need a cast. I'll have someone take you to a healer in the city center."

"OK."

"Mekial, would you alert Thom?" Sean asked, glancing up at the sudden gust of wind with a flicker of recognition.

"Sure."

"Ciarenn, help Lena," Sean added. "I'll carry Leesha."

Samiltun watched as the healer carried her across the courtyard with the others following. Once they rounded the warehouse corner, he said, "Connemara, get yourself taken care of. I need to check my other business."

"OK, Lord Samiltun," he whispered.

Noting where the constables stood, Samiltun slipped away in the opposite direction. Had anyone overheard? That girl, Mekial, had been nearby. If she'd heard and told the authorities, they'd come for him. He needed to leave Freasa.

With what he carried, he could go anywhere. He'd have to stop by his manor to collect a few things, including Phoenix. Hopefully, his manor was standing.

Thom was wiping down Kami after delivering the last patient when Mekial ran up. "Another?"

"Yes. But there's more. Samiltun's at the healing station." She quickly explained how she knew and what his companion had asked about the shake.

Thom was stunned. He'd forgotten about the man. The notion that he might've caused the earthshake disturbed him. He needed to tell Noiri and the monarchs.

When Sean arrived with the unconscious patient, he helped him secure her. At least she didn't need sedation like the others, since she wouldn't remember flying on Kami. "I'd better get going."

"There's another passenger," Mekial said.

"Leesha's twin," Sean added, as Ciarenn came through the gate carrying a girl.

"Sorry we're late, Finn. Lena nearly passed out."

"No worries."

"Is that a draaa… " Lena began.

"She is," Thom interrupted, not wanting anyone to overhear. Kami had made herself visible to help load the patients. He needed to tell Lena to keep quiet, like he had Sean.

"Lena, up you go, behind Leesha," Sean said, trying to distract her. "You can help steady your sister if she wakes."

"I can do that."

Ciarenn called Sean, 'Finn,' Thom realized. Must be a nickname. That had also been the name of one of his abductors in Glakkadeth. Was he still in prison, cooking? He was glad he'd helped Finn remember that passion. Shaking off the memory, Thom saw Lena was secure.

"Up Kami."

A large boy tried to see through the warehouse fence. Taking a shortcut home with food from the Royal Guard headquarters, he'd stopped when he heard Macirdan's voice. His family's kitchen lay in ruins, his father screaming at him as if it were his fault. Ever since their first-year training assessment, when he saw Macirdan fall, Niall had felt strange around him. He'd watched Barran test him, then lead him to Dek for the same. Both had seemed impressed.

Niall's tester had praised his strength, but he hadn't been taken to Dek. It wasn't fair. He looked down, admiring his muscular arms, hardened by summers on the Lodan horse ranch hauling feed, tools, and saddles. His Ma said a great-aunt had married into the family. Swatting a fly from his dusty blond curls, he pressed his ear to the fence. Were there other voices? What were they doing?

A shout nearby made him flinch. It sounded like his father, always threatening punishment. Home had never felt safe. He'd better get back. "I'm gonna find out what you're doing, Macirdan."

Chapter 43

The morning after the shake, Dermot rode toward Lord Samiltun's manor. Now managing the family business, he planned to gift a prized horse to win favor and secure introductions to other nobles. He dreamed of joining their ranks.

Earlier, he'd consoled his mother and sister-in-law. An old stable had collapsed in the shake, killing his father and brother. His mother, devastated and withdrawn, refused to eat. His sister-in-law, pregnant with her second child, wasn't much better. Thankfully, a servant had taken charge of her crying toddler. Dermot had no patience for that.

Being in charge suited him. Dermot knew as much as his brother, named after his father and equally narrow-minded. Entering the manor gates, he spotted a servant sweeping up glass and rubble where a tree had crashed through a front window.

Worried Lord Samiltun might've been hurt, he called, "You! Is Lord Samiltun, all right... and... uh...everyone else?" he added, not wanting to sound callous.

"Mostly, sir. Everyone's shaken. The cook's got a lump from a falling pot."

"And Lord Samiltun," Dermot pressed, annoyed he hadn't been mentioned.

"Haven't seen him."

"What do you mean?"

"My wife saw him yesterday. He rushed in, told her to pack two saddlebags with his things, and rode off."

"Do you know where he went?"

"A stablehand said east."

"When's he returning?"

"He didn't say."

"You're no help," Dermot muttered.

"Sorry, sir. May I get back to work?"

"Go ahead. I'm not stopping you."

Dermot was about to leave when a thought struck him. "Were any horses injured?"

"One. Another ran off."

"When your lord returns, tell him I'll bring replacements." He figured that would earn him favor.

"I will, sir."

Thom stepped into the Rejuvenary after a quick bite in the dining hall. Kami slept, thanks to Oddi, who'd fed her. The day before had been long. They'd flown back and forth until it was too dark to see, then resumed at first light until all critical patients were delivered.

On his way out of the dining hall, Thom had run into Eran carrying two satchels of pasties and fruit. She and a few classmates had been distributing food across the city.

His next patient was a young mother with a broken back—injured while shielding her infant from falling masonry. A diplomat, she lived in the Clereigh Hall wing that collapsed. Calling on Rafe and his healing angels, Thom repaired the internal damage. He assured her husband, who ran in afterward and had been away from the suite when the earthshake struck, that she was no longer critical. He then directed him, now holding their unharmed infant, to the dining hall.

After they left, Thom asked a volunteer to fetch leeches. The woman's back was mottled with black, purple, and reddish-blue bruises. The leeches would reduce swelling and speed recovery. He'd removed the last one when a shout rang out.

Through the front window, Thom saw Jonathan lifting someone off Apollo, while a guard directed another figure out of view.

Redik burst in, followed by Jonathan and Nedd, both streaked with soot. They held the corners of a blanket, carrying someone gasping in pain.

"Thom," Redik called. "It's Meli! She's badly burned."

If Redik hadn't said her name, he wouldn't have known. Her hair was gone; her face blistered beyond recognition.

"Lay her there," Mac said, pointing to a bed halfway down the room. "Gently. Flo," she called to a woman with long ash brown hair, "burn ointment and bandages. A lot of it."

"Yes, Mac."

"Thom," Jonathan said from across the bed, "she's barely breathing. We need to open her airway."

Thom placed his hands over Jonathan's, above her lungs. As their gifts merged, a green mist formed. Sensing that Rafe and the healing angels were feeding them, he whispered, "Thanks."

"It's helping," Jonathan said. "What if I put her to sleep. At least she won't feel anything."

"Do it," Thom answered. But when he checked, she was unconscious.

"We need to get her clothes off," Mac advised.

Without hesitation, Thom helped cut them away, pushing aside any discomfort at seeing his sister's nakedness. Her arms and torso were blackened, skin flaking off. This was ghastly.

When Flo arrived with the supplies, Meli began to shake.

"She's seizing," Mac warned. "Her blood pressure must be dangerously low."

Thom and Jonathan instinctively joined hands, channeling healing to boost circulation. Nothing changed.

"She's burning up," Jonathan said.

"Save her, Thom!" Redik cried.

Help advisors!

Suddenly, Thom was no longer in the Rujuvenary, but in the divine realm, gazing at his higher self, Rel. Jonathan sat beside him, another divine being in front. Rafe was to their right.

Before you ask, Rafe said, *your sister's not dead. My associates and I are keeping her alive.*

Why'd you pull us out?

We didn't. You came here yourselves... in your desperation.

Rel?

True. And before you start worrying, remember that time doesn't apply here.

Thom exhaled, slightly relieved.

Let me introduce Lightworker-Sens, Rel continued. *Jonathan, this is your higher self.*

Oh... uh, he stammered, *Nice to meet... me?*

Nice to meet you, in person, Jonathan, Sens echoed.

Where's Metatron? Thom asked.

With your sister. She acted bravely—ran into a burning building to save children.

Oh, my God.

I'm here too, said a voice as a figure formed on their left. *Jonathan and Nedd dragged her out. Both got burned. Not to mention your brother.*

I'm sorry I didn't notice, Jonathan, Thom said.

That's OK. Just first-degree.

And you're sure no time is passing?

Yes, God replied. *As Rafe said, your desperation brought you. Since you're here, we'll answer your plea directly.*

Rafe continued. *You already know healing involves sending energy into your patients.*

Thom and Jonathan nodded.

We want you to add sound.

Sound? Jonathan repeated.

Music, really. Song and music are energy, too. Combine them with your healing pulses.

But we don't have instruments, Thom said.

Use your voices, God suggested. *They're powerful instruments. Jonathan's a beautiful tenor, and your baritone isn't bad either, Thom.*

Thanks, Jonathan said, meeting Sens' eyes, who smiled.

Yeah, thanks, Thom added. *But singing? That helps healing?*

Don't you remember the phrase 'sing choirs of angels' from the Solstice Day hymn?

Yeah.

Think about it. Singing channels healing through vocal vibrations.

I get it, Jonathan said.

I'm sure, Sens replied. That's how I got my name. As a light-worker, I help people make sense of the insensible.

I like that.

And before you ask, Thom, God continued, remember the hymn sung a few months ago at the Chapel of the One?

Uh huh.

That's the one I want you to sing, God added, humming a few notes.

Oh... yes.

Can I mention one more thing, God? Sens asked.

Go ahead. I know what you're going to say.

You've probably noticed you have complementary gifts.

Flip-flop gifts, Thom and Jonathan said together.

Rel and I knew this before you were born.

And Sens showed up unexpectedly at my pre-incarnation meeting because of it, Rel explained.

Oh, Thom said. I've seen parts of my meeting, but not that.

Your gifts evolve as your... connection... matures, Sens continued.

When you sing over Meli, you may feel a sudden shift, Rel added. And notice a significant... release.

Release? Thom asked. And given this place, you can't say more, huh?

No, God said. It has to unfold naturally. That's all we wanted to say. We'll be watching.

And the healing angels and I will continue supporting your work, Rafe added. I must admit... I'm looking forward to hearing you sing.

Chapter 44

Thom blinked. He and Jonathan were back, standing over Meli. No time had passed.

"Lay cold cloths on her," Mac said.

Thom met Jonathan's eyes. "You start."

Jonathan began to sing. His warm, velvety voice blanketed Meli with healing, touching everyone present. The room quieted.

Thom was briefly lost in the sound before he joined in. His harmony added depth, drawing gasps. Their voices blended majestically. With each note, Thom's bond with Jonathan grew.

At the hymn's peak, as they called on beings of goodwill to heal creation, especially Meli, Thom felt a pop. Unlike Samiltun's probe years ago, this one broke through a wall around his heart.

When they finished singing, silence continued. No footsteps, coughs, or clatter.

Thom felt divine presence more intensely—a choir of angels humming in the background. One glance at Jonathan confirmed he also heard them.

"I don't understand how you did this," Mac said, "but her fever's down, her pulse is stronger, and her skin's healing. Something tells me the other patients are also improving. Check them," she told the other healers.

"Meli's kidneys and lungs are much better," Thom said.

"I agree," Jonathan added. "She'll need more treatment to fully restore them. And more singing, if Thom's up for it."

"You don't even have to ask." Tears filled Thom's eyes—of relief for Meli and gratitude for their shared love.

"Is Meli going to be OK?" Redik asked, his hands now bandaged.

"Yes," Mac said. "Thom and Jonathan healed her."

"It was all of us," Thom corrected. "Mac, Flo, Nedd, Rafe, a bunch of angels, and you too, Redik."

At that, he broke down into sobs.

"I understand," Thom said, pulling him into a hug.

When he quieted, Redik whispered. "I thought she was gonna... Mam and Da told me to keep her safe. I told her it was too late, but she wouldn't listen."

Thom held him tightly, his heart aching like his brother's.

"Let's finish placing the cooling cloths," Jonathan directed. "I wish we had a way to raise her blood pressure."

"I think we do," Sean said, hurrying over. "Last month, Flo introduced me to two academs; one studies glassblowing, the other metallurgy."

Flo reddened, embarrassed by the attention.

"They designed a small glass tube with a hollow metal pin. Ingenious, really. Didn't they leave the sample with you, Flo?"

"Yeah."

After retrieving the device, she handed it to Mac.

"This could be very useful," she said, inspecting it. "We'll need to adjust some medicines to work through veins, but that's doable. Tavi certainly has an impressive metallurgy crew, given the recent inkstave invention."

Thom couldn't debate that.

"Finn, will you help?"

"Of course. We'll need adrenal extract. It'll raise her pressure and help her body circulate what it needs. Since it's already liquid, you won't have to adjust that."

"Let's get it into her."

The extract took effect almost immediately.

"Meli will sleep comfortably now," Mac continued. "Redik, take the bed beside her and call if she stirs. I doubt she will before morning. Nedd, how's your burn?"

"Minimal. Another healer bandaged it. Can I stay overnight?"

"Of course," Mac replied.

"Jonathan, if I don't see you before I leave tomorrow, I'll let the family know what's happened."

"Thanks," Jonathan said, giving him a hug.

Thom also embraced him. "Thanks, Nedd."

"Now, Thom and Jonathan," Mac said sternly, "you're clearly drained. Strangely, your auras are brighter. Rest. We'll wake you if needed."

"You're sure?" Thom asked.

"Yes. She's out of danger."

"Good. Redik, I'll come back later to check you both."

"Would you come in?" Thom asked, opening his door.

"Sure."

Side by side on the bed, Thom and Jonathan gazed at each other, keenly aware their energies remained in harmony.

Thom's heart swelled with love and gratitude, a grin tugging at his lips.

"What's your smile about?"

"How happy I am to have met such an incredible man."

"Same here," Jonathan replied, matching his expression.

They sat quietly. Thom placed his hand over Jonathan's heart, a tear sliding down his cheek.

Jonathan wiped it away, leaned in, and kissed where it had fallen.

Thom cupped his face and kissed him back. On his mouth.

"Thank you."

"You're welcome. Do you think this was what Rel meant by a… significant release?"

"You'd know better than me."

"My intuition says yes."

"I've wanted to do that for so long."

"Is that why you were mad?"

"Yes. It wasn't my place to tell you, but it hurt. You'd say how much you liked me and brush your hand against mine—it felt like teasing. Or worse."

"Sorry. I never meant to hurt you. Do you hate me?"

"No," he replied, thinking. "The summer I turned thirteen, a neighbor boy led me on. I felt betrayed. Even my fathers couldn't comfort me. It took forever to get past. When I visited my aunt and uncle before the shake, I told them what happened between us."

"Oh, Jonathan…." Thom dropped his gaze.

"Look at me." When he didn't, Jonathan lifted his chin. "What you did… it still hurts. But I understand."

"What can I do?"

"Let me have my feelings. That's what my fathers said."

"OK."

"Thom, I love you. I sensed your feelings for me when we were singing."

"Aren't we too young to say that? I mean, you're not even sixteen."

"Who says? It's not like we're getting married."

"I guess." While Thom believed it was OK to love someone of the same gender, a judgmental voice lingered in the back of his mind, calling those feelings disordered. And damning if acted on.

"Thinking about the Iosan elders?"

"How'd you know?"

"Because I heard it as well. My fathers used to talk to us about bigotry and small-mindedness. But can we set that aside for now? I just want to be with you."

"OK," Thom said, his heart fluttering. "Mac told us to rest. Want to stay here... with me?"

"I do."

They lay on Thom's bed—Thom on the left and Jonathan on the right.

Jonathan laced his fingers through Thom's. "I knew I'd love you when I first saw you, and you shouted, 'Ho, the horse' outside the dragon sanctuary."

"Really"

"Mm hmm."

"What would you have said?" Thom's asked, his eyes twinkling.

"Ho, the human?" Jonathan chuckled.

"Not much better." Thom let the moment stretch before adding, "So you knew you liked boys from a young age."

"Yeah."

"I started wondering in Glakkadeth after Mekial told me she liked girls and boys."

They lay quietly until Thom noticed Jonathan's eyes drooping. "We should sleep."

"Sweet dreams."

"You too. Feels like my dream is next to me."

This time, Jonathan kissed him on the mouth.

When Thom next opened his eyes, the light told him it was mid-morning. Looking over, he saw Jonathan sleeping peacefully, and a flood of love filled his heart.

Thank you, advisors, for bringing him into my life, he mind-spoke.

You're welcome, came the reply.

He wanted to touch Jonathan's face, but he didn't want to wake him.

"Hey, you," Jonathan whispered, opening his eyes.

"Sorry I woke you."

"I was half awake. Go ahead."

"What?"

"Touch my face. That's what you wanted, wasn't it?"

"Yeah," he said, stroking Jonathan's cheeks.

"Sorry, it's rough. I haven't shaved for two days."

"It's perfect. Mine's the same. That's something..." he started to say when his door burst open.

"Are you...?" Mekial began, then stopped.

"Um," Thom said, quickly sitting up.

"It's about time," she added, eyeing Jonathan as he reached for Thom's hand. She leaned out and called, "Tovah, they're here."

"You knew?"

"Of course. How could I not, what with the way you acted around each other? Tovah agrees."

"About what?" she said, stepping in.

"Them."

"Ah. Yeah," she said, noting their location and slipping her hand into Mekial's. "And, if you haven't figured it out, we're together."

"Oh," Thom replied, stunned.

"Not the most perceptive," Mekial teased. "Since second year. We've been discreet. But we think Jonathan knew."

"I did. I wasn't sure how to tell you."

"Well, now you both do. And we know about you."

"Close the door," Thom said. "I don't want everyone finding out."

The two sat on the end of the bed.

"How do you feel?" Mekial asked. "I heard you sang to Meli."

"How is she?" Thom asked. "I meant to visit last night."

"I guess we were more exhausted than we realized," Jonathan said.

"Probably. Meli?"

"She's awake and asking for you," Mekial said. "So's Redik."

"We gotta go," Thom announced, standing, then dropped when he lost his balance.

"Easy," Jonathan cautioned. "The healing was quite draining. Eating should help."

"Mac suggested the staff dining room," Tovah added. "They always keep food out. You have permission, in case you were worried."

Days passed, and Dermot hadn't heard from Samiltun. During that time, he'd even selected three purebreds for him.

He was in his grandfather's room, untouched since Deda's death. His mother had once suggested converting it into a guest room, but Dermot's outburst ended that. He wanted to study his papers to learn the strategies Deda had used to build the business, except the one that got him caught.

Dermot finished sorting the desk, setting aside a few papers with trade contacts. His gaze drifted to the wardrobe. Deda hadn't been a trusting man. Maybe he'd hidden something valuable there.

When he opened it, the clothes inside were musty, but Deda's scent lingered. Breathing it in, Dermot felt his presence. At the far right hung a black uniform jacket; pulling it out, he saw a red emblem on its sleeve—a clenched fist ringed by five gold stars.

"Where did this come from? It's not a constable or Royal Guard issue."

He hung it back and opened the top drawer: underthings. In the bottom one, he found a box.

His breath quickened. "This must be important."

Inside were papers covered with unfamiliar characters. He'd need an expert to identify the language and translate them. But not now. He had other things to attend to. Certain stablehands weren't showing him proper respect.

Chapter 45

A week passed. On Fwi-dae afternoon, Thom, Mekial, Jonathan, and Tovah were summoned to the monarchs' sitting room in Cleirigh Hall. Tovah was a nervous wreck.

"It'll be OK," Mekial said. "Niamh and Peth are kind. You saved lives after the shake when you warned people about the smaller ones."

"Oddi did that too."

"He did," Jonathan agreed, "but you went into dangerous areas to help guards evacuate people before the buildings came down."

"Anyone would've done it."

"That's what I said in Glakkadeth," Thom added. "But it wasn't true. And this... 'anyone' doesn't have your gift."

"Well... ," Tovah began, stopping when the sitting room door opened and a guard stepped out.

"The monarchs will see you now."

Inside, the queen and king sat on a sofa with cups and plates before them. In front of them was a muscular woman in uniform.

"And Commander," Peth continued, "make sure the food pantries and soup kitchens stay well stocked. People are depending on them."

"Check the orphanages, as well," Niamh added. "The children could be on edge, even though the smaller tremors stopped a few days ago. It might be a bit much for the wardens to keep them settled."

"Certainly, Your Majesties," the Commander replied, bowing before exiting the same door that the four entered.

"Come in," Niamh said, as she and Peth rose.

"Tovah," Mekial whispered, "your hand's shaking."

Niamh stepped forward, offering her hand. "Tovah, I'm glad to finally meet you."

"Welcome," Peth added. "We're in your debt."

"Um, thank you, Your Maj..." she began, blushing as she tried to curtsy.

"None of that," Niamh said. "We're in private. Please call us Niamh and Peth."

"OK," she whispered, barely meeting her gaze.

"And thank you three as well," Peth said. "You're quite the foursome. What you did was a great service for Docha-leigh."

"Help yourself to drinks and snacks," Niamh added. "Oddi will join us shortly."

When he arrived, he squeezed between his parents on the sofa. The others sat in the padded chairs across from them.

"Like we said," Niamh began, "we wanted to thank you and hear more about what you did. You really are a remarkable foursome."

"We need a better name for them," Peth added. "You've clearly become a tight-knit team."

"We have," Thom agreed.

"I know," Oddi piped up, "what about Quad Squad? It rhymes."

"I like it," Jonathan said. "We're not on the same quad, but we live on the same floor, and spend time in the Gallean common room. What do you think?"

Everyone agreed it was perfect.

"The Quad Squad. We'll remember that," Peth said. "Now, who'd like to start?"

Each of them shared their experiences, Niamh, Peth, and Oddi included. When they finished, a quiet settled over the room.

Thom stared at the floor, thinking of the hundreds who had died, the many injured, and all those left homeless.

God, he mind-spoke, *why didn't you stop it? Or at least warn everyone? Many were kids... who'll never live out their purpose. And the ones left behind? How are they supposed to bear it?* He didn't expect a reply.

Thom, it's G. I recognize it's awful. I'm sorry for the suffering. Disasters like earthshakes, fires, and floods are part of an evolving creation. Many are made worse by human choices. Your higher selves understand and accept this before incarnating.

But it's not fair.

Fairness doesn't quite apply here. I get your frustration. What matters is helping those in need, including listening, like Brother Lamen does for you. And maybe reflecting on what this can teach you about yourself and others.

OK, Thom replied, troubled.

"Thom?" a male voice asked. "Thom?"

"Sorry. Did someone ask me a question?"

"Yes," Mekial said. "Were you talking to a divine advisor? He does that sometimes."

"Divine advisor?" Peth asked. "Would you tell me who?"

"God. Iosan's call him Deu."

"That's interesting," Niamh remarked. "Peth was asking if you had anything more to share, even about what Deu said, if you don't mind."

Thom briefly told them.

With nothing more to add, the newly named Quad Squad headed out, bound for the Acadium and dinner.

Chapter 46

Late Tas-dae morning, Thom sat across from Brother Lamen in his office, a warm autumn breeze drifting through the window. He'd wanted to talk about Jonathan since the end of Jauna, but hadn't found the words. In their first two meetings after the shake, the focus had been on trauma and grief.

Thom knew Lamen belonged to a Glakkadian religious community founded by two same-gender couples. Surely God must be OK with it. Yet, he continued hearing the elders' condemnation.

He needed to talk. But his thoughts kept circling. It should've been easy. He hadn't even spoken with Jeshua. At least he'd written about it in his journal.

"Thom," Lamen said, "you've been quiet for a while. What's on your mind?"

"You're not gonna like it."

"That's a good start. Say more."

Thom's leg started bouncing. Each time he tried to stop it, it resumed, like it had a mind of its own.

"You're anxious. Don't fight it. Your body's trying to release energy."

He let his right leg bounce. The left remained motionless. Odd.

"You might imagine your energy sinking into the floor."

After a time, Thom felt more at ease, but his stomach churned.

"Just say it," Lamen encouraged. "If it helps... I think I already know."

Thom inhaled and said in a rush, "I'm in love with Jonathan, and I think I want to marry him someday."

"Good. Now breathe, and say it again, slower."

He did.

"How did that feel?"

"Hard. I was afraid lightning might strike me down."

"Sounds like Iosan teachings continue to haunt you, even if it comes from a misreading of your good book."

Thom didn't really consider himself Iosan anymore; too many teachings didn't fit. The elders would be outraged if they knew he believed every soul shared the same divine essence as Jeshua. But he didn't see himself as Aaliswan either; he railed against being bound by a single set of beliefs. Sestra B's elephant analogy about God came to mind, and he wanted to stay open to other ways of understanding life and the divine.

Lamen studied him, letting the moment be.

"It's worse when I hear insults," Thom continued. "They bring back memories of Kevar mocking me."

"Your childhood bully?"

"Yeah. Sometimes I want to scream at people, and tell them how hateful they are. Other times, I want to prove I'm a good person. But then I hear the elders quoting the good book."

"I understand. I've studied this for years—read religious scholars' interpretations and even compared them to earlier versions of the Aaliswan book."

"What'd you find?"

"First, the good book was written for specific times and people with a limited understanding of sexuality and gender identity. They couldn't comprehend someone naturally being drawn to the same gender. So they view it as breaking God's law and rejecting God."

"But isn't the good book inspired?"

"It is. But the writers weren't transcribing God's or Iosa's literal words. The stories were meant to teach love, respect, and justice."

"You sort of mentioned natural law. The elders said Deu created it. They also use it to argue that the purpose of marriage is to have children."

"About that, if your elders truly studied nature, they'd see countless examples of same-gender behavior. When I was a child, our class visited an animal sanctuary. Some of the monkeys and sheep had same-gender partners. Our teacher even told us about two male penguins who adopted an egg and raised the chick. And guess what? The male seahorse gives birth."

"No," Thom said, his jaw dropping.

"Now, saying marriage is only for children is a narrow view; one most reject. What about couples unable to bear them? Or the procreative aspects of love people share regardless of their marital status?"

"That helps. I doubt God would forbid marriage to a couple who couldn't have kids. But what about same-gender couples who want them?"

"Biologically, a male and female are needed. But many same-gender couples live in diverse communities that support those who want children and can't, including infertile male-female couples."

"That's what Mekial's mothers did. But... is God OK with that? I mean, I don't want to..."

"Thom, are you afraid you'll be damned for holding beliefs the elders never would?"

"I guess."

"You'll need to make your own peace with that. But you said Rel hinted at your relationship during your visitation, and God was there. That suggests approval. Give it time. Chat with Jeshua and God... and even Jonathan."

"I will."

"Anything else?"

"Is there a word for someone like me and Jonathan?"

"A beautiful, heartfelt question, Thom," Lamen said. "My great-uncle told me that when his grandsire was a boy, people began accepting other kinds of attraction—including none... as well as a range of gender identities. Words like solbonded, moonsestra, dualhearted, shiftwoven, and enby came into use following a raid by constables in a Rohan tavern. Many patrons were injured."

"Rohan's where I lived."

"You told me. Our founders' children were part of that protest."

"What do they mean?"

"Solbonded refers to a man drawn to men. Moonsestra, a woman to women, and dualhearted to both."

"I have a friend who's dualhearted. What about the others?"

"Shiftwoven describes someone born the wrong gender. And enbies don't identify as strictly male or female. They find the two-gender definition limiting."

"That's a lot to take in."

"It is. The terms were important because they let people, once unseen or called abnormal, name and celebrate who they were."

"I get that," Thom replied, sighing. "But you said 'were important.' Aren't they used anymore?"

"No. A generation later, most realized even those labels didn't reflect our dynamic nature as incarnated divine beings. Personally, I'm grateful for that."

"Personally?"

"Yes. To use the old term, I identify as enby, though I'm mostly attracted to men."

"I'd wondered. I saw you hugging a man from your community who... well, shares my complexion."

"My husband, Callum. We've been married six years."

"Is he Dochalan?"

"Yes, from a town up north."

"I'd like to meet him, if that's OK."

"Of course. I'd introduce you today, but he's running errands."

"OK. I'll see you in a couple weeks. I need to get to mage class."

"How about a hug?"

Chapter 47

"**S**orry, I'm late," Thom panted as he rushed into the classroom and stopped short. "Rin?"

"Hi, Thom."

"Weren't you traveling around Docha-leigh to assess earthshake damage?"

"Yes. I even checked on your family; they're fine. A little bird told me that you were worried their letter didn't tell the whole story. They felt the shake, nothing more. I told them you were OK. Other towns weren't as lucky."

A throat cleared nearby.

"Sorry, Kee," Thom said, "I wasn't expecting to see Rin."

"I understand. Tovah was telling us what she discovered. Please go on."

"You all know my earth-sensing gift's been changing. When the shake hit, I could feel it, and even sense when buildings were about to collapse."

"Sorry to interrupt," Rin said, "but thank you. Your gift helped us reach the most affected towns. You saved many lives."

"Um, thanks. Well, the other day I was testing my gift's sensitivity. We haven't had any more tremors, but I scanned the plateaus anyway. I detected large chambers beneath the Keep."

"Neat," Mardu said.

"I'm amazed that more of the Keep didn't collapse if that's true," Rin ventured. "Sorry, Tovah, I don't doubt you."

"That's OK," she said. "I could be wrong."

" I believe her," Mekial added, squeezing her hand.

"Is there a way to check?" Thom asked. "Could there be a hidden entrance behind the plateaus?"

"Let's hear from the rest of you about changes with your gifts," Kee said. "Jonathan?"

"Since Thom and I healed Meli, I've been using my voice more during healing. I've experimented with different pitches, and even borrowed a tuning fork from the music teacher. Lower pitches help those recovering. It relaxes them, maybe even eases the trauma. Is that the correct word, Thom?"

"Yes. Lamen told me trauma can get stuck in the body and needs to be released. Sound helps. And before you ask, Kee, I can see sound waves. It's energy. Jonathan and I used it on Meli a few times. She's being released tomorrow and will live with my brother, Redik, here in the city. The monarchs are awarding her the Medal of Bravery.

"I heard. You must be proud."

"I am. Meli really was a hero. She told me she'd heard kids crying next door. The oldest, a young teen, was watching her brothers, but Meli noticed the shake had left the girl frozen in fear. Disregarding her own safety, she pushed them out the door when the ceiling fell and trapped her."

"I wish I'd been there," Mekial said.

"If you had, you wouldn't have saved that other family," Jonathan replied.

"I still feel bad."

"I understand," Kee replied. "Oddi, what about you? You've been working with the foreseers. Even if you're not an academ, I wanted you here."

"No more visions since the day after the shake. But Lalia's been helping me get used to them. My first one was really scary."

"I'm sure," Rin said, glancing at Thom. "Another lad struggled when his gifts first appeared."

"What about the rest of you? Cat? Mekial? Mardu?" Kee asked.

All three shook their heads.

"OK. If anything comes up, find me. Otherwise, let's end early."

After Cat and Mardu left, Rin said, "Shall we go find those chambers now?"

Kee, Rin, and the Quad Squad dismounted a few yards behind the Keep plateau.

"I'm not sure how long we'll be," Thom told Apollo, looping his reins over a branch. "Plenty of grass for you and the other horses."

Apollo neighed and lowered his head to graze.

"The back of the plateau's covered in vines," Mekial observed.

"Maybe there's an opening behind them," Jonathan suggested.

They'd searched a quarter of the wall when Tovah yelped and disappeared, leaving the soles of her shoes in view.

"Are you OK?" Mekial called.

"I found the way in," she laughed, standing up and pulling vines aside.

Thom entered last and ran into someone.

"Ouch! Who ran into me... me... me...?" Mekial shouted, her voice echoing.

"Sorry. It's Thom... Thom... Thom. I can't see."

"We should tie back some vines," Rin whispered.

The others instinctively lowered their voices.

"I've got rope in my saddlebag," Kee offered.

"I brought a firestarter and a few torches."

"Now that's preparation, Jonathan," Rin said.

Once the vines were tied back and the torches lit, they stepped deeper inside and discovered a vast chamber.

"This is huge... huge... huge," Thom exclaimed, forgetting to be quiet.

"Volume," Kee warned.

"Let's split into pairs and explore," Rin suggested. "Meet back here."

When they regrouped, everyone shared what they'd found.

"The vines cover an opening about forty feet wide and nearly fifty high," Kee explained.

"The walls are thick," Rin added. "A few rocks fell during the shake, but there's no real damage."

"We think the chamber's at least twenty-five feet taller than the opening," Thom noted.

"Mekial and I found smaller chambers off to the right," Tovah reported. "The ceilings were lower, and it got warmer the farther in we went."

"Tell them what else we found," Mekial urged.

Tovah frowned. "I was getting to that."

"Sorry."

"Anyway," she continued, "many had hot vapor escaping from a small hole in the ground. I sensed it was the start of a long tube running beneath the mountain that ends in a magma chamber. Professor Petra Creag taught us about that in geology. I think this mountain's a dormant, or mostly dormant, volcano."

"Does that mean it might erupt?" Thom asked, gulping.

"When she talked about them, Petra said a ground shake could trigger that. Since ours didn't, it's unlikely it will."

"Not exactly comforting."

"The steam's very hot," Mekial added.

Thom fell quiet.

"What are you thinking?" Jonathan asked, giving him a poke.

"Oh," he replied, snapping back. "Tovah, Kee, you've had to reheat Kami's sands for almost three years. It's a shame one of those tubes doesn't run near them."

"I've never tried moving earth or rock," Tovah said, "but I could check for a tube nearby. Kee, can we talk about it?"

"Certainly. I like the way you think, Thom."

A voice sounded in Thom's mind.

Kami?

Yes. I can see through your eyes.

"Really," he said aloud.

"Really... what?" Rin asked.

"Kami's mind-speaking to me. She says she can see through my eyes.

"That's amazing," Kee said. "Did she say anything else?"

Kami, would you mind-speak with everyone here?

Yes. As I told Thom, Kami repeated, *I can see through his eyes. And the chamber's triggered a memory.*

"That's incredible," Tovah said. "I heard her like she was next to me. What memory?"

Thom relayed her question to Kami.

Dragons once lived there.

"Wow," Thom said aloud. *Did you learn anything more?* He repeated his question to the others.

Actually, I think I can help.

About wha.., Thom began.

"What was that?"

"Ouch!"

"I felt a pop."

Kami, did you do something? Thom asked.

"I heard you ask that," Rin said.

"Me, too," Mekial added.

"And me," said Tovah and Kee together.

To answer your question, Kami said, *it was inefficient for Thom to repeat everything. You can now hear each other mind-speak and not just me.*

Dare I ask? Rin cut in. *Is it limited to us here?*

No, but I have to extend it to others. And even then, just to those with mage ability. I think that's what you call it, Kee.

It is, she replied, shaking her head. *You'd think I'd be used to gifts suddenly appearing.*

Can I mind-speak to my family in Glakkadeth? Mekial asked.

I'm not sure.

After a brief pause, she said, *I just tried, but didn't hear anything. How could I tell if they heard me?*

You'd probably get a reaction, like a yell.

I didn't, Mekial added, sounding disappointed.

Kami, Thom asked, *was there other information in the chamber memories?*

Yes. Did you notice any plants?

In the chambers with the tubes, Mekial said, leading them to one.

A plant grew in the corner; its iridescent flowers glowed softly, with teardrop-shaped petals and a translucent green stem.

It's over a tube, Jonathan said. *And part of it extends down into it. I've never seen anything like this.*

Nor have I, Rin added.

Kami, why did you want to see it? Thom asked.

Parent-dragons feed it to their young to spark their fire-breathing.

Their what? his eyes widened.

If I eat the flowers, it releases an oily hormone that lets me breathe fire. Then I'm called a flareling.

Thom was speechless. *That's in the book. I didn't realize that's what it meant. The plant's called aurixen.*

How much do you need? Jonathan asked.

I don't know.

Sorry to interrupt again, Rin said, *but I need to share this with Peth and Niamh. Let's head back. Kee, can you get Noiri and Mac and meet me at the monarchs' sitting room?*

Absolutely.

"Rin, would you mind if we stayed longer?" Thom asked. "I'd like to search for more of the plant."

"Go ahead."

Chapter 48

It was Fwi-dae, Nuvima 22, and the sky was overcast. Classes were suspended for a teacher training on trauma. Since the earthshake, several academs and one teacher hadn't fully recovered. They were physically fine, but emotionally skittish, and flinching at the smallest sound. Brother Lamen had offered to run a session to address it.

Thom was on his own. Jonathan was at his aunt and uncle's, helping repair a barn damaged in the shake. Thom had been invited, but he needed a day to recharge.

Three weeks earlier, a respiratory virus swept through the school. Over twenty cases were severe, two nearly fatal. Every healer worked nonstop until they developed an effective treatment a week ago: fennel, echinacea, and peppermint teas, eucalyptus baths, and chest ointments. The last patient left the Rejuvenary yesterday.

Thom pulled the blanket around himself as he curled up in his stuffed chair wondering why Jonathan wasn't as tired. All he wanted to do was rest while diving into the ninth *Demba's Chronicles* book. Unbeknownst to Mekial, this one featured characters based on them. The author had introduced them briefly in the previous book after meeting them in Glakkadeth. Khali had sent him this installment for his recent birthday.

He inhaled its scent. Books always soothed him. Thom opened to the first page and lost himself in the story.

When the supper bell rang, Thom was shocked. Had he been reading for two hours?

His stomach growled in reply. Mac, aware of how tired Thom was, had suggested eating in the staff dining room. Instead, he decided to grab food and return to his room. He wanted to keep reading.

In the serving line, Thom ended up behind Kee and two girls.

"Hi, Kee."

"Hi, Thom. I heard you were worn out."

"Yeah."

"Remember Leesha and Lena?"

"I haven't seen you two since... well. How are you?"

"OK," Leesha immediately answered.

"Kee got us from home," Lena added.

Thom guessed they were about eleven. After Samiltun disappeared, the monarchs had helped their parents find better-paying work and moved them into a larger house.

"We're meeting another teacher after supper," Leesha said. "Professor..."

"Ashlin," Lena supplied, as if they shared the same thought.

"It's a quick meeting before Ash and I get back to training," Kee explained. "The girls can detect minerals, diamonds, and gems. They'll work with Ash every few months until they're thirteen, then start here on scholarship."

"Our parents are really grateful," Lena said.

"Did you know the stuff we found helped fix the houses and shops that got wrecked?" Leesha added.

"No." Thom knew the city and Cleirigh Hall had been rebuilt quickly. They must've found diamond deposits to fund it.

Now carrying a tray with a plate of roast chicken, green beans, herb rice—plus a cinnamon biscuit and a mug of Timbu—he called, "Good seeing you."

"Bye."

Back in his room, Thom set the tray on his desk. A feather lay on his chair. How did that get in here? Not from his closed windows now that winter was coming.

"Sereh? Was that from you?" he asked, and immediately sensed a confirmation.

He hadn't spoken with her during the outbreak. He'd called on her and his divine advisors for help, but not for a heart-to-heart. The feather was a not-so-subtle reminder. Sereh had sent one nearly seven years ago to introduce herself. Hard to believe it'd been that long. His life had changed dramatically. He'd better eat before his food got cold.

After finishing, Thom got comfortable. Closing his eyes, he visualized his Sanctuary. As always, he found himself beneath his tree, gazing at the mountain and flower-covered meadow. The sound of the river and the burbling hot spring calmed him. The air smelled of roses and lavender. Here, it was always spring.

Hey gang, he called. *Anyone who wants to come is welcome.*

Sereh appeared first, with a male figure beside her.

Hi, Thom, she greeted, giving him a hug. *Before you ask, this is Nebli. We call him Neb. He's your second guardian angel.*

Two?

That's pretty common. Most don't realize it.

Nice to meet you, Thom said, shaking his hand.

Would you mind a hug instead?

Not at all.

After they embraced, they sat.

Neb wants to tell you something, Sereh explained.

Did I do something wrong? Am I getting kicked out? Or is it Samiltun?

Slow down. You continue assuming the worst, Neb said.

You know that, huh? I try not to.

We understand. Before the others arrive, I wanted to explain a few things. Sereh's kind of a generalist guardian angel. But I'm here to support your spirit-healer abilities, especially as your beliefs evolve.

I'm not sure what to say. Wait... yes, I do. Were you at my... or Rel's pre-incarnation?

Yes, but I stayed in the background.

Without warning, three shimmering spheres appeared, transforming into Jeshua, Archangel Metatron, and Rel. Thom stood, as did the others.

Hello, Thom, they said. Metatron and Rel hugged him. Thom and Jeshua did their usual greeting: slapping hands, tapping each foot, twisting, bumping their rumps, and ending with a hug. Rel had taught that to him.

Well done, he said.

Thanks. Shall we sit?

Once they got comfortable, Metatron spoke, *We haven't chatted much this year.*

Sorry, he replied. *I've given you updates.*

True. But it was time for a longer conversation. And, as Neb said, it's not because you've done anything wrong.

OK.

Talk to us, Rel said. *How do you feel about what happened with your sister?*

Hopeful... and sad.

Say more, Jeshua encouraged.

I'm glad she's doing better. Her face has healed but it's been six months and she won't paint. She loves painting. Redik even fixed up a studio above his shop for her. Oh, and he and Brigid are engaged.

That's wonderful, Sereh remarked.

The thing is, Meli won't go near that room. She's talking with Lamen. He suggested she try painting with her mouth until her hands heal, but she's not interested. I'm worried. She hides in her room. Even Mam and Da's visit didn't help. Lamen won't tell me if she's improving. I'm hoping...

That must be difficult, Metatron said. *Is that where your sadness comes from?*

Yeah. Meli used to be so lively and outspoken. I remember how she got in trouble for talking back to an elder. Now... it's like her spirit's broken.

Give it time. Lamen's a talented soul.

Anything more about Meli? Jeshua asked.

Jonathan and I've been working together to heal her skin and muscles. We combine our energy and ask Rafe and the healing angels to sing with us. It helps, but the scars haven't faded yet.

Rafe? Neb asked.

My nickname for Archangel Raphael.

Healing third-degree burns can take two years or more, Jeshua added.

Yeah. But to Meli, it feels like forever.

There's more, isn't there? Jeshua prompted. *About something else.*

A fourth sphere appeared beside Sereh, transforming into an androgynous, seated figure.

God? Thom asked, shifting uncomfortably.

Perfect timing, Metatron said.

Go ahead, Thom, Jeshua encouraged.

In the visitation before Jonathan and I healed Meli, he said, eyes downcast, *Rel mentioned our relationship might change. Or I'd change. Or I'd finally realize the truth. I'm not saying this well.*

Thom, God interrupted. *May I step in... or should I say sit in?*

God, is now the best time for your questionable sense of humor? Jeshua asked.

Maybe not, but Thom's not looking at any of us.

God reached out and lifted Thom's chin.

You're a beautiful soul. That doesn't change because you're attracted to Jonathan. It takes courage to admit that, especially with people around like the Iosan elders.

So... you're OK with me being... solbonded? That's what Lamen called it.

Yes. And I commend Brother Lamen for explaining sexuality and gender identity with such clarity and compassion.

Thom let out a breath he hadn't realized he'd been holding. Which was strange—did he even need to breathe here?

It's good you let that go. You'll face insults, rejection, and perhaps violence. You'll need to carefully choose who you share this with.

Jonathan told me.

He's another good one, God said. I'm happy Sens agreed to the arrangement with Rel.

As am I, Rel replied. Thom, you probably won't be surprised, but there's more ahead for you.

Because of the relationship?

That's part of it, Neb explained, but the path ahead will come in response to your paired gifts.

And of course, you can't say more, Thom smirked.

You've caught on, Metatron said. Is there more you want to talk about?

The epidemic. I heard people say the shake and the virus were punishments from you, God. I knew that wasn't true, but I couldn't figure out how to respond.

I'm glad you realize that. The human body is miraculous but complex. Some illnesses come from poor hygiene or neglect. Others are inherited. And, still others might be linked with unresolved issues from previous lives.

Thom shook his head, struggling to grasp it all. He noticed Rel nodding and wondered why.

Anything about Kami? Sereh prompted.

Thom told them the latest developments, including the growing number of people able to use mind-speech. Mac, Niamh, Oddi, and the foreseers were among them. Peth and Noiri were frustrated that it didn't work for them. While they could hear mind-speakers, the catch was that in order to be heard in return, they had to shout their reply in their minds, which wasn't natural.

Staring at the five before him, Thom realized how much he'd missed chats like this. He was about to suggest meeting more often when he felt pressure in his lower body.

Uh... I have to um... go.

Go? Neb asked. *Aren't we in your Sanctuary?*

He has to pee, Jeshua explained. You wouldn't recognize the feeling unless you've incarnated.

Bye, Thom blurted as the Sanctuary faded, and he ran for the washroom.

Chapter 49

After Founding Day supper—an annual celebration of the Acadium's opening 170 years ago—the Quad Squad headed to their rooms. All wore formal uniforms. Much to his chagrin, Thom had to ask Jonathan to tie his ascot again, even after four years.

The day had started with a language class for just the four of them. Thom and Mekial were studying three: Gallic (spoken in Eiren and neighboring lands), Aboj-paskee (spoken in Aboja-pas, northwest of Docha-leigh), and Vlodinian. Tovah and Jonathan were also learning Glakkadian. Oddly, Noiri had enrolled them in a cultural awareness course usually reserved for sixth-levels. On the first day, a few academs even told them they were in the wrong room.

The afternoon was equally full. Since Jonathan and Thom only had healing classes once a week this semester, Dek increased their training time and introduced a new challenge: pitting each against multiple attackers. Only Mekial had experience with that. The extra bruises meant longer soaks in the hot pools and liberal use of ointment made from arnica, ginger, and eucalyptus. Classmates often remarked on their potent scent when the four were together.

By evening, they struggled to stay awake through the Acadium concert. Performances by the music and vocal academs blurred together. Only the sing-along prevented them from nodding off. Since he and Jonathan now used their voices regularly in healing, their vocal range had grown.

The next day, after another language class, the four cut through the quad toward the stairwell. The early Mercha air was cool, but at least it wasn't raining... or snowing, as it had two weeks earlier. Mekial walked a few steps ahead of Thom, with Jonathan and Tovah trailing. Jonathan was asking her about a Vlodinian verb conjugation.

Like Tovah, Thom and Mekial offered guidance, albeit in Glakkadian. Thom's set of *Demba's Chronicles* helped. Many evenings, he and Mekial read aloud from them, reminding Thom of his time with Khali. They were on book three now. Thom couldn't wait until they read the one with the characters based on them. Neither had said a word.

Reaching the third-floor landing, he paused. Even months later, their class changes seemed odd. Suddenly, Rin's image popped into Thom's mind. *Sereh, Neb, did Rin have something to do with this?* he mind-spoke. No response.

"You," a voice from ahead called.

It was Niall with Oran. He rarely saw them outside weapons training.

"Macirdan, I'm talking to you," Niall repeated.

"Was there something you needed?" Thom asked cautiously.

"What are you up to?"

"What do you mean?"

"I've been following you since the shake. Why do you go over to the Keep?

"Following me?" Thom repeated. Did he know about Kami? They'd been careful. She stayed invisible once airborne. This wasn't good.

"Yeah. What are you trying to hide?"

"You must have me confused with someone else. Messengers go back and forth all the time."

"I know it's you," he insisted.

"Maybe you're wrong, Niall," Oran said.

"I'm not."

By then, Mekial was beside him, and Tovah and Jonathan had caught up.

"What's going on?" Mekial asked.

"Niall's been following me."

"Why?" Tovah asked.

"Because he's been acting suspicious," Niall said accusingly.

"If anyone's suspicious, it's you," Jonathan shot back.

"Shut it. You think you're special 'cause you're a gifted healer."

"You're jealous," Mekial said.

As barbs flew, Thom was reminded of Kevar. What did Niall's aura look like? Muddy pink swirls, signs of insecurity, rejection, and confusion, mingled with competing shades of blue. He had to ask.

"Niall, are things bad at home?"

"What are you talking about? Nothing's wrong."

Thom's gift confirmed the lie. "You can tell me."

"None of your business. What is my business is why you go to the Keep. What's over there?"

"Maybe he's got a horse?" Oran suggested.

"Academs aren't supposed to have horses. And if he did, why would it be at the Keep?"

"Dunno."

"We need to go," Tovah cut in. "I have to get my books for geology."

"I'm watching you, Macirdan," Niall muttered as they passed.

Approaching his room, Thom was struck by a flash of a pre-incarnation meeting. Niall's calling was to be a protector. But how could he be, acting like that? Thom motioned for his friends to enter.

Once inside, he asked, "Do you think Niall saw Kami during the shake?"

"I don't remember seeing him," Mekial said.

"I don't want Peth and Niamh mad at me."

"Before you get worked up," Jonathan interrupted, "he didn't even say what he saw."

"He mentioned the shake."

"Yeah," Mekial agreed. "But if he saw Kami, he would've said so."

"Maybe."

"How about one of us always goes with you when you visit her," Jonathan suggested. "We can watch for Niall or anyone else."

"I guess."

"I really do need to go," Tovah said.

"What's happening with your ability, Mekial?" Kee asked, as they sat in their usual circle in mage class. "I know Dek's been working with you privately."

"He keeps throwing heavier and heavier things at me. Last week, we went to the Keep and he dropped grain bags on me from Draganni Hall's tower. We warned... um... Keelin about the noise."

That was close, Thom breathed. Mardu didn't know about Kami. Helean had graduated, and no new academs had shown unusual abilities.

"Any problems?" Kee asked.

"At first, yes," Mekial replied, and explained what happened.

Since Thom already knew about them, his thoughts wandered. It was a beautiful day in early Mei, and classes would end the following week. He longed to fly home, though this time he'd spend only a few weeks there. The rest would be spent with Jonathan's family and a chance to celebrate Jonathan's seventeenth birthday. He couldn't wait to walk through their town holding hands, something he didn't feel safe doing here. The other day, he'd heard comments accusing people like him of trying to recruit others, as if that were even possible. Refocusing on the class, he heard Kee ask.

"Will you be able to keep working over the summer?"

"Yes. I'll be with Tovah's family, camping at a nature preserve and refuge—with cliffs."

"You'll be careful?"

"Of course."

"Tovah, can I assume those plans are also tied to your gifts?"

"Yes. With fewer buildings and people, I can focus on what nature can teach me. And now, with my whole body involved, I'm bound to pick up more. I know it's connected to energy."

"I believe it," Thom said. "Lamen told me that everything in nature shares a common energy. I've been working with him to experience that oneness."

"Can I presume this comes from your spirit-healer gift?" Kee asked.

"Mostly. And a little from my earth sense."

"Oddi, anything new?" Kee asked.

"Well...um," Oddi said, "I've been getting cloudy visions. Two of them. Maybe they're nothing."

"What does Trethy say?" Mekial prompted.

"That they might be about things farther in the future."

"Interesting," Kee said.

"Would you tell us?" Jonathan asked.

"The first was a glimpse of the Quad Squad on a road. For a moment, I saw you clearly. I don't think it's near Freasa. It felt like you were doing something important. Someone else was there, but I couldn't see them."

"You sensed intent," Kee commented. "That's unusual."

"Trethy said the same thing."

"What about the other?"

"All foggy. And I mostly heard things—people walking, like they were stepping at the same time."

"Do you mean pacing?" Tovah asked.

"Yeah. It could've been like when the Royal Guard march."

"If they come back, write down anything you see or hear, " Kee advised. "Good job."

"I will."

"Mardu?" Kee prompted.

He shared how he could selectively see through structures, even those not nearby.

Everyone marveled.

"Thanks, all," Kee said. "And congratulations, Mardu, on your upcoming graduation. I'll see the rest of you in Siptema."

Chapter 50

"Thanks for coming," Noiri said, glancing at those in her office. "Sorry for calling a meeting after dinner, but it was the only time everyone was free."

"That's fine," Dek said. "I was going to soak, but I can do that later. A few of our older academs got careless with sandbags."

"Need salve?" Mac asked.

"No, I've got some. Anyway, it turned into a nice autumn day."

"It was," Kee agreed.

"Let's refocus," Noiri said. "This involves Rin, but he couldn't join us."

"Isn't he off on another 'errand' for Peth and Niamh," Mac said.

"As always."

Everyone understood.

"Kee," Noiri continued, "Any updates on the tension between Niall and Thom?"

"No. I've kept an eye on Niall since last spring. For those of you who don't know, I was near the stairwell when their argument broke out. Are you sure you don't want to tell Niamh and Peth? If Niall saw Kami and spoke to his family, it could cause trouble."

"I'm sure. They're still dealing with last month's scandal. A trader hoarded lamp oil after the earthshake. The fires destroyed local supplies, so people relied on imports. Niamh and Peth were furious that neither the trading council nor COM caught it sooner."

"I'd imagine," Dek said.

"Now, to business, and the reason for the meeting: the Quad Squad. Except for Tovah, who's in sixth level, the rest are starting their fifth. How are they doing? Kee?"

"Mekial's shielding has grown, not just in strength, but control. She can shield herself or others, and last month, she even used it to move objects. She's clumsy, but I expect it'll improve."

"Good. And Tovah?"

"Her sensitivity to nature continues expanding. She's been releasing pressure points around the city to lower the risks of new shakes. It would help if she got experience with other land types—to learn their condition and how she can offer healing."

"Healing the land. I hadn't thought of it that way," Mac mused. "Mind if I sit in the next time you meet with her?"

"Not at all."

"What about Thom and Jonathan?"

"Mac, why don't you start?" Kee prompted.

"Certainly. Their physical-healing gifts have advanced—Jonathan's more than Thom's—but together, they're nothing short of miraculous. Their combined abilities, including spirit healing, have saved patients who wouldn't have survived the night. And their singing is unusually effective. I even sent them into the city to assist healers and midwives. Honestly, I'm not sure how much more I can teach them."

"And Thom's ability to sense people's callings?" Noiri asked.

"Strong, according to Lamen," Kee said. "Apparently, Ailsa Ferran switched from metalworking—her family's craft—to history."

Mac and Noiri exchanged raised eyebrows.

"Yeah, it's unusual. But Ailsa lights up studying founders' lives and how other lands developed. Thom saw how her spirit glowed when she spoke about her passion, and told her."

"Amazing," Noiri said.

"I have to admit," Dek cut in, "that gift gives me the willies. Last spring, I was discussing improvements to the self-defense regimen with Mekial, now one of my top assistants. Thom over-heard, then said he had a flash from my pre-incarnation meeting and kept hearing the words 'lead and defend' tied to my purpose. Like I said, it gave me the willies."

"He is unique," Noiri admitted.

"Besides that," Kee went on, "Lamen said Thom continues to doubt himself and often feels he should be doing more."

"I've noticed," Mac said.

"As for Jonathan, his sensitivity to spirit has grown, but it's hard to say how strong it'll become."

"What about their training, Dek? Noiri asked.

"Well. Even Jonathan, who started with little skill. They've sparred against multiple opponents, but I'm thinking of having them face several attackers together to test their teamwork."

"Do it. That fits with an idea I've been considering—sending them on an internship next year to explore ways to expand their gifts."

"By themselves?" Mac asked. "They've faced trials, but they're so young. Someone clever could fool them."

"Did you forget Thom's truth-sensing ability?"

"Oh. Even so, I'm concerned, especially without a mentor."

"That brings me to Rin. Before he left, I asked him to consider that role."

"And he didn't outright reject it? Kee asked.

"No. I also asked whether they might be suited for COM."

"So during the internship, Rin could teach them related skills," Dek said. "And thanks to Kami, their mind-speaking ability will be a great asset."

"About her," Kee said, "she likely can't go. She's hard enough to keep secret as it is."

"Good point," Noiri said. "Let's think about it. I'm tailoring their studies this year around the internship, so keep that in mind as you plan lessons."

"Will do," Mac said, as the others agreed.

"Now I get why the Quad Squad had language classes," Dek added. "I overheard Mekial speaking to Jonathan in Glakkadian, and she told me."

"I had them take cultural awareness, in addition to that. This has been in the works for a while. That's all for now. Thanks for coming."

After the others left, Kee lingered. "I do think you should tell Niamh and Peth about Niall."

A tree branch scraped against Thom's window as he gathered his books for Culture and Politics. Colorful leaves swirled outside, carrying the musky scent of decay. His seventeenth birthday was days away, and he was excited about the party in their quad's common room. It wouldn't be for him alone but for all four of them, despite the others having summer birthdays. He hoped Redik and Meli would come. Meli had finally begun painting again.

At least he was no longer sick. He dreaded facing Dek at his weapons class that afternoon. Not because of his discomfort with swords but because of his own stupidity.

Ten days earlier, Dek had insisted they train in all weather conditions. Rain had pelted the yard, and though the class was dismissed, he remained behind. Determined to improve his archery skills, he hoped to repeat the bullseye he'd hit the week before. Dek had warned him not to stay out long. He didn't listen and paid the price.

Exhausted when he came in, he stopped by the Rejuvenary to ask Mac if she needed him that evening. She scolded him for being soaked. Unbeknownst to Thom, an academ down the hall had the flu. He caught it and caught it bad. Not just cough, fever, and body aches, but diarrhea as well.

Mac confined Thom to his room, with Jonathan tending him masked. Despite Jonathan and Mac's efforts, the flu hung on, requiring endless trips to the washroom. His quad-mates were forced to use a neighboring one, not only to avoid infection but to escape the stench: sour and putrid, like rotting vegetables. Thom shivered at the memory of those nightmarish days.

He'd just stepped out of his room when Oddi ran up, out of breath.

"Thom," he gasped.

"What's wrong?"

"Not sure. Mamie and Da asked me to get you. They've got a meeting soon but needed to see you first."

"I have a class. Can't it wait until after supper?"

Oddi shook his head.

"OK." He'd have to explain why he was late to his teacher. "Are they in Cleirigh Hall?"

"Home, in the dining room."

Thom stepped inside and saw Peth and Niamh in their usual spots. The twins sat in booster chairs near their parents, being urged to eat. Terrin seemed more cooperative.

"Unca," he cried, on seeing him. "Horsey ride! Horsey ride!"

"Sure, but a short one."

"Me first," Tressa demanded.

He'd been giving them rides for over a year.

"Neither of you gets one until you're done," Peth said.

Both promptly dug into their porridge.

"Thom," Niamh added, "thanks for coming so quickly. And thanks for getting him, Oddi. While we talk with Thom in the sitting room, can you make sure your sister and brother finish their breakfast? They each can have a small cup of Timbu."

"Timbu!" the twins shouted.

Keelin entered. "Noiri's arrived."

"Thanks," Peth said. "Please show her to the sitting room. We'll meet her there."

"Oddi, bring the twins afterward," Niamh added.

Thom followed them into the room. Noiri was already seated.

"Don't get up," she said. "Let's all sit."

Thom chose a chair beside Noiri; Peth and Niamh sat across from them.

"Again, thanks for coming," Niamh said. "We wanted to talk with you."

"What's going on?" Thom asked.

"Elspeth dropped us a note late last night," Peth began. "She had an interesting conversation downtown."

"The falconer?" Thom asked, confused. He hadn't seen her since his first year.

"Yes," Niamh said.

"About what?"

"An academ's mother asked her if she was overseeing a wild beast. Her son had gotten near the back of the Keep and heard repeated thudding."

"Niall," Thom whispered, horrified.

"Yes, that was his name," Niamh confirmed.

"Oh, no," Noiri muttered.

"Noiri?" Peth asked.

"Thom, is this the boy you argued with in Mercha?"

"Yes. How'd you know?"

"Kee overheard it. She promised to keep an eye on him back in Siptema."

Niamh stiffened. "You knew, and didn't tell us?"

"You were dealing with the trader scandal, and I didn't want to add to your burdens."

"That wasn't your decision to make," Peth said, his voice hard.

"I didn't think it was serious enough to trouble you."

"You were wrong," Niamh snapped.

Thom shifted uncomfortably, wishing he could disappear. He'd never imagined a teacher being scolded.

Noticing Thom's reaction, Peth said, "Niamh, let's talk with Noiri privately."

Niamh drew a breath. "About Niall..."

"Did... um..." Thom ventured hesitantly, afraid he might get yelled at too. "Did he actually see Kami?"

"Elspeth didn't think so," Peth said. "You've been careful when visiting her?"

"Yes," he replied, then described his encounter in Mercha and the Quad's Squad agreement to keep watch.

"Good," Niamh said. "Perhaps Niall explored on his own."

"Maybe. What should I do?" Thom fought to keep his knee from bouncing.

"Nothing," Peth said. "You've shown you take this seriously.

Thom let out his breath.

"Niamh," Peth continued, "it might be time we tell everyone."

"What if we post guards at the side passage?" she suggested.

Lowering his head, Thom said, "I guess I shouldn't have brought Kami here."

"No. I'm glad you did," Niamh replied. "With the books, artifacts, and chambers under the plateau, we're recovering an important part of our history."

"I agree," Peth added. "And there's so much we can learn from her, especially once she accesses the full trove of dragon knowledge. I wish we had more contact with dragons. But that would complicate things, wouldn't it, Niamh?"

She didn't respond. Thom also noticed Noiri hadn't spoken since the reprimand.

"Niamh?" Peth prompted.

She shook her head. "Well, that never happened before."

"What?"

"I had a strong prescient sense that Kami's kind will be important—even more than we realize."

"Because of what they know?" Peth asked.

"Not just that."

Thom cleared his throat.

"Sorry, Thom," Niamh said. "We'll post guards but keep being careful. We'll keep an eye on things from our side."

"OK," he said, relieved. He needed to tell Jonathan, Mekial, and Tovah.

"Horsey ride!" the twins shouted, racing in.

"Go ahead, Thom," Niamh said. Fixing her gaze on Noiri, she sharpened her voice. "Let's talk."

He didn't need to be told twice.

Thom and Mekial were in the residence kitchen getting food for Kami. They'd come from visiting Apollo, who was content to be indoors after the snowfall a few days earlier. Thom couldn't wait until spring. Fibre felt endless.

"Keelin was extra nice to cut the meat the way Kami likes."

"Yeah," Mekial agreed. "How's her new leg?"

"Good. She showed me the other day. The metalworkers made it with knee and ankle joints almost as flexible as a real one, and wrapped it in soft leather that nearly matched her skin.

"Impressive."

They were about to leave when a young voice shouted.

"I'm sor. I'm sor."

"Uh oh," Thom said, "Something's wrong."

Terrin ran in, distressed.

"Are you hurt?" Thom asked, as Tressa followed close behind.

"I'm sor!"

"Where are you hurt?" he repeated, scanning for bumps or scratches.

"No... I'm sor. Sor years old."

"What?" Mekial asked. "You're four?"

"Tressie says she's older but I'm sor too."

"I am older," she insisted, stamping her foot.

"Ah," Thom said, hiding a grin. "You're both four... even if she's a few minutes older."

"Now off you go. And be nice, Tressa," Mekial added.

When they left, Thom said, "That was cute, even if Terrin was upset."

"Yeah. Tressa does speak her mind."

Thom nodded, knowingly. "Let's bring Kami her breakfast."

"I can't figure out why they canceled classes," Mekial said as she and Thom climbed the stairs. "Sure, there's a lot of snow, but since the teachers live here, that shouldn't matter."

Thom groaned.

"You OK?"

"Training mishap yesterday. I let my guard down, and Barran got me in the hip with his staff. Makes the stairs challenging."

"I understand."

"Worse was losing my balance and slamming into the salle's mirrored wall. Cracked it."

"Ouch."

"Hard way to learn. As for the teachers, some had to check on their families outside the city. The storm brought down a few trees, and some homes were hit."

"Good point. What are you doing next?"

"Soaking tub. My right arm's stiff from where you got me with your staff a few days ago."

"Sorry. I didn't mean to hit that hard."

"That's OK. My mistake. I was distracted, thinking about Niall."

"We're being careful. I didn't see him today. The guards are doing a great job keeping unauthorized people from getting through the side entrance."

"Hey, Macirdan," a male voice called.

"Oh, no."

"Stop. I need to talk to you."

Thom reluctantly did. Snow covered Niall's woolen cloak. Did he bury himself under it?

"You went to the Keep again. I saw you."

"What's it to you?" Mekial shot back.

Thom checked Niall's aura—still muddy pink with patches of light blue, but now streaked with dark red. Thom noticed his stiff posture. Reaching out with his healing sense, he detected bruises along Niall's back. Training injury? No.

You're correct, Thom.

Sereh, is that you?

Yes.

It happened at his home, didn't it? His father?

Sadly true.

How awful. Is that why Niall lashes out?

Partly.

What should I do?

Remember what I told you to do for Samiltun?

Love him?

And?

Oh, call in Uri.

And?

There's more?

Yes. Be understanding.

I'll try. Please help me with my words.

We all will. But ask Archangels Haniel and Muriel as well, who also support empaths.

OK.

Thom's focus returned to Niall, who was shouting.

"Tell me what you're doing in the Keep!"

"I'm sorry things are hard at home," Thom said.

"You don't know anything!"

"Your Da hurt you," he pressed.

"How do... ?" Mekial whispered.

"Later."

"Back off, Macirdan! My Pa's an important man. And he's powerful."

Thom felt a wave of sympathy. What more could he do?

"I'll find out what you're up to and tell. You'll be in trouble."

Gang, I'm stuck, Thom called to his advisors.

Listen to your intuition, Rel said.

Thanks.

Thom considered Rel's suggestion. Humans were divine essences in physical form. Niall needed to grasp that. But if he used those words, he wouldn't understand. His family was likely Iosan.

"Thom, what are you going to do?" Mekial asked in Glakkadian.

"That's inspired." Thom faced Niall and, in the same tongue, said, "You carry the divine inside you. You're beautiful... and don't deserve to be hurt, no matter who your Pa is."

"What are you saying?" he demanded, edging back. "Are you cursing me?"

"Niall, you're innately good. Feel your blessedness. Know you're not alone."

"Stop. Get away," he said, bolting up the stairs.

"Tell someone, Niall," Thom yelled after him, now in Dochalan.

"That was beautiful," Mekial said. "But why in Glakkadian?"

"So his heart could feel it, even if his mind couldn't accept it."

"I hope your words reach him. I don't always understand your spirit-healing gift."

"Me either. Now, I'm getting that hot soak."

Chapter 51

Rin rode back from a village where he'd spent the past two months. Now that it was spring, the air was alive with the scent of flowers. A healer friend had broken her leg, leaving no one to tend her patients. It had been refreshing to focus on healing, instead of investigating greedy traders or abusive landlords.

He mulled over Noiri's suggestion to mentor the Quad Squad during their internship. Their Acadium studies had been broad, but mostly local. It was time to stretch beyond Docha-leigh and discover what other lands, peoples, and beliefs could teach them. That couldn't happen in Freasa. But was he the best person for the job? Was he too old? This time, travel wouldn't be limited to one land, and his body no longer tolerated sleeping on the ground. He'd assumed another teacher would jump at the chance, but none had.

He smiled, recalling his time with Thom in Glakkadeth. The boy felt like a grandson. A good lad, though trouble seemed to follow him. Yet Thom's gifts had saved many, as had Jonathan's, Mekial's, and Tovah's. It would be interesting to see what new abilities emerged. If he were honest, Rin had to admit the journey might help him grow, even at his age. After all, he'd gained the mind-speech ability last year.

As for romance, though—not his. He'd never found a mate and didn't expect to. But the foursome. He knew of the budding relationships between Thom and Jonathan and between Mekial and Tovah. Was he willing to manage that dynamic? And what about the prejudice they might face?

On the other hand, Noiri had said they'd be strong candidates for COM. The group needed younger members, and the four had learned other languages. Rin was fluent in three of the four they'd studied. And learning about other cultures was a solid foundation for the role.

Rin crested a hill with a clear view of Cleirigh Hall's towers and the Acadium gleaming in the sun. His floppy hat shaded him from its burning rays—the same one Thom had once teased him about. This was where they'd stopped when Thom first came to Freasa. He remembered the awe on the boy's face as he gazed at the city that would become his new home. At that moment, a white feather drifted onto his saddle, drawing him back to the present.

"Now, that's a clear sign. Tomorrow, I'll tell Noiri I'm in."

Thom stepped outside. It was mid-afternoon, the same day, and he'd just treated a patient who'd left a cut unattended. The wound reeked, thick with whitish-yellow pus. After cleansing it and applying a poultice of echinacea, goldenseal, and yarrow, he wrapped it and sent healing energy into the area.

He breathed deeply, grateful for the fresh air. Above him, the sky was a rich blue, dotted with a few puffy clouds.

"Thanks for the nice day, Tuwatsi," he whispered. Cat had told him that's what her people called the sacred earth mother.

Thinking back to the patient, he mused, Why do people ignore their injuries? Some cuts healed on their own, but this one had to have hurt for a while. Men often clung to the belief in pushing through pain. Yet this worker was a woman.

Summer break was a few weeks away. He and Jonathan had agreed to spend half apart with their families. Thom wondered about telling his parents about his feelings for Jonathan. He'd already confided in Meli and Redik, though his nerves from the confession lingered. Meli said she'd always known. Redik had been shocked until Meli pointed out the signs, starting with Thom and Jonathan finishing each other's sentences. Not surprisingly, Thom teared up, touched that she'd noticed.

Thom was about to step back inside when Jonathan ran up.

"We've been summoned to the sitting room in Cleirigh Hall. Tovah and Mekial as well."

"Why?"

"No one said. We're to meet Oddi and the others by the side entrance."

"Let me wash up."

Soon after Thom and Jonathan got there, the three appeared.

"Oddi, is this about our guest?" Thom asked, uneasy.

"Yeah. Mamie was real upset and asked me to get you."

"We'd better not keep them waiting," Jonathan warned.

Oddi led them to the hidden entrance, usually reserved for COM agents and special messengers, as Rin had once told Thom.

"They're here, Mamie," Oddi called.

Inside, Noiri waited off to the side, wringing her hands. Niamh paced, muttering. "The gall of that man. He may be my fourth cousin, which is debatable, but he had no right to demand to see me."

"Hon," Peth said, "take a breath. You're wearing a path in the carpet."

"What?" she snapped, then kept ranting. "He accused us of endangering Freasa, let alone Docha-leigh, by harboring a dangerous beast. How did that boy see Kami, anyway? Who failed to do their duty!"

Thom's legs trembled, and Tovah's eyes went wide as she clutched Mekial's hand.

"Niamh, it's not certain anyone did," Peth said, gesturing for them to sit. "The Quad Squad's done an excellent job keeping her hidden, and the guards confirmed no one breached the side passage."

"Then how?"

"He could've come with his father for a merchant's meeting. Then slipped away while the man was occupied. No one's at fault."

"Maybe," Niamh said, finally coming to a halt. "He was yelling dragon at the top of his lungs. Why would anyone believe we had one, when most think they're myths?"

"They'd think him mad. Fortunately, Ciarenn, the nearest guard, already knew about Kami and pulled him into our office."

"I guess," she said, slumping onto the sofa beside him.

"Hon, the squad's here," Peth reminded her.

"Oh... how much did you hear?"

"Um," Jonathan mumbled.

"All of it, Mamie," Oddi volunteered.

"First, you're not in trouble," Peth assured them. "As I said before, we know you've been careful."

"We have," Thom said.

"And we believe you. Don't we, Niamh?"

"Yes," she answered, now calmer.

"Do you think Niall saw Kami?" Thom asked.

"Yes," Peth said. "His father, Merchant Campbell, described her exactly."

"Oh, no. What now?"

"Peth and I will speak with a few people to weigh our options," Niamh explained. "But she may need to be moved."

"Where?" Thom asked, alarmed.

"No idea," Peth said. "Give us time. But we'd like you to talk with Kami about it."

"In the meantime," Niamh added, "it's unlikely anyone will take Campbell seriously."

"OK," Thom said, still uncertain.

Peth sighed. "We'll sort it out. For now, let's focus on less troubling matters, starting with snacks and drinks."

Thom grounded himself as he reached for the food, picturing a rope stretching from his heart into the earth, anchoring him. His stomach remained uneasy, so he cautiously sipped the Timbu and nibbled his cinnamon biscuit. "Help," he whispered to his advisors.

Once they were settled again, Peth continued, "You're fifth level now, except you, Tovah. Tell us what most surprised you during your time at the Acadium. At the welcome assembly,

I'm certain Noiri said you'd discover things about yourselves, maybe even new gifts. We'd like to hear what that was, including anything that's, say... developed in the relationship department," he added with a wink.

"Huh?" Oddi asked, confused.

The next morning, Thom begged Keelin for heart, liver, and kidney meat, along with the usual beef chunks. A cow had died in a freak fall the day before. He wanted to give Kami a special meal before he broke the news.

Good morning, Kami, Thom mind-spoke as he entered Dragan-ni Hall and found her lounging in her nest. He didn't dare speak aloud—not after Niall's discovery. The temperature inside felt like a mild summer day; he remembered stepping in one winter morning and instantly breaking into a sweat.

Good morning.

You're not in the play yard.

The vents Tovah made pull more heat from the dormant volcano. They're nice. I'll move outside once I eat. Speaking of food, is that organ meat I smell?

Yes. I need to tell you something.

As Kami devoured her meal, he explained what he'd learned the day before.

This Niall person saw me in the yard?

Seems like it. I'm not certain how, but he convinced his father. I get the feeling the man thinks little of his son... and beats him when he doesn't measure up.

Thom recalled Niall's calling as a protector. Maybe he should've told him. But Niall wouldn't have believed him. That's why he'd spoken in Glakkadian.

That's terrible. A skyforger should never beat his firespawn. What a wretch!

Skyforger? Firespawn? Is that how your kind refers to father and child?

Yes.

What's a mother called?

Lifeweaver.

They sound nice. You haven't used them before.

No. I must be connecting more to our collective consciousness.

Do you know when you'll have full access? The books don't say.

I'm not sure. I get glimpses, but they fade when I try to focus.

That's frustrating. I've felt that way. My advisors keep saying it'll come when the time's right.

Wise.

Yeah, and I'm grateful. About the meeting, what do we do? School ends in a month. I hope Niall stays quiet until then, but since he's seen you, what's to stop him from bringing a friend? Niamh said you might need to move. Maybe the chambers below? It'd be harder to bring food, so you might need to hunt more often.

Let me think about it.

My advisors also told me to trust, watch for signs, and listen to my intuition. But my mind tries so hard to help, and it ends up spinning.

I've noticed.

I'd better run. I'm off to the pottery. Professor Creagh asked if I'd help teach her academs since I'm free. She saw Da's pottery at Redik's store, and he sent her my way. It feels wonderful to be working with clay again.

It's good to keep up that skill. You never know when you might need it.

Are you showing signs of prescience?

Maybe.

I'll see you at the end of the day. Are you hunting for your supper?

Yes. Bye Thom.

Dermot now sat in his office, having just finished noon supper in the head chair at the dining table, once his father's place of honor. The office too had been his, now furnished with worn but familiar pieces from Deda's room.

"The Vlodan Republic? He thinks Lord Samiltun went there?" he asked his hired hand.

"Yes, saor."

He remembered returning to Samiltun's manor weeks after the shake. That time, he'd gone inside, and the sight of it made him frown. Rumor blamed Samiltun for the earthshake. The monarchs had seized the property and converted it into a haven for orphans. Absurd. That house was meant for someone of means, not a swarm of loud, messy kids. He knew the type, his niece and nephew.

Turning back to the servant, he asked, "Why the Republic?"

"'Cause that's where his dealer sent most of the lord's sparklies."

Dermot grunted. Samiltun could've fled there and resumed his business. "Can the dealer get a message to him?"

"Don' know, saor."

"Find out, and give him an incentive," he said, pulling coins from a box.

"Yes, saor."

Chapter 52

Two weeks remained in the school year. Thom left the monastery behind the Chapel of the One. Brother Lamen had invited him to supper after their last session before summer. He could hardly believe he was finishing fifth level—one more year until graduation. Then, an apprenticeship.

Saddled and mounted, Thom let Apollo find his way, his thoughts drifting back to the meeting. He'd shared how much he loved visits from his advisors in his Sanctuary, especially the hugs with Jeshua, Rel, and Sereh. But he remained stiff when hugging God, shaped by the wrathful image taught by the elders. That brought to mind another teaching: God's plan. The elders claimed human wishes often opposed it. Thom now believed that God's plan was the one people made with God before birth. So they should trust their intuition, which comes from their divine soul.

Regarding hugs again, Thom had told Lamen he always felt tingling during them, a sensation that left him calm—the same feeling he experienced during meditation. Lamen explained it meant his body was vibrating at the divine frequency. He gave Thom an assignment: when the tingling arose, he was to imagine his advisors gathered around him, enveloping him in love, and feel any doubts and fears melt away. Thom was eager to try it.

It was just after dinner the next day when Thom trudged up the stairs, yawning. He, Tovah, Mekial, and Jonathan had eaten in silence, worn out from Dek's brutal training: sprints up and down all ten floors of the Acadium until their legs wobbled, followed by sparring. It was their fifth match as a unit, this time against six opponents—Dek, three assistants, and two sixth-level academs bound for the Royal Guard. Mekial had also been told not to use her shield gift.

Even so, the Quad Squad fared better, sharper and more in sync. Why push them so hard before vacation, when their edge would fade over break?

Fresh bruises covered Thom, including one on his arm from diving to avoid Dek's sword. He was proud of how Tovah held Dek off long enough for him to retrieve his weapon and knock the blade from his hand. Each step upstairs was slow and heavy, and he wished there were an easier way to reach his floor. At least he hadn't seen Niall lately; he wasn't sure he could keep his temper in check.

Once in his room, he would slather on ointment and collapse in bed, despite the sun not having set. Maybe by next week, he'd stop walking funny.

Thom had just slipped under the covers when a knock came.

"Go away!"

Probably another guard academ asking about healing herbs. Every guard had to learn the basics.

The knock came again, more insistent.

"I said, go away. I'm too tired to think."

"It's Jonathan. Noiri wants us in her office."

Thom stumbled to the door.

"Nice under-drawers."

"Oops," he said, flushing.

While he dressed, Jonathan added, "Tovah and Mekial are waiting at the stairs."

"Turg!"

"Come in," a woman's voice called.

Thom was last to enter. "Rin!" he shouted, pushing past his friends to hug him.

"Hi, Thom. Noiri told me you looked like the walking dead. Honestly, you all do."

"Tough training this afternoon."

"Good to see you, Jonathan, Tovah, Mekial."

"Have a seat?" Noiri said. "I'm expecting a few more."

The four sat side by side. Rin next to Thom.

When the others arrived—Kee, Mac, and Lamen—Noiri continued, "I'm sorry to call another meeting after dinner, especially given the Quad Squad's condition, but this was when Brother Lamen could join us. He and his husband are returning to Glakkadeth for the summer, catching a riverboat in the morning."

Interesting, Thom mused. No one blinked at the mention of Lamen's husband. He already knew Lamen was leaving. He'd asked him to say hello to Sestra B, and Mekial had given him a letter for her family.

"I see you're wondering why everyone's here. That'll become clear shortly."

Thom frowned. Was this about Kami and Niall again?

"You four have done well in your studies, including in language, culture, and weapons training. Dek, who couldn't join us, stopped by before leaving. He was quite pleased with how you played to each other's strengths, even when exhausted. And yes, that was intentional."

"I was here when he stopped by," Rin added. "He mentioned a few stumbles, literally, but saw great improvement."

"Why mention it now?" Thom asked. "Won't Dek tell us next Siptema?"

"Perfect segue," Noiri replied. "You three won't be here for your final year. Tovah, congratulations on your graduation next week."

"Thanks."

"I don't understand," Mekial said. "Did we lose our scholarships?"

Jonathan jumped in. "I'm not a full healer, but maybe someone will want my help."

"Hold on," Mac said.

"It's not about money." Kee added.

"This is about Kami, isn't it," Thom cut in. "Don't punish them for what I did."

"It's not that either," Noiri said.

"Stop!" Lamen interrupted. "Everyone, breathe. You're all over the place."

Once the room quieted, Noiri continued, "You're not returning because you're all going on an internship... together."

"An internship," Mekial echoed.

"And together?" Tovah asked.

"Yes. Normally, you'd begin one alone after graduation, which is why Kee didn't bring yours up."

"I see."

"As for the rest of you," Noiri continued, "you've reached the limits of what we can offer. It's time to broaden your training, and an internship is the best way to accelerate your growth."

"Even for our mage gifts?" Mekial asked.

"Especially those," Kee replied. "Mekial, you need to test your gift in new situations, something less dramatic than an earthshake. Tovah, your sensitivity to nature requires exposure to a range of environments. Jonathan and Thom, the same goes for your paired gifts and... your relationship."

"You know?" Thom asked, blushing.

"Of course," Noiri said. "And about Tovah and Mekial."

"We tried to be discreet," Jonathan said.

"You were," Mac replied, "but it became evident a few months after you healed your sister, Thom."

"Who else knows? Niamh and Peth?"

"Yes," Rin replied. "And they're fully supportive."

"Oh." Thom sagged with relief.

"And Thom, about our work," Lamen said, "I've been impressed by your courage to face painful experiences. Many struggle with trauma. Having someone who understands what it's like, and how to heal it, will be invaluable."

"What about my spirit-healing gift?"

"Your connection to your advisors is stronger than any I've seen. My job was to build on what Sestra B taught and support you as new abilities emerged."

Thom lifted his head in acknowledgement.

"As for you, Jonathan," he continued, "I don't know you as well as Thom, since we only started meeting after the earthshake and our schedules haven't always aligned. Still, I admire your commitment to your calling. Like Thom said, your touch is healing in itself."

"Thanks."

"I know you also have a strong bond with Archangel Raphael," Lamen added. "But you haven't established your advisory group."

"I don't know how. Thom, will you help me?"

"Of course."

"What about our healing studies, Mac?" Jonathan asked.

"You're a natural healer; divinely touched, like Thom. I've seen how you both treat patients: with tenderness, respect, and the occasional reprimand when needed. Rin and I agreed it's time you explore other healing paths. Teaching you's been an honor. There are a few things I didn't cover, but Rin can.

"Rin?" Thom gasped.

"Yes. Would you mind having me as your teacher again?"

"Oh my God, no," *Sorry, G. Hope you don't mind me using your name like that.*

Not at all, a voice replied in his mind.

"And the rest of you?" Rin asked. "Are you comfortable with me?"

They all answered, yes.

"Now to practical details," Noiri said. "Your internship begins this summer, after you've had time with your families."

"Which we understand you can't do, Mekial," Rin added, "but one of our destinations is your home."

"Oh, wow. I haven't seen my family since the end of my second year. I even miss Budaj, Thom. Can you believe it?"

"I can. Bratty younger brothers usually grow out of their attitude problems."

"I hope you get to meet my older brother, Sefu. Technically, my half-brother. Ma was married before she met Mamie."

"Rin, are we catching a ship from Dridley?" Thom asked.

"Yes, but not immediately."

"Jonathan and Tovah will get to meet Khali," Thom said excitedly. "Do you think we might see Nuala, Rin?"

"Not sure. You could ask Khali. I hear they're friends."

"I will. How long will we be away?"

"Over a year. It depends on where we go and what you need to learn."

"What should we bring?" Jonathan asked.

"Before you set out, I'll supply you with plenty of herbs, poultices, and other portable treatments," Mac explained. "When you run low, you can restock locally. You might even find new remedies."

"Will we continue weapons and defense training?" Mekial asked.

"Absolutely," Rin said. "If we stay in one place for a while, I'll find guards or constables willing to help. And when we sail to Glakkadeth, maybe a few sailors."

Thom groaned.

"What?" Jonathan asked.

"He's remembering the aches he got from his training on his first voyage there."

"You had to mention that," Mekial added. "They didn't fight fair either. I assume we'll bring weapons."

"Yes," Noiri confirmed.

"With our belongings, won't that be too much?" Tovah asked.

"Good point," Rin replied. "We'll have a caravan pulled by two horses, and one of us will need to drive. I'll start out, but you'll each need to learn. If we can't find travel shelters or affordable inns, we'll sleep inside the caravan, which, I'll admit, will be tight."

"Since only Thom and Rin have horses, Niamh and Peth have agreed to loan you three more, including Aponi," Noiri added. "I hear Apollo and Aponi are often together."

"They are," Thom admitted, having a sudden realization. *Kami. Could they even bring a dragon on the internship?* She could become invisible, but she'd need a place to hide. He couldn't abandon her. He'd promised Ariel.

Kami was nearly five. She could hunt on her own, so food wasn't an issue. *What about cleaning her? Maybe he could teach Oddi. Mac could monitor her health. But Niall... oh God. That would be a disaster.*

"Thom, are you all right?" Lamen asked. "You seem shaken."

"Kami. I can't leave... what with Niall and everything."

"Ask her... mind-to-mind," Jonathan suggested.

Kami, Thom mind-spoke.

I hope you don't mind, but I've been listening. I have a solution.

So quickly?

Meet me in the play yard tomorrow morning, after I hunt.

OK.

"That was amazing," Lamen remarked. "I heard everything."

"We all did," Mac said.

"Thom," Rin said, "tell us what she says."

"You all could come."

"No," Jonathan replied. "That should be between you and her."

The others nodded.

"Before we end," Kee said, "have you chosen any stops besides Dridley and Glakkadeth?"

"No," Rin replied. "We'll let our intuition... and our divine companions guide us."

Thom groaned again.

"That makes two," Mekial noted.

"What do I tell my parents? It's like the first time I left home—no idea where we're going or for how long."

"Good morning, Kami," Thom greeted his charge, half-buried in the play yard sand. It was safe to speak aloud now; that morning, Niamh had told him Niall's father had withdrawn his son from school after she didn't respond to his complaint to his satisfaction.

"Buuurp."

"That's an interesting greeting."

Excuse me. I had a big breakfast. Found a dying black bear by a broken branch. Must've fallen from a tree.

"You hunted? That's good. But a bear? I haven't seen any around."

Northwest of here. I left before sunrise. Wanted to test my flight endurance.

"How'd it go?"

Very well.

"Why were you testing it?"

Because it's time for me to return to my family.

"That's the solution you mentioned yesterday?"

Yes.

"This is because I'm leaving. Maybe I could talk to Noiri and Rin; see if I can stay. Then you wouldn't have to go. Unless... you want to."

You need to go on your internship. I need to go home to keep learning.

"What do you mean?"

I'm more connected to my kind's consciousness. But I sense I need their help to fully access it.

"Oh. OK."

There's more. Remember the aurixen plant you found last year?

"Yeah. We've fed you its flowers, but all you manage is a little smoke."

That hasn't changed, she said, demonstrating.

"Does that mean there's not enough ignitropin being released?"

Oddi had found another anatomy book in the dragonry, as they were calling the hidden room. It mentioned the hormone.

I'm not sure. I'm hoping my mother can help. I should've become a flareling by now.

"Ariel did say you might have to go home. She didn't say when. Strange you're feeling that now, just as I'm leaving."

Maybe ask your advisors?

Why didn't I think of that?

Because you're a muffin-head?

"Kami, did you call me a muffin-head?"

Not me, she said, shaking her head.

Jesh?

Yepper.

The last time you called me that was...

When you were worried about bringing Kami back to the Acadium.

That was ages ago. Didn't you also mention synchronicity?

I did, Jeshua confirmed. I told you to trust when things line up. This is one of those times.

Did you know about this internship?

Only when you heard. But even before that, I knew you and the rest of the Quad Squad were close to outgrowing your teachers. Jeshua paused. Looks like Kami wants to join.

Huh?

She wants to listen. Is that OK?

Of course.

I wanted to know what you're talking about, Kami cut in.

OK. Thom replied, and then explained that Jeshua had called him a muffin-head, and why.

Greetings, Kamael*Ariraz, Jeshua said. Thom's told me a great deal about you. I've spoken with your advisors in my realm.

Jeshua used Kami's full name, Thom noted. Wait. You have advisors?

A small group, including a guardian angel.

Why didn't you tell me?

It never came up.

So dragons have divine beings watching over them.

All beings do, Jeshua added. Even to a degree, the rest of nature.

I need to tell Tovah.

Go ahead. But start by sharing your beliefs first. Her family's been private about theirs since before they escaped from the Vlodan Republic.

Escaped?

Not my story to tell. Back to your internship and Kami rejoining her family.

Oh, Thom said, his heart sinking. *Will I ever see you again?*

Don't be a muffin-head. Of course. I just don't know when. You didn't say how long you'll be gone.

Rin didn't. More than a year.

Sounds like you're being asked to trust divine timing again. Jeshua suggested.

I still hate that.

We haven't forgotten. I'll let you two finish your chat.

Thanks, Jesh.

Yes, thank you, Kami added. *I'm glad we finally met.*

Speaking aloud again, Thom said, "I'm going to miss you, Kami."

Me too.

"Say hello to your mother, brother and sister."

I will. But don't worry, I'm not leaving until you do.

"OK. I'd better head out. I'm working in the Rejuvenary this morning. I love you, Kami."

I love you, too, Thom.

Chapter 53

Thom was in the family stable grooming Apollo. He'd risen early, unable to sleep with his mind spinning over their internship. With no one else awake, he'd carried his porridge to the bench overlooking the valley. The sun was cresting the horizon. This was where he'd first met Ariel as a toddler, and many years later, where he and Deena had argued about faith.

He sat quietly, sensing the presence of his advisors. As he breathed in the brisk air, his anxiety eased. All was peaceful.

Eventually, he stirred. Tasks awaited. After dropping his bowl off in the kitchen, he loaded his things into the caravan and went to the stable, where he was now.

They'd be leaving in a few hours. Jonathan and the others would join him after breakfast. He brushed Apollo's withers, making sure his chestnut coat gleamed, as beautiful on the outside as he was within. The others had arrived three days earlier. After school ended, Mekial had stayed with Tovah's family. Jonathan had gone home. Mid-Jauna, they'd met Rin at the Acadium and traveled to Thom's.

Reta, Kavan, and Alli had graciously given up their beds and moved back to the loft. After Bedum married, Reta took his old room; when Redik and Meli moved to the city, Kavan and Alli claimed theirs. Mam apologized for not having a separate room for everyone. Aware of the Quad Squad's relationships, Rin suggested Thom share with Jonathan and Tovah with Mekial. Thom had kept his expression neutral as he assured her no one minded.

Thom still hadn't told his parents about his relationship. He wasn't ashamed, just unsure how they felt about same-gender attraction. After returning from Glakkadeth, the topic had come up briefly when Rin mentioned that its Prezdan was married to a man. His Da had known such relationships existed in Docha-leigh and hadn't seemed repulsed. Even so, the same elders who taught Thom as a boy led services in the local chapel. He'd gone once since coming home. Thankfully, the elder wasn't Oona or the one Mam disliked.

He found himself thinking of Deena again. He'd seen her twice. She still clung to her fear-based beliefs, but at least she wasn't trying to change him. Her husband and daughters seemed more open. Deena kept thanking him for saving Liv, which grew annoying. Now he understood why she'd been irritated when, as a child, he begged her to retell the story of Ariel's scale.

"Hey, Archangel Uriel," Thom whispered, "bless them with your light and love."

His thoughts shifted back to his parents and their talk about his internship. They hadn't been pleased he couldn't tell them how long he'd be away, but they accepted that his unique calling might lead him elsewhere. Promising to write regularly had helped.

Apparently, Mam had started chatting with Deu. The summer before he entered the Acadium, she'd asked about his chats with God and Archangel Raphael. She admitted she didn't speak with them often now, and usually received their responses through others. The experience brought her peace and helped her better recognize her patients' emotional needs while tending to their physical ones.

Mam genuinely cared about people. That was clear from the birthday party she threw yesterday for Jonathan's eighteenth. His family had already celebrated before he left home, but he appreciated the gesture. Mam baked Jonathan's favorite chocolate cake with raspberry filling and made Thom's lemon curd buns ahead of his eighteenth. Not wanting to leave anyone out, she also honored Mekial, who turned eighteen in Mei, and Tovah, whose birthday was in Aprali. It became a send-off celebration. With the exception of Redik and Meli, his whole family was there. Thom had already said goodbye to them in Freasa.

During the party, Tovah had shocked them by saying she was twenty. That meant she'd started at the Acadium at fourteen instead of the usual thirteen. Thom wondered if her escape from the Vlodan Republic had played a role.

She'd spoken to Reta yesterday, urging her to enroll in the Acadium. Reta's earth sense had grown; she could now read the condition of the land, much like Tovah. But Reta remained reluctant, despite Da saying they could afford it now and Rin assuring her she'd easily earn a scholarship.

As Thom finished currying Apollo, laughter and raised voices drifted from the house. Kavan's stood out—his pitch bouncing between squeaky highs and deeper tones. Saying goodbye would be hard, especially to Alli. He'd missed most of her growing up. At least, she wasn't bashful anymore.

Thoughts of goodbyes brought him back to the day Kami left, nearly sunrise on the morning of Thom's departure. Kami wanted an early start. She'd be heading in the same direction she'd flown when she caught the bear, guided, he imagined, by her connection to her kin. He'd made her promise not to push herself, a lesson he continued to learn. She had assured him she'd rest and use her invisibility gift to stay hidden.

Before Kami took flight, they embraced—his arms wrapped around her long neck, her wings folded over him. It was special. As he watched her fly off, he wondered whether they'd be able to speak across the distance. Coming out of his reverie, he considered reaching out now, but decided to give her time with her family.

A gentle nudge brought him back. "Sorry, Apollo. I'm glad you're coming... and Aponi. I know you like her." He paused. What if she gets pregnant during the internship?

Footsteps approached.

"Thom, are you in the stable?" Jonathan called.

"Yeah. About to saddle Apollo."

"The rest of us are coming to do the same," he said, stepping inside. "Rin wants us to watch how he hitches the horses to the caravan."

He's wearing my gift, Thom noted. "Thanks for telling me."

"My things are already in. The others are putting theirs in now. I'll start currying Aponi. I still can't believe Niamh and Peth gave her to me."

"I suggested it. I didn't want to tell you sooner and make it seem like I was showing off, as if I had an in with them."

"I'm touched. And you're not one to show off."

"Thanks."

"Aponi's a sweet animal."

They heard a whinny from the next stall.

"The vest you gave me is beautiful," Jonathan said, brushing his hand over the fabric. "I love the symbol of the hand with a spiral. The spiral's your symbol, and you always talk about my healing hands. It feels right, like it represents both of us. How'd you come up with it?"

"Riding back from Lamen's one day, I passed a weaver's shop. The vest was in the window. I had them add the symbol. I'm glad you like it."

"Thanks again," Jonathan said, giving him a lingering kiss.

"Caught you," Mekial teased as she and Tovah entered. "Nicely done."

"Um," Thom replied, blushing. "I'd better get Apollo saddled.

Not long after, Thom's family gathered outside to say goodbye. He hugged them tightly. As expected, his parents had tears in their eyes. So did he. He loved them all, even Deena.

Rin and Tovah sat on the box seat at the front of the caravan, with Rin driving. Tovah would be the first to learn. Mekial rode Blaze, a dun-colored horse with a black mane, named for her fiery spirit, according to Duncan. Jonathan sat tall on Aponi. Thom, of course, rode Apollo.

The night before, Rin said his divine guides advised beginning their journey by heading south. Metatron and Rel had hinted at the same when Thom spoke with them. Placing his hand over a tunic pocket, he felt Ariel's scale. He carried it at the start of every new stage in his life, a good-luck talisman.

"Let's be on our way," Rin called, setting the caravan in motion. Mekial brought Blaze alongside, with Thom and Jonathan riding behind.

Everyone called their goodbyes again.

"Don't get into any trouble, Thom!" Kavan shouted.

"Hey," he protested.

"He's not wrong, Thom," Reta called.

"We'll see," he said. Trouble? He hoped not.

Last night, he'd filled the final page of his current journal. For weeks, he'd written small and brief to make it last. Tonight, he'd begin a new one, marking a new chapter of his life. The journal was a gift from his parents, who now understood why he kept one.

His mind returned to his first journey to the Acadium, when he'd wondered if he'd make any friends. Mekial and Tovah's laughter up ahead was one sign he had. Glancing at Jonathan, he smiled. He'd never imagined loving anyone this much.

His stomach lurched as a purple feather drifted onto his saddle.

"Oh turg," Thom mumbled. "What are we in for now?"

Acknowledgements

Writing this second book in the series was every bit as enjoyable as the first—though this time, the editing process proved more rewarding. As always, it would not have been possible without the unwavering support of my husband, Michael, who never uttered a word of complaint when I monopolized our computer.

My creative process was emboldened by my spiritual teachers—Denise Linn, Terry Bowen, Dougall Fraser, Radleigh Valentine, Liz Dawn, and Kyle Gray. I was further inspired and guided by Gabi, Luke, Dad, and my advisors in the divine realm, who encouraged me to follow my intuition, trust divine timing, and cultivate patience—a virtue I sometimes struggle to embody.

That encouragement was strengthened by the love of my family, the companionship of my mindfulness group (Jeanne, Joan, Karen, and Kimberly), and the steady encouragement of my friends.

Finally, I owe special thanks to those who were instrumental in bringing this book to life: my beta readers (Karen, Deborah, Bill, JoAnn, Lori, Jay, Dave, and Tom), whose thoughtful suggestions enriched the story; the cover artist, John, for his beautiful design; and the publishers, Kyra and Todd at As You Wish Publishing, for shepherding the book into print.

I hadn't expected to embark on this journey at my age, yet it has been a blessing. Book 3 in the series is now underway.

May you, too, follow your passion and discover the possibilities waiting just around the corner.

About the Author

Joe McMonagle is a spirit healer who uses storytelling and blogs to help people reconnect with their innate goodness, deepen their relationship with the divine, and discover healing and insight into their life's purpose. He holds degrees in Architectural Engineering (B.A.E.), Divinity (M.Div.), and Counseling Psychology (M.A.), reflecting a diverse educational background that grounds both his spiritual and professional work.

Joe's journey spans 12 years as a religious seminarian and priest, followed by 26 years in the software industry. He is the author of *Shadows and Light: Journeys of a Spirit Healer*, the first in this five-book spiritual fantasy series. His short story, *Not Yet Skyborne*, set in the same world, is freely available on his website. He has also contributed chapters to *Awaken Your Magic: Real Life Manifestation Journeys*; *Guided By Spirit: A Quest for Self-Discovery, Insight & Illumination*; and *The Power of Vision: Inspiring Possibilities, Creating Change*, published by As You Wish Publishing.

Committed to ongoing personal and spiritual growth, Joe continues to explore belief systems and healing practices while studying under the guidance of esteemed spiritual teachers, whom he thanked in the acknowledgments.

Visit www.joemcmonaglehsp.com to connect with Joe and explore his work.